Nightmare Beauty

Nightmare Beauty

Ileen Martin

E.L.I.
PUBLISHING
& LITERARY SERVICES

Published by E.L.I. Publishing & Literary Services, 2024.
NIGHTMARE BEAUTY
Second Edition. January 17, 2024.
Written by Ileen Martin.
ISBN: 979-8-9911956-0-7

To my son, who's written and drawn more books in his twelve years of life than I could possibly generate.

Contents

1

As the Fire Burns, A Fairy Gets Its Wings

PROLOGUE
1725 - Elmridge,
Rhode Island

A hush fell over the crowd of the makeshift courtroom as two young women, with hands bound before them, were shuffled inside. They stopped before the pulpit that now served as the judge's seat. The taller of the two, Abigail, held her head high, though her wide, frightened amber eyes betrayed her courage. A week in the dungeon had unraveled her long, raven black hair from its high bun. The smaller girl, Emily, buried her face in her older sister's shoulder, weeping dismally, her chestnut brown hair falling like a curtain, hiding her from the merciless stares.

"Be brave, Emily," Abigail whispered into her ear.

Emily could only turn her tear-soaked face and peer at all the faces she'd known her whole life of eighteen years, all staring back at them. There was the jolly village butcher who'd occasionally slipped her cubes of sweet ham in his shop, but looked at them now like they were next on his butchering block; Mrs. Stacey, their school teacher who'd once visited their home to compliment their parents "on such fine daughters with admirably voracious minds for reading," but now glared at the girls like they'd just set fire to the school house.

And their own childhood friends... It didn't matter that Emily had once socked an apple at Jacob's face when he'd gotten impertinent with her friend, Sarah, looking a little too long at her bare legs when her dress had ripped on sharp bramble. Because there, he and Sarah sat together now, side by side, mutual looks of disdain in their eyes, all aimed at Emily.

It was official, then. Emily and her sister were officially outcasts. Never again to be welcomed in any social circle.

But there was something even worse...

"Where are Mama and Papa?" Emily whispered, alarmed.

"I do not know," Abigail replied in a hushed voice, scanning the crowd. "Perhaps, they are being held against their will."

Abigail didn't think her heart could take it if their own parents had abandoned them too. Only one last shred of hope remained for her and Emily now. Rubbing her naked ring finger, she thought back to last week.

"One minute only," the jailor growled.

William shoved past him. "You will pay for your part in this, Matheson."

The jailor, a scrubby mammoth of a man, merely snorted in response.

"My love!" Abigail cried out, thrusting her hands through the iron cell bars.

"Abby!" Emily called out from another dark corner of the dungeon. "What is happening? Is William here?"

William clasped Abigail's hands to his lips. "Are you hurt, my darling? I came as soon as I heard."

"Your father—"

"Has gone too far." Fury and anguish coursed through him. He touched the faint purple spot on her pale cheek—an injury, he swore, that her captors would pay back a hundredfold with blood.

Feral rage glittered in his emerald green eyes, a look Abigail had only seen once in her peace-loving fiancée. A prelude to violence. Like the bloody-pulp kind Charlie Jones received at the ends of William's fists when he'd foolishly tried to assault her chastity. She'd ended up having to throw herself on top of Charlie's body to keep William from pummeling him to death.

Once again, she knew she'd need to save him from the noose, even if she was the one behind bars.

"We should call it off," she began, trying to steady her voice. "Perhaps, if we had not been so sudden about it—"

"No. He does not get to decide who I love, who I spend the rest of my life with."

He touched the garnet engagement ring he'd slid onto her finger just a few days ago, just after they had shared their long-awaited first kiss together. The satisfaction had been exquisite. They'd decided to save their next biggest step for their wedding night, which was supposed to be a month away.

He kissed the ring and cupped her face. "I will make this right."

She kissed the center of his palm and pressed it against her cheek. A tear escaped, and William drew in her face and captured the stray tear with a kiss. His mouth found hers and he drank her in, and when she opened for him, he felt his heart would explode in his chest.

Their second kiss.

"Minute's up, boy," Matheson snarled.

Abigail ripped her lips away, but William held her face in place, resting his forehead against hers and ignoring the cold bars pressing into their heated cheeks.

"I love you," William breathed out. "I would do anything for you. If anybody—"

"Please, my love, please. Don't do anything that would draw harm to yourself."

A heavy hand landed on his shoulder. "I said, minute's—"

William turned and smashed his fist into Matheson's face, the burly man's head snapping back as he fell with a thud against the stone wall.

"William!" Abigail cried.

"What on earth is going on, Abby?!" Emily yelled from her cell.

William lunged toward the keys hanging from Matheson's belt, but as soon as his hand closed over them, Matheson's hand clamped down on his. William's other hand latched onto Matheson's throat and squeezed.

"William, no!"

"Do it, boy." Matheson grunted out. "And you'll hang." He flashed a row of yellowed teeth as if the thought delighted him.

"William, please!"

With a guttural groan of frustration, William shoved off Matheson, and the guard's head bounced back against the wall with a resounding smack.

Abigail gripped the merciless bars tighter, the frigid steel biting into her palms, as she watched William visibly trembling with restraint. The conviction behind his next words as he held her gaze with a searing tenacity filled her with hope.

"We will overcome this. Together. Nothing will keep me from you. I will be back for you and Emily." And he did the most difficult thing he'd ever had to do. He turned around and stormed out, leaving her behind.

Matheson sneered out over his shoulder, "Make sure that you do, boy." He pushed against the wall to haul himself onto his feet. "For your daddy will see to it that these witches burn."

Now, the tears burned in Abigail's eyes as she searched through the hostile faces of the congregation. As if reading her mind, Emily whispered, "William is not here either."

"He will come," was Abigail's immediate reply. But she sucked in her bottom lip and chewed anxiously. That time a week ago had been the last she'd seen of him, and she'd refused to believe the rumors about him that Matheson had delivered to her: *Gone. On a business errand. For his father.*

Matheson, standing behind them as guard, brusquely nudged their shoulders forward as if signaling for them to pay attention up front.

The buzzing murmur of the congregation died down as the Reverend Judge Jonas Rawlins stepped up behind the wooden pulpit. His white sepulchral-colored robes with a royal blue coverlet and freshly powdered wig were in stark contrast to the dark, dreary shabbiness of his own congregation's attire. The reverend's piercing gaze slid down his long, crooked nose and pinned the two young, trembling women before him.

"Abigail and Emily Prynn," he boomed sonorously. "You two stand before us today accused by the governor's daughter, Lady Violet Wickeby, of consorting with Beezlebub through means of witchcraft. In accordance with the charter laws of Elmridge, unless a confession be wrought, persons found guilty of witchcraft and sorcery are to be burned alive at the stake in the public square immediately following the verdict of trial."

At this, a collective tittering spread among the people as Abigail inhaled sharply and Emily swayed into her sister's side. Besides the terrifying prospects of the reverend's words, a mysterious pain began to throb dully in the sisters' backs.

The reverend's fist thudded heavily against the pulpit like a mallet. "Silence!" A bulging blue vein pulsed in his temple as he turned back to the accused. "Do you, Abigail Prynn, deny these charges to be true?"

Abigail drew herself up tall. "We are not witches. We have never consorted with the Devil. Simply put, Violet Wickeby is a conniving liar."

Shocked gasps, sideways glances, and mutterings such as "But she's the governor's daughter..." all escaped from the audience.

Before Rawlins could intervene, Emily burst out, "Violet is simply jealous that William chose my sister and not her!"

"Emily!" Abigail chided.

The muttering rose to a cacophony before the reverend's heavy hand once again squashed out the din.

Thump, thump, thump throbbed the pain in the sisters' backs. They rolled their shoulders with the discomfort.

The scowl on the reverend's face was replaced with a look of sinister amusement. "Is this true? My son, William, has declared his love for you? Why isn't he here now to vouch for you?"

All heads swiveled to Abigail.

"Because you have detained him somehow."

All eyes were back on Rawlins.

"Of course, that must be it. Unfortunately for you, my dear, that is not the case." He reached into the folds of his robe and drew out a letter-sized parchment. "Mrs. Stacey?" he called out.

The teacher's eyes sprung round as saucers.

"Will you so kindly come forth and read this letter out loud for all to hear?"

She clambered out of her seat and took the outstretched letter. Facing the audience, she cleared her throat and read:

To the esteemed Reverend Judge Jonas Rawlins of Elmridge,

I am aware that you desire a station for your son, William Rawlins, at the capitol, preferably under my care. After having reviewed your son's skills and credentials, I have found him worthy of a post to serve as clerk to my brother, Sir Harold Wickeby, an estimable and world-class merchant. If he can be here within a fortnight's time, he can meet Sir Wickeby at the annual governor's ball at my estate and seal his future. You and your wife are happily invited to attend as well. Please excuse the ill haste with which this letter was penned, since the mail post will arrive any minute to deliver this letter.

With warm regards, Governor Josiah Wickeby

Mrs. Stacey handed the letter back and resumed her seat, as Rawlins rolled the parchment up and slid it back into his robes. "This letter was received last night. And being the judicious man I have raised him to be, William has left immediately for the capitol."

Tears sprang to Abigail's eyes and threatened to spill over. "I don't believe it for one minute," she replied, trying to keep the anguish out of her voice.

But where is he, really? Is he confined? Hurt? The doubt gnawed at her. *Or, has he really abandoned me?*

"Believe it, my dear," was the reverend's snarling reply. "And now I call forth the witness to present her evidence, Lady Violet Wickeby."

All heads turned toward the entrance as Ms. Wickeby entered in a simple white sundress quite en vogue with the high fashion of the day. Her golden curls were pinned up into a crown of ringlets inlayed with wild flowers. The audience murmured their approval, and Ms. Wickeby rewarded them with a blush and an endearing smile. After Rawlins directed her to come up onto the platform beside him and share her story, she looked into the steely faces of the two sisters, and with a wicked glint in her eye, casually brought up her left hand and brushed a curl away from her face.

Abigail's gaze landed on a gold ring with a glittering garnet stone encircled by tiny diamonds, and like a fuse being lit, she exploded in outrage, "My engagement ring! William gave it to me. It was wrenched from my finger during my incarceration this past week."

Violet looked taken aback. "William proposed to *me* with this *very* ring in the presence of his family just before he left." She looked to Rawlins for confirmation.

"It is true. I can attest to this claim."

A small bubbling of excitement spread among the women of the audience.

"A wedding!"

"I wonder when it will take place."

"Do you think it will happen here?"

"No, you goose, it ought to be at the capitol on the Wickeby Estate."

Men silenced their women, but one penetrating glare from their reverend doused the remaining embers of excitement to ashes.

Abigail spoke slowly, her voice trembling with rage, "So then *I* am made to be the liar."

Thunder rippled menacingly overhead and she winced at the sudden jab of pain in the center of her back. *What* was going on with her back? It felt like it wanted to split right open. She cast a look at Emily and saw the same bleached expression of pain. Abigail could only blame the aches on the toll a week of confinement in a frigid dungeon had wreaked upon their bodies.

Nonetheless, she straightened and ignoring the pain, continued evenly, looking Rawlins squarely in the eye, "You white-washed hypocrite...." The audience gasped. "You would force William to marry Violet simply to improve your connection in society. You would trample upon, even *murder* innocent—"

But Abigail was not to finish, for with a wave of the reverend's hand, she had been forcibly gagged by the jailer. Emily's protesting cries were silenced as well.

"You have had your turn Ms. Prynn. Now, let us hear what Ms. Wickeby has to say," Rawlins drawled.

Emily sobbed quietly while Abigail glared daggers at Violet, who ignored her and began her performance for the audience. "About a fortnight ago, my mother and I were returning home from our visit to Mrs. Norris's shop right here in the town square. We were out buying ribbons and doilies for the upcoming governor's ball, you see, which is why my mother is quite indisposed at the moment with preparations for it. I, myself, must hurry back this evening to rejoin my William"—Matheson restrained Abigail by the elbow—"and help with the preparations. There is just so much to do!

"Well, as we were walking back to the Rawlins family's home, our gracious host for the summer," she cast a quick, charming smile at Reverend Rawlins, "the overcast sky began to thunder something terrible. We sought the quickest way home, my mother and I, which we had heard once before was through the forest. So, into the forest we went.

A little ways in, we heard something that chilled us right to our very bones."

The audience inched closer to the edges of their seats as Violet wrung her hands.

"Two women's voices shouting incantations in a strange language. And a third voice: deep, gravelly, and masculine. The whole forest was filled with their words. It was sickening to the soul to hear. My mother suddenly grew weak and could no longer stand. She could not go on, you see. But I knew I had to. I willed myself to move forward.

"The air felt more and more oppressive, you see, and, by and by, I felt as if all the happiness I had ever known in the world was being over-shadowed with a terrible misery. I had so many depressing thoughts in a minute than I ever thought I could entertain in a lifetime. It was...it was dreadful!" Violet gulped. "Then, finally...finally...." But here, she faltered, as if the memory was too distressing to share.

"Go on, dear," a woman from the audience encouraged.

"Yes, do," said another.

Clearly, Ms. Wickeby held the audience spellbound.

Taking a deep breath and avoiding the older Prynn sister's murderous stare, Violet continued, "While I hid behind a tree, I saw the Prynn sisters dancing around an enormous, strange, glittering rock, whilst shouting foreign incantations and holding hands with, with—oh! I dare not say it!" Violet cried, an uplifted palm to her forehead, as if about to swoon.

"Who, child, who?!" an elderly woman cried out from the audience.

Emily shook her head in tearful disbelief, and one wouldn't dare look upon Abigail's face in that moment.

Thunder continued to growl outside.

The reverend placed a consoling hand on Violet's shoulder. "Go on, Violet. No harm shall befall thee. We are in the Lord's house."

Clutching her chest and taking a deep, steadying breath, Violet finished tremulously, "The Man in Black."

Gasps and exclamations from the audience filled the room, some crossed themselves, and a flash of lightning illuminated the entryway, followed by a thunderous roar that rattled the small church as if it were made of matchsticks.

"It's the Man in Black himself, come to join his two servants!" wailed a panicked voice.

"Evidence" for an evil presence in the village was spilling freely from the audience's mouths now:

"My cows feed on the pasture by that very forest and for exactly a fortnight now, they won't be milked!"

"I saw a black cat staring at me from the fence last night!"

"My pocket mirror has cracked!"

"My mother-in-law wants to move in!"

"My cabbage patch rotted overnight exactly two weeks ago!"

"I swear I spied a shadow lurking behind me in broad daylight!"

"My Wilhelmina took ill just after the Prynn sisters departed from their visit!"

Reverend Rawlins hung back for a moment, allowing the hysteria to sweep over the congregation. When it reached a fever pitch, he lazily lifted his hands and drawled, "Now, now... Calm yourselves everyone. Calm yourselves!"

The clamor fizzled out.

Turning to the ashen-faced woman beside him, he asked gently, "What happened next, Ms. Wickeby?"

"Well, when I saw...what I saw," she continued quavering, wringing her hands, "I made to run away back to my mother, but-but then I saw that Abigail had stopped and, and she was looking right at me."

Here, Violet looked right at Abigail.

Abigail could not help raising a questioning eyebrow despite the cold fury that clouded her face and the inexplicable pain that pounded in her back.

"She had this expression in her eyes of-of sheer hatred just like she has now."

Abigail sensed a trap about to spring and immediately regretted displaying her temper at the trial. Her strong-willed temperament had always fueled her fighting spirit, but now it would be used against her to nail the coffin shut.

Still gazing at Abigail as if entranced, Violet continued, "I suddenly felt ice-cold and weak, and...and...then, I—" She suddenly gripped the edge of the pulpit with one hand and swayed.

Rawlins caught her by the elbow. "Violet? Are you ill?"

To everyone's horror, Violet's eyes rolled up into the back of her head. She collapsed sideways onto the platform, convulsing violently.

The effect was instantaneous. Several of the young men leapt out of their seats and engulfed Violet. One held her head, another placed a thick, wooden quill in her mouth lest she bite off her tongue, two held her hands on either side, while others stood around her protectively shielding her from Abigail's view. At the same time, mothers clasped their children to their bosoms, and some scrambled over their seats and exited the building in fear. Hysterical voices cried out.

"Witches!"

"Burn the abominations!"

Objects were now being hurled at the Prynn sisters, who were huddled together in fear of the crowd's mania. A belt buckle slashed its way across Emily's pallid cheek, while a potato struck Abigail hard in the shoulder.

Matheson sneered as he took several steps away from the cross-fire, while Reverend Rawlins pounded his fist and called for order until the tumult simmered down to a buzz. Violet stirred, was helped up, and ordered by Rawlins to be escorted back to his home.

Facing the two sisters, he bellowed his verdict, "Abigail and Emily Prynn, by the power vested in me as the appointed overseer and judge of Elmridge, as well as one of the Lord's ordained reverends, and based on the evidence presented here today, I hereby find the accused guilty of witchcraft and of abetting the forces of darkness. Should you now confess to these crimes and repent, the Lord will forgive you and you will be shown mercy. You will be spared the purification of your soul by fire and will instead be blinded and branded an outcast as a lifetime penance. Matheson, uncover the mouth of the elder one. Abigail Prynn, do you confess to being a witch and hereby repent of this sinful crime?"

Abigail merely spat on the ground before the pulpit, a look of utter disgust on her face.

A wave of the reverend's hand and Abigail was gagged again. He now turned his attention to Emily, bright red blood seeping from the fresh cut across her pale cheek and mingling with the tears that ran dolefully throughout the entire proceeding. "Emily Prynn, do you confess to being a witch and hereby repent of this sinful crime?" He nodded for Matheson to ungag her.

Immediately, Emily let out a wail akin to the cry of a fawn separated from its mother and caught in the mouth of a ravenous wolf. "Mama! Papa!"

A hush blanketed the audience, and Abigail hung her head and wept.

A light rain began to fall outside.

Ignoring the stirrings of conscience inside him, Rawlins proceeded to give the jailer a meaningful glance and so Emily's cries were muffled into silence. Driving in the final nail, he boomed, "Since no confessions will be given, the Prynn sisters have chosen the way of fire."

~~*~~

There are many kinds of fire. There is the fire that will blanket a person with its warmth and defend her from the biting cold, and there is the friendly fire that will light the way in the darkness, or heat and cook one's food for sustenance. These are the kinds of charitable fires the Prynn sisters have known and welcomed all their lives.

The fire that they are about to meet is of the feral and gluttonous sort. Made up entirely of flaming tongues, its appetite never satisfied. It licks and feeds, swelling larger and wilder, devouring all in its path and leaving only a smoldering trail of ashes in its wake.

Sometimes, though, what was meant for evil is mercifully used for good: like the fresh green buds that grow from the charred remains of a forest fire, or like the phoenix's spontaneous fiery death and its subsequent miraculous birth from the ashes. So, too, would the Prynn sisters experience a new birth from this infernal fire.

~~*~~

Abigail and Emily clasped hands as they stood at the stake, tied back-to-back. The crowd encircled them, some jeering and some quiet with apprehension at what they were about to witness. The light rain continued to fall from the iron sky as it soothed the Prynn sisters' hot cheeks and mingled with the tears that poured freely from their eyes.

Reverend Rawlins stepped onto a box and towered above the crowd as he held out his arms. "We are gathered here today to serve as witnesses to the purification of Abigail and Emily Prynn's sinful souls by fire, so that they may be made commendable to enter the kingdom of Heaven." He read their last rites and, after a meaningful look at Matheson, stepped off the box and joined the crowd of spectators.

Matheson ignited the brush encircling the base of the stake and stepped back. The flames spread rapidly, and within seconds, had already consumed the base and were licking at the Prynn sisters' feet.

"It burns!" Emily wailed, the fire creeping up her skirts.

"Heavenly Father, be merciful and release us from this agony!" Abigail cried.

While the sisters screamed in absolute torment before the transfixed crowd, something strange began to occur. The horrendous burning sensation that was torturously eating them alive was slowly being overtaken by a cooling, tingling sensation that felt like tiny explosions bursting pleasantly all over their skin.

What's more, the sky was blackening and the gray clouds were being impossibly drawn together into a dark swirling mass, right above the Prynn sisters. The light rain turned into a pounding torrent and a mighty wind began to blow that swept some of the flames onto nearby onlookers, who screamed and frantically worked to put them out. Although the sudden ferocity of the weather was enough to frighten half the crowd away, the rest remained rooted to their spots, staring gapingly at the two sisters, who were now glittering with a golden sheen from head to toe.

Abigail concentrated on the dark whirlpool in the sky above their heads, while Emily grew paler and paler until she seemed almost translucent.

The reverend's voice thundered madly above the howling wind, "Matheson, rekindle the flames! The witches must burn!!"

But Matheson was nowhere to be found. With a roar of exasperation, Rawlins flung a burning branch at the base, but this, too, was doused by the drenching rain. In a wildly desperate act, he snatched a pistol from the holster of the man next to him and pointed it at Abigail.

Screams punctuated the air.

But just as quickly as Rawlins had moved, a bolt of lightning directed by Abigail's gaze zapped from the sky and struck him with a deafening crash that left a charred, smoking hole where his black heart had once been.

Pandemonium ensued as people scrambled over each other to escape.

Emily, who looked as if she had been fading away in her increasing pallor, suddenly disappeared completely from view, leaving behind a cloud of shimmering gold dust, while Abigail let out a gut-wrenching cry of agony as her back indeed split open and a pair of enormous glittering, golden wings burst out, cutting through her bonds.

Another agonizing howl pierced the air and Emily reappeared on the ground on all fours, a pair of massive golden, glittering wings also protruding from her back.

Strangled gasps and screams escaped from the remaining witnesses, and some fainted as the Prynn sisters grabbed each other's hands and took off into the air, growing impossibly smaller, until they resembled two golden lights being swallowed up by the tempest, leaving only a trail of glittering dust in their wake.

2

Why the Caged Girl Reads

**Today - Littleton,
Kentucky**

Lisselle Montague let the last page (Today – Littleton, Kentucky) of the fairy tale book close with a whisper. "And they lived happily...ever...after." She smiled at the dreamy-eyed, ragtag children sitting at her feet.

Her next words released them from the spell. "The end."

A collective sigh arose from the group, but a few scowled deeply.

Little Sally Jenkins embraced herself with her long, blonde pigtails. "*I* want to marry a prince when I grow up."

Lee Jackson snorted. "Awww, miss, can't we read a story about the Wild, Wild West?"

"Yeah, talking animals and magic ain't real," added another boy, a finger digging around in his nose.

Several others grumbled in agreement.

"Alright, then," Lisselle said. "We'll meet again next week, and we'll make up something about gun-slinging princesses and magical cowboys. And maybe we'll even act some of it out. What do you all think?"

The children cheered.

"I'm gonna have the sheriff put a warrant out for the prince and set traps for them talking critters," Lee called out.

"Oh no, you won't!" Beatrice, the tallest, pudgiest child of the group, got in his face. "Prince Charming is the best swordsman there is, so y'all won't be able to touch him!"

"I'd like to see 'em swipe aside the sheriff's bullets with his sword!" Lee yelled back, then quickly dodged Beatrice's fist.

Lisselle quickly stepped in between them. "Ookay, children, take a breather. Same time again next month and have those story ideas ready. Everyone, get on home."

The children dispersed in a chattering frenzy from the makeshift library of the O'Tooles' living room. It was the biggest air-conditioned room in the little poor, farming community of Littleton, Kentucky, which seemed to be stuck a few decades behind the times. Story-time for these children was like movie-night for "them uppity city kids."

Replacing the last fairy tale book into its gap on the shelf, Lisselle turned to gather her belongings, but clutched her chest and screeched at the scarecrow standing in the doorway. It took a step forward and her breath whooshed out in annoyance. "Geez, Tommy, you scared me."

The oldest and lankiest O'Toole son. His overalls were covered in farm-dirt and he stood shifting his weight between his two feet. His ears stuck out through his straw-colored hair as red as the apples he'd been picking. "Uh, hi Lissi.... Didn't mean to scare ya."

"It's alright. How've you been?" She began packing her things more quickly.

"Been just fine."

She couldn't keep out the suspicion that'd been growing since he'd volunteered to do all the yard work at her house for free. At first, she'd looked forward to a friendly face to talk to, but once that face started peering through her windows and searching her out, the heebie-jeebies had started settling in. And the bundles of wildflowers she'd started finding beneath her window sure didn't help. She'd tossed them out before her father could discover them.

She was so embarrassed, she couldn't even complain to her father. Besides, she was afraid he'd do something crazy to chase Tommy away like leave a bear trap where he raked leaves or something. Her father was infamous for being over-protective of her. Ever since then, she'd been successfully avoiding Tommy.

Until now.

Lisselle hitched her bag over her shoulder and turned to go, but Tommy didn't move out of the way. When she looked up into his face, icy dread gripped her. He was gazing at her with this painfully shy smile, twisting and untwisting his hat in his hands, a deep blush spreading across his face from his tomato-red ears.

She gulped. *Oh no, please no.* As her eyes darted around for some means of escape, he began talking, but she listened like Charlie Brown did with grown-ups.

Soon enough, Tommy was waving his hand in her face. "You alright? You checked out on me for a second there."

"Yes. It's just that, um..." an idea came to her, "my condition! I have this thing where I just, you know, sort of space out for long periods of time like a trance and, um, yeah, there's no cure."

"Old man Pollack told you this?"

Rats! she thought. He was the only doctor around for miles and miles and everyone went to him. It didn't matter that he was a veterinarian. "People are animals, too," the doctor always said.

"Well, anyhoo," Tommy continued. "What I was trying to say...I mean, what I'm trying to ask you is, uh...." He fell to tracing a pattern on the rug with his boot.

"Hey, well," she announced a bit too loudly, "I've really got to get going. Papa'll be home soon and I've got to get dinner ready." She moved towards the doorway, but he planted himself in her path. A flash of impatience went off in her chest. *I'm going to count to three and if he doesn't move, I'm going to kick—*

"I've been wondering if, if, well…if I…." His hat was now a twisted mess in his hands and his face was getting redder and splotchier by the second.

"Yes?" She asked, desperate to be done with this.

"Can I take you to Betsy's cookout next weekend?"

She huffed out impatiently. "Tommy, you know I'm not allowed to go to those things."

"Well, I know, but I thought since your Pa' knows me and I hope trusts me that he wouldn't mind you going, as long as I was there to keep an eye on you."

Lisselle thought that that might actually be a good plan, despite the fact that she'd show up with Tommy. She could always slip away from him once there. Maybe her father *would* finally let her out of the house to socialize. After all, he did appreciate Tommy for his work and he *was* the son of his biggest client, Mr. O'Toole, who ordered special medicine from her father on a monthly basis, which is what mainly kept food on the table at her house.

Just as Lisselle was about to agree, Tommy had to go and ruin it.

"You know, to protect you from the herd of scary folks that'll turn on you and trample you underfoot."

She narrowed her eyes. "Bye, Tommy." And pushed past him.

"Awww c'mon, Lissi, I'm sorry. You know, it's true though. What's your Pa' so afraid of that he can't let you out and mingle with everyone? You know, people been wondering if there's something wrong with you, but those of us that know you say that ain't it. So, everyone's been saying that maybe your Pa's been cooking up illegal "medicines" in that chemistry lab of his, or more likely he's just got a few loose screws—oww!"

Tommy had made two mistakes that left him crumpled on the floor cradling his injured parts: one, he'd grabbed her arm when she'd tried to get past him for the third time, and two, he'd insulted her father.

"Don't you *ever* insult my family!" She stepped over him as he looked up at her through one eye, wincing in pain. "He's a pharmacist! And, he's *not* crazy—I'm just all he's got!"

Thwack! She let the screen door slap shut behind her.

Immediately, Lisselle heard, "Thomas Beuford O'Toole! What did I tell you about slamming that door?!"

"It weren't me, Momma!"

~~*~~

Angry tears stung Lisselle's cheeks as she trampled home through the fields, sending a startled flock of swallows scattering into the sky. *Stupid Tommy, who does he think he is? He had no right to make fun of me and Papa.* She kicked at a cluster of rocks that lay in her path.

Although Lisselle hated to admit it, what really hurt the most about what Tommy said was that it was mostly true. She wasn't allowed to participate in the community. Or even leave the area around her house, except once a month as a "treat" to take orders to the O'Toole house. A family her father had deemed safe enough to expose his daughter to. And that had taken years. He would spaz if he knew that she'd taken up to reading stories to the neighborhood kids that would gather there to meet her, and not Mr. O'Toole's ailing mother like he thought.

Once a month was all she had to mingle with civilization. All because of her father's paranoia with "Big Brother" watching. Or of the pharmaceutical corporations who might send agents to steal his secret medicinal ingredient—a secret he kept from her too. He would never elaborate. Never explain to her why he'd moved them when she was a baby from France to Kentucky to live off the grid. Her mother had died giving birth to her and he hadn't bothered to bring any photographs with him. Apparently, they had left in a hurry. Once, she asked him to describe what she looked like. He was awestruck as he remembered: vivacious and aloof all at once, never aging, forever beautiful.

"Never aging?" she repeated perplexed.

He snapped out of his reverie and pinned her with wary eyes, as if he'd said too much. "It is still too painful to speak of her. It always will be."

"But am I anything like her?"

"No," he said quickly, but then smiling nervously, he backtracked. "I mean…I see in you, all that was good in her." She bristled at the insinuation that she couldn't say aloud: then what was bad about her mother?

The only other details about her that Lisselle had gleaned over the years were that her mother had long black hair and light brown eyes. And they had no other family. It was just her and Papa now.

She reached that fork in the path: the right one, which was Papa-approved, led to their tiny 2/1 house through the woods, and then there was the left one that led to the main road and to definite contact with strangers—hence, Papa-forbidden. So forbidden, he'd threatened to burn all her books if she defied him on this. That's how serious he was about sheltering her from the "dangerous world" around them. He was willing to incinerate the only friends and experiences she'd made in the imaginary worlds she'd constructed from reading books. To lose her books was to lose her only means of escape. She couldn't even dream at night as an escape. It was an oddity about her—the fact that she never dreamed. But she'd made peace with it. Kind of had to since there was no explanation for it. So literature became the world that she thrived in.

But at 15 years old, even the latest books her father brought home for her from his business trips (driving his 1997 Oldsmobile into the nearest towns to sell his medicines) were leaving her shrouded in bitterness. She knew now: books were no substitute for real people and experiences. She wanted to live and feel in the here and now. In this skin, not just in her mind. Imagining heart-to-heart conversations through characters…dances, swimming, a circus, exploring a city, exploring *anything*, through books wasn't enough anymore. She wanted a real Mr. Darcy to kiss, a real Anne Shirley to befriend….

Lisselle squeezed her eyes shut and took in a deep breath, letting it out slowly and counting away the raging storm brewing inside her. It usually only took up to 10 or 12, but today, she felt a little better at 56. It was a technique that her father had taught her when she was very little. Come to think of it, he'd taught her right after the only extraordinary incident that had ever happened in her life. It was a memory she had allowed to fade away into her imaginary world because that's where that kind of incident belonged. Even now, thinking back on it, she still couldn't explain it.

When she was four years old, a playmate broke the head off her only doll and so she cried and howled, but when he laughed and threw the doll's head at her, she'd retaliated in a blinding rage, screaming as she rushed at him and pushed him down. The light bulbs had shattered, plunging the house into shadows. The boy's mother, who'd been stopping by to buy one of Papa's medicines, screamed in horror as she found her son slumped under the window, breathing raggedly with two small, charcoal handprints burnt through his shirt, branding his little chest.

Papa hadn't allowed anyone into their house after that and had taken his business on the road.

Lisselle blinked. The memory was all too real. How could she have forgotten? She turned it over in her mind, over and over, as a realization took form that made her blood run cold.

Was her father protecting her from everyone? Or...was he protecting everyone else from her?

Lisselle shook her head and made her decision—the main road it was. She headed left. Papa could have her books.

3

Papa, I Just Killed A Man

"This is it?" Lisselle said, unimpressed.

The main road didn't look like much: it was a worn-out gravel road flanked by grass fields fallowing as far as the eye could see. For now, she relished her private rebellion, especially since Papa wasn't about to find out. But for next time, she'd take the original way since the view was better. She figured it would be about a good half-hour walk now before she could cut through the woods to get home.

After a bit of walking, her sour mood dispersed and she fell into her usual habit of fantasizing. Looking around to ensure no one was watching, she began humming the "Follow the Yellow Brick Road" song and skipping to the beat. She was Dorothy now, linked arm-in-arm with the Tin Man and Scarecrow, while Toto ran and yapped before them. Eventually though, before she could reach the Emerald City, a rumbling noise in the distance interrupted her reverie.

She immediately stopped her prancing and started walking normally. "They'd think I was an escaped mental patient," she muttered.

A truck appeared on the horizon and got louder and larger as it grew nearer, spewing a black cloud of smoke behind it.

Lisselle couldn't explain it, but an icy foreboding settled in her chest. "I must be catching Papa's paranoia," she scoffed at herself.

Run, a gravelly voice rasped in her mind.

She froze in her tracks, rattled. "And now officially hearing things." She swallowed and looked off warily to the side. There was a homestead a ways off in the distance. If she took off now, she could make it there before the truck had time to reach her. I mean, they wouldn't drive off the road and follow her through the fields, right?

"Stop!" she chided herself. "I'll just move off to the side and they'll pass." She continued walking on the grass, ignoring the chill spreading inside her.

The rusty green truck roared closer and she could make out two passengers inside the cab and a third sitting back in the cargo bed. As they passed her now, they slowed down with their eyes glued to her as if she were a prime rib meal.

She snapped her attention forward, picking up her pace and feeling as if she'd been undressed with their eyes. They were grimy-looking with red, sun-burnt faces. The two men in the front wore wife-beater shirts and the one in the back was bare-chested and bald. They reminded her of three stray dogs wandering the road, panting in the heat, sniffing out an unlucky little rabbit to cross their path.

But, thankfully, they hadn't stopped, and as the rumbling grew farther away, she breathed a giant sigh of relief. Still maintaining her brisk pace though, all she could think about was getting home. She'd never wanted to be home so badly as she did right now.

"Argh! Stop stressing!" she admonished herself. "They're gone, relax!" But her steps felt unsteady now and she tripped over a tuft of grass, crashing into her knees. And then she heard it: the rumbling of a truck growing louder as it came closer.

The voice in her head screeched, *Run! Before it's too late!*

Lisselle launched herself off the grass and broke into a run. Panting, she didn't even bother to look back. Her sixth sense screamed that the men in the truck were coming back for her. It drowned out the scolding her practical side was giving her for running for no reason.

And then she heard them:

"Where you running off to, baby?"

"Yeah, whoo! Look at 'er go!"

She ran faster, kicking up blades of grass behind her. Her lungs burning.

But she was not quick enough.

The truck swerved in front of her, cutting off her path, and coming to a stop. The driver leaned his arm over the door and blew a kiss at her. She spotted the barrel of a rifle leaning against the dashboard.

Lisselle backed away slowly, as if retreating from a circling pack of wolves.

When the man in the back hopped out of the truck, she turned and began running again. She heard pounding footsteps behind her and roaring laughter from the truck. Before long, her arm was seized and she was wheeled around into the tight embrace of a sweaty, gap-toothed redneck.

"You're a pretty little thing," he grinned, spraying her with spit and revealing a line of yellow, crusted teeth. She turned her face away in disgust—the stench of rotten breath and alcohol was like a slap in the face.

Before she had a chance to struggle, he spun her forward, twisting her arm painfully behind her back and started marching her back toward the truck. With every fiber of her being riddled with fear and increasing panic, she screamed as loud as she could and struggled to get away, but her captor enveloped her in closer and clamped his hand over her mouth so hard she couldn't even move her mouth to bite him.

Oh God, oh God, oh God! Please help me! she thought frantically.

The man in the passenger seat got out, a thick coil of rope in his hand, and called out, "C'mon, Cal, hurry up! We ain't got all day!"

Grunting with the effort of restraining her, Cal called back, "She's fightin' me tooth and nail, this one. She's a lively one!"

The driver leaned a skull-tattooed arm out the window and produced a long knife blade. He waved it around menacingly, the blade's steel glinting in the sun, and purred, "Don't worry, fellas. I'll teach her to behave. Isn't that what I always do? Tame little pussycats they become."

Something strange was happening inside Lisselle. It was as if the sight of the knife and the driver's words had cranked a lever inside her all the way to max and now she felt as if the overheated concoction of fear and adrenaline fueling her body was about to blow. She trembled violently as every nerve in her body felt electrified, her vision growing hazier.

Oh no, she thought panicking. *I'm passing out!*

She willed herself to continue fighting. The sensation of thousands of hot, sharp needles began pricking at her skin from the inside, as if trying to pierce through from every square-millimeter of her body.

"What the hell?!" Cal cried out in alarm, shucking her to the ground. "She's burnin' hot!"

Lisselle cursed herself for being so incapacitated with fear. Her body was crackling with as much energy as a high-voltage wire, but she felt her consciousness fading. She heard the driver curse and yell at the other two, "Quit playin' around and tie 'er up!"

As soon as the two men grabbed her and lifted her off the ground, two things happened at once: everything went white and she felt a hot pulse explode from her out through her fingertips. The crunching and rumbling of what sounded like a giant boulder tumbling away and the sickening *crick-cracks* of two large heavy sacks landing in the distance met her ears. Just as quickly as the world had gone blank, her strength and full-color vision returned. Instinctively, she was on her feet and lunged out of the men's reach. But just as she was about to turn and run, Lisselle froze.

Cal and the other guy were lying immobile, far away in opposite directions from each other, their limbs splayed at odd angles with a thin column of black smoke rising from their bodies.

Her breath stalled in her lungs.

The truck lay upside down nearby, its wheels still spinning in the air. She scrunched her eyes to focus better and then clapped her hand over her mouth: the driver hung upside down, in a bloody crumpled heap, fish-eyed and staring blankly at her.

She turned and ran, as if the ghost of the truck was barreling after her.

4

The Voices Told Me To

Lisselle slammed the house-door behind her and fell back against it, sinking to the floor as she gasped for breath. "I killed them," she whispered raggedly, panic clawing up her throat. "I killed them all." She hugged her knees to her chest recalling the slimy, steel-trap arms of her captor, dragging her back to the truck, until suddenly—impossibly—she was free and they were dead.

Better them than you, the voice rasped like nails scraping down her mind.

Lisselle pressed her palms hard against her ears, as if that would help shut the voice out. "How is this even happening?!" she cried. She'd been fainting and then the men grabbed her and it was like she'd exploded awake. In that incredible second, she'd felt more alive than ever before. Remnants of that electrifying energy still buzzed through her body. "I-It has to be adrenaline. Super adrenaline!" She rambled on to herself, trying to make sense of everything. "L-Like that mom on the news once who lifted a truck off her child's leg or something."

A picture of the dead driver hanging upside down flashed in her mind.

She gulped nervously. She knew no amount of adrenaline from a wispy teenaged girl could toss a truck across a field like a skipping stone. Or the other two guys who were zapped back like a mile away. How in tarnation had she done that?! The smoke coming off them? Like she literally zapped them with some energy blast or something.

Holy. Moly. She was a freak! Maybe this was why her father kept her in the house. That beheaded doll incident made sense now. Her father was protecting everyone else from *her*.

There was a faint, wry laugh in her mind.

Lisselle gasped and jumped to her feet, moving away from the spot as if that would help put distance between herself and that voice. She wore down a path in the living room rug, trying to outpace the alarming thoughts that hounded her. Trying to keep them from arriving at a terrible conclusion about herself: she'd killed three people and that made her a murderer; she was hearing voices and that made her psychotic.

She was a psychotic murderer.

It was self-defense, little Prynn.

Lisselle let out an anguished scream. Squeezing her eyes shut and clenching her fists, she shouted in a shrilly voice, "Go away! Leave me alone!!"

Because her eyes were closed, she did not see how the lights flickered on and off in the house as she screamed. Slowly, she opened her eyes, expecting the voice to laugh or retort. But after a few minutes...nothing. Drawing in a long breath, she let it out and counted.

206.

Her breathing was even now and her headspace calm as glass. She became acutely aware of her hair sticking to her damp face like a cobweb and a burning sensation in her nostrils—the stench of alcohol-laced, roadkill breath still lodged in her nose. Her stomach turned over and she ran to the bathroom and threw up in the toilet. After a few heaves, her insides felt better, but she needed to erase the dead men from her skin.

She showered in scalding, hot water and winced as she scrubbed her skin with soap over and over, until her skin shone bright pink.

Soon, she lay curled up in her bed under the covers. She left a note for Papa in the kitchen for whenever he came home from his business trip that day.

Microwaveable dinner today. I'm not feeling well (girl issue), so I'm turning in early today. Love you to the moon.

Thinking of Papa made her realize that he was right. The world was dangerous. She'd almost been kidnapped and God knows what else.

She shivered at the thought and tightened the comforter around her shoulders. Tears burned in her eyes. *And* <u>I'm</u> *dangerous. I deserve to remain locked up in this house.*

Her heart feeling completely empty, she closed her eyes and drifted off into her very first dream.

~~*~~

Lisselle brought the hookah pipe to her mouth and took in a lengthy draw before exhaling a stream of purple perfumed smoke. The hand that she saw before her was tan and tipped with long, tiger-striped fingernails. A dainty bracelet of black stones encircled her wrist. Shocked, she wanted to verify her reflection in a mirror, but her body ignored her. She was trapped. As if she was an alien body-snatcher hitching a ride in this stranger. She had no control of her actions—she was a silent, passive observer through the eyes of this woman.

From the plush black chaise on which she lounged on, Lisselle could see through the haze of the hookah smoke that she was in an opulent room filled with exotic artifacts from around the world. The whole floor was covered in a white shag rug with a large black jaguar skin laid out in the center. Its petrified yawn revealed a swollen pink tongue and four sharp incisors, its glassy green eyes staring right at her.

She sighed loudly in an exceedingly bored mood. R-rated thoughts of ways to entertain herself crossed her mind, but while Lisselle gagged at the images, the woman dismissed them with a "been there, done that" attitude.

A knock sounded at the door. The woman narrowed her eyes at the door and thought about whether to answer it. Finally, another knock and the ho-hum feeling of nothing else to do made her rise off the chaise, but not before taking in another long draw from her hookah pipe. When she pulled open the door, a pair of college-aged male twins, in brown slacks and stiff white-collared shirts stood before her. She frowned darkly at the brown leather Bibles in their hands and exhaled the hookah smoke into their faces. They coughed and sputtered.

The shaggy-haired one choked out, "Good morning, m'am." *Cough, cough.* "We'd like to share an important message with you."

She looked them over as if savoring a juicy filet mignon. The boys were tall and lanky with chocolate brown eyes. One of them had a mop of black hair that fell in layers beneath his chin while the other had a closely cropped head of black curls. *I think I've found my entertainment for the day,* she thought with satisfaction. She leaned casually against the doorframe, allowing a sliver of white breast to peek from her silk black bathrobe.

The curly-haired twin nervously cleared his throat. "Uh, maybe, we should come back tomorrow like, um, in the afternoon so that you'll have more time to be like—*cough*—not naked."

The shaggy-haired twin, however, was not to be routed. "Ahem. You see, m'am—"

"Don't call me, m'am," she interrupted with a demurring smile.

He flushed a deeper red. "Right, um, I'm sorry, m'am, I mean, uh, Miss."

She rolled her eyes.

He continued, visibly flustered, "It says here—"

As soon as he opened his Bible, she recoiled with a loud hiss and the book suddenly snapped shut on its own. The boys looked up at her, as if a monster—witch or sorceress—loomed before them. They started backing away, but when she lifted her palms and flared out her fingers, the boys froze in place, their eyes darting around in horror as they realized they couldn't move a muscle. As she raised her hands a fraction, so did they until only the toes of their shoes touched the floor.

"Come, my pets," she drawled, and as she walked backwards into the room with her hands raised, they, too, followed, hovering in the air with their shoes scraping against the floor.

A voice boomed through what seemed like the ceiling of the room, "The pancakes are ready! Come and get 'em!" It was Papa's voice!

The sorceress stopped abruptly in her tracks, the boys frozen and dangling before her just above the jaguar hide. She peered slowly around the room. Her eyes narrowed as a realization dawned on her. She clapped her hands once, the movement effectively knocking the twins' heads together and sending them crashing to the floor. She smirked as she stepped over their crumpled KO'ed forms and slinked toward the grand, jewel-encrusted mirror on the wall.

The woman Lisselle saw reflecting back was astonishingly beautiful with wide amber eyes and waist-length, raven hair so unnaturally black it seemed to gleam in dark purple patches in the light. She was staring coldly and steadily at her reflection in the mirror. Actually, Lisselle got the uneasy feeling that the woman was somehow staring at *her*. She gasped as the woman's hand shot forward to the height of her own neck in the mirror and clenched her hand as if squeezing the throat. At the same time, Lisselle felt her own throat closing with excruciating pain and found herself struggling to breathe. Her vision swam in and out, but the witch only smiled as if unaffected—an evil exultant smile, her eyes gleaming with wicked pleasure.

Lisselle heard Papa's voice reverberating throughout the room again, this time, with an obvious note of impatience in it. "Lisselle Montague, your breakfast is getting cold! Now, for the last time, get up!"

The witch gasped, and inexplicably, her sinister expression melted away into a look of utter surprise and humane concern. She snatched her hand away, releasing Lisselle.

5

As He Lay Dying

Lisselle shot straight up and sucked in a giant gulp of air, feeling as if she'd been yanked out from nearly drowning in deep, black waters. Her fingers flew to her throat as she looked around trying to orient herself. She was still in her bed, sweaty and entangled in her long, brown curly hair, and the mirror on her dresser next to her showed her own hazel eyes staring back at her and not that of the witch's.

What. Was. That? She rubbed her throat and found it painful to swallow. *Was that supposed to be a dream?*

"Holy cow, I had a dream!" she cried aloud.

"Mmmm, yum! I guess I have *two* plates of blueberry pancakes to eat!" her father beckoned from the kitchen.

Lisselle called back, "I'll be out in a sec!" She fell back onto the bed and gazed up at the plastic glow-in-the-dark stars glued to her ceiling. Ever since she'd made that left turn on the field, her life had changed. Her first time out on her own in stranger-danger world had opened a floodgate of bad in her life. So far, she'd almost been kidnapped, somehow killed three men, and then almost gotten choked to death in her very first dream.

Papa really was onto something when he chose to have them live off the grid.

A small *boom* and a brief rattling of the other side of the house signaled that Papa had retired to his lab. Which meant she could now eat without having to explain the odd behavior she would undoubtedly display. He would've probably known right away that something was up. She took a deep breath and closing her eyes, told herself, "You can do this. Just act normal." Without bothering to brush her hair, she wrestled the mane of tight curls into a long, thick braid down her back, said a quick prayer, and then went out to face her new reality.

A loud clang and the sound of glass shattering came from the lab. There was a brief silence followed by a roaring "Dagnabbit!" from Papa. There was coughing and then the sound of the window being thrown open. She could hear her father continue to mutter curses in French and shuffle about the room. She didn't know what new medicine he was working on now, but from the sounds of his frustration these past few weeks in the lab, it wasn't going too well.

Lisselle picked at the cold pancakes and tried to think about what she was going to do today. It was difficult to even think since behind her, the TV's only working channel, a world news network that made every event seem like Dooms Day, was blaring some news about government officials running human trafficking rings. Another stomach-turning reason for her to never venture out.

Just as she was about to get up to switch off the TV, the "Breaking News" jingle sounded and the reporter announced, "Ladies and gentlemen, this just in: the Hammerson brothers, three fugitives who escaped from Pilsom's maximum security prison last month, were found dead yesterday."

Lisselle nearly fell backwards over her chair. She scrambled to her knees in front of the TV, so that she was at eye-level with the thickly-mustached reporter.

"Once again, the Hammerson brothers are dead."

Black and white mug shots of three familiar scowling men flashed onto the screen. She shrieked as she fell back onto her elbows, her heart threatening to burst out of her chest.

"Here is Tyler with the details."

The scene cut to an immaculate dark-skinned young man holding a mic, standing in a very familiar-looking field marked off with yellow tape and crawling with policemen. "Thank you, Tom. Now behind me"—he moved out of the way and Lisselle gasped— "you'll see a green, overturned truck with a yellow tarp covering the side door and two more tarps lying on the field. These tarps are covering, what has officially been confirmed as, the lifeless bodies of the Hammerson brothers. They had been on the run from the Feds for a month now, heading south of the border and leaving behind a trail of missing young women." She stopped breathing. "Now, their cause of death will not be officially determined until the coroner's report comes out. But for now, Chief Roberts has released the following statement."

The scene changed to a big, burly cop in aviator glasses with several mics in his face. "Based on the evidence we've seen so far and from our sole witness and various weather experts, it seems that their vehicle was impacted by a dry lightning strike." Her breathing resumed. "Although we cannot determine where the lightning bolt actually landed, the burn marks on the two victims' chests on that field and the force with which the truck was apparently struck from the road, all point to the possibility that a multi-branching lightning strike may have been the culprit. But, of course, please keep in mind that this is all speculation until the coroner's report is released."

The scene cut back to the reporter who was now accompanied by a tall, lanky man in overalls. "I'm here with Mr. Joe Wilcox who has a farm nearby and who is the witness that Chief Roberts referred to." Then, turning to Joe with the mic, Tyler asked, "What exactly was it that you witnessed?"

Joe had been smiling and waving at the camera. "This is real live national news, not just local, right?"

Tyler nodded.

"Well, I'll be. Cousin Nathaniel, if you're watching, just know that I haven't forgotten about that $300 you still owe me and the next time you set foot—"

Tyler pulled the mic away and spoke into it while looking at the camera with an embarrassed grin, "Sir, we're on a timetable here. Please, just tell us: what did you witness?"

"Sorry. It's just the man doesn't pick up the phone and when he does, he pretends to be a voicemail machine—"

"Sir?"

"Alright, alright. Well, it wasn't what I'd seen, it's what I'd heard. It was a clear, blue day, I was out feeding the chickens and there weren't a cloud in the sky, well except for the little puffy ones that announce the cold's coming. And then out of nowhere, I heard a great big BOOM! And then a low rumble. I could swear I felt the ground shake a little too. The chickens were besides themselves and my animals were all making a commotion. It sounded like it come from this direction too."

"Is that all, sir?"

"Well you know, about those Hammerson fellas, that was the hand of justice that struck 'em down. I say, good riddance! All them poor girls.... If I'd gotten my hands on them, why I'd wring their necks like—"

"Thank you, Mr. Wilcox. And so...." The reporter slowly walked away from Joe, who was waving and smiling again at the camera, until he was the only one in the frame. "Dry lightning strike? The 'hand of justice'? Whatever the cause, families everywhere can breathe a little easier tonight. The Hammerson brothers"—the camera zoomed in—"are dead. This is Tyler Jackson reporting live for WCN. Back to you, Tom."

A voice from behind Lisselle said, "That is—"

Lisselle shrieked as she whipped around.

Her father stood there like a tall thin reed, the tight curls of his white hair reduced to soft wisps over the years. His white lab coat was peppered with chemical stains and burnt holes, and the lab goggles he wore magnified his eyes to big round saucers, which were blinking at her with concern.

"I was saying," he continued in his thick French accent so that his 'th's sounded like 'z's, "that 'good riddance' quite sums it up." He bent down to her level. "Are you okay, Lissi?" When he said her name, he always accented the last syllable so it sounded like "Lis-seé."

"I was just—I didn't know you were standing there. How long have you been standing there?" She couldn't help sounding a bit accusatory.

"Well, naturally, I came out when you screamed." He touched her cheek. "There's nothing to be afraid of. Those evil men can't hurt anyone anymore." He pressed his hand more firmly against her cheek and then felt her forehead. "Lissi, sweetie, you're burning up."

"I'm still not feeling well from yesterday." *Two near-death experiences in a row can do that to a person,* she thought.

"I'm getting the thermometer. Stay put."

Sitting on the couch and resting her head against her hand, she tried to absorb what she'd just seen on the news. She had to find *some* comfort in the fact that she'd put a stop to those murderers. She could give herself a pep talk and say that it was self-defense, that she saved future women from dying at their hands, but if she technically wasn't a murderer, her actions still labeled her a killer. *A psychotic killer.* Before she could launch off the couch and escape that thought, Papa returned with the thermometer, goggles drawn up over his forehead. He was wheezing and coughing.

"Are you okay, Papa? You should go to one of the doctors in town. You know, a people-doctor. Not Dr. Pollack."

With a hand, he waved aside her concern. "It's just a cold. And besides, town doctors want you to register with the system."

"But you sound worse."

He popped the thermometer into her mouth.

Looking over at the TV, she pointed out, "Papa, that happened right by here." He tapped her nose for her to keep quiet while the thermometer worked its science.

"Yes. And around the same time you were supposed to be making your way back from the O'Tooles. Rendre grâce à Dieu (Thanks be to God) you never take the main road. Or it might have been *you* on that news."

Lisselle nodded and shivered.

He suddenly stood ramrod straight and stared at her. She could see the gears whirring in his mind as he continued. Finally, he muttered, "Dry lightning strike." She looked away quickly, his words like being doused with a bucket of iced water. He was figuring it out!

But he merely shook his head after a moment and forced a smile at her as he retrieved the thermometer from her mouth. His eyes went wide as he read the result, and he stumbled backward gripping his chest. "No!"

She went to him. "Papa, what's wrong?"

He gripped her shoulders, his eyes wild. "Did you take the main road yesterday?"

"What?" *How does he know?!* she thought, panicking.

"Please, Lissi, the truth."

She broke down. "I'm so sorry, Papa—I'll never do it again. I was just curious. Besides, the road's a boring view and the woods are much prettier."

A coughing fit seized him. She retrieved a glass of water for him, but he refused. "Did anything *happen* on the road?" He pointed at the TV. "Those men?"

Her mouth gaped open and she paled. And then he knew.

He gripped the back of the kitchen chair to steady himself. "They'll come for you now," he said raggedly.

"The police?" she squeaked.

He scrubbed his hand down his face. "Worse." Another round of violent coughs erupted from him.

"What?" No. This wasn't happening. The police already think it was a lightning strike that killed them. The worse that could happen now was Papa not ever letting her see the light of day. She would truly become a prisoner here.

Deny and lie. She *couldn't* let him think she had anything to do with the Hammerson brothers.

"Honestly, Papa," she helped him into the chair as the coughing subsided, "I didn't see those guys. I was, I was lucky." Distract, distract. "Besides, I have some good news: I finally had my first dream last night."

He jumped in his seat, his hand falling with a slap on the table as he turned to look at her. He was blanched with fear as if he was staring at a ghost.

She took a step away. "Papa, what's wrong? You're scaring me...I thought dreaming was a good thing—healthy."

And then as if a heavy yoke fell on his shoulders, he crumpled forward into his hands, gripping his forehead in despair. The thermometer lay beside his elbow on the table and when she reached for it, he came alive and tried to grab it before she did.

But she was faster. She blinked once, twice as she read it: 125°. "I-I should be dead right now!" She turned to him and pleaded, "Papa, please, *what* is going on?"

"C'est la façon dont cela a commencé avec votre mère (That's the way it started with your mother)," her father said, his head bowed.

All Lisselle understood was the word "mère," which meant "mother."

"What *about* my mother?" she demanded.

This time it was her father's turn to plead. He lifted his head and there seemed to be tears in his eyes. "Why, Lissi, why did you not listen to me?" He took a few steps closer to her, but seemed to be purposefully keeping his distance from her. "This is not the life I wanted for you. I tried to protect you." Another coughing fit made it difficult for him to get his words out. "To shield you from anything," *cough, cough,* "that may excite you into this state, so they wouldn't find—"

"By not having a life at all?" Lisselle cut in. "I'm 15 years old and the only thing I know about life comes from old books, th-that terrible news station, and you!" She was shaking uncontrollably now.

"Lissi, dear," *cough, cough,* "you must remain calm," he pleaded.

But it was too late. The little crack in the dam had spread until it split open and all the years' worth of pent up frustration came flooding out.

"Papa, you've always known something about me, especially since I was 4 years old, and you never tried to help me. You just shut me away, so you wouldn't have to deal with it. You weren't trying to protect me, you—you were just ashamed of me! I'm a freak somehow and you know it!"

The lights in the house flickered on and off.

Lisselle looked at her father as if daring him to say differently.

"Y-You don't understand. You're special." *Cough, cough, cough.* "But it can go wrong. Very wrong. You have to stay calm." Her father was coughing uncontrollably now. "Lissi, please, listen to me: there are dangerous people—" He reached for her but fell with a crash to the ground, bringing the chair on top of him.

She rushed to his side. "Papa!"

He was gasping for air now, struggling to speak. Focusing on her face, he held her cheek. "Lisselle, ma belle princesse (my beautiful princess)...."

"Papa, no! Why didn't you tell me you were this sick?"

"I've known for a while now, but...it...happened too soon. Too quickly."

Lisselle clasped his hand to her wet cheek.

"Listen," he gestured for her to come closer. "There's...a letter...in my desk drawer.... You must mail it," he gasped out.

"I love you, Papa. Please, don't leave me! I'm so sorry for those horrible things I said!"

"She can answer...all your questions."

"Who, Papa?"

His head fell limply against her hand.

"Papa, no!" She buried her head in his chest and sobbed, but soon felt his fingers stirring in her hair.

His lips moved silently as if trying to say something. Lowering her ear to his lips, she could barely make out his ragged whisper, "The woman in your dream...stay away from her." And with the final word dying on his last breath, he exhaled, "Beware the J—"

6

Halfway House

"You think she did it?"

"Oh, I know she did."

"How can you be so sure?"

"Do I need to remind you again about what that devil-child did to my nephew?"

"Oh, I've heard it before, but just always thought it was some odd little incident that got spun into a tall tale."

"You callin' my family a liar?"

"Now, Janice, there's no need to get all offended—"

"My sister's little boy had that, that *thing's* handprints charcoaled onto his baby chest. It was weeks before them scabs fell off. And now she gone done in her father. Heart-attack? Pfft! Heart-attack, my eye! I'll be glad when her dead-beat aunt sends word for her. Then maybe we'll finally be rid of that scourge!"

She hushed when a door clicked open followed by a loud thudding of heavy boots down the hall. A calm male voice boomed into the room, "Ladies, I think this book meeting's over. Your discussion of this most exciting chapter has reached my office and possibly some other ears in this house. I cannot allow my sleeping children nor our guest to be disturbed, so if you would all please bid each other goodnight."

"Oh, George! There's no need for that!" Janice O'Toole complained.

"Now, woman," he said simply, and thudded back down the hall to his office.

A bustle of complaints and goodbyes erupted among the six women downstairs before the front door expelled them into the night.

"Ooooh, that man. Who does he think he is?" Janice seethed. Lisselle could imagine her narrowing her eyes and was sure that the *click, click* of the heels was leading straight to the office. A few seconds later, she'd guessed right. A door slammed open and then, "George O'Toole! You've humiliated me in front of my friends!"

"Woman! How many times have I told you that malicious gossip is not welcomed in this house?!"

Lisselle clamped her pillow down firmly over her ears. She sighed and sunk deeper into her covers. Well, Tommy's covers. She'd been holed up in his room for over a month now. An idea that had Tommy practically walking on air nowadays. The O'Tooles had taken her in after her father's funeral until she got a response from her aunt, which was supposed to be any day now. At least, that's what she had told them.

The fact was she had lied.

Lisselle opened the bedside drawer and gingerly pulled Papa's crumpled envelope. She dropped it onto the night table and stared at it: *Emily Prynn. 8472 Sycamore Lane, Elmridge Estates, RI.* She felt a painful jab at the sight of her father's short, quick scrawl and she once again let the warm tears slip down their familiar trails.

Images of the funeral flashed in her mind: Papa lying all too still in a fresh pine box (he'd looked like a human doll), the *slam, slam, slam* of the hammer and nails sealing him away forever, the wildflowers and then shovels of dirt raining down onto the box, until a large wreath was laid on top of the fresh mound. It had begun to rain then. And the few people who had shown up started to trickle away. A few patted her shoulder. One whispered condolences in her ear. When she'd been fairly soaked through but still hadn't budged from her spot, Janice had wrapped an arm around her shoulders and drawn her away. Tommy had retrieved all her belongings from her house and then sealed up the windows with boards.

Since then, she'd hardly left his room. Her birthday came and went. 16 years old now. She hadn't even realized until days later when she noticed the date on a news program. But she didn't care. She'd taken up to staring at the bright television screen until she eventually started watching the programs. And the movies! Like books coming to life before her eyes! The more she watched, the angrier she grew at Papa. He'd lied to her! Her whole life was a lie! The world was not how he'd painted it. She learned there was plenty of good to experience in the world, and that it wasn't consumed by violence and crime everywhere. It made her blood boil to think that he must have rigged their own TV to show that one doomsday-style news channel. He went to reprehensible lengths to keep her in the dark and to keep her scared witless of the world. Making up stories about battling thieves on the road or outrunning packs of wolves.... All lies. And then, there was the proverbial salt jammed into the wound: they *did* have other family. An "Aunt Emily" who seemed to be in cahoots with her father to some extent.

Lisselle reached for the envelope and pulled out Papa's letter.

Emily,

I can no longer take care of my precious Lisselle because I am no longer physically able to. I am most likely dead. It is time for you to take in your niece. By this time, I do not know how much she knows, but I am entrusting her into your capable hands. Keep her safe. Remember, she does not dream. You know what happens when she does.

Enzo Montague

Lisselle crushed the letter back into its envelope. How much did she know? Just that she was kept hidden all her life because, apparently, she's an electric zapper that can kill people. What happens when she dreams? Nothing. Except for one hyper-realistic nightmare. Since then, though, her dreams had returned to darkness. And for this, she was grateful. She didn't want another run in with the nightmare witch, especially since her father's dying wish was for Lisselle to stay away from her. Something that puzzled and disturbed her to no end. How had Papa known? And "beware" of something that started with a 'J.' She couldn't think of anything dangerous that started with "J," except for a few animals. She'd asked Mr. O'Toole and he'd frowned sternly and said, "I can think of a few demon liquors that'll make some dangerous life choices look mighty attractive." So that was a dead end. She didn't think her father's last words to her would be to stay away from alcohol. But just in case he really meant it, she swore it off for the future.

She had so many toxic emotions festering inside her that she felt she was going to explode. She cried out through clenched teeth, "What's *wrong* with me?!" She clutched fistfuls of blanket as she suppressed the scream threatening to burst out. When the light in the room began to flicker, she swallowed her scream and didn't move a muscle until the light stilled.

Soon, she heard the clicking of heels growing louder in the hallway, until her door swung open and Janice emerged into the room. She took in Lisselle's wide, terrified eyes and rigid posture, still gripping the sheets. "I heard you cry out and then the lights decided to do a dance of their own." Janice's voice dripped with suspicion. "There's nothing to be afraid of, girl. Thomas says it was just an electrical shortage." But she had narrowed her eyes, as if she was looking right at the problem. The sweet Janice that had welcomed her into this house had eventually been poisoned towards her by the gossip. She had taken to calling her "girl."

The envelope! Lisselle silently panicked. She couldn't stop herself. Her eyes slowly came to rest on the crumpled envelope perched on the night table. She reached for it, but not quickly enough. Janice snatched it up and read the address. Her eyes narrowed further into slits. "You said you had mailed this, girl. It's been a month and here it is still. You lied to us!"

Lisselle opened her mouth, but no words came out.

Janice drew herself up tall and huffed, "This is going out first thing tomorrow. Overnight express!" She turned on her heels and slammed the door behind her just as Lisselle croaked out, "Please, don't!"

"The audacity of that girl! What did she think? That she would stay here forever?! I can't believe...." But Janice's outrage mercifully faded away down the hall.

~~*~~

A few days later, Lisselle sat next to Tommy in his truck, and through the rearview mirror, watched Littleton fade away into the dusty horizon. After the awkward goodbyes with the O'Tooles and the tearful hugs with the community children who, despite their parents' objections, had run over to the house as soon as the news of her departure had spread, she and Tommy headed out toward the Glenville train set to depart in exactly two hours. She reached into her pocket and pulled out the letter that had arrived from Aunt Emily last night. She inhaled it. *Mmm, still smells like gardenia.* Her eyes roamed over the ornate cursive writing that looked like artwork.

Dearest Lisselle,

I apologize. I apologize for the isolation you have endured all these years.... for the thousand questions I am sure you could never find answers to. I am most sorry for the loss of your dear father... the only man in the world who ever understood us. My deepest regret, though, is being kept apart from you. This was my and your father's decision for reasons that were only ever in your best interest. But now that you are ready, we can be together as family. I have done everything in my power to make your transition into Elmridge as smooth as possible. I have to warn you: your new world may come as a bit of a shock.

I am counting the hours.

Your aunt,

Emily Prynn

And just like that. Lisselle's aunt had reached through lost time and unknown miles and given her a long healing hug. For the first time, Lisselle felt as if she had a beacon of light to swim toward, away from the despair and confusion that she'd been drowning in.

Hope. That's what that new sensation was that had spread its wings in her chest.

She clutched the plaid green carpet bag that Papa had used for his travels and pulled it into a hug. If she breathed deeply into it, she could still smell their old house. She felt better enough now that she could begin to forgive him. Knowing there was one more thing she needed to do before she could close this chapter of her life forever, she turned to Tommy, who was dressed in his church suit with his hair slicked over, "Tommy?"

He sat up straighter. "Yes?"

"There's someone else I need to say goodbye to."

Understanding her request, he referenced his watch. "We could spare about ten minutes." He smiled gallantly at her.

She returned an appreciative smile before retreating into her lonely world again, gazing back out the window at the endless sea of plains.

Tommy, though, was not going to be pushed to the backburner again. He had given her plenty of space; first, because his mother demanded it, and then, because Lisselle had wanted it. Whenever he'd had a chance to speak with her on the occasional times he'd caught her leaving the bathroom, she would just smile sadly and absently at him and then quickly move past him and shut herself up in his room. Even now, in the cab of this truck, Tommy felt as if she had managed to exit into another room again. If this was the last time he would get to spend in this elusive goddess's presence, he wanted to make it count.

"So Elmridge, huh?" he asked, his voice coming out in a high pitch.

It took a few seconds for Lisselle to realize that Tommy was addressing her. "Huh?" she replied, somewhat dazed.

"Elmridge? You excited?" Tommy cringed just as soon as he said it and gave himself a mental smack on the forehead. *How can she be excited about anything? She just lost her father and was leaving behind everything she ever knew.*

"Um..." Lisselle tried to scramble her thoughts into a coherent response. "I guess," was all she could manage.

Tommy simply nodded sympathetically and when it was clear he would get no further response, sighed dejectedly and surrendered to the heavy silence.

Yet, his question had diverted her focus from the overcast skies of her depression to the promise of sun behind it. She began to think about her newfound family and her new home, a place her aunt had promised would be shocking. *Shocking good or shocking bad?* she wondered to herself.

"Tommy?"

"Yeah?" he replied eagerly.

"Do you know anything about Elmridge? I mean, have you even heard of it before?"

"Jeez, who *hasn't* heard of it?" was the surprising reply.

Lisselle flushed with embarrassment. *Me, of course,* she thought drily.

"You mean, you don't know *anything* about the place?" he continued incredulously. Her chagrined silence prompted him to continue more tactfully. "Not sure you're gonna like this too much, but the rich and famous folks send their kids there for some special school that's supposed to be the most elite in the country. They keep the list of students a secret, but I heard that the president's daughter goes there and even that singing fool that all the girls go nuts over—what's his name? Prince? Jack? Jared Prince, that's it."

Lisselle sank her head into one hand. "Great," she muttered. "The grass will never actually be greener anywhere else." How could she not stick out like a freak there with her raggedy t-shirt and jeans ensemble and country ways? And not to mention her mutant powers. It was a wonder Professor X hadn't called her yet. She could already envision herself walking down the high school corridor with her radioactive presence, students dropping dead as she passed, heads banging against lockers as they went down, papers scattering into the air.

"You don't have a thing to worry about, Lissi," he continued, breaking into her thoughts. "You're just so—" he swallowed. "You're smart and *prettier* than any girl I've ever seen in my life and that includes movies." He was bright red.

It was Lisselle's turn to squirm with embarrassment, but she couldn't deny that his compliment had warmed her up inside. Guess she just wasn't used to being told nice things about herself. When she rewarded him with a smile, Tommy continued, encouraged, "And I just wish that—" But he would never finish his sentence to her immense relief because, at that moment, a giant stone statue of an angel soared into view up ahead.

"We're here," she announced, unnaturally loud.

He pulled the truck to a stop underneath the rusted archway of Littleton Cemetery. "I'll wait here," he said, looking wistfully at her.

"Thanks, I won't be long." She shut the car door behind her and exhaled with relief at escaping another painfully awkward Tommy-moment. She walked past various cherubs perched atop small crumbling headstones until she reached the latest addition: a small rectangular slab of concrete. It still looked new and the ground beneath her feet still felt quite loose. She crouched down and gently caressed her father's name. "I miss you, Papa." The tears slipped down her cheeks like raindrops onto the gravestone and any anger she harbored toward him dissolved away. A slight breeze scattered dead leaves across the slab. She brushed them away and read the inscription again:

Enzo Montague

Survived by:

Lisselle,

Keep the dust, keep it safe.

She remembered overhearing a guest at the funeral snidely remark, "How morbid," after reading the inscription aloud. She had mentally passed off her father's choice of words as part of his eccentric ways, but for some reason, she kept reading the inscription over and over. For the first time, something struck her as odd about it, more so than her father's usual level. Papa was a stickler for written grammar... so what was off about this? The comma after her name was unnecessary, unless...he was addressing her! He must have actually been *telling* her, "Keep the dust, keep it safe."

She kissed her father's name on the gravestone. "I understand, Papa." She lingered there for a moment, basking in the warmth of this new communication from her father. It felt good to "hear" from him again.

But a growing sense of urgency pulled her away. She wasn't sure she'd make the train now, but it was a risk she had to take. She returned to the truck, only to discover that Tommy was nowhere to be found. She stuck her head in the truck's cab, the back, the other side, and did a 360° scan of the area, but no Tommy. "Oh, sugar!!" She could feel the seconds thudding by as fast as her racing pulse. "Tommy?!" she called. They had to leave *now* in order to make the detour *and* the train, but the only reply was the wind whispering through the trees.

Just as she was beginning to conjure up some horrible vision of Tommy being snatched by aliens, she breathed a sigh of relief as he emerged out of the cemetery. He was concealing something behind his back. "Hey! That was fast," he exclaimed cheerily. As he came closer to where she was, she noticed that his face was flaming red. "I thought it'd be *me* waiting by the truck."

Lisselle didn't care at the moment. She could only focus on her race against time. "Listen, we don't have time. I need to—"

"Whoa, whoa. Hold your horses, pretty lady. You mean, we don't even have a minute for *this*?" He whipped out what he'd been concealing: a bouquet of flowers.

She was beyond annoyance right now. She wanted to snatch up the flowers and shred them in his face. But her father raised her better than that. Through her teeth, she ground out as politely as she could, "Wow, they're beautiful."

He beamed and held them out for her to take. She noticed the different-colored mix of roses and carnations and just stopped short of taking them. "Wait a minute," she exclaimed. "You picked these off the graves!"

His face exploded into splotches of the deepest red as he burst out with, "Did not!"

Lisselle sighed with exasperation and tried the gentle route. "Tommy, thank you kindly for your thoughtfulness"—she grabbed him by the shoulders—"but I really need you to focus right now: I need you to take me back to my house."

"And then afterwards, we might as well drive back to *my* house because there's no way you're gonna make the train."

"We'll make it," she said simply, crossing her fingers behind her back.

A hectic 20 minutes later, Tommy was roaring down the road, muttering about trains not waiting for anybody. Lisselle couldn't help thinking that as sweet as Tommy wanted to be, he sure had some of his mother in him. She had waited until her old house and then the last tree from her beloved woods had disappeared from view, before turning around and settling back into her seat.

She braced herself against Tommy's mad dash: one hand gripping her seat and the other, clutching the carpet bag in her lap which now contained her father's mysterious jar of dust. On her father's gravestone, she knew exactly what her father had meant by the "dust."

When she was younger, she had gone into his lab while he was napping on the couch to look for a glue bottle, and when she'd moved aside a jar in one of the cupboards, the innocuous black dirt in the jar had shimmered brightly for a second, as if it had responded to her touch. She'd wrapped her hand around the jar again and a golden light had beamed brightly inside: the black dust transforming into a shimmering gold swirling around in the jar. She could feel a tingling warmth creep in through her hand, up her arm, until Papa had walked in on her and roared, "NO!! GET AWAY FROM THERE!!" At which she'd slammed the cupboard door shut and almost fallen off the counter she'd been standing on. He'd convinced her it was a jar of experimental manure and had made her promise to never touch it again.

"Sorry, Papa," Lisselle whispered, looking down at her bag in her lap.

Her hand was wrapped along the bulge of the jar, and for some reason, the dust in the jar had not reacted to her touch when she'd grabbed it from the house. She was disappointed—she'd been looking forward to that warm golden glow again. Now, it was just a jar of "manure," or more likely, Papa's secret medicinal ingredient. She knew it was valuable, so she promised to herself and her dead father to keep it safe.

A bump in the road jostled her from her thoughts and to her current predicament. The agonizing possibility that she had most definitely missed her train and would have to return to her cave as the Thing of Littleton hollowed out her stomach. Only now did she truly feel how desperately she wanted a new start as a new person, and she definitely couldn't do that in Littleton.

"Ah, there it is!" Tommy exclaimed, pointing at the tiny train station growing larger as they neared.

It was five minutes past the train's departure time.

"Wow!" he marveled as they pulled into its parking lot. "Ain't you lucky the train's still here." Behind the building, a rather sleek black train with the words *Rawlins Enterprises* imprinted on its side in gold lettering still stood miraculously parked on its tracks.

Lisselle breathed such a sigh of relief, she felt her stiffness melt away into the floor. "Luck? I don't know *what* this is. How can the train still be here?" she remarked incredulously, but gratefully.

"Who cares? Let's hightail it over there and not push our luck."

Lisselle couldn't agree more. He opened her cab door and grabbing the carpet bag from her hands, they rushed into the building together.

It was really happening! She was heading for a new life!

But her bubble of joy popped as soon as she saw the commotion in the building: a crowd of angry people were clamoring at the ticket window. She and Tommy exchanged looks.

"I'll go see what's going on," Tommy offered, handing back her bag.

Is the train broken? she wondered painfully.

Her anxiety climbed higher as she watched Tommy approach a member of the crowd and exchange words with her. She was a stocky woman in a purple coat and hat adorned with a long peacock feather. Lisselle could see the outrage coloring her face as she explained the situation to him, her fist clenching a train ticket and repeatedly pumping it into the air like exclamation points.

Tommy glanced back at Lisselle and she could swear she saw him gulp nervously. He then managed to squeeze through the crowd up to the harried ticketmaster behind the window and speak with him, pressing her train ticket up to the glass and pointing back at Lisselle. She expected the ticketmaster to wave him off and tell him to get in line, but was taken aback when he threw his hands up in relief and directed a tall, thickly mustached porter to follow Tommy back to Lisselle.

Quickly taking her bag in one hand and wrapping a protective arm around her shoulders, Tommy said panicking, "We have to go *now.*"

The porter acted as a barrier between Lisselle and the crowd, which had started to press in on her and yell insults.

"What's so special about *her*?"

"We can't take the train because of *her*?"

"Who's *that* girl?"

"Wait 'til my lawyer hears about this!"

"Tommy, *what* is going on?" she demanded, avoiding eye contact with the angry crowd.

They'd emerged out of the building, onto the platform, the porter locking the doors behind them. Tommy turned her by the shoulders to face him, his eyes round with concern. "The train's for you, Lissi. Only for you. The other folks are being delayed onto the next train."

Her mouth dropped. "Wha- why?"

"Your aunt, uh, she bought out all the seats."

"On the entire train?!"

He nodded and looked at her as if he was impressed and perplexed at the same time.

But she knew what this was. The word sunk in like a dead weight: isolation. Her aunt was continuing her father's imprisonment. It was drawing the shades closed inside of her again.

The porter took her bag and gestured for her to board the train. "M'am?"

An avalanche of panic rushed over her as she suddenly stood to exchange the familiar for the strange unknown.

Tommy had one hand on her arm, looking sad and wistful. "I guess this is goodbye."

The train blew its whistle. The porter leaned out of the doorway, and looking pointedly at Lisselle, said in a normal pitch, "All aboard." He pointed his finger at her and mouthed, "That's you."

Lisselle threw her arms around Tommy. "I am much obliged to you. You've been the kindest friend." And with that, she planted a firm kiss on his cheek and then swept onto the train.

Tommy stood rooted to his spot, blissfully touching the wet spot on his cheek as the train zoomed out of sight.

7

Nightmare in Paris

The only excitement aboard the train was the ever-changing scenery outside. For the first time, Lisselle saw cities with their maze of skyscrapers and lines of cars weaving throughout; residential areas with cloned homes so packed together that she imagined people could reach through their windows and borrow sugar directly from their neighbors; and then there were the various mountains that occasionally loomed into view framed imperiously against the sky, some capped with snow and others blanketed by forests.

She hoped there were mountains or a forest in Elmridge. She had a feeling she was going to need the refuge.

Lisselle still couldn't get over the fact that Aunt Emily had bought out the entire train. That was so unnecessary. If her aunt had wanted her to stay away from everyone, then she could have just asked Lisselle to stay in her compartment. But then again, she had not stayed put (she had checked out the entire train already), and probably would not have if her aunt had asked her to. So maybe her aunt had anticipated this and taken drastic measures.

She shook her head in disbelief at the thought. Her indignation grew as she dwelled again on the recent revelation that her aunt had been in league with Papa from the beginning in keeping her isolated from people, and here she was, still at it again! What's more, they knew about her mutant ability, kept her in the dark, and never even tried to prepare her for it! She had not even met her aunt yet, and she was already imagining a screaming match between them.

Lisselle had begun to tremble like a heated pot of water boiling over. She wrinkled her nose at a sudden burning smell and gasped when she noticed the train ticket had caught fire in her hand. She tried to put it out. The fire alarm let out an ear-piercing squeal, and then hurried footsteps sounded in the corridor until her compartment door flew open. A pixie-haired stewardess assigned to her cabin, Amy, burst in wielding a fire extinguisher and, after pulling Lisselle out of the compartment, swiftly put out the flaming ticket and small fire that had spread to the seat cushion.

"Are you alright?" Amy asked breathlessly. But her eyes really demanded, *How did this happen?!*

"Yes, I just—I- I- I don't know what happened," Lisselle sputtered out.

Amy narrowed her eyes disapprovingly, while her lips spread into a tight smile. "Let's just move you over to this compartment here." She retrieved Lisselle's bag from the scorched compartment and ushered her in to the new one. Amy scrunched up her nose, adding, "You don't think there'll be any further mishaps, right?"

Lisselle ardently shook her head.

"Good." Amy flashed that mechanical smile, and after closing the door behind her, Lisselle could hear her muttering as she walked away, "A pyromaniac. Humph! No wonder."

Humiliated, Lisselle sank into her seat and hopelessly consented that maybe her father and aunt *did* know what they were doing.

The late afternoon hours soon melted away into evening as the train raced steadily along. Amy had informed her that they would be arriving at 6:00 p.m. the next day. She had been popping in every now and then, no doubt ensuring Lisselle wasn't trying to burn down the train again. Soon, there was nothing left to do but sleep.

~~*~~

Lisselle found herself sitting at an open-air café, with the Eiffel tower looming in the background, next to an astonishingly handsome man. He looked like a French TV star out of a glamorous soap opera show. His black hair was gelled back, a thin black mustache lining his upper lip, and he was busy planting a trail of kisses along her arm, inching ever so slowly towards her neck while he murmured the most embarrassing romantic nonsense.

She instinctively wanted to yank herself away, but instead felt herself cuddle up closer to him and even slide her hand along his thigh. Her mind reeled in horror as Lisselle realized she was stuck inside the sorceress again. Soap-opera-man's mirrored sunglasses also confirmed this as she could also see the reflection of the supermodel-like witch gazing demurely back at her, but instead of the long midnight hair, she sported a short blonde bob.

The witch purred, "Et puis quoi?" Which Lisselle understood to mean, "And then what?" At this, soap-opera-man reached into his jacket and pulled out a little black velvet box. She drew back in feigned surprise.

"Will you marry me?" he asked huskily in French. He snapped the box open, revealing a substantially large and brilliantly red diamond ring cut in the shape of a heart.

She gasped in earnest now and asked breathlessly, "Is this really the Queen of Hearts diamond?"

The man leaned back with a slight smirk, and with an air of importance replied, "The very one. It has been in my family for many generations, and it is yours now...."

She instantly reached for the ring, but stopped mid-air when he added, "*If* you will have me."

A wave of annoyance swept through her. She felt as if she was on the brink of finally attaining something she had secretly worked so hard for. With great effort, she gazed into his deep brown eyes and with all the lovey-mushiness she could muster, asked tenderly, "Is it really mine, then?"

He hesitated for a fraction of a second at this unconventional reply before responding, "Of course, mon amour."

An explosion of triumph erupted inside her as she snatched the ring from the box and slid it on to her hand. She gazed jubilantly upon it, caressing the ring as if it was the most important thing in the universe. "At last, you are mine now," she murmured to it. "And we only need a few more pieces before we are unstoppable."

Soap-opera-man shifted nervously in his seat. He cleared his throat. "I will take that as a yes," he chuckled awkwardly.

She turned her eyes upon him in such a way that the poor man straightened up and leaned quickly away from her. She narrowed her eyes and simply said, "No."

In a second, his face displayed a wave of emotions: confusion, shock, hurt, shame, and, finally, anger. "If that is how you truly feel... give me back the ring then." He laid his hand open on the table, waiting.

She raised one eyebrow and looked scornfully at his waiting palm. "No," she repeated more icily.

He continued, "You are very mistaken if you think—"

She snatched the butter knife off the table and drove it into the center of his palm, pinning it to the table. His scream pierced through the Parisian chatter of the café. She leaned in and whispered, her voice edged like a blade, "It's MINE."

Lisselle watched in terror as she lifted keys out of his pocket and strolled over to a red Ferrari sitting at the curb. Blissfully ignoring the chaotic cries behind her and calls for her to halt, she unlocked the car and slid into the driver's seat. She tossed her purse beside her onto the passenger seat, landing on top of a real-estate magazine that seared Lisselle's memory in the second that she glanced at it. Its headline read, "Elmridge: The Town of Dreams."

The Ferrari roared to life and before pealing out, she opened the sun visor and checked her reflection in its mirror. Lisselle saw the same cold toffee-colored eyes peering smugly back at her from her first dream. She smirked as she reached beneath her scalp and peeled off the blonde wig. After shaking out her mane of black hair, she blew a red-lipped kiss into the mirror and said, "See you soon...ma fille."

Lisselle felt her blood run cold as the meaning of her words became clear. She snapped awake. Soaked in sweat and trembling with cold, she breathed hard and clutched the mattress to steady herself.

"Mom?" she gasped aloud into the darkness.

8

We're Not in Kansas Anymore

Beeeep. "Good morning, esteemed guest and crew." The voice blasted through the speaker in her cabin, jarring her awake. "This is your conductor speaking. It is currently 8:00 a.m. and we shall be arriving at Elmridge in approximately 10 hours. The weather is forecasted to be clear, with 5% chance of precipitation...."

The hours flew by as she watched TV in her cabin: a scary movie marathon called *Halloween* that kept her blissfully distracted. She had stayed up for the better part of the night frozen on her bed, fistfuls of blanket, staring into the blackness of the room, replaying the nightmare in her head over and over, the last sentence echoing into oblivion.

It was impossible. Her mother was dead. But a gnawing, ominous feeling made her stomach feel queasy. What else had her father kept from her? Was her *whole* life a lie? Mercifully, her skeptical side had taken over and attempted to retain her sanity. "No, no, there's no way. Those dreams are just me *wishing* she was alive."

And she had simply left it at that.

Now, with one hour left before arrival, Lisselle watched as the train sped through a dark labyrinth of endless trees thick enough to hide the sun. She sat in the main dining car, her belly filled with a fancy meat and vegetables dish. A glossy silver brochure that the waiter had silently deposited next to her dinner plate grabbed her attention. *Elmridge* was emblazoned in gold across the top and underneath it read, "Foremost Town of the Times." She was intrigued by the accompanying image: a golden silhouetted woman carrying a clear sphere in one hand and a lightning bolt in the other. Fairy or angel wings were outlined in gold behind the figure. *That's interesting,* she mused. She wondered if it was the town's personal Statue-of-Liberty-type monument. But monument to what? The answer was inside the brochure.

The Legend of the Elmridge Fairies

Two centuries ago, sisters Abigail (20 years old) and Emily Prynn (18 years old)—"Oooh, my aunt has the same last name...maybe these are my ancestors"—*discovered a shimmering metallic boulder in Wychblack Forest, and according to witness Violet Wickeby, the Prynn sisters were overcome by a supernatural force upon touching the glowing rock. Soon after, the Prynn sisters were condemned to burn at the stake as witches by Reverend Jonas Rawlins.*

As the community looked on and the fires crept up their dresses, the Prynn sisters suddenly transformed: golden wings sprouted from their backs, freeing them from the stake. According to onlookers, Emily displayed the power of invisibility when she disappeared from her spot, and Abigail harnessed the power of lightning to strike Reverend Rawlins dead. Lisselle bristled. She was having an uncomfortable case of déjà vu. *The two sisters flew away into the night sky, leaving behind a trail of shimmering gold dust.*

She snorted derisively, "Yeah, right." But then the dead Hammerson man's face flashed in her mind, effectively squashing her skepticism. She couldn't deny that the limits of what she thought possible had been obliterated a month ago. But still, fairies? She could at least draw the line there. Plus, this is a self-proclaimed legend, a fairy tale. But her aunt had the same name: Emily Prynn. Ancestors? Coincidence? She shook her head and satisfied herself with the knowledge that there was only ever a shred of truth in legends to get them started anyways. And she'd ask her aunt later about that name-sharing too.

She continued reading.

The astounded Elmridge community soon created the Fairy Prynn, a golden statue of a fairy woman with a crystal sphere to symbolize Emily's power of invisibility and a bolt of lightning for Abigail's power. It was with the hope that if the Prynn sisters were to ever return, they would be merciful and forgiving of the community that had ignorantly stood by as their death sentence was carried out. It was also to memorialize the event and serve as a lasting reminder to never be quick to judge, and to turn struggles into golden opportunities, just as the Prynn sisters did.

Today, Elmridge is the embodiment of this ideal as it is internationally recognized as one of the most progressive small towns in the world, seamlessly integrating the latest advances in technology into everyday life (see page 8 for list of innovations).

On her way to page 8, she was distracted by an illustrated map of the town, with numbered 3D-like mini-drawings corresponding to a legend explaining each location. As she poured over the map, her imagination left the Prynn fairies and took off on a tour of Elmridge as she first envisioned herself at location #9, zooming down the ice-skating rink dressed in a dazzling, electric blue unitard, jumping into an acrobatic spin while the blurred audience erupted into cheers and applause; she saw herself at #12, lounging on the deck of a sailboat gliding across the smooth, glassy Merry Lake, which occupied the center of town; she was trekking through #6, Wychblack Forest, and making her way towards those glorious mountains which towered just beyond a fence that enclosed the whole town; #14 was the school, which—

The train's whistle pierced through her reverie, and Amy's mega-smiling face stole her entire view. "We're here! Welcome to Elmridge!" She handed Lisselle her father's carpetbag and couldn't usher her off the train fast enough.

A blast of warm air greeted her as she beheld the busy commotion of the other trains unloading on the rows of tracks and platforms before her. Dozens of workers bustled about moving large crates to and fro. One particular person stood out among the blur of blue and gray jump-suits: a few platforms across, in front of another sleek *Rawlins Enterprises* train like hers, there stood an impressive-looking young man with blonde hair pulled up into a messy man-bun. He wore gray sweat pants and a royal blue football jersey, which she realized as her cheeks reddened, he filled out quite nicely with his noticeably muscular stature. The jersey had a large powder blue *3* on both sides and the name BEAST on the back. He looked as if he had just rolled out of bed, but he carried a clipboard and seemed to be conducting some business. In flip-flops.

He was listening intently to a worker, who wrung a hat in his hands and spoke quickly with an extremely apologetic face. Then, before Lisselle's blush could spread even further, she gasped as "Beast" snatched the worker and slammed him up against the side of the train. The worker put his hands up as if pleading before he was just as suddenly lowered to the ground again. Beast gruffly straightened the worker's collar as if apologizing and the worker soon bowed away and retreated into the hustle and bustle. He turned away cradling his forehead and stooped to pick up the clipboard that had fallen.

When he straightened up, his eyes locked on Lisselle across the way and neither of them moved. She wanted to look away, but was petrified at having been caught staring. Her face flushed an even deeper red and she could feel her heart beating in her ears, but still she could not break from his penetrating gaze. She now clearly saw that he couldn't be more than a few years older than her and, oh Mylanta, was he handsome! He reminded her of a teen-version of Thor.

But insecurity started to creep into her. What was he staring at? Did she look that much out of place? She glanced down at her outfit: blue jeans and a funny t-shirt Papa had gifted her when she was little but now fit her like a baby tee so some of her stomach showed. The shirt had the table of periodic elements on it and read, "I wear this shirt periodically." She and her father had thought it hilarious, but now it suddenly made her feel childish. Her hair was definitely a mess of brown curls that stuck out everywhere on top and fell down to her back. Ugh, she must look like a frazzled Raggedy Anne compared to the "rich and famous" folk in this place.

He was *still* watching her, but this time smiling as if amused. And, oh my word, was that a dimple in his chin? She checked to see if there was something behind her that held his attention, but then made the mistake of meeting his eyes again and found that he was now laughing. Her face began heating up for a different reason now. So, okay, she may not be from around here, but that is just plain rude to—

A loud *ahem* next to her interrupted her silent tirade.

A much older man stood next to her and she did a double-take: he looked like a 60 year-old version of Ivan Drago from one of the *Rocky* movies she saw at Tommy's house, but with salt-and-copper hair. He looked as if he was dressed for a business meeting, minus the jacket. "That's Liam Rawlins," he said in a thick exotic accent she couldn't quite place.

"Pardon?" She instinctively clutched her carpetbag closer.

The stranger gestured toward Beast and the two men stared soberly at each other from across the tracks. "A dangerous young man," he added grimly, still watching him until a moving train obstructed their view and then Liam was gone.

Lisselle couldn't help feeling a twinge of disappointment. Even if this Liam-guy did laugh at her. She started when the stranger addressed her by name.

"Ms. Lisselle Montague?"

"Yes?"

"I am Ernesto Panzinski, a close friend of your aunt. I am here to escort you home."

His smile was so warm and friendly now, and the way he said "home" sounded so sincere that she immediately felt at ease. She smiled and offered her hand, but just before speaking, she shut her mouth again. The realization struck her that she was now beginning a new life, a new identity. She could be who she wanted to be. What that was, she still wasn't sure, but it definitely didn't involve the freak of Littleton. A new name, maybe that would be a proper start. Her last moments with Papa resurfaced in her mind, his last term of endearment to her: "Ma belle princesse."

She smiled again and lifted her chin as she shook Ernesto's hand. "Please, call me Belle." *Better than "Princess,"* she reasoned with herself.

"Belle," he repeated thoughtfully. "I think it suits you." He gestured towards her carpetbag. "May I?"

She handed it over and thanked him.

"It is a pleasure to finally meet you. Shall we?" He swept his arm towards their exit.

She shot one last glance across the tracks, before following Ernesto out.

~~*~~

"Do those mountains have a name?" Belle asked, gazing rapturously at the view of the sun setting over the mountains in the distance.

Ernesto glanced sideways at her and smiled. They traveled in what he proudly said was "a 1967 Chevy Impala," but to her just meant they were in an oddly long black car that looked nothing like the tiny electric cars that passed them.

"Stony Peaks," he answered.

Belle scrunched up her face in disapproval. "That's like naming a child 'Boy' or 'Girl.'"

Ernesto chuckled.

"No," she sighed dreamily. "Those are the Misty Mountains and that forest of evergreens is called Shirewood."

"That sounds better than Wychblack Forest."

At that moment, they arrived at an immense solid gate that was part of a high concrete wall enclosing the town. "Just like trying to enter a real Emerald City," she said weakly, but felt troubled by the wall's prison-vibe.

A military-type man in black camouflage and dark sunglasses approached their car. When Ernesto slid the window down, she could see that the man had a formidable-looking gun strapped to his side.

"Buenos días (Good day), Sergio," Ernesto greeted him.

"Oh, you're Spanish!" Belle blurted out.

He grinned back at her. "Russian, actually."

"But—"

"I speak many languages. Though I did live in Cuba long enough."

Sergio flipped up the lens of his sunglasses as he stooped to peer through the open window. "Que lo que hay, compadre (How's it going, my friend)?" He wore a wide grin that contrasted sharply with the dark red scar that ran down one side of his face. He clapped Ernesto on the shoulder. "I see you've brought the famous package."

She frowned.

Ernesto smiled over at Belle reassuringly, and nodded to Sergio. "How is your Lucita?"

Sergio's face lit up. "Her 5th birthday's coming up. You'll be there, right?"

"Of course, cómo no (for sure)!"

Sergio looked at his watch. "Bueno, jefe, adiós (Well, boss, bye)."

"Vaya con Dios (Go with God)," Ernesto replied.

"It was a pleasure to meet you, Señorita Montague." He smiled with genuine respect at Belle and then pounded a goodbye on the roof of the car. He turned towards the gate and waved a signal at some men, whom she just noticed, had been watching from dark windows within the wall. The gates slowly opened and they were waved through.

To Belle, those gates became giant stage curtains drawn back to reveal an exquisite set. Short of pressing her whole face to the window, she ogled the view of the small town in all its fairy tale-like glory.

Ernesto narrated the main sights as they drove through. To her right, was another formidably high wall covered in climbing ivy and an entrance with elaborate scroll-worked iron gates. An armed guard booth sat underneath a prominent sign that read "Manor Hill." As Ernesto returned the guard's wave, Belle gasped as she caught a brief glimpse through the gate of a row of splendid mansions.

Ernesto answered the question that caught in her throat with a question of his own, "The rich and famous have to live somewhere, right?"

"Of course," she squeaked.

Stony turrets and a tower in the distance caught her eye. "Is that a- a castle?!"

"Yes. Rawlins Castle." His face darkened when he added, "A place of death." He crossed himself as if warding off evil.

Naturally, Belle immediately lost herself in a vision of gothic romance as she fell just within the gates of the castle into the arms of a brooding and handsome stranger with blonde hair and dimpled chin. A streak of lightning tore through the sky as he enfolded her into his arms.

The reverie lasted until an abrupt stop at an intersection. They were on a small hill at a red light: straight ahead was a giant lake surrounded by white beach sand. To her right, the road led to a complex of buildings huddled closely together. She gasped with delight as she recognized the group of large iridescent blue birds strolling around the fringes of the school. "Are those—?"

"Elmridge High. Home of the Peacocks," Ernesto pointed out. "With real peacocks. They're natural to this area." He pointed towards the left view from the hill. "Over there is where you youngsters like to get into trouble."

In the distance, she could make out a long boardwalk outlining the edge of the lake, and a line of shops and some complex of larger buildings behind them. "What is that spherical building?"

"Planetarium."

An "ooooh!" escaped from her. She'd been suppressing them this whole ride, but this was just too much. Too much amazing.

The light at the intersection turned green. "I normally take the shortcut, but, for you, we need the scenic route." He proceeded forward towards the lake as her eyes grew wider. They approached an edge that rose over the lake until it suddenly dipped and the car continued into a tunnel that ran right through the lake. Ernesto could only smile as she pressed her forehead against the window and stared, slack-jawed at the aquarium-like tunnel. A stream of lights illuminated behind the glass ensured that the lake-life was visible to passer-byes. All manner of fish she'd only studied in books swam in and out of view.

A low vibrating hum interrupted the reverent silence. Ernesto pulled a cell phone out of his shirt pocket and before he could speak a greeting into it, a hysterical, shrieking voice caused him to jerk the phone away from his ear. He held the phone in front of his mouth and tried to speak over the sound of screeching cats, "Calm- calm down. I will be there in 5 minutes. Stay put." He ended the call and dropped it back into his shirt pocket. "I am sorry to have to do this to you, Maria," he said sadly, rubbing the dashboard.

"You named your car 'Maria'?"

Instead of responding, he flipped a switch on the dashboard and the car screamed to life with a loud siren and flashing blue and red lights that were hidden behind the rearview mirror.

She almost banged her head against the roof. "You're a cop!"

"Sheriff," he corrected with a wink.

A picture of the fish-eyed Hammerson brother hanging upside down dead in the truck, flashed in her mind. Feeling like a wanted criminal, she felt herself shrivel up inside.

"I'm not supposed to do this in the tunnel," he continued. "Scares the fish away." Then, with his face contorted in worry, he added, "But there's an emergency."

Belle watched as the cars ahead scrambled out of his way. "Was that Aunt Emily you were speaking with?"

His face tightened. "Yes."

"Is she ok?"

"She's fine," he said curtly.

Feeling thoroughly unsettled, she held onto the sides of her seat as Ernesto wove his way out of the tunnel. Soon they emerged out into another intersection where he made a hard right. She was anxious. Any minute now they would pull up to her new home. And for the first time, she'd meet her aunt. Her mysterious aunt. Her possibly demented aunt. She forced herself to be positive, but she couldn't help wondering, *Maybe Papa was keeping her away from me and not the other way around.*

Ernesto pulled up to a two-story Victorian-style house, that looked much like the Isaac Bell house she'd admired in an encyclopedia. It was complete with a wrap-around porch, a swinging bench by the door, and second-story balconies. A prominent, bronze sign post by the brick walkway leading to the house read, *Historical Society of Elmridge: Founded in 1810.* Underneath were the hours of operation, but they had been covered over with a sign that read, *Closed Until Further Notice.*

"I live in the museum?" she asked incredulously.

But when Ernesto turned to her, his face was lined with worry. "Please, wait here while I go inside. I'll be right out. Just give me a few minutes."

"What's going on? Is she sick?"

He sighed and hung his head once before he looked at her again. "Actually...." He pursed his lips together as if thinking. His cell phone buzzed again. Looking at it, the harried expression returned and he opened the door and exited. Before closing it, he bent inside once more and pleaded, "Please, just—wait here."

Belle's mouth hung open as she watched him take the front porch steps, unlock the front door with a key, and disappear inside. This was all very strange to her.

After ten minutes and still no sign of Ernesto, she stepped out of the car. She had reached the conclusion that Ernesto was her aunt's boyfriend or husband, and that her aunt was either psychotic or was having second thoughts about having a freak-of-nature-niece stay with her. If Belle had to choose, she hoped for the former. She could handle crazy; she couldn't handle being unwanted. She'd had enough of that in Littleton.

Just as she was about to mount the porch steps, the little hairs on the back of her neck stood up with the uneasy feeling of being watched. She stepped back, eyeing the house, and froze. There, in the top right window was a small feminine face peering at her. It seemed to flicker in and out.

At that moment, Ernesto opened the front door and waved her in with a much calmer, albeit apologetic, expression. Belle half-rushed at him. "I saw a girl in the top window! She- she faded in and out like a g-g-" She couldn't say it.

Ernesto's eyes went wide, but then he burst out into an unnaturally loud laugh that could only be characterized as forced. "Not to worry. There are no ghosts here. Although being an extremely old house, you might come to think it is with all the creaks and groans it makes."

"Are you my uncle?" she asked, looking him squarely in the face.

He looked taken aback and didn't seem to know how to respond at first. "Well..." he looked pensive and sighed deeply before relenting. "I guess you can say that I am."

It was Belle's turn to be surprised. "So, you're married to my aunt?"

"No."

When he didn't volunteer any further explanation, she asked, "So, you're *with* my aunt."

"I am *with* your aunt," he confirmed.

"So, then you're not *really* my uncle," she clarified.

"We've been together for forty-two years," he countered with a benevolent smirk.

Her eyebrows shot up. "O-o-kay, so you're my uncle." And with unmistakable hurt in her voice, she asked, "Why didn't you tell me so at the train station?"

He pressed his lips together as if thinking carefully of what to say next. "Emily is what people would label a recluse. She hasn't openly left this house in over 20 years. If she needs to travel, she wears a disguise.

If she needs to run errands, conduct business matters, I'm her man. Founding Council meetings? I sit in for her."

Belle gaped at him.

"There's more. And I hope you will forgive me, but...I lied to you in the car."

The hurt registered on her face.

"The woman on the phone was not Emily. It was"—he shook his head, as if it was difficult for him to continue—"it was her 18 year-old daughter, Emilia, who recently came to visit with us from abroad. And she is...well, she is not well. You'll see for yourself when you meet her." She opened her mouth to speak, but Ernesto held up a hand. "Please, let me finish. I need to get this all out there." He sighed raggedly and sweat beaded his brow. "No one in Elmridge has met Emilia. Your aunt wants to keep her stay private until Emilia goes back to, uh, to...her father in France."

"You're not her father?" she asked in a small voice.

He shook his head. "One last thing: your aunt is away on business, so you'll meet her sometime soon. Hopefully, in a few days." He exhaled and stood up straighter, studying Belle's reaction.

"So the girl in the window was Emilia?"

Ernesto smiled with relief. He'd expected an outburst of some sort. "Yes, that was Emilia."

She touched her forehead, conflicting emotions swirling inside her as she tried to make sense of what he'd told her. It was like forcing mismatched puzzle pieces to fit together, resulting in a nonsensical picture. "Why? Why all the lies and secrecy?"

He reached to touch her shoulder in sympathy, but she stepped away. "I told you," he reminded gently. "Emily is paranoid about her privacy. Again, I am truly sorry for how this is affecting you."

"Papa was paranoid like that," she said softly. A horrifying thought struck her, "Will she try to keep me hidden too?"

"No, of course not. You'll live like a normal teenager here: going to school, making friends."

Relief blossomed in her chest, and something else too, as if she'd just been handed a lovely surprise gift. Thinking of Emilia, though, outrage colored her tone when she spoke, "But what about my cousin Emilia?"

Ernesto sighed patiently. "Emilia is only visiting and she is not in a proper state of health, so your aunt would simply like to avoid public involvement and gossip. Being the wealthiest resident of Elmridge, anything new involving your aunt, especially the arrival of a never-before-seen daughter would start a frenzy of international tabloid stories. So, as I hope you can understand, your aunt values her privacy to no end."

"Oh," she said, feeling somewhat mollified. "Wait, what about *my* arrival?" Panic started crawling up her throat. Suddenly, privacy seemed like a really swell idea.

"Reporters have already been legally gagged."

"Oh. Okay. 'Legally gagged'," she repeated numbly, trying to comfort herself. "Is that why she bought out the entire train? For my *secret* arrival?"

He nodded as if glad she was finally getting it.

She remembered something else he'd said. "Aunt Emily is the richest person in town?"

He nodded again, but arched an eyebrow as if that fact was something to be impressed about.

"Hmm." She'd always been content with the little that she and her father had, so she wondered what kind of difference having wealth would make in her life.

Ernesto opened the front door again and gestured toward the inside. "Would you like to come in and meet your cousin now?"

Feeling more settled about the situation, she grinned brightly. "I'd be delighted," and she added meaningfully, "Uncle Ernesto."

Inside, the entire first floor of the house was a museum full of relics and displays chronicling the founding of Elmridge and its evolution to the present day. He informed her as they headed upstairs that she would eventually be tasked as curator and that she needed to memorize all the history in the museum, and it would be a paying job. Excitement zinged through her at the news. Getting paid to read sounded exactly like her dream job. The museum was one big tantalizing book she couldn't wait to get her hands on.

They reached the second floor and she could see that it had the open-floor layout of a cozy home, but she was baffled by the starkly different designs in each section of the room. Ernesto read her thoughts because he explained as he pointed, "Victorian-style dining room, 1950s-Deco kitchen, and African tribal living room." He shrugged his shoulders. "I had no say. As long as I have Maria, she can do whatever she wants with these spaces."

"I love it!" she exclaimed, gazing the most at the ornate Victorian dining room.

"Then you two are truly related," he quipped. He pointed towards a wall with an archway. "Through there is the hallway with the three bedrooms. The first one on the left is yours, then there's the guest room, and the master. Each room has its own bathroom."

The sound of a door handle clicking open silenced them. Soon Emilia emerged barefoot from the archway and cautiously approached Belle. She was dressed in a white flowing nightgown with a sheer, black shawl wrapped around herself. Her hair was a dark brown like Belle's, but as she noted with a pinch of envy, Emilia's hair fell in smooth wavy, cascades down to her waist. She had a pretty, elfish quality to her face, but her eyes—they were big, brown doe eyes with the vacant, haunted expression of someone who was lost in their own world. Belle now understood what Ernesto meant by Emilia not being well.

"Hi," Belle called out cheerfully.

Emilia's eyes sparked with life. "Speak again," she whispered intensely.

"I'm your cousin, Belle." When she didn't get a response, she shifted on her feet and added, "I'm really happy to meet you."

Emilia stared at her wondrously as if watching a unicorn in an exhibit.

Belle tried again. "I- I didn't know I even had a cousin."

Emilia closed her eyes and smiled dreamily. "You *sound* like her," she breathed.

Ernesto flinched.

"Like who?" Belle asked.

"Shhh," she angled her head sideways as if speaking to someone beside her. "Don't tell her, Peter."

Cold goosebumps ran along Belle's arms.

Ernesto cleared his throat loudly, which seemed to draw Emilia back to reality. She cocked her head sideways as she looked at Belle. "Your mother named you Lisselle, but you call yourself Belle?"

Belle nodded.

She smiled strangely. "I like the name Emilia." She closed her eyes as if recounting a sweet memory. "I had a beau once in Italy who called me that." She snapped her eyes open toward Ernesto. "It was a long, long time ago Ernie."

O-kaaay.

Ernesto had been fidgeting in his spot and took this last statement from Emilia as his cue to exit. "Let me get your bag for you," he told Belle as he headed toward the door. "We left it in the car."

Emilia continued staring dreamily at her.

Belle squirmed in her spot, until deciding that awkward small talk would be better than awkward silence. "I'm so glad I have a cousin. It's nice to have family. I'm really looking forward to meeting your mom." She flushed pink at her own rambling.

A faraway look came into her eyes. "My mother..." She dazed off to one side. "I can scarcely remember her face...."

Belle's confusion skyrocketed, until she remembered Emilia's condition and then she just felt sorry for her.

Ernesto came tramping up the stairs and through the door. He lay the carpetbag at Belle's feet and turned to Emilia. "Do you want to give Belle a tour of the house? Show her to her bedroom, maybe?"

While still staring off into space, she replied, "No, Ernie, I'm done for today. I will retire to my room." She broke suddenly from her trance and locked eyes with Belle, "You are *never* to come into my room."

The severity of her tone caught Belle off-guard. She took a step back. "Sure, no problem."

Emilia's face relaxed into a warm smile. "We will have breakfast tomorrow. And if you are anything like your mother, you will tell me all about the boys who are madly in love with you." And she actually giggled.

Emilia looked at the spot next to her, and with an ushering wave of the hand, beckoned, "Come along, Peter." Her ghostly nightgown trailed behind her as she disappeared beneath the archway and into her room. Several loud clicks of locks bolting shut were stern reminders of Belle's boundaries within the house.

Belle stared after her, at a loss for what to even think.

"She's a sweet girl," Ernesto said softly. He turned to her. "I have to get back to work. If you need anything let me know. I don't think she's coming out of her room tonight, so you may as well help yourself in the kitchen."

"Um, okay," she replied uncertainly.

He gave her shoulder a reassuring squeeze and then turned to go.

"I am much obliged to you," she said, reaching out and touching his arm, "for everything. I mean, taking me in and all into your very private lives as a member of this family. I've only ever just had Papa."

He beamed, the corners of his coffee-brown eyes crinkling. "You two will be good for each other," he remarked, pinching her cheek, and then he disappeared down the stairs.

Of course we will, she thought with a pang. *Like calls to like.*

9

A Balcony With A View

Later that night, Belle sat ensconced in a large window nook of her posh new room, gazing out at the night sky. The house was on a small hill, so she could see the school complex and beyond. She could make out the dark turrets of Rawlins Castle piercing the sky above the twinkling wealthy community of Manor Hill.

Peering behind her, her room looked like a page out of a *Ladies Home Journal* for teens. She had matching bubblegum-pink TV and telescope; lavendar-colored walls with nature scene paintings framed in ornate silver frames; a bed topped with a plush white comforter that felt like a cloud; a chair and white desk with a laptop and a vase of lilac flowers sitting on it; and the final touch that really made Belle feel like she was still in a dream was a small crystal chandelier hanging from the center of the ceiling that softly lit up the room.

The giant closet looked empty, though, even with the few outfits she'd unpacked and hung up. She saw some students on her way into town earlier sporting school uniforms, so she wondered what to wear tomorrow to her first day of school if she had no uniform. Before bidding her goodnight, Ernesto had informed her that she'd be starting tomorrow. He might as well have told her she was going to be on *Naked and Afraid* what with no uniform and no clue on what to expect. Hopefully, though, she'll blend in over time here and make a few friends of the "kindred spirits" kind. It would be miracle enough for her.

Her new life here still felt so surreal, as if it was made of beautiful Murano glass and could shatter at any moment and she'd be shipped back to the Littleton penitentiary. While her senses were still reeling from the upgrades in her life, her heart and mind were trying to come up for air. Too much had happened way too fast lately, and her emotions and thoughts were still floundering to collect the pieces of this new puzzle she'd been handed in life. Electric, fire-starter hands? Her mother possibly being alive? And as an evil supermodel sorceress of some kind? Of course, the *Ripley's* weird-list didn't stop there: dead dad, Nell-like cousin, mysterious missing aunt, and, now, she lived in a super-rich and famous community with Fort Knox-like security headed by her surrogate uncle. She'd traded a life as an attic-imprisoned-Bertha for her own personal *Twilight Zone* episode. Admittedly, though, the latter was preferable any day. What would make this transition easier, she realized, was having someone to confide in, someone who'd understand her—understand everything, including all the weird.

Belle rubbed her temples and squeezed her eyes shut. *Uh, brain overload.* She needed a distraction. She glanced at the TV, but rejected the temptation. TV reminded her of the two long dark months in the O'Toole house. She missed books. And she wanted modern books since Papa had only ever brought home old classics. She needed to start recreating her Fortress of Solitude. Yes, that would definitely help. She glanced at the laptop—curious—but had no idea how to use it.

Her eyes widened as she caught sight of a shooting star streaking across the night sky. She closed her eyes and just as she was about to wish for the same thing she wished every time, she realized it had come true—freedom—and Papa's death had been the cost. She wondered for a split-second if the stars had a dark magic in them or if it was a cosmic balance-of-nature act. Shaking her head to clear the grim thoughts, she closed her eyes again quickly, not wanting the shooting star's make-a-wish magic to pass, and said aloud, "I wish for a true confidante who'll really care about me."

Opening her eyes, she immediately noticed something new in her view: the turrets of Rawlins Castle were lit up. A familiar excitement filled Belle: *Northanger Abbey* was now cuing up on her mind's movie screen. This was exactly what she needed right now. She eyed her telescope. Soon, she was gazing at a titillating assortment of cherubim and gargoyles perched on the castle ledges. She was now Catherine, exploring the dark, drafty halls for clues of Henry's mother's murder.

"Whoa—" A bare muscular chest filled her view. She scrambled for the dial and zoomed back a bit. She gasped. It was the blonde Beast-guy from the train station! Liam Rawlins! He was in the doorframe of a balcony, arms stretched above, gripping the overhead arch. He was leaning slightly forward so that his whole rippling frame stretched taut. His sweatpants dipped low, revealing the deep "v" contours of his hips. "Oh Mylanta...."

Belle snapped back from the telescope, her cheeks flaming-red and her breathing a bit erratic. "This is so wrong."

But the alluring sight pulled her in again, and this time, he had walked out onto the balcony and was gazing up at the sky with his arms crossed over his chest. His hair was not in the bun and hung just beneath his ears in messy pieces. Belle studied his face. His looks were so striking, he could easily have been a descendant of Adonis. But, he looked...incredibly sad. His lips were moving now as if he was talking out loud. The only words Belle could make out were "Mom" and "Dad." He dragged his arm across his eyes as if he were wiping away tears.

Belle pulled away again. This was a moment she couldn't spy on. She didn't know the reason for his melancholy, but she found her own eyes watering and felt a familiar painful clutch in her chest.

"Papa," she whispered.

The little girl that used to crawl into her father's lap resurfaced. She mourned him, and seeing now how much beauty and excitement this world really had to offer, she cried bitterly for the lonely girl in Littleton who was stuck in a tiny world that existed only of her father and her fantasies. This would be her last cry as Lisselle, before Belle buried her forever.

~~*~~

Belle found herself standing alone before her father's headstone in Littleton. An exasperated sigh escaped her and she was caught off-guard by the cool nonchalance bordering on impatience that filled her. She glanced at her diamond-encrusted watch.

Oh no! she thought, panicking. *I'm dreaming with Lady Macbeth again!*

She recognized the long smooth hands tipped this time with violet-colored nails. A giant red heart-shaped ring and a dainty bracelet of black stones adorned her hand.

And what was she doing at Papa's grave?!

A silky female voice drawled aloud, "Don't ever say that I don't do anything for you, Abigail."

There wasn't anyone else around, so who was the witch talking to? Belle still couldn't quite believe that this woman was supposed to be her mother, even if she did have the black hair and light brown eyes that her father had described. So 'witch' was what Belle would call her—she wasn't calling her 'mom' anytime soon. And was Abigail her name? Was she talking to herself?

The witch continued, "Remember how you used to say, 'Oh that conniving Violet Wickeby?' Well, don't you forget this. You see, this Ms. Violet"—she thumbed her chest—"didn't need to come all this way to Hicktown just so you could lay eyes on a dead lover. But something *did* wake you. So just out of boredom, I followed your pull. And now we're here...." She tapped her chin and rested a hand on one hip. "Hmmm. You're still restless. Actually, you're even worse. Are you *nervous,* Abigail?"

Strangely enough, Belle felt a tightening sensation around her. The witch must have felt it too.

"My, my. Is it that daughter of yours?" she teased, a shadow of a threat in her voice.

Belle felt a surge of fear and protectiveness further tightening like walls around her, insulating her from the witch's slimy toxic presence.

"Oh relax, Abigail, I haven't forgotten your condition, you see—I'm not to lay a finger on your daughter. You'd think with all this time we've spent together we'd be friends by now."

'*We*'? Belle thought, confused. *She was talking to herself as if she was two people: Abigail and Violet.*

But, a memory suddenly surfaced that wasn't Belle's: a handsome young man in his thirties with dark shaggy hair and the clearest green eyes, his colonial-style white blouse half-opened and askew, revealing a powerfully-built chest. He stood teetering precariously at the edge of a cliff, large bottle in hand, looking downward at the crashing waves below. He raised tear-stricken eyes to the gray sky and closed them. Holding his arms outward like a 'T', he fell forward into the depths below.

"But we will never be friends," the witch's voice sliced through, her voice thick with anger and agony. "I will *never* forgive you for what you did to William. I truly loved him, and you didn't." She inhaled a shaky breath and suddenly threw on a cheerful grin. "But, not to worry." She turned her eyes upon the red diamond ring on her hand. "That's water under the bridge now, you see. Life goes on, new opportunities arise. You'll be free, Abigail dear, as soon as I have all my special gems. Then, I won't need to keep punishing you anymore—I'll have my own unlimited power." She laughed wickedly as she stroked the bracelet, "This one was to die for!"

Belle tried desperately not to think or feel anything. She did not want the witch to discover her presence, but she felt that if she didn't wake up soon, her brain would explode with the questions that were piling up.

"*Enzo Montague.*" The woman read aloud the death date on the tombstone, and then as if gears were clicking into place, she said, "Isn't that the very day you—" She let out a raucous laugh that chilled Belle's heart. "Oh my, oh my," she said in between bales of laughter. "The day he died is the day you awoke again, but—" She laughed again. "Oh, this is just too perfect. You awoke because *her* powers emerged, and it happened the day her father died." She took on a sarcastically sweet tone. "Did daughter dearest accidentally kill daddy?" And then, in a cruel voice, she added, "Or, perhaps, it *wasn't* so accidental."

Like a floodgate bursting open, Belle's confusion and outrage gushed out of her.

The witch sucked in a breath. "How long have you been eavesdropping, little girl?"

Belle felt that defensive layer constrict around her even further.

"Go to sleep, Abigail, or I *will* kill her. You know the deal. Better yet, I'll let *them* do it."

Belle felt as if the protective embrace was loosening, as if being slowly released from a bear hug. In its place, the slimy-feeling that made her soul feel ghastly in this skin crept back in. *"Who's 'them'?"* Belle asked tentatively.

The witch paused before answering, as if sizing her up. "I will give you this, little Prynn, and only because Abigail has been an obedient little servant and this will keep her quiet: the day your powers emerged, you see, was the day you awakened your hunter. He'll find you soon enough. Or she. The more you use your power, the closer they'll draw to you."

"Why? Why would I be hunted?"

"Uh-uh," she chided, as if Belle was trying to steal a cookie from the jar. "Class is over."

A pair of strong arms wrapped around her from behind and she felt her neck being nuzzled. "Are you done talking to yourself, Violet?" a husky, male voice teased. "We're gonna miss that train." He pulled her in tighter and lust swirled through her, sickening Belle. But at least she learned the witch's name: Violet. And Abigail was her mother, who was somehow trapped...*inside* this body? And how and why does Belle keep popping in as third-wheel in this party?

"One minute, my pet."

The arms pulled away, and she glanced backwards. A red Ferrari sat in front of the entrance to Littleton Cemetery with a young man dressed in all black and a punk hairdo leaning against the side of the car. The face was so familiar. The other guy, the "friendly" one, was walking back towards the car. He looked clean-cut and preppy, like he belonged to an exclusive country club. He turned around and winked at her. Both guys had the same face.

Shock punched Belle in the gut. They were the Bible-twins from her very first dream.

Violet smirked and pointed as she spoke, "Ah, yes, my very fine minions." She began strolling back towards the car, talking to Belle now in a low voice. "You'll meet them soon enough. Just don't get in our way. You or your crazy aunt and no one will get hurt...too badly." Her voice dipped ominously, "I *will* find out how you're spying on me."

Goth-guy, wearing a ton of black eyeliner, was waiting in the back seat, while the preppy twin held the passenger door open.

Violet steadily held Preppy's gaze as she approached, and a series of R-rated scenes with him flooded her mind, causing Belle to recoil in shock. Violet snickered at her reaction. "Wearing a purity ring?"

Preppy thought she was talking to him. He snorted, "That came off a while ago, remember?"

Belle felt like she was going to hurl when Violet encircled her arms around his neck and leaned into him. "How could I forget?" she crooned. As his eyes closed and his mouth zoomed in, Violet shut her eyes, and Belle snapped hers open.

10

The Ghost and the Girl

Belle had recited the Lord's Prayer over and over, trying to avoid the barrage of frightening questions and re-plays that were instigating electrical sparks from her hands, until she had fallen asleep again, hoping she didn't return to the *Nightmare on Elmridge Street*.

Now, a few hours later, she lay awake in bed, drenched in sweat, the room a-glow with the morning light. A glance at her alarm clock told her she'd woken up too soon.

"....I'm not to lay a finger on your daughter."

Vivid details of the disturbing dream were already dissipating, but snippets of Violet's words kept coming back to haunt her.

"Better yet, I'll let 'them' kill her."

Belle squeezed her eyes shut, trying to steel her mind against the connections that were forming on their own. She'd felt that inner protection when Abigail, her mother's name, was mentioned, and she'd noticed how it left when Violet threatened harm if she'd remained. Was her mother trying to protect her somehow? And who was Violet? Violet Wickeby—it sounded familiar as if she'd heard it somewhere. And how could Violet be talking to Abigail when they both seemed to be the same person?

The only conclusion she couldn't help reaching was that her mother was, in fact, alive and suffered from a split personality disorder. It made sense that her father wouldn't want her to have anything to do with her then if one of the personalities was apparently a psychopathic sorceress who stabbed people with knives and kidnapped and brainwashed young men. It seemed this family was full of Berthas-in-the-closet: a schizophrenic mother, paranoid reclusive aunt, mentally unstable cousin, and herself included with her firecracker hands and mind-melding dreams. Seemed 'crazy' ran in the family.

She took a deep breath and exhaled slowly, trying to subdue the heat flaring in her palms. She couldn't deny her own curious condition and insane family drama, but perhaps dreams—nightmares more like—were just dreams. She decided, for the sake of her sanity, not to worry about these dreams anymore, unless something *real* from these dreams happened. She brushed aside the memory of almost dying in one.

All thoughts flew from her mind, though, as her bedroom door creaked open.

She blinked, expecting Ernesto or Emilia to follow in, and feeling half-outraged at this intrusion and yet half-hoping for one of them to actually appear.

But there was no one.

The door seemed to have opened completely on its own. She would have gladly believed that the door had a faulty lock, if it weren't for the growing and alarming sense that someone, or something, was watching her. She wanted to spring out of bed and look out the door, but her body was petrified. She could only stare at the spot by the door, of which she was sure was the source of the phantom eyes.

She finally croaked out, "Who's there?"

Immediately, the smallest of whispers, "Come, Peter," and then the door shut again.

It was a moment before her body thawed from the unnatural fright and her muscles could work again. She bounced out of bed and stuck her head out the door. Only Emilia could be seen in the kitchen moving about in an outfit reminiscent of a first-class lady on the Titanic, complete with the fancy up-do hair style.

She was so weird.

Look who's talking, Belle thought to herself, *especially now that I'm imagining ghosts.* She rubbed her temples. *Stay sane. Focus on normal.*

She pointed at the door. "Faulty lock," she said aloud. Pointing in the direction of the kitchen, "Emilia calling for Peter from the kitchen," at her head, "Mommy-deprivation dreams," and finally she held up her hands, "And...I'm a mutant."

She shook her head at the only undeniable proof she had of the unnaturally weird. *Maybe us Prynns are aliens from outer space and it's impossible to completely blend in among the humans. It would account for all the secrecy in the family.*

Belle palmed her forehead. She had watched too much of the *Syfy* channel at Tommy's house.

But she did feel better. She decided to ignore the inexplicable, freakish drama for her sanity's sake and just try to keep her electric-zapper skills hidden. She needed to focus on being normal. She did have her very first day of school today after all, and that in itself was a more terrifying beast to tackle than imaginary hunters and body-snatchers.

At the mention of 'beast,' she thought with a blush about the disturbingly good-looking blonde "Beast," of which she'd already seen too much. At the memory, she pulled at her shirt collar as if letting in some air to cool herself. Liam Rawlins. That was his name, according to Ernesto, who'd also said he was dangerous.

And since her uncle is looking out for her best interests, she wasn't going to be entertaining any further musings about this Liam Rawlins fellow. Nope. No, sirree. She glanced at the telescope and swallowed.

She'd have to get rid of that telescope though.

Sometime later, at Emilia's insistence that school could wait, Belle sat at the dining table admiring her plate of egg benedict in hollandaise sauce with a thin slice of ham expertly curled into a heart-shaped ribbon, results of Emilia's surprisingly phenomenal culinary skills.

"Coffee?" Emilia chirped, standing before her in a white apron that read, *Antoine's Restaurant*.

Belle nodded enthusiastically.

Emilia's cheerful mood was infectious. She hummed while she worked a small elaborate machine. The mental patient act that had disturbed Belle yesterday seemed to disappear when Emilia was busy in the kitchen.

"Mmmm," Belle marveled aloud, savoring a heavenly bite of her dish. "Ooooh!" she exclaimed as a coffee in a beautiful China cup and saucer was placed before her. The coffee had a white foam with a thin chocolate artwork design drizzled on top.

"I am a coffee artist," Emilia beamed. "Trained in France's Le Procope café." She sat across from Belle with her own cup and plate. She watched as Belle made fast work of her plate. "That is the truest compliment of my cooking." Emilia grinned, watching her now trying to scrape up the last bit of sauce from her plate, and then Emilia sighed and her eyes drifted off into a daydream.

Belle didn't want her to go "Nell" again, so she promptly asked a question she'd been wondering about, "Do you go to school?"

Emilia laughed in earnest, a giggly girly laugh, but then quickly sobered when she realized Belle was serious. "Oh. Well." She cleared her throat, after taking a long draw from her cup. "I graduated."

Belle was surprised. Emilia didn't look any older than her. "How old are you?"

"18." Emilia hid behind her cup again, the inexplicable awkwardness growing heavier. A long moment passed and then Emilia cocked her head as if remembering something important. "I need to tell you something." She leaned forward as if about to share a secret. "It is the most important advice in our family."

Belle stopped drinking the coffee and listened intently. Maybe now she would get some answers.

Emilia's round eyes shone. "Think happy thoughts," she said, and then leaned back in her chair with a satisfied air.

Belle blinked twice, hoping she was kidding.

"Even Peter knows that," Emilia added with a smile.

Belle's disappointment turned into pity. "Who is Peter?"

Emilia's smile evaporated. Avoiding the question, she asked with sudden urgency, "Have you studied the books on the Elmridge History shelf downstairs, yet?"

Belle perked up. "Books?"

Emilia sighed, as if deflated. "You haven't."

"Don't worry. I'll get on it this afternoon."

Emilia looked slightly mollified. "Very well then."

Belle was genuinely looking forward to that task now, though she wondered at Emilia's insistence. Aunt Emily and Emilia must take the running of the Elmridge Historical Society very seriously. Speaking of Aunt Emily... "Do you know when your mother will be back?" Belle asked.

Emilia looked flabbergasted. "My mother?!"

Belle was completely thrown off by this. Does she also have selective amnesia? She tried again, "Aunt Emily?"

"Oh, dear." Emilia suddenly rose and began clearing the plates from the table. "These questions vex me."

"I'm sorry, I just—" Belle accidently knocked her coffee over on the table in trying to hand it to her. "Goodness, I'm such a klutz."

"No, no, you remain. You're my guest at this table." Emilia automatically rolled up her sleeves and then corrected with a smile, "Excuse me, *family*, not guest." Belle could not reply to this because she was busy staring at Emilia's exposed forearms: her porcelain white skin was etched in angry, red branch-like scars. Emilia gasped and quickly drew her sleeves down again. She stood stock still, her lips tightly pursed.

"What happened?" Belle whispered.

Her face was stony as she stared straight ahead, but her eyes glistened. "France. Lightning strike."

Belle's heart froze. Lightning. That murderous motif that haunted her steps.

The upstairs door clicked open, and Ernesto called out, "Good morning, ladies." His cheerful countenance melted away when he saw the serious tableau in the kitchen.

"I'm tired, Ernie. I need to lie down." And then Emilia disappeared behind her locked bedroom door.

Belle waited for the sound of several locks clicking in place to cease. *What* was she hiding in there? And why was Emilia staying in her mother's room and not the guest room?

Soundlessly, Ernesto helped Belle clear the table. "When will Aunt Emily be back?" she asked, sounding more demanding than she meant to.

He stiffened as he placed the last plate in the dish washer. "I'm not sure," he said turning and smiling at her as he dried his hands with the dish towel. His Elmridge Police Department badge hung on a chain around his neck, something that made her nervous to look at. Then, with a simple question, he careened her attention elsewhere. After a quick study of her appearance, he asked, "Is that what you're wearing to school?"

But before she could look down with mortification at the white starchy blouse and long navy skirt she was wearing (the nicest outfit she owned), Ernesto pulled a clear square package out of his briefcase and set it down on the kitchen table before her.

She squealed with delight when she recognized what was inside. She wasted no time tearing the package open, gingerly removing the school uniform—a white short-sleeved button-down shirt and khaki pants. She breathed in its crisp, linen scent, and exhaled with satisfaction. Finally, she would belong somewhere and blend in with its people. With her finger, she traced the outline of the shirt's golden, circular patch: it had the school's name embroidered in gold cursive and a royal blue peacock with the glimmering feathers forming the field. She read aloud the motto beneath the peacock, "Golden dreams and all that gleams are not what it all seems." *Odd,* she thought. It came across as cautionary, not inspiring, and it hit home for her in a way, but she couldn't quite put her finger on it.

"A nice reminder for this town to stay humble," Ernesto remarked. He motioned toward the uniform. "Go ahead, put it on." Picking up his briefcase, he turned to go. "I won't be back until after dinner tonight, so let me give you the rundown: check in at the school's main office-they're expecting you, and then—as per your aunt's orders before she, uh, left—go to the mall after school, pick up a new cell phone at Q's and then there's a certain store you're supposed to go to for all your clothes. Candace will know. She's outside right now waiting for you. She'll walk you to school and then help you at the mall as well."

"Who's Candace?" Belle said, wary of having to trust a total stranger.

"Her grandmother is good friends with your aunt, and, well, she's a nice girl, you'll see," he finished with a wink. "Oh, I almost forgot." He pulled a key out of his shirt pocket and handed it to her. "House key." His eyes crinkled as he grinned widely. "Welcome to the family."

~~*~~

After getting past the initial awkward introductions, Candace and Belle had become fast friends as they walked to school. Candy, as she liked to be called by her friends, exuded such a good-natured charisma that immediately put Belle at ease and won her over. She was a rich coffee color with a voluminous dark curly afro that grazed her shoulders.

"You're a Nature-gal, huh?" Candy noted, as Belle seemed more enthralled by the peacocks ambling in the nearby field than by any of the other snazzy town sights.

She gave a sheepish shrug of the shoulders. "I can't help it. The only excitement back in Littleton was Nature," she responded. "And books." A memory of her father surfaced of them playing Silly Scrabble, a version they'd invented in which they could only use made-up words with ridiculous definitions. He once won with "Spittlicious," which "meant" something worth drooling over.

"Well, you're not going to find any books around here," Candy remarked. "Everything's digital."

Belle stopped in her tracks and stared at her as if she'd just announced the end of the world.

Candy quickly added, "Don't look like that, girl. You can still read books—just online. Besides, there are far better ways to entertain yourself in this town." She winked conspiratorially. "Starting with this afternoon." She linked arms with Belle to get her walking again and then continued about the "entertaining eye candy" at school. "You arrived yesterday, right? Have *you* spotted any 'eye candy' since then?"

"Well..." Belle began, thinking of Liam Rawlins.

"Oooh, I knew it! You can't step foot in this town without spotting one. Spill it, girl. Tell me about the U.F.G.?"

"The what?" Belle countered, perplexed.

"Like a U.F.O., but U.F.G.," Candy repeated, as if it was common knowledge. "Unidentified Fine Guy. You sight a rare fine guy but don't know his name."

"Okaay." Her mind was already on Liam before Candy had finished explaining. "Well, there was this guy—" She paused, reddening as she recalled spying on his half-nakedness last night.

"Oh, honey, this is going to be good. What does he look like?"

"Well, I only saw him from a distance at the train station...." *And from my bedroom window.*

"Uh-huuuh?"

"He's tall, broad, and—"

"Let me guess," Candy interjected. "Dmitri? Reddish, curly hair? He could win a Mr. Universe contest?"

Belle shook her head. "No."

"Good." Candy continued, with a hint of relief in her voice that turned into annoyance, "Because he is locked down and chained to a pit bull named Katerina." She gave Belle a look of caution. "And watch out too because she is quick to mark her territory around potential threats." Sadness softened her tone as she added, "It's a shame, too. He's such a sweetie pie."

Candy's shift had not escaped Belle's notice. "Looks like *you've* got your eye on a certain guy."

Candy waved her hand dismissively. "Whoa, whoa, whoa." She turned an accusatory finger at Belle. "Nice try, girl. Finish telling me about Mr. Tall-and-Broad."

"Okay, well, I saw him at the train station last night ordering some workers around with a clipboard—"

"And he's blonde and looks like he could be on the cover of a trashy romance novel?"

"Yes!" Belle agreed, a bit too enthusiastically. Just as she was about to name him, Candy beat her to it.

"That's Liam Rawlins. He's a senior and I heard he takes all his classes online now, but they're still trying to get him to play quarterback for the football team." Belle was surprised to find Candy's tone had gone from teasing to cautionary. "Up until last year, he was the most popular guy in the school and sure acted like it. Went through the Princess Posse like popcorn. Now he's an enigma and no one hardly ever sees him anymore. He's supposedly running his father's business now, Rawlins Enterprises." Candy stopped and turned Belle by the shoulders to face in the direction she pointed. "See those turrets over there? Kind of hidden behind Rich Row?" Belle nodded, feeling like some bomb was about to drop. "That's his *castle*. On a cliff. By the ocean." Candy spoke as if accusing him of being disgustingly rich.

The sea, Belle repeated in her mind, finally pinpointing the foreign feel of the air. She was inwardly drooling now. *Spittlicious.* She'd already been fantasizing about that castle, but now that she knew it sat on a cliff by the ocean, if given the opportunity, she doubted she'd be able to resist its siren call, even if it was inhabited by a dangerous Beast. *A rare fine Beast,* she admitted using Candy's words.

"The Rawlins family castle," Candy clarified. "He lives alone now, though."

They continued walking. "Alone? Where's his family?"

Candy hesitated before speaking. "Dead."

"What happened?!" Belle gushed out, stopping in her tracks.

"No one really knows, except Liam. He was there when it happened." Candy continued walking silently while Belle followed, hanging onto her every word. Candy took a deep breath and said, "I hate to think the worst of the guy. I mean, nobody wants to, but the explanation that the police and the newspapers put out there is really hard to swallow."

"What?" Belle prodded desperately.

Candy stopped and faced her point blank. "I mean, c'mon. Would you believe that lightning could smash through the roof of a castle and strike two people dead?"

Belle blanched. Actually, she could.

11

A Kat With Claws

"**H**ey, beautiful!"

Instinctively, Belle looked up.

Click. A skinny guy wearing a dark beanie hat and a red-and-white striped shirt had snapped a photo of her and then hurried off before she could even respond like she'd wanted to (but wouldn't), which was to snatch the camera from his hands, smash it on the ground, and scream out, *Why is everyone looking at me?!*

"Get outta here, Waldo!" Candy yelled after him. She turned to Belle and explained, "We all call him that for obvious reasons. He's the year-book photographer, and of course, as you can see"—she gestured at the gawking students, and raised her voice as she spoke—"everyone likes to be nosy!"

Most of the gawkers returned to their business.

"Thanks," Belle said, giving her new best friend a grateful smile.

"I got your back, girl. Now, listen, you see that main entrance right there?" she asked, pointing.

Belle nodded.

"You need to go straight through those doors and you'll find the main office on the right. You can't miss it. Your schedule and stuff are in there."

Panic started setting in for Belle. "You're not walking me in?"

Candy pointed to a smaller building adjacent to the main one. "I can't be late for Mr. Connelly's class again, or Momma will tan my behind. But just a quick tip on survival here...." Candy leaned closer as Belle swallowed nervously. "Stay away from the girls that think they're supermodels. I have a feeling they're going to try to eat you alive."

"What?!" Belle squeaked.

"You're a threat," she said, her face not revealing an ounce of humor. Sensing the panic grow in her new friend, Candy smiled brightly and gave her a reassuring hug. "But, you'll be fine, baby girl. I'll see you later for some epic shopping!" She waggled her eyebrows as she walked away and faded into the herd.

With her heart pumping in her ears, Belle felt like she'd been dumped into one of those *Survivor* episodes: a treacherous jungle of concrete and glass, overrun by buzzing white and khaki bodies scurrying toward the buildings. A girl with long, shimmering blonde hair walked by and Belle instinctively reached up and tried to smooth down her bushy mane. She sighed hopelessly, but thought with comfort about being dressed like everyone else. She just couldn't stretch her arms out too much since the shirt buttons over her chest would start playing tug-of-war, and she definitely couldn't sit too low or she'd very possibly rip a hole in the back of her pants. She felt like she had the most awkward body dimensions, which she normally kept hidden in her father's oversized shirts.

A male voice in the distance cried out, "Holy mother of Greyskull!"

Belle's head whipped toward the sound. A short brunette male had one arm clutching his chest and the other thrown out to the side as if holding his two friends back from walking out in front of a truck. The three were staring wide-eyed at her. Then the short one came to life and started heading directly towards her. He said something to his two friends who followed closely.

The tan, dark-haired one responded, "Dude, I'm a married man."

The short leader snapped back, "She doesn't even know you exist."

"So?"

The short one paused long enough to stare at him in disbelief. "Seriously?" He shook his head and then continued his beeline towards Belle.

The second friend, who towered over the other two and who looked like he could easily bench a tree, said, "Yo, just don't get me in trouble with Kat, man."

Belle stiffened as the three came to a stop before her.

The short one assumed an air of cool reminiscent of the *Grease Lightning* gang. "Hey. Name's Hans." He gestured to the tan one. "This is Amir."

Amir smiled politely. "Hi."

Hans continued, "And this is Dmitri."

Dmitri who'd been allowing his eyes to roam freely over Belle, looked up, nodded a "What's up?" and then looked away muttering repeatedly under his breath, "Kat, Kat, Kat...."

"I'm Belle," she said, smiling tightly at them. Wanting to escape this quasi-ambush, she started moving away from them. "I need to get to the main office. Nice to meet y'all."

"Oh!" Hans threw his hands up and rolled his eyes dramatically as if saying *Why didn't you say so?* "I am an *expert* at finding the main office."

Amir snorted. "Yeah, 'cause you've got your nose so far up the principal's—"

"Shut the frack up," Hans cut in.

Dmitri was anxiously looking around.

"Um, thanks, that's really kind of you, but I think I can find my own way," she said, stepping farther away.

"Buuurn," Amir muttered to Hans.

But Hans simply gestured for the others to follow him as he tagged behind Belle like an eager dog yapping at her heels. "Hey, so I can't help but notice you have an accent. Where are you from?"

Belle made a full stop and faced him. "I do?"

Pleased that he had her full attention, he continued walking as he responded so that Belle unconsciously followed him. He smirked at his success. "Yeah, I mean, it's a hint of Southern with something else."

"Oh, wow. I guess it's from my father's French accent and from growing up in Kentucky." She wasn't particularly happy about sounding different.

"Well, it's sexy," he said, giving her an approving grin.

"Oh, please, don't do that," she said, feeling put off.

"Do what?"

Dmitri stepped in and attempted to explain. "Dude, she doesn't know you."

"C'mon, she had to at least have heard of me." He turned to Belle, jutting his thumbs at himself. "Hans Events? I throw the sickest parties on the Eastern seaboard." He reached into his pocket and handed her a business card.

"No, sorry, haven't heard." But since she didn't want to deny herself any friendships, something that had been a rare commodity in her life, she added with an appeasing smile, "But I'd love to go to one of your parties."

A grin broke across Hans's face and Amir clapped him on the shoulder. "Alriiight, you got it! You are officially on my guest list," he said with a wink.

As soon as they passed through the main entrance's double doors, an outraged female's shriek cut through the morning buzz and literally froze everyone in their tracks.

"Dmitri Marino!!"

Dmitri cursed under his breath.

Belle didn't need Hans to tell her who the girl was that suddenly loomed into Dmitri's face and made his knees knock together.

"What are you doing with *her*?" Kat jutted an angry finger in Belle's direction and threw her a death glare. Her big brown eyes, outlined in thick eyeliner, flared, and her long bushy ponytail reminded her of a red fox's tail. It whipped around as Kat looked back at Dmitri, waiting for his answer.

He had his hands up as if surrendering to a cop. "*Hans* was with her. Not me."

Amir vocalized the sound of a whip cracking. Some bystanders watching the free entertainment laughed.

Kat looked at Belle again, as if sizing her up. She had long bangs swept to the side, big hot pink hoop earrings, matching hot pink lipstick, and neon colored bangles running up the length of her forearm. She looked like a roller-skating girl who'd pump to '80's retro music at a glow-in-the-dark rink.

Belle blinked and Kat's face was inches away from hers.

"What are *you* staring at, skank?" Kat seethed.

Belle's eyes flashed and dangerous warmth tingled in her fingers. She didn't know what a "skank" was, but it sure sounded like an insult.

Before she could reply, Hans cut in, creating breathable space between the girls. "Ladies, ladies...peace and love, peace and love." He looked meaningfully at Dmitri and added, gesturing towards Kat, "Please, handle your woman?"

"Handle *this*, pipsqueak!" Kat retorted, shoving hard past Hans and slapping away Dmitri's peace-offering hand. She stormed off with a few neon-accessorized girls in tow.

"Ouch," Hans feigned, dramatically placing his hand over his heart.

Someone was heard saying, "Awww man, I was ready to bust out the mud and inflatable pool. My bet was on Kat...." The crowd buzzed back to life and the busy rush to class resumed.

Amir patted Dmitri's shoulder sympathetically, but his attention was stolen away when a stunning Arabic girl passed him by and disappeared into the crowd. "Gotta go," Amir said, dashing off after her.

Dmitri stalked away. A burst of students scattered away from him when he suddenly punched a locker, leaving a frisbee-sized dent.

Belle jumped at the sound and her heart dropped. "Oh my word, I am so sorry if I caused any trouble."

Hans politely shushed her. "Nonsense, sweetheart. Just another episode in *Days of Our Lives*."

Belle scowled. The shushing and the "sweetheart" comment rubbed her the wrong way.

"Kat gets jealous if Dmitri even talks to Mrs. Schwarts the librarian and she's like 90."

He'd been gently steering her through the crowd by her elbow, greeting others along the way, especially as so many heads turned to look at them. She felt uncomfortable at the attention and the possible insinuations about the two of them, while Hans seemed to bask in it.

She pulled her elbow away.

As they came to a stop under the Main Office sign, he winked at her and said, "Here you are, sweetheart."

"Thanks," she called out over her shoulder as she turned and finally escaped through the heavy glass doors of the main office.

A cooler blast of A/C greeted her. Several matronly women sat behind various office desks shuffling back and forth between computers, telephones, and stacks of papers.

Belle approached the front counter and almost missed the tiny, pudgy woman behind it whose dark head was bent over a large electronic pad. Alerted by Belle's presence, the woman raised her head and blinked owl-like through large round glasses. With a pang, Belle was reminded of her father.

"Can I help you, dearie?"

"It's my first day here. I was told to come to the main office." She felt her words were on a loop.

The lady's eyes lit up as she sucked in a breath. "You must be Mrs. Prynn's niece." She leaned forward as if about to digest a piece of juicy gossip. "How *is* she?"

"I don't know. I haven't seen her yet." She bit her lip. "She's out of town."

Owl-lady cocked her head to the side. "Is that so?" She eyed Belle, waiting for her to elaborate, but when Belle didn't oblige, she took on an official air. "Well, Lisselle Montague?"

Belle nodded.

She briefly scanned through the electronic pad. "It seems your registration is already in order. Mrs. Steifschwester has your schedule." She gestured behind her towards a door that read "Principal" on its frosted glass window. Leaning forward as if divulging a secret, owl-lady whispered, "She refuses to believe a Prynn exists until she actually meets one."

Huh? Belle thought, nonplussed. *What was that supposed to mean?*

She hopped off the stool she was on, revealing her to be much wider than she was tall, and opened a small barrier in the counter for Belle to pass through. The hustle and bustle of the office suddenly ceased as all eyes were trained on Belle's approach to the principal's door.

"Emily Prynn's niece," someone whispered with awe. "The Stiff is going to have a heart attack when she sees her."

"Dear God, let it be so," someone else countered non-too-discreetly.

A shrilly, giggly voice squealed, "Did you hear? Flo just got the phone call: Jared Prince is returning from his world tour today. He's supposed to—" The principal's door swung open and all office heads whipped around to face their computers, the *click-clacketing* of keyboards resuming.

Belle gaped as she beheld Mrs. Steifshwester, a knee-buckling force in the flesh. Black pantsuit, her neck and fingers dripping with extravagant jewelry, and salt-and-pepper hair turned up into one of those fancy 1800's-style bun. Belle watched mesmerized as the marble-like face's eyebrow arched up a mile high as it slowly scanned the room. The principal's eyes narrowed on an elderly red-head in a violet cardigan, who diverted her eyes and sunk down a few inches behind her computer monitor.

Mrs. Steifshwester's voice dripped with derision, as she said in a thick German accent, "I'm sure Mr. Prince would be charmed to know his #1 fan could be his grandmother. Ya, not disturbing at all." Her piercing gaze finally landed on Belle and scrutinized her slowly from head to toe, her left nostril rising higher, as if inhaling a putrid odor. "*You* are Emily Prynn's niece?"

Dread replaced Belle's amusement. With the obvious disgust on the principal's face, and the fact that her aunt was apparently some famous mystery, she felt increasingly more like an ignorant outsider. The latter she still was, but the former she hoped to clear up as soon as possible. Belle cleared her throat and lifting her chin, replied, "Yes, I am Lisselle Montague. I was told you have my schedule."

Mrs. Steifshwester smiled, but it didn't reach her eyes as she side-stepped and motioned for her to pass through. "Come in. Have a seat."

Belle passed underneath her heavy stare. She was now in an impressive CEO-style office with the entire wall behind her sleek desk covered in what appeared to be signed souvenirs and a bunch of framed photographs of her smiling ecstatically next to a different person in each one.

A cherry red electric guitar on the wall caught Belle's eye. It brandished a signed message that read,

To Lena Steifshwester,
Keep my school poppin'!
–Jared Prince

The framed photo next to the guitar showed the principal grinning crazily while holding the red guitar in one hand, and with the other, shaking the hand of a tall, gorgeous boy wearing a sheepish grin. His black hair was styled into a tall swirl, and he wore dark skinny jeans and a white t-shirt with a black vest that had about 50 different message buttons pinned on.

Belle couldn't help thinking snidely, *Guess we know which grandma is his #1 fan.*

Other pictures showed the principal shaking hands with a demure-looking Arabic girl that looked just like the one Belle had seen earlier in the hallway. Another was of a pretty girl in a wheelchair who had thick, red long hair that—

Ahem.

Belle jumped at the sound that came from behind.

Mrs. Steifshwester gestured towards an uncomfortable looking metallic chair shaped like a wide S. Belle took it, and as the principal sat in the leather executive chair across from her, she swiveled and gestured to the wall behind her. "See this wall?" *How could I not?* Belle thought. "These photos are of our most notable students and alumni." Belle wondered what classified as "notable" for her. "They have all graduated or will be graduating from this prestigious preparatory academy to become movers and shakers of society. See this one?" She slid over and pointed to a photograph of a much younger looking, but unmistakable, version of her shaking another teen boy's hand. "This is the current vice president of the country." She continued, pointing at another, "And this one is the curator of the Louvre." She waved her hand dismissively. "The list goes on and on."

Belle shifted uncomfortably in her seat. She wasn't sure where she was going with this. She just wanted her schedule and to be shown the door already.

"The problem is I don't know what to make of you." Mrs. Steifshwester gave her a scrutinizing glare.

Belle squirmed and offered with a sheepish smile, "You could just get to know me."

The principal laughed. "A sense of humor"—her face turned stony—"only spells trouble." She leaned back in her chair, and with her elbows on the desk, tented her hands beneath her chin. "You are a Prynn, ya? One of the two oldest founding families of Elmridge, and no one, except Sheriff Panzinski, has ever seen a Prynn. Only a paper trail and orders carried out by this man for the supposed Emily Prynn confirm her existence. My curiosity can't be helped if this Ernesto also happens to be the chief of police and security in this town, ya?" She exploded with emotion, as if it had been simmering under the surface for too long. "Do you think it fair not being able to meet and greet your employer?"

Belle was confused.

"Oh, ya," she continued, "your aunt is the real boss lady, but she has some education committee running the show that pops up unannounced to perform inspections and audits at *my* school!" Frazzled, she ran a hand along her hair and took a deep breath.

And because Belle didn't think sometimes before she spoke, she said, "I thought you said it was my aunt's school."

Mrs. Steifshwester looked mildly surprised, and then her lips slowly curled into a venomous smile. "Ah, boss lady attitude, ya?"

Belle swallowed nervously, the taste of foot still in her mouth.

The principal leaned forward, flattening both palms on the desk, revealing long blood-red fingernails that reminded her of claws. "Perhaps, you *are* a Prynn." There was a visible tick along her jaw. "Or perhaps you are *not*, and Emily Prynn really *is* a ghost as many in this town believe." She leaned in even closer and dropped her voice, "Or, maybe, Ernesto *is* Mrs. Prynn, in which case you will both be locked up as imposters. And, believe me, I will discover the truth."

Belle's jaw dropped in disbelief. She pinched her thigh to make sure she wasn't in some nightmarish *Twilight Zone* episode.

The principal pressed an intercom button on her desk and spoke into it, "Odette, we're ready."

The office door swung open and the pudgy woman from the front desk waddled in. She had a large camera in one hand and motioned for the two to stand in front of a bare gray wall.

Mrs. Steifshwester took her place first and as Belle joined her, completely weirded out, the principal took hold of her hand in a simulated handshake. They both looked forward at the camera as the principal plastered on her infamous fake grin and commanded, "Now, smile."

12

Prince of Pop

After taking a few quick exams for subject-level placement, Odette finally handed Belle a school-embroidered canvas shoulder bag (which she absolutely fell in love with). Inside was her class schedule, a school-issued laptop, a school map, and another school uniform package.

Finally! Freedom from that suffocating room! she thought, exasperated and relieved at the same time.

She looked down at her schedule to see which class she was supposed to be in right now, but the instant she pushed the right-hand door to exit the office, someone else pulled open the other door to enter, sending a blast of musky evergreen scented-A/C that fanned her curls back and made her heart skip a beat.

The next two seconds seemed to slow down into eternity as Liam Rawlins passed through, his eyes widening with surprise and then changing into something else that caused a flash of heat to swell in her chest and fan outward. The warmth reached her cheeks as his eyes traveled the length of her body back up to where they rested on her face. He paused, a question in his clear green eyes as they met hers, but she kept going, allowing the doors to close behind her.

Oh Mylanta. Out in the hallway, Belle took a moment to process this assault of the senses. She was a flustered mess of heat as she recalled his chiseled cheeks and strong jawline with a light stubble, and her eyes hadn't even made it down past the white button-down school uniform shirt that framed a broad chest with sleeves that were too tight around the upper arms. And he had totally checked her out! And that smile, those lips, and—

The school bell screamed, sounding the end of another class. As students began pouring out of the classrooms, her heart thundered in her chest as she frantically looked around for a quick exit. She suddenly did not want 500 eyes on her again.

She lucked out. She didn't have to search long and ducked into a girls' bathroom right by the office. She locked herself into a stall and stood motionless as girls streamed in and out. The only talk she could decipher among the feminine gaggle had to do with Homecoming: who was going with who, an upcoming football game, and who was entering the beauty pageant. Belle hadn't recognized any names, except from a frenzied chatter that erupted when someone exclaimed "Jared Prince is back!" followed by squeals of rapture.

Another girl sighed loudly, "I wonder who he's going out with this month."

Someone else interjected a bit too ardently, "I'd *kill* for him to pick me."

Other girls began announcing what *they* would do to get his attention, some of it making Belle blush.

Her ears perked up when she heard, "There's a new girl, did you hear?"

"Yeah, I heard she was flirting with Dmitri and Kat ripped a fistful of the girl's hair out!"

What? Belle thought, outraged.

"Well, I want to know who her boob doc is so *I* can go to him. Apparently, *she* didn't have to wait until she was 18."

The late bell rang, sending the girls scurrying out of the bathroom.

Belle peered at her schedule again, flustered and wondering how many classes she'd missed already. From glancing at the clock before leaving the main office, she figured she should be in Chemistry right now. Exiting the bathroom, a map on the back of her schedule guided her upstairs. She admired the school's grandeur/high-tech style, an eclectic mesh of fancy, old Victorian and Star Trek-style that somehow worked. She passed a few glittery banners in neon colors (she wondered if that was the work of Kat's Clone Club) announcing various Homecoming events before coming to a stop outside her classroom. Before she could knock, though, her nerves got to her and her stomach hollowed out. A familiar current of electricity rippled through her and she felt her palms getting hot.

"Oh no," she whimpered, panic rising. "Not now!" She stuffed her schedule into her back pocket before she could torch it and squeezed her hands and eyes closed, forcing herself to calm down and get control of herself. Being expelled for arson on her first day was not what she had in mind.

Think happy thoughts: Papa, the Littleton children, her new family.... Slowly, her dangerous jitters subsided.

Huh, Emilia's odd advice had worked. Her palms were finally cool enough that she took a deep breath and tentatively knocked on the door.

A male teacher paused his lecture and boomed, "Come in!"

She pulled the door open and the first thought she had when she saw the room took her back home. *Papa would've spazzed over this lab.* The people in the classroom blurred out as she wistfully took in the shiny metallic lab tables adorned with mazes of chemistry equipment that would make any mad scientist drool.

"I think she's having one of those silent seizures."

And just like that, the people slammed into focus, specifically a girl with a red-fox pony-tail surrounded by neon-clad clones. Kat was smirking as a small titter of laughter broke out.

The teacher, a tall reed-like man in a lab coat, held up a hand, silencing everyone. "You must be our newest Peacock. I am Dr. Battersby. Please introduce yourself to the class and quickly take your seat next to your lab partner." Belle's eyes widened when she saw who the only seat in the back was next to. "Because this chemical reaction won't wait"—he lifted a flask of foaming liquid—"unless you're an inhibitor!" He winked at the class and chortled at his own joke.

Several students groaned.

Belle, however, had found it genuinely funny. A joke Papa surely would've appreciated. So she quickly cleared her throat in embarrassment when the rest of the students had looked at her strangely for laughing out loud. "I'm Belle," she said quickly.

"Diiing dooong!" was heard from a corner.

Another round of laughter, but Belle noticed that it only came from Kat's group, and the rest of the students were looking at Belle as if interested or sympathetic. This eased her a bit.

Kat snorted again after the teacher gave her a warning.

As Belle walked down the aisle between the two rows of lab tables, it was difficult to ignore the murmuring complaints of some of the girls, and her heartbeat quickened as she came closer to who she was about to sit next to.

"Hey babe." Jared Prince was flashing this lop-sided grin that set off a flurry of butterflies in her stomach, although she was vaguely annoyed by "babe." His characteristic black hair swirl was relaxed into a side-swept look and his eyes were startling dark blue.

Belle acknowledged him with a smile and slid into the seat next to him. A fresh cologne scent invaded her nostrils and she could still feel his eyes on her, as well as everyone else's watching their interaction. Her faced burned and she felt the heat creeping down her neck. She dipped her head so that a curtain of curls fell between them, shielding her face from him.

She knew the guy was famous on many levels and although deep down she was thrilled to be sitting next to his Royal Hotness, the last thing she wanted today was any share of limelight. Especially on her first day. All she wanted was to blend in and quietly adapt while she figured herself out. Once she felt strong or "together" enough, she'd gladly get her feet wet in the social world with her newfound, secure self.

While Belle was lost in her thoughts, blankly watching the teacher demonstrate chemical equations on the board, Jared had been discreetly trying to get her attention by drumming his fingers on the desk, inching closer and closer to her side until she'd look at him. He'd absolutely never had a girl ignore him before and a gorgeous one at that. He felt Belle's burrs sticking deeper into his ego until he started wondering with a pang if she was a bonafide member of the "Prissy Prince Club," an online hate group that claimed his rival, Daemon King, was the king of pop.

He couldn't take it anymore.

Belle felt her curtain of hair being lifted. She turned her face to see Jared's grinning one.

"Hi," he whispered. He had an eyebrow arched as if waiting.

Wow, he really is adorable, she thought, admiring his baby-faced looks. She felt herself being drawn into that dazzling smile of his. Her mind blanked and she found herself grinning back.

"Were you hurt?" he asked with concern.

She was baffled. "Hurt? From what?"

"I thought the fall from Heaven might've hurt a bit."

"Oh, that's clever," she responded, amused at the metaphor and not seeing the pick-up line.

"Mrs. Montague?" Dr. Battersby called. "Care to balance this equation for us?" He stood at the front pointing to a chemical equation on what looked-like an oversized computer screen that covered half the wall.

Jared spoke up for her, "C'mon, Dr. B. Cut her some slack—it's her first day. She doesn't know that stuff yet."

The teacher ignored him and looked at her expectantly.

Thanks to Papa, she'd known how to solve chemical equations since she was eight years old, so when she rattled off the answer effortlessly, she turned beet red as several jaws dropped.

Jared murmured, "I guess I found my new Chemistry buddy."

Dr. Battersby, however, seemed annoyed, as if his plan to embarrass her as punishment for talking during class had backfired. "And where is your laptop?"

Belle looked at the other students' laptops lit up on their desks displaying the same formula from the giant screen. She quickly pulled the school-issued device out of her bag, laid it on the desk in front of her and smiled sheepishly at the teacher.

As Dr. Battersby resumed teaching, Jared leaned over and whispered, "It's dead. You've got to take it over there and charge it." He pointed to a cart with the sign *Charging Station* over it.

Only problem was that it was by Kat's group.

Jared watched as Belle half tip-toed over to the cart, admiring a certain view of her. He wasn't sure what to make of her unusual response to him. He was used to hysterics, catatonic states, and downright sluttiness from girls, but never this kind of lukewarm response. Even King fans couldn't resist him in person.

He frowned as Kat and her girls threw tiny wads of paper at Belle's hair, her back turned to them as she struggled to connect the wire to the laptop. When Kat took the gum out of her mouth, he *ahemmed* loudly getting everyone's attention. He locked eyes with Kat and pointedly shook his head. She scowled and jammed the gum back in her mouth.

He winked at the girl with a long, blonde ponytail sitting next to Kat. The girl beamed back at him. He sighed with satisfaction, confident that the girl would continue doing his chemistry homework now that he was back from his world tour. That is...if Belle didn't want the honor.

When Belle returned to her seat, he scooted closer with his laptop and whispered, "Here, we can share."

The smell of "hot guy" cologne enveloped her, and for the next few minutes, she couldn't concentrate on anything else. She was flattered, but at the same time, she'd already gotten in trouble with the teacher once and this guy seemed like he enjoyed trouble. She scooted away from him a little, pretending she was trying to get a better view of an instructional poster on the wall.

Soon enough, she heard the slight screech of his chair moving closer and his breath tickling her cheek, "Are you free tonight?"

She looked at him, not sure whether to admire his persistence or be alarmed at his borderline stalker vibe. Admittedly, she could imagine herself enjoying a personal tour from him of the new town, but then she didn't want to be accosted by the throng of fans and gawkers that would surely follow them. Yeah, she was not up for that. She definitely couldn't handle another set of anxieties right now, at least not until she had settled in properly.

Her eyes never leaving the teacher, she whispered back, "I'm not." She glanced at him when he didn't respond and was met with a look of pained confusion. She took a deep breath and offered him her most gracious smile. "But could you ask me again another time?"

He gave her a lopsided smile. "Definitely," he replied, dropping his voice an octave.

She held her breath when he lifted his hand and reached towards her face, but all he did was proceed to pick out the little paper wedges that were lodged in her hair.

"You'd look spectacular with straight hair," he commented lightly.

She felt a twinge of disappointment; she had no control over her hair. There was no telling these Medusa curls what to do.

Flicking the last piece out, he swept one side of her hair back, casually letting his fingertips graze her neck. She inhaled sharply and it didn't help when he flashed her a knowing, heart-stopping grin. She forced herself to stop ogling him and slowly turn back to the lecture.

For the rest of class, Belle judiciously focused on the teacher up front and mercifully, Jared left her alone until the bell sounded the end of class.

He immediately got up and retrieved her laptop from the charging station and handed it to her. "Just saving my new friend some trouble," he explained, purposefully brushing his fingers with hers as she took it from him. She hoped he didn't feel that current that just zapped through her.

"Au revoir, Belle." He put his hands in his pockets and stood there looking at her bag the laptop, a roguish half-smile on his face.

Gosh, he was cute. She finally tore herself away and followed the line towards the door. Her vanity demanded to know if he was still watching her, so just before exiting, she turned to look and froze.

Across the classroom, Jared had just wrapped his arms around a girl with a long, blonde ponytail and squeezed her in from behind. She felt a sharp stab of annoyance when he planted a kiss on the girl's neck. Without meaning to, she caught Kat's eye in the group, who was smirking and shaking her head at her as if saying, *You fool.*

Belle whipped around and left. *Ask me again later, my eye,* she thought viciously.

13

Watering Hole

Lunch was next. Her trusty map led her to a large courtyard surrounded by a variety of food vendors. A massive glass-domed ceiling allowed the sunlight to provide natural lighting to the room. Students streaming in from several entrances, quickly filled up the lines and tables.

Her stomach grumbled, but since she didn't have any money to buy food, she just sat at the nearest table to wait out the lunch period and study her schedule some more.

"You're in my spot."

Belle looked up to see a guy in a forest green army jacket, a mop of reddish hair and tortoise-shell glasses. He was heavy-set with his left shoulder jutting higher than the other. Tucked underneath one arm was a large black laptop with a gray alien-head sticker glowing at its center.

She looked around at the other empty chairs at the table. "I'm in your spot?" she repeated incredulously.

He set his lunch tray down and pointed at a spot on the table right in front of her.

She hadn't noticed it before, but there was a large letter in faded blue ink. "Q?" she read aloud.

He smiled robotically. "You're still in my spot."

Shaking her head, she moved two seats down. *What a jerk,* she thought.

Out of curiosity, though, she looked over at him again when he snapped open the laptop. Different boxes with random sequences of letters began running across each of them. He peered closely at them as if reading, and then sighing contentedly, he pushed the laptop away and centered his attention on his lunch, closely inspecting each item on his plate, including every leaf-lettuce, holding each one up as if expecting to find something.

Belle couldn't help asking, "What are you doing?"

"The FDA allows a small percentage of contaminants in our food, including insect body parts and feces."

Belle blinked. All she could think to say was, "Well, we could use the extra protein, right?"

That fell flat. Q looked at her as if she'd sprouted horns. He gestured to the empty spot in front of her. "Why aren't you eating?"

"I didn't bring any money today," she said, feeling embarrassed.

"You must be new here. Food's included in tuition." She perked up and started eyeballing her choices now. Q pointed at the tacos and burritos vendor and said, "You have a choice of heartburn with a side of Tums." He pointed next at the burgers and fries place. "Heart disease." Then at pasta and pizza, "obesity," at ethnic food, "gas, or—" and pointing at salads and wraps, he finished, "and still feeling hungry."

Belle decided to humor him. "That heart disease takes a while, right? I'll live if I have a burger."

"Actually, being the new girl today in an unfamiliar setting decreases your overall chances of survival by 13% compared to the rest of the student population."

Belle gaped at him. "I'll be extra careful then."

His face relaxed a little. "I don't know your name," he said matter-of-factly.

She smiled and extended her hand. "I'm Belle. And Q stands for...?"

He frowned at her hand. "No, thank you. We're not swapping 5,000 germs."

She quickly stuffed her "dirty" hand into her back pocket.

"Q *is* my name," he continued. "Would you mind if I added you to my list of friends?"

Belle blinked twice. This friendly request from him came out of left field, but she had a sneaking suspicion that this guy only kept two kinds of lists and she most definitely wanted to be on the good list. She broke into exaggerated enthusiasm. "Of course!"

"Excellent," he replied flatly. He turned back to his lunch and laptop and without looking up, remarked, "You only have 11 minutes left to eat."

When she returned to the table with a cheeseburger, fries, and vanilla milkshake (her stomach was rumbling like an earthquake), someone else had joined their table. A girl about her age with blonde bangs and hair framed her face. She wore a gray hoodie zipped up to the neck with the hood drawn up around her head. She sat hunched over her food and only briefly looked up when Belle said "hi" and introduced herself. The girl had a beautiful face, one that reminded Belle of those fresh, clean faces in acne product commercials. But this face was closed off and only interested in shoving food into her mouth.

Belle looked to Q, whose fingers were zooming over the laptop keys, for an introduction. Without looking away from his screen, he uttered matter-of-factly, "Cindy doesn't talk. I'm positive she has selective mutism caused by some severe social anxiety disorder."

Belle's jaw dropped. Talk about insensitive.

Cindy stopped eating and glared at Q, who still seemed like a Borg at one with his computer.

Belle caught Cindy's eye, pointed at Q and twirled her finger next to her ear in the "cuckoo" gesture.

Cindy's guarded expression briefly cracked into the smallest smile.

Without looking up, Q said, "I saw that."

Belle made a "yikes" face that elicited a full smile from Cindy.

After a few minutes of Belle sinking her teeth into burger heaven, a commotion of squeals erupted from one side of the food court. A harassed-looking Jared Prince pulled himself out of a throng of fans, as school security quickly showed up and dispersed the girls.

He lurched himself into a seat at a table in which a few stunningly beautiful girls sat. The girl next to him sat in a wheelchair and had waves of deep red hair, and from across the room, Belle could see she had big, wide blue eyes that shone with pure joy when they landed on Jared. His reaction matched hers and he planted a kiss on her forehead and drew her into a bear hug. They seemed as ecstatic to see each other as...as would a puppy-love couple that hadn't seen each other in a while.

Belle waited for some sort of lip-lock to confirm her theory, but none came. They only spoke animatedly to each other as if none other in the room existed. *Huh*, Belle thought, not quite sure what to make of it.

"Hey, Belle!" a familiar male voice called out. It was Hans, straddling the chair next to her backwards and facing her. As he did, Belle noticed that Cindy seemed to retreat further into herself. As soon as Hans opened his mouth to speak again, Q cut in, "You have 10 seconds to go away."

Hans stared at him in disbelief. "Dude, that was over a year ago. And I already apologized, remember?" He suddenly looked to Cindy. "Right, Cindy?" She bowed her head away from him.

Q's fingers were flying furiously over the laptop keys.

Hans knit his eyebrows in genuine worry. He turned to Belle and spoke quickly, "There's a lake party this Saturday—"

Q cut in again, swiveling his laptop screen to face Hans, revealing his picture and all his personal private information. "This time, I will erase your identity." He moved the cursor to the red delete button on the screen.

"Tomorrow 3:00," Hans told Belle, clearly panicked.

A click was heard.

"No!" Hans cried out.

The screen displayed a new message, *Are you sure you want to delete?*

"Last chance," Q said flatly.

Belle thought Hans was going to land his balled-up fist in Q's face, but he simply glared darkly at Q. "Nice friends you've made," he said coldly to Belle, and walked away.

"What was *that* about?" She couldn't help feeling some outrage toward Q, but at the same time she knew there had to be some sort of justification in it based on Cindy's reaction to Hans's presence.

"He made Cindy cry last year," he replied, snapping his laptop shut and sliding it into a camo-style messenger bag. "So, I legally changed his gender. You can imagine the difficulty he had trying to convince the football coach that he was still eligible to play for the team. He used the only masculine proof he had to convince the coach he wasn't a girl." Q smirked, "He apologized rather quickly to Cindy."

Cindy was also smiling now.

Belle didn't know what to think.

When she looked across the room again, she saw that Hans had joined Jared's table. He was deep in conversation with Jared, when Hans suddenly pointed at her own table and she ended up locking eyes with Jared. He grinned at her, and her face betrayed her and smiled back. She noticed that the red-head sitting next to Jared wore an expression that was half-angry, half-sad.

Then, icy horror seized Belle.

All the beautiful girls were staring at her: sizing her up and whispering to each other. She felt as if she had somehow stolen all their boyfriends, even though she had never even had so much as a first kiss. Not desiring the ire of another girl-mafia, she quickly looked away and became engrossed in the plate before her.

She glanced up at Cindy and even she looked like she felt sorry for her.

14

Darcy Drama

Musical Theater flew by quickly. The teacher had made her organize and clean up the Costume Room the whole period as a way of keeping her out of the way of a full-fledged dress rehearsal in progress. That was perfectly fine with Belle. In fact, it was a welcomed relief. She'd sing and dance and pretend she was other characters when no one was looking, but she shut it down when there were people around. It was enough that she got lost in her own fantasies in front of others, but she wasn't about to purposely act them out for an audience.

In Littleton, she craved more company, but just her second day in Elmridge, and she was already missing her "me-time." She was starting to not like people en masse. The only thing keeping Belle from running home at this point and curling up into a ball under the blankets was the prospect of talking about books in her next class: Senior Literature. Even though she was only a sophomore, the test she took earlier placed her at the senior level for literature.

This time, she breezed in to class before it started and took her seat with the other students. No awkward introductions, no spotlight, and, she looked around at the faces: she didn't recognize anyone. *Hip-hip-hooray.* She sighed contentedly.

But, of course, that wasn't going to last.

"Welcome Belle," Dr. Helsing announced as he took his position at the front of the class. He had the look of a reformed pirate dressed in a suit. His face was rough for wear: his cheeks were pockmarked with a long scar running down the length of his face, and he even had a thin mustache and a small pointed goatee.

Her mind slipped into a vision of Dr. Helsing on the bow of a pirate ship, a hooked hand holding up a long telescope to one eye and the other hand at the wheel, no doubt seeking revenge on the foe that carved up his face. *"Faster, you maggots!" he roared at his crew.*

"Belle?" Dr. Helsing broke in.

"Aye, aye Captain," she automatically responded.

The class giggled. She turned scarlet red.

He chuckled. "So you *are* enjoying Elmridge so far?"

"Oh," Belle caught on. "It's definitely a new, interesting chapter in my life." She sunk a little lower in her seat.

"Seems we have something in common. This is my first week here as well."

Another student piped up, "What brought you to Elmridge, Dr. Helsing?"

Belle breathed a sigh of relief, grateful to have the attention off her.

He clasped his hands and perched against his desk. "Well, several things actually. But I'll have to be discreet though because I am on a top-secret mission. If you knew the full details, I'd have to kill you." He waggled his eyebrows dramatically and everyone, except Belle, laughed. "Teaching is my day job. As for my *other* job..." he paused dramatically. "I'll just say this: witches, treasure, lightning and"—he drew out the last word slowly—"muuurder."

Belle gasped audibly.

"You're a Winchester from *Supernatural*!" a girl squealed.

Dr. Helsing laughed out loud. "Close! I do like those guys, though."

Belle had seen a few of those episodes in Tommy's house. "You're a monster hunter?" she asked, at almost a whisper.

"He's a writer. My dad told me," someone declared from the back.

"Bingo!" the teacher exclaimed. "And this town offers plenty of material."

Belle squirmed uncomfortably in her seat. He'd been looking right at her when he "bingo-ed." Was she the one with the right answer? Or was it the kid in the back? And how did Dr. Helsing know she wanted to be called Belle? Any school records he had on her should've read "Lisselle."

Whatever anxieties she harbored right now though were obliterated when Liam Rawlins walked in through the door. He was about to walk past the teacher, but Dr. Helsing reached out and caught him, flat-palmed, on the chest. A few people gasped as Liam froze and slowly looked up at him.

She was reminded of the phrase, "*If looks could kill.*"

A jock-type seated next to Belle called out, "Yo, Dr. Helsing, you just don't come at the Beast like that."

Another jock behind him, with a look of pity, pantomimed the Catholic crossing of oneself for Dr. Helsing.

The teacher merely frowned at the two, but quickly pulled his hand away and stood up straight, facing Liam. "And just who might you be?"

Liam stood up straighter and pulled his shoulders back, towering impressively over the teacher. In that instant, Belle sized him up: his stature up-close was mesmerizing, like Mother Nature's own statue of David. He was broad-shouldered with a muscular silhouette clearly evident beneath the white uniform shirt, which ended neatly tucked into a small waistline. Belle's eyes trailed back up to his face. His blonde hair was pulled back into a messy twist with some loose strands grazing his face, and his jaw was set in a hard line. She pictured him as the divine Apollo in an ancient Greek chariot glowing brilliantly like the sun, fire flashing from his emerald green eyes, beads of sweat glistening on his golden bare-chest....

"Wooow," Belle breathed out.

Whatever harsh words Liam had for this dead-man-walking of a teacher were quickly swallowed because all eyes were on the new girl, who used a hand to half-cover her red face.

A very pretty girl with dark blonde curls expertly woven up with a fancy head scarf, who Belle now recognized as part of the Princess Posse, called out gleefully, "Belle meet Beast. Beast meet Belle." She had a thick, European-sort of accent.

A shadow of a smile softened Liam's face and the mood in the room lightened considerably. He even shook hands with the teacher and introduced himself, "Liam Rawlins. I'm supposed to come in here once a week."

It was the first time Belle heard his voice. It was a smooth baritone that elicited delicious shivers down her spine. She could listen to *his* audiobooks all day.

What in tarnation am I thinking?! she chastised herself. *Get a grip, Ms. Hormones!*

"Ah, yes, Ms. Silva left a note about that. Our virtual student." Dr. Helsing gestured for him to take a seat. With a nod, Liam moved past him and headed towards the only remaining desk. In the back. Right in front of Belle.

She avoided looking at him as he approached and pretended to fiddle with her laptop. She felt everyone's eyes upon them, as if waiting to see if she'd have another outburst. Finally, she had to look up because Liam had stopped right in front of her, as if waiting. He gestured towards the empty seat and asked, "Would you like to switch?"

"Wha- why?" she half-demanded incredulously, thinking back to her earlier run-in with Q.

He spoke carefully, "Because if I sit here, you won't be able to see."

"Oh." Belle was caught off-guard by his consideration for her. Even though it warmed her, she knew that if she made any big movements now, she would somehow end up tripping over something, breaking a bone, and inadvertently starting a fire. "Um, thanks, but I'll be fine right here."

Liam shrugged his shoulders and sat in front of her.

And now she regretted not taking him up on his offer. She couldn't see a thing, except the students next to her. Just a big, white wall of shirt before her.

She exhaled gruffly.

Liam's shoulders shook a fraction and she guessed he was laughing at her.

"Yo, Beast," the jocks traded tricky handshakes with Liam across the aisle. "I spoke with Coach. He says you're welcome back on the team anytime."

The other one jumped in, "Yeah, the new quarterback's trying, but he's not you, bro. We need that cannon back. Especially now with the Homecoming game coming up next month."

"I've been thinking about it, but we'll see, man," Liam replied. "I've got a lot on my plate still."

With a pang, Belle remembered what Candy had said about his murdered parents.

Dr. Helsing called out, "Ok, class, open up *Pride and Prejudice*"—Belle barely contained her shriek of delight—"to where we left off yesterday." Then the teacher muttered audibly to himself, "Few more chapters of this nonsense and we'll be done with this dreadful unit she started."

While everyone lit up their laptop screens and Belle struggled to even find the power button, Liam whispered across the aisle, "What happened to Ms. Silva?"

Jock #1 shrugged. "Dunno, man."

A girl's voice sounding pouty from somewhere in the front floated back, "I've missed you, Liam."

Belle wondered with rising aggravation if it was the head scarf-girl, and also, *How did this dagnabbit thing turn on?!*

Jock #2 snickered and elbowed the other one. "At least he's still getting some action."

"Ugh," Belle muttered angrily to herself. "Useless!" She pushed the device to the farthest corner of her desk. The white wall moved and she could see everyone now: Dr. Helsing leaning against his desk, tablet in hand, and it *was* the head-scarf girl since she was looking right at Liam with a coy smile. But Liam wasn't looking back because his eyes were trained on Belle's face.

"Need help?" he said in a low voice, looking meaningfully between the rejected laptop and Belle. He was completely turned towards her and, while she tried to remain dignified, she was struck a bit deaf and dumb by this skin-tingling, up-close view of him. She caught a whiff of a heavy evergreen musk that immediately took her back to the woods by her house in Littleton. Without thinking, she leaned in a bit closer and inhaled deeply. "Mmmm," she smiled, nostalgia flooding her.

"What an odd little duck," head-scarf girl said.

Belle snapped her eyes open and flushed deeply again.

The jocks were elbowing each other and laughing.

When she dared to meet Liam's eyes, she expected to encounter ridicule or even pity there, but, instead, she found herself locked into his smoldering gaze. She felt much warmer and her insides did funny things.

Dr. Helsing's voice sounded somewhere in the background, "Can anyone tell me why Elizabeth rejected Darcy's proposal?"

Someone replied, "Because she's an idiot."

The fiery connection immediately severed. Belle sucked in air—she had forgotten to breathe. *Who's calling Lizzy an idiot?*

Liam shifted in his seat enough to allow Belle a view. Her heart skipped a beat, as he was still thinking of her.

"Kim, would you care to elaborate, please?" Dr. Helsing asked.

"Well, Darcy's filthy rich and frickin' hot. So, yeah, she's an idiot."

Belle just had to see who was speaking. She stuck her head into the aisle to get a better view. A girl with lime green and hot pink accessories and a big sideways pony tail. *Hmmm, figures. A Kat-clone.* She raised her hand.

"Yes, Belle?" Dr. Helsing called.

She was acutely aware of several pairs of eyes, especially Liam's, turning to her again. She ignored his tantalizing scent. "Elizabeth respected herself and her family too much to accept his proposal."

Kim challenged, "You mean, she thought she was better than him?"

"No," Belle said carefully. "*Darcy* thought he was better than her. He claims he proposed to her despite his best judgment. Lizzy and her family were poor and odd and didn't meet the expectations of high society. He says he loves her, but clearly implies he doesn't value her as an equal. How *could* she be with someone like that?"

She had everyone's attention now, except Kim's, who'd whipped her pony tail around and faced forward. "And then there were the rumors surrounding Darcy," Belle continued. "He was accused of some terrible things, but kept to himself so much that people had no choice but to believe the unfair things said about him. He was prideful, and Lizzy and everyone else were prejudiced against him."

"Bro," Jock #1 grabbed his friend's arm. "That's why it's called *Pride and Prejudice!*"

"Get off me, man!" Jock #2 shrugged him off.

"Excellent analysis, Belle. Now—" Dr. Helsing began, but Liam cut him off.

"So then how does Darcy redeem himself?" He was looking expectantly at Belle, his expression dark and penetrating.

"What was that, Liam?" Dr. Helsing asked.

"I mean, we can tell from the cover of the story they end up happily ever after. So, how does he do it?" Liam pressed.

Jock #1 rolled his eyes. "Bro, you're supposed to *read* to find out, or watch the movie—"

But Liam viciously cut him off without breaking eye-contact with Belle, "Shut up, Shawn."

A pin-drop could've been heard in the room.

Belle didn't understand this sudden front of hostility from him. "Well..." she began slowly. "He started off by addressing each rumor with truth. Then, she visited his estate and got to hear all the wonderful things about him from his servants—"

Liam cut in, "And she believed him?"

His aggression jarred her. "What do you mean?" she asked softly.

"The truth," he said impatiently.

"Yes, especially after—"

"Well, that's just the problem," Liam said, eyes narrowing. "In the real world, no one believes the truth anymore." He shoved out of his chair and walked out of the classroom.

The back of Belle's eyes suddenly burned. *What a jerk!*

Head-scarf girl caught her eye and actually smiled sympathetically at her.

"You know what, ladies and gents?" Dr. Helsing announced loudly, slicing through the awkward tension in the room. "Thanks to this enlightening discussion, we now officially know how *Pride and Prejudice* turns out. By a show of hands, who would be opposed to wrapping up this unit next class by watching the movie, huh? Only three? Well, majority rules. That settles it." He slapped the desk enthusiastically. "Let's turn our attention now to my personal favorite: using investigative field work to dig up our family histories."

15

Lightning and Glass

Belle rushed to her last class of the day in a simmering sour mood. She couldn't stop thinking about how she had offended Liam and driven him to walk out. But her inner drill sergeant piped up: *You did nothing wrong, Belle. Liam's the one being ultra-sensitive.* Still, he had a right to be sensitive what with his family history and all. *But not a right to be rude!*

Crash! Belle had suddenly tripped over a foot and careened into a locker.

"Ha! What a klutz," a familiar snooty voice drawled. Kat leaned against the locker in front of her with her neon clones clustering around, smirking. "Not looking like the wildcard Homecoming candidate anymore, huh?"

Belle could feel her anger and confusion rising. She'd been purposefully and violently tripped. "What are you talking about?" she responded measuredly.

Kat pushed off the locker as her clones closed in and got in Belle's face. "What? You think you have a chance at beating me for the sophomore spot in the Homecoming court?" she scoffed.

The crowd of course had stopped to watch. Cell phones were taken out to record. Some students egged Kat on while others seemed to be supportive of Belle.

Belle's mind reeled. "I have no idea what you're talking about."

Kat sneered, "Drop the doe-eyed innocent act, skank."

Belle had to think fast. She was not worried about Kat's nasty pettiness; rather, she was terrified of exposing herself. Those hot-needles were starting to poke through from all over her body, her hands were burning hot, and her vision was starting to go white. Just like with the Hammerson brothers...Belle was about to blow.

"Hey, what'cha doin', babe? Why don't you come over with me?"

Belle could just barely make out the voice from her growing haze. *Dmitri?*

This seemed to enrage Kat even more. She seethed out in Belle's ear, "You're nobody, you hear? You're just a shiny new nobody that these losers have never seen before."

Everything that happened next was instantaneous. Belle knew she couldn't stop it. She could only squeeze her eyes shut and try as hard as she might to control its release. Kat had her hand on the locker while she was in Belle's face and an old science lesson resurfaced in her mind, *Metals conduct electricity.* Discreetly dropping her hand, she planted her palm on the locker and let go.

A crackling and several loud pops followed by screams punctuated the air. Kat and two of her friends, who'd been leaning on the locker, flew off and crashed into some bystanders.

Belle's vision returned, and she exhaled with relief: she hadn't killed them, thank God. They even appeared unhurt, just in shock as they gaped back at her.

The crowd started murmuring.

She quietly and quickly made her escape through the crowd, which parted for her, allowing her to duck into the nearest girls' bathroom. Her heart had chilled at a word that reached her ear from the commotion: "*Freak.*"

~~*~~

Perched on a toilet seat, Belle squeezed her eyes shut and focused on Emilia's all-important advice: "*Think happy thoughts.*" Memories and promises came to mind: board game night with Papa, meeting Candy at the mall later.... Belle breathed a sigh of relief as the last *snap, crackle, pop* disappeared from her quivering hands. She hugged her knees to her chest, grateful her cousin's advice actually turned out to be useful.

It was hard to think above the gaggle of girl chatter in the restroom. The same topics as last time floated around, including the latest addition of how "the new girl is packing a Taser" and how they thought Kat, Sheila, and Chloe were going to retaliate. Someone predicted a *Carrie* stunt at Homecoming. Whatever that meant.

Belle groaned, letting her head sink to her knees. She needed to see Candy, stat. The only clue she had about all the sudden attention and Kat's ire was that she was now somehow involved with the Homecoming court. Hopefully, Candy could explain this new mystery to her.

Ugh, her new life felt like a TV soap opera marathon of melodrama with a side of weird. Actually, a large artery-clogging dose of weird. She recalled watching a movie on Tommy's TV once called the *The Truman Show*, and she couldn't help wishing right now that the director of her show would yell "Cut!" already. She couldn't believe she was thinking this, but...she really, *really* missed Littleton right now. And Papa. She was now starting to appreciate her former isolation as precious solitude.

She humphed at the irony.

Before the tears could work themselves back up, the alarm sounded the beginning of next class and the restroom quickly emptied out. She sighed. Another tardy. Another dreadful classroom spotlight. Just as she was about to set down off the toilet, the restroom door slammed open, and a familiar thick German-accent made her freeze.

"Where are you, girl?" Mrs. Steifshwester hissed. "You thought you would get away with it, ya?"

How did she find out so quickly? Belle thought panicking. *How am I going to explain this?!* It was at this moment that she realized how utterly alone she was in her mess. There was no one she could think of who truly understood her and could help.

"Come out here this instant. I know you're in one of these stalls." She added in a slow, menacing tone that made Belle's skin crawl, "You know what I could do to you—what I *will* do to you—if you don't obey me at once."

Right before Belle was about to step down, another small foot in the stall next to hers touched onto the floor. And then the other foot. They wore a pair of glittery, but dirty, light blue sneakers with the brand-name "Glass" etched onto the sides.

Belle remained frozen right where she was, dumbstruck that she hadn't been the one being addressed. Who could the principal have possibly been talking to then? She watched as the Glass shoes came to a stop in front of the principal's black pumps and listened.

"So, what is this that Stella and Mona are telling me? A large package came in the mail for you, ya? A dress from Fairy Godmother Boutique? How did you pay for it, you little thief?" There was a short, strained silence interrupted by a powerful *smack!* "Speak!" she demanded.

An abrupt sob escaped from the girl. "It was—it was free. A contest. I submitted a ball gown design and- and I won. They created my dress and sent it to me."

Mrs. Steifshwester scoffed in derision. "Ha! How pathetic. You actually think you're going to this Homecoming dance, ya? You are going nowhere."

The girl barely whispered, "I am."

"Excuse me, what was that? I'll have none of your insolence."

The girl rushed on, a growing mix of desperation and boldness in her voice, "They're selling my dress in their catalogue and then I will have my own money. I'll be free of you—I will! My father and I, both. And then you'll never be able to hurt him again!"

The girl suddenly gasped in pain.

Belle clapped her hand over her mouth. The old woman must have physically gotten ahold of her.

"You will *never* be free. I will write to that company and tell them it was Stella's idea and that you are an envious, no-good thief and liar. Who are they going to believe, ya? A girl who's practically failing school, or the principal of the most prestigious high school in the country?"

The girl sobbed.

"In fact," the principal continued, her tone more snakelike than ever, "you and Stella are about the same build, ya? I think *she* will wear the dress to the dance while you stay home."

"No!" the girl cried out.

"Get off me, girl!" the woman replied with disgust.

Belle heard a scuffle and then a deafening *smack!* She couldn't take it anymore—she had to do something.

She flushed the toilet.

"Silence!" Mrs. Steifshwester hissed. "Or I will *finish* your father! Go, disappear."

Belle listened as they scrambled out and the restroom door closed with a heavy *swoosh*. She waited a full minute before exiting the stall. There, in the middle of the floor of the empty restroom was one of the girl's Glass shoes left behind in the scuffle. Belle felt sick to her stomach, reeling from the mental replay that shoe brought on. She had to find a way to help this poor girl. She had some major clues already, which she'd made up her mind to reveal to Ernesto when she got home and get him to mount a full-scale investigation.

Determined, Belle packed the lone shoe in her bag. Evidence. As she exited the restroom, she nearly stepped on the snake—Mrs. Steifshwester had been waiting for her. Belle backed up quickly, fully knowing how capable it was of striking out.

"So, skipping class, ya? I come out of my office just *now* to find you here and not in class." The principal glanced down at a very expensive looking watch. "You are going on 8 minutes late now. What have you to say for yourself?"

What a liar, Belle thought, and she could tell that the true question in her eyes was really *How much did you hear?* She raised her chin and answered, "Enough to interest the Sheriff."

Mrs. Steifshwester's eye merely twitched, and then she moved to block Belle's attempt to sidestep her. "So, tell me, how is your aunt?" she asked cruelly, as if already knowing the answer. "Any words from the boss-lady?" She sneered when Belle avoided her gaze. "I see. So, she *is* a ghost."

Belle felt the heat flare in her palms. She tried to walk away again, but, this time, the principal grabbed her by the upper arm. Hard. The snake leaned in as if to hiss in her ear, but Belle did not give her a chance. A loud *crack! pop!* was heard as Belle forcefully ripped her arm away and put distance between them. She hid her buzzing hands behind her back and glared at the principal, who was watching her now with a dangerous regard.

Just like with Katerina's attack, Belle realized she wasn't afraid of this woman; rather, Belle feared what *she* could do to the hag and that she'd be outed as a freak. And more than that, she was outraged! How dare the old witch put her hands on her! She thought of the girl in the bathroom and of the Glass shoe still in her bag and her indignation rose even higher. But Belle had to calm down. She could hear the snapping and popping coming from her lava hands hidden behind her back. A fire would soon be next.

"Actually, I do have words from the 'boss-lady,'" Belle lied boldly, looking her squarely in the eye. "My aunt says the writing's on the wall for you: there'll be a new principal at this school soon."

Mrs. Steifshwester's eyes narrowed as she stared at Belle in defiant disbelief. But as Belle calmly held her own, her steely gaze broke into genuine surprise and worry.

Belle felt her hands cool enough now to stuff into her front pockets. "You might as well start packing," she added, in feigned sympathy.

"You lie," she countered weakly.

Belle shrugged her shoulders apologetically, hitched her bag up higher, and walked away, leaving a befuddled principal to fly back into her office.

~~*~~

"Are you okay?" asked a small girl's voice.

Belle blinked rapidly and a pair of round blue eyes framed by pretty, blonde ringlets adorned with mini-butterfly clips swam into focus. Grace Darling, the sixth grader who she was assigned to tutor during her alternate days of Study Hall/Work Experience, tapped her pencil expectantly over the unfinished long-division problem.

Belle tried to rein in her thoughts, which were on a constant, torturous replay of the nerve-racking events of the school day mixed with the nightmare she'd had last night. *Ugh.* She rubbed her temples and squeezed her eyes shut, the million unanswered questions stomping around in her head gave her a migraine. She wished she could unload this burden somehow, but she couldn't think of anyone she could safely talk to without sounding like she was paranoid or psychotic or both.

"And my teachers complain that *I'm* distracted," Grace muttered.

Distractions. That's it. She just needed to stop thinking about all this stuff until she could...could get a journal or something. Actually, Aunt Emily was the only one who could really answer all of her questions. She had to know about Belle's powers and dreams and her mother. So until Emily returned from the other side of the universe, Belle would have to push the puzzle to the backburner.

School, lake party, new friends, books, boys... distractions. That would be her new focus. The tension in her head started to subside, especially when she thought of meeting Candy after school at the mall to shop. Normal, teenage stuff. That's what she needed right now.

A long sigh drew Belle's glance across the table. Grace was dreamily engrossed in a picture she was doodling on the paper.

"Did you finish that problem?" Belle asked.

Grace looked up from her drawing, a faraway look in her eyes. "Hmmm?"

"Hey," Belle reached for the drawing. "That's rather"—she scrutinized the stick figures—"unique."

Grace suddenly held on to the paper, her rosy cheeks flooding with embarrassment.

Belle gave her a questioning look.

"Fine," Grace relented. "No one believes me anyway."

"What do you mean?" Belle looked at the drawing again.

Grace remained silent.

Belle's eyebrows shot up as she made sense of the picture. "Who's that?" She pointed at a winged stick-figure boy hovering over a stick-figure girl in bed.

"That's Peter," Grace replied matter-of-factly.

"And that's you?" Belle hoped for a 'no.' She wasn't so sure a 12-year-old should already be imagining boys in her bedroom.

Grace slowly nodded her head.

"Hey, can you tell *me* about this Peter? I promise to take you seriously." She meant it.

Peter... The name unsettled her.

Grace's eyes brightened. "Well, okay." She began hesitantly, but soon her words came tumbling out over each other, "Peter's my age and he's really, really cute. But he's only my friend. He's kinda weird though. It's like he's searching for his mom and he wants *me* to pretend to be his mom. And he's not from Elmridge. He comes to my room at night sometimes, through my window—"

From looking at Belle's shocked expression, she quickly added, "Nothing bad happens! I swear! At first, he wanted me to tell him stories, but I was like 'no way, I suck at that,' so I just show him funny Youtube videos on my laptop instead. He loves the epic fails."

She began giggling uncontrollably as she continued, "His favorite video is this squirrel that's trying to eat at this spinning birdfeeder, but it can't because it keeps spinning and spinning and he's hanging on for dear life for like five minutes and then when it finally lets go and hits the ground, it's trying to dash away, but it just keeps walking in circles and bashing its head into the ground!" She finally gave into a big belly-laugh. "That just kills Peter!" She guffawed holding her stomach.

Other students around were shushing them now.

Behind the teacher's desk up front, Mr. Chet, the Study Hall monitor, who looked like a sour 30-something-year-old still living in his mother's basement, looked up from a hand-held gaming device and frowned in the girls' direction.

Peter. Peter. Belle was so close to putting her finger on it. She gasped aloud, "Emilia!" She keeps pretending like she's talking to a Peter.

"Who's Emilia?" Grace asked, wiping away tears.

"Um, nobody. I mean, my cousin." Belle proceeded cautiously, "Hey, Grace, can you *see* Peter?"

"Uh, yeah," Grace replied, looking at her like she was crazy.

Mr. Chet sighed loudly as if supremely annoyed and withdrew his Converse-clad feet from off the desk. He headed down the aisle towards them.

Belle quickly shook her head. "Of course, you can. I mean, can *other* people see Peter?"

"Well, he doesn't trust grown-ups. And he says he only comes to see me, so...." She was blushing bright pink. "I guess I'm not sure how to answer that."

Belle rushed to wrap up the conversation, "Does he *have* to use the window? You should tell him to walk through the front door next time."

Grace shrugged. "I did, but he says he'd rather fly."

Mr. Chet slapped his palms on the table, making both girls jump in their seats. "Dudettes, please!" He whisper-screeched, "I was *just* about to level up to wizard. Do you know how difficult it is to find the Arcadian gemstone in the Dagmor realm?"

The girls stared blankly at him.

A heavy-set student sitting across the aisle weighed in, "Almost impossible, sir."

"Thank you, Fatty Bags," Mr. Chet responded, never breaking eye-contact with the girls.

Belle's mouth hung open.

"You're welcome, sir," the student replied as if all was completely normal.

"Goldilocks," he jutted his finger in Grace's face. "If I hear your asinine giggles again, you can take a hike to the principal's." He turned sharply. "And you..." he waved his hand around her face, searching for what to call her. "Hair!" he finally spit out. "Shut your pie-hole!" He turned back on his heels and strode back to the front, muttering something about now having to fight a troll for the 8th time.

Belle was too stunned for words, but her palms were itching with heat as she glared after his back.

Grace whispered, "Don't worry about him. He's a nitwit."

"There seems to be plenty of those around here," Belle said bitterly, thinking back to English class again. "How does he even *work* here?"

"He's the principal's nephew."

Belle groaned, "Figures."

16

Peacock Plaza

Belle dragged in a deep breath of freedom as she put more distance between herself and the school. Students streamed out in every direction, piling into those tiny cars, on bicycles, on foot, and some on those motorized-looking skateboards which she later learned were called hoverboards.

This had to be the single most eventful day in her life and it still was far from over. She blocked out these past few hours from her mind and focused on following a current of students on a sidewalk headed towards Peacock Plaza, the mall where Candy was supposed to be working in for her Work Experience class, which meant that she was already there waiting for Belle.

Although she was tiring of new experiences and longing for her old routine of curling up with a good book on the couch, shopping was something she had never done before. From watching a shopping network on Tommy's TV, the hosts made it seem like it was more exciting than Christmas.

"Ouch," she cried out. A sharp pain radiated from her foot. Her old sneakers were becoming unbearable to walk in. New shoes were definitely on her shopping list.

"Hey, beautiful!"

Jared Prince.

Several squeals erupted from a few girls walking near Belle.

He slowed down next to her in a tiny two-seater convertible car. He inched down his black sunglasses, revealing electric blue eyes. And they were aimed right at Belle.

A few girls groaned in disappointment.

"Comment allez-vous (How are you), Belle?"

"I only know French curse words, sorry," she responded.

Jared laughed. "Then you don't know that 'Belle' means 'beautiful' in French? Alright, how about I just call you Beauty then."

She blushed and a tiny smile appeared. "Belle's fine." She kept walking while he slowly followed in the car beside her.

Some girl wailed enviously, "What's wrong with her? Why doesn't she talk to him?"

Belle hated being put on the spot again and truth was she had no idea how to flirt back. It felt unnatural.

"Do you need a ride? Where you headed?" he persisted.

"I'm meeting a friend at the mall," she replied looking straight ahead. "I'm told it's a short walk."

The girls nearby would not stop with their outrage.

Jared was not used to being rebuffed. He quickly checked the mirror, wondering if he had anything hanging out of his nose or something. All clear. "It's a 20-minute walk from here. I can get you there in 5."

Belle half-grinned at him. "Thanks, but I'm sure one of your fans here would be more than grateful to take you up on your offer."

"Look, sweetie, you can either put up with me for 20 minutes while I follow you or get rid of me in 5."

She had cringed at "sweetie," but, nonetheless, he did have a point.

He flashed her a charming grin. "Hey, I'm just trying to meet the new girl that everyone's been talking about all day."

Belle stopped dead in her tracks. "*Why* is everyone talking about me?" What Kat said about being the "shiny, new toy" shot across her mind.

"Get in and I'll tell you all about it."

Belle still hesitated. It was clear he was baiting her.

He pretended to pout. "Pleeease."

Those blue eyes sure did sparkle prettily. "Well, fine. These shoes *are* choking my feet. Straight to the mall, right?"

He held up two fingers. "Scout's honor."

"Yeah, I don't take you for a Boy Scout," she said, not believing his sincerity.

"Really? Well then, 'cross my heart and hope to die.' How's that?"

Belle smiled genuinely this time. "Ok." That charm, however suspicious she was of it, was growing on her. Her teenage ego wasn't invincible to flattery.

Jared reached over and threw the passenger door open. She slid in and she could just hear the gossip mill operating at max now. As they pulled away, she heard someone shout, "Good luck, Ms. September!"

"What's that supposed to mean?"

"Never mind them," he said dismissively.

"So—" they both had started speaking at the same time.

"Go ahead," Belle laughed, embarrassed. She felt so alien in this car with its fancy-looking white interior, sitting next to a world-famous heartthrob. His fresh cologne scent was a bit dizzying. But he promised her some answers, so she was determined to brave through the awkwardness.

Jared rubbed the dashboard like it was a pet. "So, what do you think of this ride, huh? I got this baby yesterday. Figured I'd reclaim my throne at this school in style."

Belle blinked. She waited for him to laugh as if joking or start talking about the rumors surrounding her like he said he would.

Jared misinterpreted her confusion. "I just finished my world tour last week," he added proudly, as if that would help. "I usually use this downtime at home to write new songs and pop out some new singles."

"Oh." Belle discerned he was fishing for the praise he must be so used to hearing. "Well, that's great," she said awkwardly, "and this car is..." *How do you compliment on cars?* "...really...shiny."

He raised an eyebrow and laughed. "You *are* different." Before Belle could respond, he continued, "Marissa doesn't like it, though. I can't take her to school in it."

"Your girlfriend?"

"No," he replied, recoiling slightly. "Mari's like my sister. Our families grew up together."

"But why can't you take her—" and then she remembered Marissa's wheelchair. "Oh, sorry."

"I'll hook up this car with the lift she needs, though," he said, speaking more to himself.

"That's really nice of you."

They made a left turn and arrived at the mall. He threw the gear into park and turned toward her. "*You're* nice," he said seriously.

Belle couldn't see his eyes behind the dark sunglasses, but from the subtle movement of his head, she could tell he was checking her out. She was semi-flattered, but relieved to be getting out of the car now. "Well, thanks for the ride."

"You're going to the Lake Party tomorrow?"

"Probably." And before he got any ideas, she added, "I'm going with Candy."

He flashed her his famous white pearls. "See you tomorrow, Beauty."

She waved back, but before he pulled away, he called out, "Hey!"

"Yeah?"

"A hundred bucks says you wear a one-piece tomorrow."

She frowned, but he just laughed before driving away.

~~*~~

Peacock Plaza was luxurious and fit for a king's shopping experience. It was u-shaped with a large cobblestoned courtyard in the opening, peppered with bistro sets. At the center was a shallow, circular pool with a giant 5-tier stone fountain lazily spilling water into its lower tiers, while the top tier held a pedestal with a tall golden Fairy Prynn statue. It looked like the one from the train brochure. One hand held a clear sphere that had lights sparkling inside of it and the other hand carried a lightning bolt with bright lights flashing through it, giving it an electrified look. Above, a criss-cross of lights and "floating" art installations connected the three floors. And from the looks of the mall directory, this place offered *everything* a person could need.

Belle was completely spellbound: she could easily spend a whole day just on the first floor.

After locating Candy's Cakes, she headed left and it wasn't too long before a familiar voice called out from behind her, "Excuse me, Belle."

When she turned, she spotted Q waving at her without a smile, his left side noticeably humped, and standing in front of a store called Q-Tech. He was wearing a black t-shirt that had a running electronic banner across the chest that blinked, *Q-Tech, Your Best Bet for the Best Tech.*

"Hey, Q! How are ya?" Belle approached him, sidestepping a young mom pushing a stroller.

Behind him were a few customers milling about in the store, checking out a variety of electronics and computers. He looked worried. "Have you seen Cindy? She's not answering her texts and she's late for work." He added, muttering to himself, "I could hack into her phone and track her, but"—he ran a hand through his ruddy hair—"I promised I wouldn't."

"I haven't, sorry," Belle said. "Does she work with you here?"

"*For* me," he corrected. "She works the register, but now *I* have todo it. And I don't like dealing with—people." He shuddered, and then as if contaminated by the very thought, he took a small hand sanitizer bottle from his pocket, squeezed a generous mound into his hands and rubbed it all over his hands up to his elbows.

Belle peeked over his shoulder, curiosity demanding how he could run a store on such a philosophy, when she discovered his solution: robotic arms and talking computer-screen smiley faces extending from the ceiling were interacting with customers, while the lone register desk sat empty in a corner.

Belle hitched her bag closer. The Glass shoe pressed into her side and she was reminded of her desire to help the poor mystery girl. A worrisome possibility tugged at her: could it be Cindy's? She was about to pull it out and ask Q, but thought better of it when she realized that Cindy couldn't talk while the shoe's owner could.

"What are you shopping for?" Q asked, interrupting her thoughts. He was frowning, as if she'd overstayed her welcome in his presence.

"Actually," Belle said, recalling her shopping list. "Maybe you can help me."

Twenty minutes later, Belle was on her way to Candy's with a brand new cell phone in her back pocket. A holographic video from a customer service robot had given her a brief tutorial on how to set up and use the phone. She was later supposed to fill it with contacts and something called "apps."

Soon, she spotted Candy across the way behind a glass counter showcasing a tantalizing assortment of goodies. She had a hot pink daisy pinned in her curly afro and a hot pink t-shirt with gold script that read, *Candy's Cakes.*

Candy spotted her and waved her over. "Hey, girl!"

In her excited scramble to get to the cake shop, Belle nearly tripped over a security guard zooming past her on a Segway.

Once inside, Candy introduced her to Millie Kwan-Yin, her best friend since she'd punched Kat on the playground for pushing Candy off the seesaw. She was Asian with bangs and straight black shoulder-length hair, light purple framed eyeglasses, and she wore the same hot pink daisy and shirt ensemble as Candy. Millie sat at a booth, where Belle joined her, sitting across from her, while Candy tended to an elderly customer trying to decide between red velvet or chocolate chip cookie cupcake.

Millie did not waste a minute. "Okay, so Candy says I'm supposed to give you the 'Who's Who' of Elmridge High." She took a deep breath, and a minute later, Millie was breathless after giving Belle a rapid-fire stream of information to digest.

Most of the Elmridge student body grew up together going to the same exclusive school since they were kids, raised mostly by nannies and being trained up according to the wishes of their super-rich, mostly absent parents, usually to follow in their footsteps. This was the main group of students, who Millie said were called the "bourgees" for bourgeois. Jared, Hans, Dmitri, Kat, and everyone in the Princess Posse, for example, were in that group.

"You're either really rich, or really talented—a whiz—to go to Elmridge High, and if you're both, like Jared Prince, then you're part of the 1% that rules the school," Millie said matter-of-factly.

"What are you?" Belle asked.

"Bourgee. My dad invented 'mood' glasses. See?" She removed her glasses and held it up to the light. They were pink now.

"Wow!" Belle was impressed.

"Yeah, everyone knows to avoid me when they're black. Usually happens in Trigonometry. What about you?"

Belle was perplexed. "'What about me,' what?"

"Are you bourgee or whiz?"

That made Belle think. "I'm not sure. I literally got here yesterday. I didn't showcase any talent to get in or anything, so...."

"Did you move in to one of those mansions on Rich Row?"

"No, I live with my aunt and cousin at the Historical Society."

It was Millie's turn to be impressed. "Emily Prynn is your aunt?"

"Yes," Belle replied, suddenly not liking the focus of conversation on herself.

"Ok, definitely bourgee. Your aunt has like the deed to this town. And you say there's a cousin?"

Belle winced. She forgot about Ernesto's request to keep Emilia's presence a secret.

When Belle hesitated, Millie pressed forward, "What does your aunt look like? No one I know has seen her, so she's kind of like an urban legend now. There aren't any pictures of her. People say that place is haunted. There is that one girl, kind of strange, who lets guests in sometimes to roam around the museum. Is she the cousin? And then there's Chief Panzinski who's always in and out of that place—"

Belle felt extremely unsettled. She liked Millie, but she seemed nosy to a fault, especially when Belle had too much to hide.

Millie finally noticed her uneasiness. "Oh, my God, I did it again! I'm so sorry." She pointed at herself. "Fast talker; impossible to have a filter." She clasped her hands together and pleaded, "Please don't unfriend me."

Her sincerity made Belle relax again. "Well, it looks like you might be a whiz detective which puts *you* in the 1%."

Millie chuckled. "Nah," but then fell into pondering. She suddenly dove into her bag, as if she remembered something important, and pulled out a laptop. "Hey, have you set up your Peacock Profile yet?"

"No," Belle said, her eyes wandering over to the counter full of cupcake temptations. A particular strawberry-frosting one looked like it knew her name.

"Well, looks like you've started setting one up...." Millie moved her face closer to the screen as her finger glided on the cursor pad.

"Um, I really don't think I have." She was alarmed that someone would know enough about her, besides her name, to put up on the Internet.

Millie swiveled the laptop screen around to face her and gushed, "You are so lucky!" Her glasses were a pale green.

"What do you mean?" She responded blankly, scanning the contents of the screen. A large glittery banner across the top read *Homecoming Court Countdown* and beneath it was what looked like a tournament chart of student photos.

Belle gasped. There was her face wearing a surprised expression, no doubt the picture that Waldo snapped of her that morning, and underneath it read *Wildcard Sophomore Princess*. She was pitted against Kat's smug face.

One of her country Littleton expressions slipped out, "How in tarnation?" She was dumbfounded. "No one even knows anything about me."

"Are you kidding?" Millie began ticking off on her fingers. "On your first day at school, you almost stole Kat's man and then tasered her and her friends; your aunt owns this town; Jared Prince wants you; and this last reason alone would have put you over the top: watch this—" She clicked on a corner image of an ornate oval mirror and the page changed to an enlarged version of the mirror that faded in and out like the rippling surface of water, with a shimmering silver sentence hovering over it, *Who's the fairest of them all?*

Belle's surprised face filled the screen with her name flashing below it.

"See?" Millie said pointedly. "*You* are now the prettiest girl in the school." She crossed her arms and leaned back. "Princess Posse will definitely be recruiting you soon." Her glasses were now a dark green.

Belle felt absolutely sick to her stomach. This was the last thing she wanted. It all felt like some cruel cosmic joke being played on her. She'd tried to gain control of her life when she'd made that rebellious left turn on the road about two months ago and it only seems as if since then, she's been a pawn of Fate, and it was still unraveling the course of her life. She still had no control. Her goal when she got to this town was to blend in and figure herself out, quietly, but no—Fate, Destiny, God would have her center stage as an exhibition. The girl with the fire hands! Vote her to be your next princess!

"Belle?" Millie's concerned voice barely penetrated her thoughts.

"Oh, I am Fortune's fool," Belle whispered, sinking down into her booth. When normally her temper would flare up and her palms would spark, she instead just felt so tired suddenly. Like all the energy had been sapped out of her.

"Oh my God, Millie, what have you been telling her?" Candy's concerned face came into view and she gently shook Belle's shoulders.

"I just showed her the HCC page!" Millie said defensively, her glasses turning white. "She's mumbling something now about being a fool with fortune."

"Shakespeare," Belle corrected softly. She felt cold.

"Here," Candy placed something in front of her. "Maybe you need some sugar in your system." Belle's eyes focused on a cupcake with a white cloud of frosting and chocolate drizzle and something else on top. Her eyes widened.

"My famous brownie s'mores cupcake," Candy announced proudly. She pushed the small plate closer to Belle. "Take a bite. I promise your *soul* will feel better."

"Your hips won't," Millie muttered, looking down critically at her own.

Belle took a bite and, for a moment, her cares melted away as she quietly savored bite after bite. "Mmmm, tastes like Heaven."

Millie whispered slyly to Candy, "She's practically making out with that cupcake."

Candy elbowed her into silence and then leaned toward Belle, folding her hands underneath her chin. "Now, honey, how else can Candy make your day better?"

"If you can make me invisible in this school, it'll be a good start," Belle replied, licking her fingers.

Candy and Millie exchanged confused looks.

Belle sat up and took a deep breath. "Back where I come from, it was just me and Papa. And I didn't realize it until recently, but with life being so much simpler then, I was actually"—she blinked back tears before continuing—"happy. Most of the time." She was feeling better. She needed this. To unload. "Then, in a single day, life got complicated." She carefully avoided any reference to her secret X-men gift/curse. "My father died and now it's *not* me and Papa anymore, but it's me and a strange family and a whole school of people who think they already know me." Belle felt her hands heating up and quickly shoved them underneath her thighs and gripped the seat. "*I* want to reinvent myself; not have strangers do it for me. And I *don't* want an audience while I do it."

Millie leaned her cheek on her hand. "Wow," she breathed. "You totally just Dr. Phill-ed yourself. Can you do me now?"

Belle replied, "Pardon?"

Candy quickly diverted Belle from Millie. "Girl, do *not* listen to my silly friend here." She leaned in with her eyes watering a bit. "And we're sorry about your daddy." Millie nodded sympathetically, her glasses turning gray. "But listen here," Candy continued, brightening, "we're going to help you get what you want. You're asking for wallflower status, and no one usually wants that, but in your case, seems you need it for a bit. First, you need to set the record straight and put these wild rumors to bed and the way to do that is to fill in your Peacock Profile. Looks like you have your photo already set up—"

"Yeah, Waldo," Belle said.

"And secondly," Candy turned towards Millie. "Let's get something straight right now: Belle did *not* try to steal Dmitri. Besides, you know he's *my* boo."

"Pretend-boo," Millie corrected.

"Yes, well, whatever," Candy said, brushing her off and turning back to Belle. "Next, we need to change your profile picture. Make you look un-pretty."

"Oooh, yes! I see where she's going with this." Millie nodded knowingly. "Trick the Mirror with a fugly picture and then the bourgee will stop obsessing over you. Here, let me see your phone." She held out her hand.

Belle passed her phone to Millie, who worked on it briefly, while Candy instructed Belle. "Ok, so one thing we noticed is the Mirror never picks a girl who's smiling. Maybe part of the algorithm is based on those runway models who never smile."

"Probably because they're always hungry," Millie muttered. "There! Your Peacock app is set up."

"And rock these glasses." Candy pulled Millie's glasses off her face and slid them onto Belle's. "Seems the Mirror is not savvy enough to recognize sophistication," Candy said, winking at Millie who blushed gratefully.

"Hmmm, what does lavender mean again?" Candy asked Millie, referencing the glasses' new color on Belle's face.

"Anxiety," Millie replied.

"Relax, trust us! It's going to be fine!" Candy reached across the table and gave Belle's shoulders a squeeze, while Millie aimed the cell phone's camera at Belle. "Now, show us your grill!" Belle arched a questioning eyebrow. "Smile!" Candy clarified with an eye roll.

"Oh." Belle flashed a wide grin and a soft click was heard.

Millie retrieved her glasses and started working the cell phone again.

When a chime sounded the entrance of a new customer, Candy's eyes magnified and a huge grin spread across her face. "Oooh, here comes my man now!" she whispered gleefully.

"Pretend-man, remember?" Millie countered, without looking up from the phone.

Belle turned in her seat and felt the odd sensation that the bench beneath her had become bumpy. When she lifted herself to check, she stifled a gasp. Her handprints had melted into the plastic seat from when she was sitting on them.

"You alright?" Millie asked.

Belle nodded slowly and sat back down to hide the spot.

"Watch this." Millie rolled her eyes and gestured towards the entrance. "He comes here for his protein shake everyday like clockwork. Only time he's sans girlfriend."

A sweaty Dmitri walked in shouldering a gym bag and wearing a tank top that showed off his powerful build.

"How's my Hercules?" Candy's voice was as sugary as her cupcakes. She perched one hand on her hip and the other on his bicep. "You've been working arms today, huh?"

He laughed, his cheeks flushing. "Yeah. This muscle exactly." He flexed his arm and pointed at a ribbon of muscle that popped out of his triceps. "Here. See if you can make a dent in that."

Candy squeezed his arm. "My, my, my," she said, fanning herself with the other hand. "Your hard work has earned you a treat, mister."

Millie whispered to Belle, "Not sure if he actually does like her or if he's using her for free cakes."

"Your protein cake and shake coming right up," Candy turned away, mouthed an ecstatic *oh-my-God* face at the two girls watching in the booth and walked behind the counter.

After watching Dmitri's eyes glued to the way Candy sashayed behind the counter, Belle whispered back, "Um, I think he likes her."

Dmitri turned and nodded towards them. "'Sup ladies."

The two girls greeted him back and then smiled conspiratorially at each other.

While Candy and Dmitri generated enough sparks to start a forest fire, Millie finished updating Belle's profile picture. Soon, the Mirror on the HCC website flashed a new "fairest one": Vasilisa Shveya. The headscarf girl! Only this time, her dark golden hair framed her flawless face while she pouted demurely.

"There, it worked. Back to normal now," Millie sighed. "She's up for Homecoming Queen. I bet Liam Rawlins will be King, even though he only shows up once a week and everyone thinks he offed his parents."

"They're both in my literature class," Belle said, her aggravation rising for some reason.

"You got Senior Lit., huh? Not sure whether to congratulate you or feel sorry for you."

Belle was absentmindedly shredding a napkin into tiny scraps. "Are Liam and Vasilisa together?" She didn't even want to think about why *that* bothered her more than anything at the moment.

"Lisa. That's what she wants to be called. She's Russian royalty in the fashion world."

And I'll be calling her Vasilisa, Belle thought, feeling petty.

"They definitely dated. They won the Homecoming court together every year so far." Millie replied with a sly, knowing smile.

Belle's palms itched and she hid them again under her thighs. There was a sweet metallic taste in her mouth now too.

Millie continued, "No one really knows what he's up to now, though. Keeps to himself. All I know is he's running his father's international shipping company from his castle and doing school online. Last year, his parents—"

"Candy told me." Belle didn't have the heart to hear that tale again.

Millie shrugged. "Well then, you know as much as anyone about it now." She leaned forward and added in a low voice, "I think he did it."

Belle's eyes went wide. "Really? Why?"

"He's got a terrible temper, and he supposedly hated his father who supposedly wasn't too kind to his mom either. And, once, during a football game, he punched out a referee for making a call that cost them a big game." She sat back and crossed her arms against her chest. "He's a beast, alright."

Belle was reminded of his sudden hostility in class and Ernesto's warning. She swallowed. Was he really dangerous?

Millie raised her eyebrows dramatically. "And this nonsense about lightning being the cause of death? Indoors?"

But Belle also couldn't forget his initial kindness in class and, given her own personal experience with bizarre and deadly lightning strikes, she suddenly felt impelled to offer Liam *some* defense. "Have you heard of how the Hammerson brothers died?" she asked, almost choking on the part of her secret she dared to utter aloud.

"That happened outside. How do you explain *inside* the Rawlins Castle?" Millie asked in a 'gotcha' tone.

Yeah, she wasn't pursuing this conversation any further. She looked away and saw Dmitri flexing a muscle in his forearm and explaining something about it, while Candy prepared his shake and hung onto his every word.

Millie swiveled the laptop towards Belle. "Anyway, your step 2: you need to start setting the record straight, right? Start typing in your profile info." A few minutes of Belle's inexperienced hunt-and-peck typing skills drove Millie to say, "Change of plans! I'll type, you dictate."

Candy slid into the booth and pretended to faint against Belle.

Without looking up from the screen, Millie asked, "Is your fake date over already?"

"I am creating a Hercules cupcake that only I can eat." Candy grinned, lost in thought as if picturing it.

"Ewww. You're sinking to a new deranged low," Millie complained.

"Banana fosters cupcake with—"

"I'm not even going to mention that innuendo—"

"—caramel and chocolate peanut butter cups."

"You're hopeless," Millie finished.

"That does sound delicious," Belle said, picturing herself sinking her teeth into it.

"*My* cupcake," Candy replied with a wink. "And you"—she pointed at Millie—"need to start your shift, while you"—she pointed at Belle—"need to start shopping."

As if on cue, a group of little leaguers stormed into the bakery and crowded around the display case. "Nuh-uh. I quit." Millie stared in horror at the kids pushing each other about.

"Ha!" Candy scoffed, grabbing a denim jacket and her purse from behind the counter. "And then let's see what your tiger ma' has to say about that."

"No fair," Millie whined, but getting up nonetheless and taking her place behind the counter. She scowled at the kids.

"Make it rain, honey!" Candy rubbed her forefingers together as a greedy Scrooge would and then gestured for Belle to follow her out.

"Thanks for helping me with the profile, Millie," Belle called.

"No problem. Don't forget to finish it, though," she answered back. She turned to the horde of gremlins before her and glowered. "What do you want?"

"No problem. Don't forget to finish it, though," she answered back. She turned to the horde of gremlins before her and glowered. "What do you want?"

17

The Girl with One Flip-Flop

Once out the door, Candy linked her arm with Belle's as they walked. "So, before I forget, *did* you taser Kat and her friends? Because if you did, I only wish I was there to see it!"

"No!" Belle countered. "I don't know what really happened. One minute, she's in my face, and the next, she got a shock from something. It seemed like it came from the lockers." She glanced at Candy's quizzical expression, hoping she bought it. "I was just glad to get out of there."

"Ok, so you're not armed and dangerous. Question #2 I've been meaning to ask: *what* is up with you and Prince?"

It was Belle's turn to eye-roll. "He talked to me a few times today—gave me a ride to the mall."

"Oooh, honey," Candy clucked her tongue. "You have got yourself in a Catch-22."

"How do you mean?"

They paused to allow an elderly lady in a motorized chair to pass.

"Well, the Prince wants you, and you say you want to be left alone, but if you ignore his 'charms,' he'll just want you more and, with all eyes on the Prince, they'll keep being on *you*."

Belle groaned. "What do I do?"

Candy stopped and turned incredulously toward her new friend. "So you're *not* interested in Jared? Not even a little bit?"

Belle dragged her forward and continued walking. "Well, he *is* handsome...."

"You mean, smoking hot." Candy touched her finger to her tongue and mimicked a sizzling sound as she pressed the finger against her shoulder.

"But he's not my type," Belle finished.

"Ok." Candy led her onto an escalator. "Then what *is* your type?"

Belle moved aside for a hurried-looking person to pass. "I guess all of my book-boyfriends rolled into one. Mainly Gilbert Blythe and Mr. Darcy."

"Uh-uh, honey. Give me Jace Wayland or Asher St. Michael. Mmmm." Candy gently nudged her in the ribs. "But I see what you're saying. You like proud and sweet. Or more like sweet and salty. And that, my friend, is an excellent flavor. Hmmm," she gazed off to the side. "A dark chocolate pretzel cupcake with caramel drizzle would be an amazing addition...."

They arrived at the next floor. A huge shoe store filled their view, which reminded Belle of the Glass shoe in her bag. She quickly filled Candy in on the disturbing bathroom incident.

Candy took the shoe from her hands and examined it. "Yeah, this brand was popular like two years ago. Definitely don't look among the bourgee for the owner; none of them will be wearing last season. This probably belongs to a whiz kid."

"How is Steifshwester even in charge of this school? She's evil!" Belle raged, her hands starting to heat up at the memory of the poor girl's abuse. She tucked the shoe back into her bag, determined to have a long talk with Ernesto that night.

"Haven't you seen the Stiff's brown-noser Hall of Fame? I'm sure she's got her head far up enough 'important' people's butts to maintain her position."

"She said my aunt was her boss," Belle said.

"Girl, do this town a service and get that woman fired!"

"Working on it."

"Here we are," Candy announced. "The Briar Rose."

The store's name was written in a glowing green script that ended with a large red rose. High-fashion mannequins formed a city scene at one window and a beach scene at the adjacent window of the wide entrance that showcased two floors of women's clothing.

Belle swallowed. "I'm more a jeans and t-shirts kinda' gal." Warily, she eyed the skin-tight geometric patterns on the mannequin.

Candy dragged her forward. "C'mon, girl. This is the one-stop shop for all your wardrobe needs. And you'll even get a personal designer." They approached the customer service desk. "Hi, my girl, Belle, here needs a whole wardrobe, under Emily Prynn's account."

The tall, thin middle-aged woman with a high, tight bun, and an attitude to match, asked, "Do you have an appointment?"

Candy laughed. "You must be new here"—she leaned in and peered at her name tag—"*Claire*. See, I bring your boss her gluten-free, vegan cupcakes every week and this is the first time I've ever seen you, so if you just call Lisa over, you'll see that I don't need an appointment."

"Lisa?" Belle asked, surprised. "As in Vas—"

As if magically summoned, Vasilisa appeared in the flesh. "It's alright, Claire. I've got this." This time, she was dressed in all black and her scarf was wrapped prettily around her throat, accentuating a low-plunge neckline. "See if Helen needs help."

"Yes, m'am," Claire said, hurrying off.

Belle muttered to Candy, "Does *every* kid have their own store here?"

Candy ignored her. "Hey, Lisa. I've brought you a project." She grabbed Belle's shoulders and gave her a gentle push forward.

Lisa crossed her arms and leaned on one hip. "I knew you'd end up in my shop." Her eyes traveled over Belle, mentally taking her dimensions.

Belle bristled under her scrutiny and self-consciously shifted her bag to cover herself. She couldn't help feeling a dash of betrayal on Candy's part, but then again, she hadn't known how this Lisa-girl had gotten under her skin. She could still see hear that cat-like voice, *"I miss you, Liam."*

And then again, so what? She needn't concern herself with Liam. Except for that family history project that Dr. Helsing had paired them up for at the end of class. The teacher had refused her request to work alone, saying, *"It's fitting that the descendants of the two oldest Elmridge families work together."*

"So, what do you think?" Now Candy joined Lisa in her assessment. "What is your fashion sense telling you? Country chic?"

Belle frowned and repeated, "Jeans and t-shirts, please."

Lisa touched a manicured finger to her rouged cheek. "Hmmm. No, nothing country. I noticed today she wouldn't stop smoothing her shirt down and rubbing her khakis and she didn't try any accessories to distract from these vanilla uniforms, so she is probably loving it. Dressing like your average Elmridge Joe would do." Lisa stepped closer and ran her nail along Belle's cheek. "But you're not average now, are you? Not with this face and this bod, and...." She leaned in and whispered in Belle's ear, "I know just the style Liam likes." She stepped back with a smug smile and clapped her hands before Belle could respond and said, "Jeans and t-shirts it is."

Candy looked dubious while Belle was half-glad, half-wanting to tighten that scarf around Lisa's skinny neck.

"Of course, I mean, *my* kind of jeans and t-shirts," Lisa corrected. She beckoned them to the counter and pulled out a catalogue, flipped it to a section that read *Urban Casual* and handed Belle a permanent marker. She pointed at the page. "Circle what you like and we'll match it here." She tapped a device in her ear that Belle hadn't notice before.

"Nieves, come to the front desk, please." And then she left to tend to a teenager with more clothes draped over her arm than her weight.

"Thanks, Lisa," Candy called out.

"Pleasure's all mine," she said without looking back. "Dosvidaniya."

"She's Queen B at the school, but she's about as nice as they come," Candy commented.

~~*~~

An hour later, Belle and Candy left the shop, talking excitedly about the large Briar Rose boxes that were going to be sent directly to her home that night. She was surprised by how lighthearted she felt.

"You know what? This was fun!" Belle marveled.

"Uh, hello? Of course, it is. It's called shopping!" Candy raised her shopping bag like a prize, not being able to resist indulging herself as well. "Ernesto ordered me to treat myself as well," she had said earlier, dropping a pair of new shoes into her shopping basket.

"Wait a minute, don't tell me this was your first time?" Candy asked incredulously. Belle shrugged her shoulders sheepishly. "Girl, how many firsts are you missing out on?" They stepped onto the downward escalator. Candy faced her. "You know what, it's going to be a blast being your friend. I get to re-experience my firsts through you. I bet tomorrow is your first time at the beach."

Belle nodded, grinning, and then suddenly becoming really worried, confessed, "Which reminds me, I don't know how to swim."

"Dear Lord, you're like a baby!" They stepped off the escalator. "Well, I'm not getting in the water tomorrow anyways. I'm gonna lay out, so you can join me if you want."

They were nearing the courtyard with the grand water fountain. A young couple sitting on the fountain's ledge, unabashedly locked in a passionate embrace, were drawing stares from passerbys.

Candy linked her arm with Belle's and spoke in a hushed tone, "Speaking of firsts. Are you...." She raised her eyebrows meaningfully.

"What?" Belle replied, clueless.

"*You* know..." And before Belle could respond, Candy backtracked, "Wait a minute, what am I saying? Of course, you are."

"Throw me a bone here, Candy, what are you talking about?"

Spotting something up ahead, Candy tucked Belle close to her side. "Oh no, don't look now, but here come Betty and Botter." Belle was about to look, but Candy quickly navigated her into hiding behind a large artificial tree. "Ugh, I think they saw us," Candy groaned, leaning her forehead against the tree.

"Who are they?" Belle asked, resisting the urge to peer around the plastic trunk.

"Hi Candy!" a nasal voice with a shrilly edge called out.

"Wannabees," Candy answered quickly. "They're the Stiff's daughters, Stella and Mona. Be nice." Candy stepped out from behind the tree with Belle and plastered on a fake grin. "Hey, Stella and Mona!"

The two girls, both with unnaturally stick-straight blonde hair, were dressed like tacky versions of Beverly Hills Barbies. Stella was the taller, older one, exuding authority, and the other, younger, mini-Stella seemed to copy her every move like a shadow. The only part of the picture missing was the poodle in the oversized handbag. They even had an unfortunate tag-along servant, her face hidden behind a tower of shopping bags and boxes she cradled in her arms. Belle's polite smile faded from her mouth as she noticed the feet: one Glass shoe and a beach sandal.

"Hi girls! What are you two doing back here?" Stella chuckled and a snort escaped. She cleared her throat in embarrassment.

"Yeah, what are you guys doing back here?" Mona chimed in.

They both had an accent like their mother's, but not as thick.

"Just showing my girl, Belle, around. Oh hey, Cindy! Didn't see you back there." Candy stopped her before she crashed into them. Several of the boxes and bags from the top slid off and clattered to the floor. Cindy's face was visible now and she looked panicked.

Stella glowered at Cindy. "You're such a klutz! If my new Burberry bottle is broken, you bet it's coming out of your allowance."

"Here, let me help you." Belle stooped to pick up the packages from the floor.

"Oh no! That's Cindy's job—don't!" Stella screeched.

"Yeah, don't," Mona echoed.

Belle's hands were beginning to tremble with anger as she balanced the new load in her arms and peered at Cindy's face, whose eyes flitted away nervously.

"Tell her you've got it," Stella said, staring Cindy down.

Belle elbowed Candy and, with her chin, gestured towards Cindy's feet. Candy glanced down and the two girls exchanged knowing looks.

"You know there are shopping cart rentals right there. I can get you one if—" Candy pointed out to the sisters.

"No thanks, Candy," Stella said. "We were leaving anyways."

"Yeah, thanks, but we're leaving," Mona mimicked.

Stella turned toward Cindy. "Actually, I think it's better that you apologize to my friends for being so rude."

Belle made a slight motion toward Stella, but Candy held her back and shook her head. Still, Belle couldn't help what she said next. "Cindy doesn't need to apologize because we"—she gestured between herself and the two sisters—"are not friends."

Stella looked Belle up and down as if appraising a new enemy. She barked as she snapped her attention back to Cindy, "Fine. Apologize to Candy then."

Belle clenched her hands together behind her back to stifle the heat that was building in her palms.

Cindy spoke up, her voice small and cracked, "Sorry, Candy. I didn't mean to run into you."

Belle stifled a gasp. She *could* talk! Cindy was, without a doubt, the girl missing the Glass shoe.

"See? She's fine." Stella grinned nastily.

"Yeah, she's fantastic," Mona chirped.

Stella looked sharply at Mona, who quickly looked down at her feet.

"So, seems like Cindy already knows you," Stella said to Belle, almost as if demanding an explanation.

Cindy wouldn't meet anyone's gaze now.

Belle looked squarely at Stella and held her stare. "Yes, she's my friend. In fact"—she turned to Cindy—"I've been meaning to give this back to you." She pulled the Glass shoe out of her bag and presented it to her.

Cindy's eyes grew wide as she stared at it.

"Oh look, she found your old, gross shoe," Stella said in mock excitement.

"Gross," Mona said.

"You left it in the girls' bathroom," Belle said pointedly, looking at Cindy. "I saw when you left it, but you went away so quickly I couldn't catch up." Cindy gasped audibly. "And I *will* be helping you," Belle said firmly as Cindy's eyes watered.

Stella and Mona exchanged quizzical glances. "Yeah, okay, whatever newbie," Stella said rolling her eyes and grinning sardonically. "Mona, take that thing."

Mona complained, but obeyed nonetheless and took the shoe from Belle.

"I need...I need the bags back now," Cindy said timidly, looking at the packages in Belle's arms. Candy started helping Belle place them back in Cindy's stack, and when Stella opened her mouth to protest, Candy impatiently cut her off, "Honey, just be quiet. Please." With one box left in Belle's hands, the one that would hide Cindy's face from view, Belle said, "I won't forget. I promise."

"Don't. You *can't* do anything," Cindy whispered with an intensity that alarmed Belle. "You'll only make things worse. *Please*, don't," she begged.

Stella snapped at Cindy, "Wow! You are so melodramatic! Always acting like the victim." And with that she snatched the box from Belle's hand to place it on the stack, but unfortunately for Stella, the box had mysteriously caught fire in her hand. She screamed and tossed it into the fountain. Other people were staring at them now and asking questions.

"What the—" Mona began, but Stella cut her off with a forced laugh and said loudly so everybody watching could hear, "I don't know *what* just happened, but watch out for combustible hat boxes!" She laughed loudly and unnaturally, slapping her knee. She then turned back to Belle with a fierce look and jutted a finger at her. "I don't know how you did that, but you are officially on my radar. You're new here, so I'll just let this be a warning."

Candy grabbed Belle's wrist and squeezed as if saying, *Stay.* She was grateful Candy hadn't grabbed her hand because they were still scalding hot. She resisted the urge to give Stella a charcoal handprint across her face.

Stella suddenly beamed an all-too-bright grin and chirped, "Ta, girls!"

With Mona's "Ta!" echoing after, the trio retreated towards the exit.

"Tell me again why we're supposed to be nice to them?" Belle asked, scowling after them.

"They'll get you kicked out of school," Candy sighed, resuming their walk.

"But my aunt is—"

"Away on vacay, apparently. Since like ever." Candy cast her a sideways glance.

Belle chewed her lip. "I have a lot of catching up at home and I'll figure out what's going on with my aunt, but in the meantime, we're Cindy's only hope."

"And what is your plan exactly, Supergirl?"

"Take down the evil hive queen," Belle replied, mulling over the various ways.

Reaching the curb outside the mall, Candy turned toward Belle. "Look, this isn't some cheese-fest sci-fi battle. You heard the girl: she doesn't want to be helped. You don't think we haven't already tried to help her? Freshman year. With how popular she was, everyone assumed she'd be Queen B by Senior year. She was already hanging out with the Princess Posse and was even Jared Prince's date for Homecoming that year." Candy paused, sadness clouding her expression.

"Then what happened?" Belle pressed gently.

Candy sighed. "At a family lake outing, her dad had a heart attack in the water and drowned."

"How terrible..." Belle felt like an old scar was threatening to rip open again.

"But he didn't die," she continued. "He's been in a coma at the hospital ever since. So, as you can probably guess, Cindy's in a dark place right now and she refuses any help from her friends. I guess we're all waiting for her to heal and come around."

"She's pushed everyone away," Belle said morosely.

"Except Q. Seems hanging out with a robot works for her."

Belle sighed gruffly. "Well, we have to do something! I told you about what happened earlier. *That* isn't part of the grieving process or acceptable in any way, so she definitely needs help. Even if she doesn't want it."

"Careful, now," Candy warned. "You're dealing with big players here. You'll need to enlist a big player of your own."

"I'll talk to Ernesto tonight."

"It's a good start," Candy agreed. "Let me know if there's anything I can do to help."

After finalizing details about when and where to meet for the lake party tomorrow, they parted ways: Candy to relieve Millie in the bakery and Belle to "follow the lights home."

18

Strangers in the Night

Belle welcomed the solitary walk home and a chance to be alone with her thoughts. Elmridge was beautiful at night. The sidewalks lit up along the edges after sunset and she could see the twinkling lights of the boardwalk beyond the lake. Plenty of people were strolling about. Some crossing her path gave her friendly nods, a few kids from school that she didn't recognize, but apparently recognized her, waved and smiled at her. If she got past all the problems that weighed on her mind like a ton of bricks, she could have a chance to really settle in and enjoy her new life in this town.

Once she turned onto the path leading to the Historical Society, the path became empty and the pretty sidewalk lights disappeared, plunging her way into darkness. She continued walking, her attention focused on following the dark gray sidewalk beneath her feet. Soon enough, the air felt charged somehow causing the hairs on the back of her neck to stand. She looked up into the pitch black night hoping to see stars, but they were strangled by the dark, ominous clouds that had gathered and grumbled menacingly. A cold, icy feeling crawled down her back. She hadn't felt this way since...the Hammerson brothers. She swallowed, wondering with apprehension if the insidious voice in her mind would return to warn her.

After a few minutes of frantic walking, she could barely see the ground beneath her feet due to how dark it was. In fact, she was sure the ground was too soft to be the sidewalk anymore. She paused in her step and reached down to feel the ground. Grass. At some point, she'd veered off the side walk.

Great. She was lost.

She shivered and rubbed her arms. It was getting colder. She had to keep moving. Perhaps, if she just came back the way she came, she'd run into the sidewalk and get back on the right path. She moved quickly, scanning around for the lights and safety of her home to appear already. But as the minutes stretched out, a chilly breeze picked up, carrying a low, steady roar with it. She tried to reassure herself as panic clawed at her throat. Worst case scenario, if she didn't find the house anytime soon, she'd just park her butt on the ground, and wait for the moonlight to rear its lazy head from out behind the clouds so she could coordinate herself. But what if there was a new moon? Then, she'd roll up into a ball and wait for the sunlight. No wild animal would bother with a dead-looking human ball, right? Isn't that what she learned somewhere in a nature survival book? Play dead if faced with a bear?

Get a grip, Belle! she practically yelled at herself.

But she doubted bears would be a problem; it was the peacocks she had to worry about. Tripping over one, stepping on one, and then getting ganged up on and being pecked to death, or maybe they were like colorful, vicious mini-ostriches that would kick and claw her to death. The roar in the air grew louder. Her footfalls started to match the hysterical frenzy of her thoughts until she broke into an outright run.

Smack!

She had crashed into something huge and solid. With legs and arms.

"Whoa!" a deep voice cried out in surprise.

A strangled cry escaped her and a light suddenly shone on her face.

"Hey, are you alright?" A hand reached for her shoulder, but she smacked it away, backing up. She still had that acidic feeling spreading in her chest like something terrible was supposed to happen.

"Go away!" she cried out. "I'll scream!" She shielded her eyes from the blinding light and prepared to turn and run in the opposite direction.

"Whoa, wait! It's Belle, right?" The voice was sounding familiar. "Here." The light now shone on the speaker's face.

As if star-struck, her heart slammed into her chest. "Liam Rawlins?" she panted out, trying to catch her breath. But wasn't he angry with her from their last encounter? Maybe he was the "bad" that was supposed to happen now.

Thunder rumbled overhead. A warning to keep her guard up.

"Just a sec," he said. The light, which she now saw came from a cell phone, grew brighter until it encompassed them. "There."

Belle couldn't help staring. He wore gray sweatpants and a partially open gray hoodie jacket revealing a glimpse of well-toned chest. The hood over his head framed his stunning face and from his minty green eyes she only saw concern. She shook her head and took a deep, calming breath. This sense of foreboding she harbored had to be some sort of false PTSD alarm.

"Do you need help?" His eyes flared vigilantly. "Is someone chasing you?" He flashed his light around them.

She could orient herself now: they were standing near a huge stone wall, which meant they had to be in that large patch of field behind her house and the school. The roaring sound was coming from the ocean right on the other side of that wall, far down below the cliff.

A hollow laugh escaped her. "I got lost! I was following the sidewalk lights like Candy had said until they disappeared and I thought I'd made the correct turn—" A cold wind swept past and the sky rumbled again. Belle shivered and wrapped her arms around herself.

"Um, why don't I help you get home?" Liam offered.

Nodding, she followed him as his cell phone lit the way. "Why were *you* out here?" she asked.

"I run this trail at night."

"It's pitch black out here. How do you not face-plant into the ground or the wall?"

Of course, Belle had to trip over some rock at that exact moment, causing her to veer straight into his side. He instinctively caught her by wrapping an arm around her waist and bringing her close. Without light, the other sensations were heightened. The feel of his rock-solid build against her soft one made her catch her breath, mirroring his own sharp inhale through his teeth. She pushed apart quickly and he held her by the elbow, steadying her.

When he brought the light to their faces, his emerald eyes were glittering. "You okay?"

Her face flushed. *Mylanta, he was beautiful.* Her eyes were automatically drawn to his lips, which were totally lush and kissable.

Stop it, young lady, she chided herself.

He must have noticed because the color of his eyes darkened, setting off a warmth in her veins. The connection held until thunder rumbled again and broke the spell. She pulled her elbow away, deciding to keep her wits about her. "We should get out of here."

He looked up at the inky night sky, clouds flashing with small bursts of lightning. Worry stole across his face. "Yeah, let's go." He gave her a meaningful look. "Stay close."

They continued walking quickly, chasing the beam of light before them. She stayed near enough so his elbow kept brushing her arm, causing jolts of static electricity each time. She knew *that* was her fault. "Sorry," she cringed. His response was just to give her a heart-stopping smile.

This man totally kept making scrambled eggs of her thoughts. A few minutes ago, she had been running from a phantom menace, and now she was trying her hardest not to romanticize this whole situation in her head. Hadn't he been positively rude to her in class earlier? Gotten in her face and then walked out? Hard to ignore now, though, his coming to her rescue when she was lost in this field, just like...like.... She sighed aloud, "Marianne and Willoughby."

"Willo-who?" Liam asked, casting her a sideways glance without slowing their pace.

Her cheeks flamed. Mental face palm. *Change the subject.* "Hey, you didn't answer my question before," she walked more quickly to keep up with him. "How can you run in this darkness without any light?"

"The sea wall starts in my backyard. I follow it, stay close to it. By now, I know the trail by heart." He smiled at her again, sending her heart into an erratic rhythm. "Plus, running in the dark sharpens my Batman reflexes."

"Who's Batman?"

Liam stopped in his tracks and stared at her. "Who's *Batman*?" Belle blinked back at him, waiting for an explanation. He barked out a laugh. "Ha! Nice poker face." He continued walking. "I hadn't pegged you for a jokester."

Belle hurried to catch up. "Ooookay." She made a mental note to search "Batman" on that Google-thing. She had assumed he was taking her back to the sidewalk, so she could follow the lights home, so imagine her surprise when the lit upper windows of the Historical Society came into view. He'd led her directly home.

They stopped in the driveway, next to the sign which doubled as an ornate lamppost. "How'd you know I live here?" Now that they'd stopped, she was breathless. Mental note #2: make exercise a routine.

He dug his hands into the pockets of his hoodie. "I'm on the Founding Families Committee. Not that I ever waste my time going to those meetings. I send Jacques in my place."

"Like a secret spy society?"

Liam threw his head back and laughed, making Belle smile. He pointed at her. "You're funny." He continued, "The FCC. It's their business to know everyone's business." Belle frowned, wondering how much of *her* business they knew. He must have read her mind because he added, "In your case, we don't know much. It helps a lot having your aunt on the FCC." He then looked as if he was going to ask her something but then thought better of it.

"What?" she prodded.

He shook his head as if letting it go.

A colder, sharper wind passed through. He shivered and zipped up his hoodie. *Boo*, Belle thought, disappointed at this downgrade in view. And then she was mortified at the thought that the sentiment might have registered on her face, especially since he suddenly held her gaze. Any longer now and her insides would melt into goo.

Another biting breeze slammed into them.

Liam pushed strands of hair out of his face. "We only had to vote on whether you should be allowed to move here or not."

Belle was taken aback. "Gee, I'm glad I met with their approval." And then, as soon as the question left her mouth, she regretted it, "What did you vote?"

He looked away, his jaw hardening as he pursed his lips. "I voted 'no'."

Belle took a step back. It was like déjà vu of English class.

"Anyway," he said, eyes hooded, nodding towards the path they had just come from. "I need to—"

Kaboom!

Belle flew into his arms as a powerful bolt of lightning crashed into the field with the explosive force of a bomb. In that split-second, the sky flashed white and the earth shook, sending the two reeling to the ground in a tangle of arms and legs.

When she looked into his face, she didn't expect the sheer terror that blanched his expression, like a war veteran reliving the trauma of battle at a fireworks show. Then it hit her: he claimed his parents had been killed by lighting. And in that moment, she believed him without a doubt, even if no one else did.

She became highly aware of how tightly he was holding her to him. Her face flushed and it was she who asked this time, "Are you okay?" He finally focused on her and swallowed. Soundlessly, he released her and helped her up. Avoiding her gaze, he began quickly collecting her things which had scattered everywhere out of her bag.

Thunder rumbled louder as if Zeus was priming to send another one.

"You can't go home through that field right now," Belle exclaimed. "Is there another way, or maybe I can call Ernesto—" As if on cue, the sky opened up and the rain came down like sheets. Liam cursed. Belle grabbed his arm and pulled him towards her house. "C'mon!"

Once inside, Belle flipped on the first-floor lights. "Wait here, I'll be back in a jiffy."

'I'll be back in a jiffy?' She definitely lost cool points with that one.

While she grabbed two towels from upstairs and dropped off her bag, she was distracted by an incessant muttering coming from Emilia's room. Belle put her ear to her door and heard a crazed stream of "She's coming, she's coming, she's coming...." Out of concern, she was about to knock, but thought better of it. With Liam downstairs, she didn't want to complicate the situation any further.

Liam's back was to her as he looked out the window, the light of the lamppost a blur in the deluge. She came down quietly, when she noticed the name on his back. "Why do they call you 'Beast'?" she asked, handing him a towel.

The mood considerably lightened, he chuckled as he let his hood fall back, most of his hair still tied back into a messy twist, and wiped his face with the towel. "I go into 'beast mode' on the field, won us a few championships before...."

She thought he had trailed off because he was about to mention his parents' deaths, but when she finished towel-dabbing at her wet curls now hanging all loose down the length of her back and looked up at him, she realized he was distracted. By her. His gaze lifted from her shirt and he briefly met her eyes with a searing look that tied her stomach into knots, before he turned away and stepped toward a display case of Elm-ridge antiques.

She looked down and was mortified to find herself donning the wet white t-shirt look, little yellow daisies in all their glory prominently on display. She still hadn't changed from her white school uniform shirt. Red-faced, she pitched the towel behind her neck and around her shoulders to reclaim her modesty.

The rain outside wasn't letting up and thunder still grumbled outside. After he rejected her offer of refreshments and snacks, she asked if he wanted to wait upstairs in the living room where he might be more comfortable. "No, thanks. The sooner I'm outta here, the better," he said, moving on to a small ancient-looking bookcase.

Ouch. Seems the surly Beast was back.

Seeing Belle's glowering face, he took a few steps toward her and added, "It's not you, it's...." He shrugged his shoulders and stuffed his hands into his pockets. "Me and Panzinski don't exactly see eye to eye, so I'm pretty sure I'm not welcomed here." He lifted a book from the shelf, and after flipping it open and snapping it shut, a cloud of dust shot up into his face causing him to sneeze into the crook of his elbow.

"God bless you," Belle responded automatically.

Liam's back suddenly straightened. He deposited the book on the shelf and turned slowly towards her. "You believe in God?" His expression was guarded.

Wondering what direction this conversation was about to take, she replied softly, "Yes." He looked down at his feet. "Don't you?" she asked.

He looked at her, a hardness in his eyes. "I used to."

She looked away, her heart suddenly feeling heavy.

He cleared his throat. "You read any of these books yet?"

Books. That just reminded her. "Not yet, but hey, we have to do this project together." She crossed to where he was. "Dr. Helsing talked about it after you left."

"Yeah, about English class," he said. "I've been meaning to apologize for being...." He seemed to be searching for the right word.

"Insensitive?" she offered.

"A jackass," he finished.

"Oh."

He smiled roguishly, setting off a swarm of butterflies in her stomach. "You're too kind."

She blushed and then without thinking, reached out and squeezed his arm reassuringly, which was like gripping a rock. Liam looked at the hand on his arm and then back at her. The smoldering look he gave immobilized her. He stepped toward her, his eyebrows drawn together in concentration as if he was reading her face, his mind sifting through all he knew about her, wondering what it was about this girl, besides the obvious, that made him want to defy the Lightning Witch's curse.

The step Liam took had closed the gap between them so that Belle was looking up into his face, which was mere inches from hers. Her heart thudded wildly against her ribcage and she worried for a second if he could hear, but she was too engrossed by the discovery of yellow flecks in his green eyes to care. His eyes suddenly dropped to her lips, which seemed to part with a mind of their own. Her head became fuzzy as she felt his warm breath on her lips. But as Belle felt the inclination to close her eyes, Liam suddenly straightened and stepped away.

Belle sucked in a breath, her cheeks on fire. *Great Jehoshaphat—we almost kissed!*

"So"—he cleared his throat—"what's this project about?" He began leaning books out from the shelf one by one before letting them fall back into place. *No way I'm putting this innocent girl's life in danger,* he thought.

Belle avoided looking at him and busied herself with collecting her hair back into a ponytail, smoothing it out and then letting it all fall loose down her back again. "Um, we're supposed to research our family histories—"

"Well, that might be a bit of a problem for me," he cut in.

"I know, but he means digging through records to see how the Prynn and Rawlins histories intertwined in Elmridge."

He looked at her sharply. "So, you know?" And then he scoffed aloud and muttered to himself, "Of course you do. It was probably in your 'welcome packet'."

Belle knew he was talking about his parents' murders. "Yes, I do know," she said meeting his stare.

"And you don't have a problem with that?" he said, half-challenging, half-incredulous.

Because I can shoot lightning bolts out of my hands, ergo it's possible for it to happen indoors. But, of course, she couldn't say that. Instead, she said steadily, "If you were guilty, Ernesto would've had you jailed."

"Ah, well, there's the rub." He picked a large volume off the shelf and opened it to the table of contents.

Did he just quote Shakespeare? Belle thought, suddenly finding herself even more attracted to him. "What do you mean?" she asked.

"Ernesto thinks I did it. Had me handcuffed and ready to press charges," he said, not looking up and skimming the page with his finger.

"Then how—?"

"Someone called him on his cell and convinced him to let me go. That I wasn't the killer." He snapped the book shut and handed it to her. Belle wafted away the cloud of dust with a frown and read the title, *Elmridge: A History, 1720-1820 (Volume One)* by A.E.P. Meeting her questioning eyes, he said, "Your homework."

Momentarily thrown off the murder-case subject, outrage started to fill her. "I'm *not* doing this whole project by myself."

He smirked before waving his hand around dismissively. "I'm sure I've got a 50-pound Rawlins family history book somewhere in that huge, useless library at home."

Belle's eyes widened with awe and disbelief. "You- you've got a library? A real one? 'Huge,' you said?"

He arched an eyebrow and an amused smile slowly pulled at the corners of his mouth. "What's it to you?"

Belle stared at him like he was the golden ticket to the Wonka factory. This ticket to bliss was dangling before her, just out of reach. At this point, she didn't care if Michael Myers owned that library. Killer or not, she *needed* to see it.

She tried to compose herself and, clearing her throat, said with as much gravity as she could muster, "You know, a library is the best place to do homework. No distractions, plenty of books to research through...." She was already picturing it: curled up on a plush Victorian couch with a giant leather-bound book in her hands, the morning sunlight streaming through those massive stained-glass castle windows, endless books covering the walls just waiting for her.

"I don't know," he began, scratching his head. "I mean, it may be too many books to look through—it's floor to ceiling. The library alone is probably bigger than this house." Belle was practically drooling. He added, his eyes twinkling, "We'd never finish."

She jumped at the chance. "All the more reason to get started as soon as possible." She looked out the window and mused aloud, "Hmm, still pouring outside, so now wouldn't be a good time."

"Yeah, probably not." A smile played at the corners of his mouth.

"What about tomorrow morning?" She offered like it was the brightest idea anyone's had all day. "I'll bring this book, and whatever else is relevant here, and I bet we can knock this assignment out in a day. In your library." She added for good measure, "Piece of cake!" She could almost smell the dusty, old leather books now.

"Aren't you forgetting something about tomorrow?"

"What?"

"Lake Party?"

"Oh," she groaned. "Why? Are you going?"

"No."

"Perfect. I'm sure Candy won't mind if I meet her there later, so in the morning we can—oh wait, I'm so sorry." She held her forehead as her face went from hopeful to disappointed in a second.

Liam moved in, concerned. "What's wrong?"

She looked up at him, her expression apologetic. "You probably, most definitely, have something already planned for tomorrow and here I am just making these plans for you."

"I most definitely do."

Belle's vision of herself in the castle's grand library went up in smoke.

"But I think this assignment is more important than my plans to sleep in," he finished with a smirk.

Her eyes lit up and she couldn't help grinning from ear to ear. She resisted the impulse to throw her arms around him.

He continued gazing at her, as if studying her face, with a tenderness that was disarming. The atmosphere shifted again and she became hyperaware of how little space there was between them. The heavy scent of an earthy fresh musk mixed with sweat rolled off him, filling her lungs and giving her a heady feeling.

"I *really* love that smile on you," he murmured, lightly touching her chin with his finger. "Happy."

Neither could look away. Like magnets, their faces drew closer, until a soft click of the front door was heard and Ernesto stepped through, shaking an umbrella closed behind him.

Liam and Belle jumped apart, jostling the small bookshelf and causing some books to clatter to the floor.

"What's this?" Ernesto asked, looking between the two of them as if they were intruders.

"We were just picking out books for our class project," Belle began, feeling strangely that she had to explain herself as if she had done something wrong.

Ernesto's face was like stone while his voice trembled with a simmering rage, "He's not welcome here." His eyes were glued to Liam, who remained motionless but kept looking toward the front door.

Liam put his hands up. "Look, Pan, she didn't—"

Crash! A powerful lightning bolt struck close by, rattling the house.

Belle instinctively jumped into Liam's side, who wrapped an arm around her, but then just as quickly they pushed away from each other.

As if triggered by this entire episode, Ernesto roared, "Get out of my house!"

"*Your* house?" Belle echoed.

Liam gave her a sideways look. "Told you." He started to leave, but Belle grabbed him by the arm and protested to Ernesto, "He can't leave now! It's dangerous out there—he can get hurt!"

Ernesto glared at him as if daring him to defy his orders.

Suddenly, a screeching wail pierced the air, "She's coming! Help us! She's coming! Hide, Peter!"

Belle dropped her hand and automatically looked towards the door at the top of the stairs, as did Ernesto, and then the front door slammed shut.

Liam was gone.

Ernesto and Belle rushed the stairs at the same time, but when they got to Emilia's door, Ernesto stopped her. "Go to your room," he said, his face strained with worry. Something shattered against the wall inside, followed by a mournful cry. When Belle defiantly stood her ground, he added gently, almost as if begging, "Please. I'm the only one who can get her right again."

She relented, but said, "You have a lot of explaining to do."

"I promise, I will." He nodded towards her room to which she went.

19

Truth or Dare

After a while of what sounded like Ernesto humming a lullaby in a foreign language to Emilia, the crying and whimpering finally subsided.

Throughout this time, Belle got ready for bed, trying to figure out what had Emilia so terrified. *Who* was coming? And why did she keep bringing up this Peter? Who was this Peter? And then the Darling girl she tutored today claimed she also saw a Peter. Maybe he was like the town's urban legend, like stories of the boogeyman that parents told to keep their children from wandering out of their beds at night.

As Belle laid back on her bed, her damp hair wrapped in a towel and still wearing an old shirt of her father's (since her new wardrobe hadn't arrived yet), her eye fell on the telescope and the memory of what she saw through it burned her cheeks and the temptation to peek through it again felt like a physical pull.

She sighed. *Liam.* How many times had they almost kissed tonight? And how many times did she also want to shove him down a flight of stairs for his rudeness? But he had the only real library in town, so she was making him her new best friend. She doubted he'd feel the same way, though, especially after the way Ernesto threw him out into the storm tonight. He probably didn't want anything to do with her after that.

Belle chewed the inside of her cheek. She couldn't leave things the way they were. Liam was owed an apology, and if Ernesto wouldn't give it, then she'd do it. She was going to keep their agreement to meet up in the morning. She'll just hike over to his castle and hope he doesn't toss her out. They did have some serious homework to do. In his library.

Now, she just had to get the message to Candy that she'd meet her at the Lake Party later instead of walking there with her. She got her laptop out. Since it was too late to call, she'd try messaging Candy and get some much-needed practice on this contraption.

After half-an-hour of trial and error and some French cursing, she'd finally made it to the school website and logged on to her Peacock Profile. She already had hundreds of views on her first day and a banner resembling the Mirror revealed the date and time that she had been "Fairest of Them All" as if it was some sort of trophy. A Homecoming banner with a tiara graphic showed a list of rankings. Next to Sophomore Princess Wildcard was her name, and right underneath, Katerina Sirtis was Sophomore Princess Candidate. She felt ill at the thought of how these rankings were even determined.

She spotted the Messaging icon and remembered why she was even on this site in the first place. The new "Message" page revealed that she had 56 people waiting for her to approve them as Chat Buddies. She only accepted the few she knew: Candy and Millie (yay!), Grace, Hans, Amir, Nieves, Jared (with some hesitation), and a few others who had smiled at her in class and looked friendly. She had a request from Vasilisa, but thinking of how she may have lip-locked with Liam in the past, Belle skipped past her. Speaking of Liam, she couldn't help pouting at not seeing a request from him. She typed his name into the Search bar and held her breath.

Liam "Beast" Rawlins. Below the name was a picture of him playing football on the beach, sunlight glistening off his ultra-toned chest and washboard abs and leaning back as if about to launch the football. In the corner of the small square picture was a group of girls sitting on beach towels as if cheering him on. Belle clicked on the picture, hoping to see more, but a message popped out claiming the profile was inactive since over a year ago. She bet those girls were the Princess Posse. A bitter taste arose in her mouth when she remembered how Candy said he'd gone through the group like "popcorn."

She snapped the laptop shut with a huff. Why did this bother her? What was wrong with her? It's like ever since she drank the water here her hormones have ignited. Geez. She had more serious things to focus on then boys with bad reputations. She shouldn't even be attracted to him in the first place. More important things deserved her attention like helping Cindy and Emilia, as well as figuring out her own case of mutant-itis. And, of course, there was homework, which brought her back to her original mission on this laptop: messaging Candy.

She opened the laptop again and was distracted by a sidebar next to Liam's picture containing a running tally of the profile with the most views, which was Jared Prince's. Curious, she clicked on what looked like his portrait painted as '50s-style pop art. His entire profile opened and it looked like fans had completely taken over it. There were constant new postings, even now, "Lisa Prince 4 Eva" just posted in what read in Belle's mind as fanatic shouting, *"YOU'RE THE PRINCE OF MY HEART!!!! #1 FOREVER!!!!!"*

Geez Louise, this site's distracting! I need to message Candy. She glanced at the clock on her desk, 1:02 a.m. Quickly, she retraced her steps back to her Chat List and finally messaged Candy. She clicked on Liam's profile again and sighed, momentarily distracted by his picture before finally closing her laptop shut.

She wasn't even sleepy and she needed her Z's for her big day tomorrow, which would start with a nature trek to the Rawlins Castle. She got goosebumps just thinking about it. She fell into a reverie as a mage making her way past treacherous creatures to the Cave of Scrolls, where she would uncover the truth of her emerging powers.

Pssst.

Belle snapped her head in the direction of the sound. She watched in petrified horror as her bedroom door slowly creaked open until it was gaping wide. Seconds ticked by. She could do nothing but stare as a cold sweat blanketed her skin. Finally, she heard the smallest of whispers, "Come."

Belle shrieked and dove from the desk chair to her bed, quickly cocooning herself with the thick comforter against any potential ghostly fingers caressing her skin. Only her eyes showed, still staring widely at the open door. For a few minutes, nothing happened, except for the icy tentacles firmly wrapping around her spine. Feeling dumb with fright, she called out, "Peter?"

No response.

This house is definitely haunted, she thought, swallowing hard. But if this was part of the family mystery, then she had to investigate. She slowly lifted off her bed and with her heart thundering in her ears, walked towards the open door.

Nothing. No cold spots. No whispers.

She poked her head out into the hallway. There, against the wall on a small decorative table was the Elmridge history book that Liam had handed her earlier. When they had been interrupted by Ernesto and then Emilia's screams, Belle had forgotten the book. Downstairs.

Now, it was sitting on that little hallway table. Looking around for who could have possibly moved it, she could also see that Emilia's door was slightly ajar but the lights were off. No was one around.

Unsettled, she walked further into the hallway, feeling like one of the doomed characters in a *Halloween* movie. The creepy jingle played in her head and she was really wishing she had skipped that movie marathon on Tommy's TV.

Her heart froze and she stopped dead in her tracks as the book on the table suddenly flipped open. She watched, petrified, as pages flew past.

Then it stopped...and the book slowly turned towards her as if prompting her to approach.

Belle had already stopped breathing, but she thought she would faint for real when she thought she heard the soft padding of feet on the floor. She jumped as Emilia's door suddenly opened and closed shut.

In an instant, she snatched the book off the table and dashed into her room, locking the door behind her. Diving into her bed with the open book clutched to her chest, she cocooned herself again, including her eyes.

After what felt like an eternity of waiting and listening for anymore bumps in the night, and her short, ragged pants finally normalizing into easy breathing, she felt brave enough to move a muscle and peek out. Her bedroom looked normal. Nothing was out of place. Loosening the blanket enough to peer at the book, she read the page that had been shown her. A title in bold, archaic script read, "The Legend of the Elmridge Fairies." She took a shaky breath and read. It was a detailed version of the Prynn Fairy story she had read in the pamphlet on the train. She read aloud the only new information that stood out to her:

Only a confession could save the Prynn sisters from the fire, but they could not give it because some of what Wickeby had said was true, only they were not witches and there was no Beezlebub. After hearing a loud boom in the forest by their homestead, the sisters had investigated and found an odd stone in the forest that glittered with gold. Both girls touched the stone, and the golden dust began to lift off the stone and swirl around them until it completely covered their skin and soaked through them. The two girls then lost consciousness.

Later, they awoke in their homes, having been found by their parents after Violet Wickeby's report spread through the community like wildfire. Abigail knew Violet had probably followed them into the forest to see if they were meeting with William, and then must have witnessed everything from behind the foliage. The Judge seized this opportunity for his own political advantage and had their trial prepared for the day after Sabbath.

Meanwhile, the Prynn sisters had awoken in their beds utterly changed: they had a knowledge of another world and its creatures and especially of a fairy race at war with themselves that was bringing misery to the inhabitants of the island on which they all lived. The Island itself was alive and had made a pact with the fairies: the Island would find them a leader who would bring them all peace and a new purpose. So it sent out meteorites of magical golden dust that would seek out candidates throughout the galaxy. Once found, the golden dust would reward the recipients for their sacrifice.

Belle slowly closed the book. Her eyes were tired, but her mind was wired. This story was supposed to be a legend, but she knew legends started from some form of truth. So, what was true? She didn't believe the whole island fairy tale, but now, because of her Abigail-ancestor, she was convinced that lightning-control was in her DNA.

And Violet Wickeby? That was the sorceress's name from her dreams, a woman who also claimed to be her mother. Her possibly schizophrenic mother, who was supposedly making her way to her. And this Peter-ghost really wanted her to know this story.

She shivered just thinking about it.

Thinking of the supernatural led her to a frightening thought: what if her mother was possessed by this centuries-old ghost, Violet Wickeby, still seeking to bring down the Prynn line? And what if having a pair of Prynn sisters today with the same names as the original pair made it worse and attracted the vengeful spirit even more?

Belle shook her head. She had to remain rational. What hard evidence did she have besides dreams and legends? Only her fire-starter hands and...the top-secret jar of gold dust from her father!

With a surge of energy, she bounced out of the bed and retrieved her old carpetbag from underneath. She took the jar out of the bag and held it up.

She shook it a little, but...nothing. Just black dust.

She knew she didn't imagine the dust turning into a shimmering gold and swirling around in the jar, warming her hands when she'd first touched it as a little girl. She rejected the idea that whispered to her that perhaps this was the same magical golden dust of the fairy legend. With a sigh, she returned the jar into the bag and pushed it back underneath her bed. Her father took this secret to the grave. Literally. She only knew she had to keep it "safe." Whatever that meant.

So, she was back to square one: still not understanding her current family's mysterious drama. But at least she had one potential explanation for her powers: it was in her blood. And Liam's family history was tied to hers. Speaking of which, if she didn't want to be turned away from Liam's front door tomorrow for sporting the haggard, witchy-look, she really needed to click her mind off and get some beauty rest.

She finally fell asleep inside her cocoon chastising herself for even caring about something like that and wondering how much of her simple, country-self was morphing into the typical Elmridge "princess." And this had only been Day Two. Wasn't it her goal to re-invent herself here? She worried now about who she was turning into, or *what* she was turning into, lightning powers and all.

She missed Papa. And even Tommy now.

~~*~~

Belle found herself sitting at a desk with a lamp shining on a book with strange writings and a picture of a mermaid with black eyes looking back over her shoulder. A feminine hand with long reddish black nails came into view and hovered over the page. A heart-shaped red diamond glittered on one finger and a delicate bracelet of smooth black stones encircled her wrist. They looked to her like black pearls.

Belle seized up, not daring to make her presence known.

But it didn't work. The hand paused above a drawing of a constellation in the sky of the mermaid's picture.

"Serendibite," Violet corrected Belle. "Not 'pearls'."

Belle willed herself desperately to wake up.

"Shhh, it's okay, dear. I have no intention of harming you. In fact, I've been waiting for you."

Belle could only listen as her dread grew.

Violet leaned back in a chair and shut the book. "I'd like to do something for you that no one has done, not even your family. And that is..."

Belle's curiosity and doubt were heightened, but she still kept trying to wake up.

"Provide you with answers."

Belle ceased struggling.

Violet smiled like a cat with a canary under its paw—she had her total attention. "This will be my gift to you, as long as you promise to give *me* a gift. Oh, don't worry, it'll be something that you will *want* to give me. Do we have a deal?"

Belle didn't make a move, which signaled she wasn't accepting.

"Well then, how about I give you a taste of the truth and let's see if you don't want more. A free sample, if you will."

Ok, Belle thought reluctantly. *How is this happening?*

"Your mother. When your powers emerged, your telepathic link with your mother was established, except she was now with me and didn't want me having access to you, so she shut her end down. Only you keep finding your way back to her when you sleep, which of course leads you to me." Violet's fingers drummed against the black leather cover of the book, its gold script in foreign letters like hieroglyphs. "So, we made a deal: as long as I didn't lay a finger on you or her sister, she wouldn't interfere with my plans."

What plans?

"Wouldn't you like to know? Just agree to give me the gift that you will *want* to give me, and I will tell you my plans." Violet passed her hand over the bracelet and the ring. "I will tell you how I will make these rarest gemstones in existence work together to free your mother, and then you, mum and her lunatic sister can be one tiny happy family. So you see, this really is a win-win for you."

Belle could feel herself giving in. The prospects of being united with her mother and aunt and finally filling in all the gaps of knowing who and what she was were too tantalizing. *All I have to do is promise to give* *you something that I will <u>want</u> to give you?* She could sense a trap in those words.

Understanding her thoughts, Violet prodded, "There's no reward without risk."

And I'll have my mother back?

"Absolutely."

Fine.

"'Fine,' what? You have to say the words. Your promise needs to be clear." There was a note of sharp impatience in her tone.

Belle hesitated again, and before she could completely back out, Violet laid out some more bait. "Wouldn't you like to know how your aunt lost her mind?"

I haven't even met my aunt yet. I don't really know if she's sane or not.

Violet laughed heartily. "Oh, dear child." She cleared her throat sharply. "Well? I'm waiting...."

Slowly, as if each word were a snake poised to bite her, she told Violet what she wanted to hear. *I promise to give you the gift that I will want to give you.* Belle felt as if she had just made a deal with the Devil. *Now tell me what I want to know.*

"Foolhardy girl, just like your mother."

Belle could feel the wolf ripping off its grandmother-mask and baring its teeth now.

"You see, I've seen all of her thoughts and memories. Your mother tried to kill you when you were a baby, and your aunt got in the way. Struck with lightning. Your father whisked you away from France and your aunt awoke from a coma, her mind scrambled. How's that for the picture-perfect Prynn family?" A note of hysteria had entered her voice as she continued, "As for my plans, the day that I come to you, you will give me the Island's fairy dust that I know you have, or I will kill someone you love. Then I can use the dust to bind the four rare gemstones to the blade and become unstoppable!"

No! It- it can't be true! Belle tried desperately to wake up again. Violet was stark, ravening mad and Belle was mind-melded to this lunatic.

A knock at Violet's door seemed to bring her hysteria down a few notches. A male's voice asked through the door, "Are you okay in there, Vi? Do you want me to make you that tea again?"

Violet let out a slow breath and replied in a syrupy, sweet voice, "Yes, my pet. Earl Grey." She returned her gaze to the ring and bracelet adorning her hand, but not before her eyes had passed over a window with a silver telescope standing before it.

"I will keep my promise as you will keep yours," she said in a calmer tone. "Now, that we've got that squared away," she leaned back in her chair and pulled a newspaper out of the desk drawer. She held it up so Belle had a full view of four mug shots plastered across the front page. Her heart stopped when she recognized the men underneath the bold title, "Hammerson Brothers Killed in Freak Lightning Storm."

"You've been a naughty girl, little Prynn," she said with a tone of approval.

I- I don't know what you're talking about.

"Oh, please." She eye-rolled. "I am giving you this one courtesy warning. Mainly because you have invited trouble upon yourself, and I cannot have anything possibly interfering with my plans."

What do you mean? What trouble?

"You killed, child. Murdered in cold blood."

I didn't—it was an accident!

"Do you know what lightning does to someone's insides?"

A strange memory flashed of a man in 1800s garb aiming a long rifle at her and firing a shot, grazing her arm painfully, while at the same time a lightning bolt blasted him clear out of his shoes.

"Well, never mind." She got up and approached the window with the telescope. "You see, you've awoken your personal hunter. He'll come for you. And he won't stop until he kills you."

Terrified, Belle felt like she couldn't breathe. And when Violet pulled the curtain open, she felt the blood freeze in her veins: in the distance, she could see the town of Elmridge over the high wall that encircled it, as if she was outside the town looking in from a high vantage point.

"Stay out of my way, little Prynn, and I won't have to kill you," she warned, and the curtain fell shut.

20

Rawlins Castle

In the morning, Belle found herself in a much more pleasant reverie than the nightmare she had last night. She had woken up to the smell of charred patches of blanket, her hands undoubtedly running an electrical fireworks number during the nightmare.

When her mind did an instant replay of the ordeal, her hands came to life again and she quickly did her "happy thoughts" exercise to regain control. The "happy thought" that was successful: seeing Liam's library soon...or was it really about seeing *him*? She wasn't sure. But she refused to dwell on the nightmare. With *no one* to talk to about this, she felt she'd implode if she thought about it any longer.

So now, she had filed last night under her list of things-to-freak-out-over-later and was currently lost in a mental episode of *Belle of Elmridge* taking a nature trek through a field filled with a few peacocks ambling about, on her way to the mysterious Castle of Enlightenment, with its young brooding, debonair master. She didn't need to borrow anyone else's story for this fantasy: her own was now deliciously intriguing and real enough.

She took a deep breath of fresh, salty air as she reached the sea wall and zipped her hoodie jacket all the way up as the temperature cooled. Following the sea wall towards the castle, she hitched her bag with the Elmridge history book higher up on her shoulder.

Her massive box of new clothes from Briar Rose had arrived in the early morning and had been waiting right outside her bedroom, courtesy of Ernesto. After gushing over the selections she'd found inside, she'd made up her mind to accept Lisa onto her Chat List so she could thank her for her fine taste.

Now, she wore a lavender-colored hoodie with the school's peacock emblem embroidered on the front and "Belle" in gold script underneath the patch; blue denim shorts; a brand of white sneakers that she noticed a lot of the girls were wearing; and, finally, she had a choice between a navy one-piece or a sea-green bikini. Remembering Jared's bet had made her bold enough to go for option 2. She'd wrangled her hair into a low bun and secured it with a gold ribbon. She even had make-up now. But she needed a makeup class from Candy lest she paint herself into a clown, so she went with some safe bubblegum-flavored lip gloss application for now.

Her heart beat sped up as she finally reached the point in which the sea wall met with the castle's outer wall. Walking further into this V, she spotted the outline of a door, the same color and material as the castle wall, but no door handle or peep hole or anything. Nonplussed, she looked around and spotted a red blinking light at the top corner of the V. It was a camera. She waved and introduced herself to it and added, "I'm here to see Liam Rawlins."

The door slid open into the wall revealing a sight that almost made Belle sink to her knees with rapture. A maze-like garden with roses of every color and at the center was a towering wisteria tree with long branches dripping ropes of white flowers and shading the entire garden. She spied a few cats zooming through the bushes.

An elderly man, who Belle assumed was the gardener based on his garb and the large shears in his hands, came over hurriedly and welcomed her in. "Just this way, m'am. Master Rawlins is waiting inside."

Belle didn't hear him. She couldn't help thinking aloud, "This is what the first glimpse in Heaven must feel like."

After the gardener apologized for having to snap his fingers in her face to get her attention, he offered to lead her down the direct side route to the entrance of the castle. Belle, however, had other plans and ventured straight into the knee-high maze of rose bushes.

"Please watch out for the thorns, m'am," the gardener called out after her.

She was giddy with excitement and after a few wrong turns, finally made it to the tree. She couldn't help becoming teary-eyed as she stared at it. It looked glorious with streams of morning sun shining through. An inviting ornate bench sat at the foot of the tree, where she could imagine herself reading tons of books or just enjoying the view of this slice of Eden, but like a child going straight for the bounce house, Belle went for the swing hanging off one of the tree's thick arms.

She didn't know for how long she swung herself at a leisurely pace completely enraptured, but by the time she recalled her original mission here, she'd already named the tree Grandmere and had an imaginary conversation with it.

Ahem.

Belle turned to look behind her. Standing there, arms at his side, was a tall, thin man who looked like a caricature of an early 1900s French butler, complete with tuxedo coattails, except his uniform seemed to be hastily thrown on while his silver hairs stood up behind the front's slick comb-over. He had one brown dress shoe on and the other black.

"Bonjour, mademoiselle. I am Jacques, the castle's head butler, and you must be Belle." He gave a slight bow.

Belle was thrilled at the accent that reminded her of her father. Hopping off the swing, she approached him. "Yes! I'm sorry I loitered here so long. It's just"—she looked around—"this place is absolutely magical!"

She clasped her hands beneath her chin and breathed out, "The stuff that dreams are made of." She totally felt like a princess in a fairy tale.

Jacques cocked his head as he looked at her, a warmth coming into his eyes. "I quite agree. Madame Rawlins certainly seemed to think so. She spent most of her mornings on that bench with a book." They gazed at the empty bench, the mood tinged with sadness.

He turned to her. "There is a small breakfast laid out for you in the library, where I am to take you." He held out his arm, gesturing toward the path on the side that skirted the maze garden and led to a pair of tall glass doors. He led her silently through these doors into a great ball-room, a long hallway filled with family portraits masterfully painted, and then through a foyer and past the grand staircase to a pair of tall, arched doors.

She had walked through it all awestruck and mouth agape, soaking it all in like a first-time tourist at the Louvre. Even though most of the furniture in the rooms were covered in white sheets, the grandeur of this castle was fit for royalty. Her jaw felt permanently unhinged.

"The Rawlins family library was started as far back as the first Rawlins colonist, the Reverend Judge Jonas Rawlins, in the 1700s."

Belle gasped and instinctively clutched her bag with her family history book in it.

"Yes, shocking. This collection is quite old." And just before he turned the ornate door handles, he paused and told her in a low voice as if not wanting to be overheard, "The young master may say differently, but my name is Jacques, *not* Alfred. It is enough he makes me wear this ridiculous uniform before guests in this day and age...."

And when he finally pushed open the doors, Belle reached out and clutched his shoulder for support as she stared wide-eyed at the vision: it was almost exactly as she'd imagined it with the tall glass windows and seemingly endless walls of shelves lined with books—real books— from floor to high ceiling.

"Are you alright, mademoiselle?" he asked, squeezing her elbow.

Belle had one hand covering her mouth, and teary-eyed, she nodded slowly.

"Well, then, let me just set you over here before your breakfast, if you choose to have it, and Master Rawlins will join you shortly." He guided her into the center of the room to a large study area with heavy wooden desks, vintage lamps, and velvety plush sofas and armchairs. Before her was a silver tray with various muffins, pastries, fruits, a tall glass of orange juice, and a small thin crystal vase with a single freshly cut red rose in it.

She looked up at him. "Thank you kindly, Jacques. I am so very much obliged."

He looked down at the most genuine show of gratitude he'd seen in a long time and replied, "You are welcome. It was truly a pleasure to make your acquaintance." And with a small bow, he faded away. The echoing click of the doors shutting, signaled she was alone.

She looked around her like a kid left alone in a toy store.

After wolfing down a cheese Danish, half a muffin and frothy orange juice, she got up and explored the books. Letting her fingers trail along the spines, she was delighted to discover that they were organized by genre, authors, and time periods. She filled her lungs with the smell of dusty, old leather and dove into the buffet of books.

By the time the soft clicks of the door opening and shutting reached her ears, she already had five books under one arm and a weighty, ancient-looking book of fairy tales from around the world balanced on one hip with the other arm. Alarmed, she looked toward the door as if she had been caught mid-heist.

"Need a shopping basket?" Liam called out. "Or a cart?"

She tried to think of a snappy response, but her mind was too occupied with his approaching hotness. The morning sunlight streaming through the windows enveloped him as he got closer, giving his skin a golden glow. That Apollo vision was filling her mind again, even with the flip-flops, camo cargo shorts, and graphic t-shirt ensemble.

Stopping in front of her, he studied her face. "You're staring." He crossed his arms over his chest, his biceps announcing their presence. "Still staring."

She blinked rapidly, and attempted to straighten up a little, "I was not star—" when the tower of books in her hand started to teeter.

Liam quickly relieved her of her load, but when he brushed his hand against hers they both recoiled at the sharp static shock that erupted between them.

"Sorry!"

"It's not your fault," he said, shrugging his shoulders.

But she knew better. She shoved her hands into her hoodie pockets while she followed him back to the study area. Last thing she wanted was to send him to the hospital next.

He laid her books on the vast wooden table and gestured towards her breakfast tray. "I see you've met Alfred."

"Uh," she looked at him like he was a child caught in a fib. "He distinctly said his name was Jacques."

"Oh, well," he said with a roguish smile. "At least he wears the costume." He ran a hand through his hair, which hung in messy layers just beneath his ears, but that arm-movement had caused his shirt to stretch taut over his chest and bicep.

Look up at his face, young lady, she told herself.

Didn't help. The yellow flecks in his sea-green eyes were beckoning to her now.

But he was the first to break the connection: the wall slid down again and his eyes became unreadable. He stepped toward the books on the table. "Let's get this over with."

Belle figured she might feel the same way if she had been tossed out into a storm. She stepped closer. "Look, I didn't come here to just work on the project."

He looked at her with a raised eyebrow. "I know. It's pretty obvious." He picked up the fairy tale book to prove his point.

She blushed. "Well, yeah, that too, and I hope it's okay—"

"It is."

She paused. She had been fully expecting to beg for a library pass here.

He continued, "You can use this library whenever you want. But just you. And if you happen to wander out into the hall for the bathroom"—a hardness came into his eyes—"stay out of the West Wing."

"What's in the West Wing?"

"You being banned from this place," he responded automatically.

"Oh."

"Just announce yourself at the back gate like you did today and ask for Jacques. He'll let you in."

Visions of future visits with Grandmere Willow and lazy afternoons lost in books flashed before her. Her heart felt like it was about to burst, and just to make sure she wasn't daydreaming, she asked, "So I can visit the garden and this library...whenever?"

He nodded, watching her face. The hardened mask was dissipating.

Overwhelmed with gratitude, she blurted out, "I want to kiss you." And then she smacked her hand over mouth as her cheeks flamed.

He threw his head back and laughed. It was a deep baritone that would've made her toes curl if she hadn't been looking for the nearest chair to crawl under and die now.

"I'm so sorry! My mouth has a mind of its own sometimes—" she began, but Liam cut her off with a dismissive wave of the hand.

"It's okay. I know you just want me for my books."

It was Belle's turn to laugh now, but when she stopped, he was watching her so intently that all humor fled the room and his smoldering gaze made her breaths deepen. He reached out and touched her chin. "There's that smile again," he said softly, as if to himself. Her gaze traveled to his lips, which looked pillow soft, and like magnets, their faces drew nearer. Then the same splash of cold reality struck them as Liam straightened and Belle drew in a sharp breath.

Avoiding her gaze, he muttered as he backed away, "I've gotta go check something."

"Okay." She gripped the back of the chair to aid her weakened knees.

He turned and, walking towards the door, called out gruffly, "I'll be back."

The door failed to close behind him all the way, so she hastened over to shut it, but stopped and held it open enough to peek. She watched as Liam strode over to the base of the grand staircase, pause at the wide hand rail, and as if burdened with the weight of the world, hunch over and lay his arm and head on it.

She jumped when he suddenly rammed his fist into a nearby wooden panel.

A flustered Jacques appeared. "What are you doing, Sir? That is the third hole we've had to patch this month. Aren't your punching bags and boxing lessons enough?"

"Have it fixed again," Liam growled. A fresh stream of blood dripped onto the floor from his hand.

Jacques cringed. "I'll fetch the first aid kit." But then turning back around, he added, "What about the girl?"

"What about her?" Liam retorted, sinking down onto the first step.

"Well, you said, you weren't going to—"

"I know." Liam ran his good hand through his hair as if frustrated. "She's different. I'm drawn to her. I- I can't help it."

Jacques laid a hand on his shoulder. "You must help it, young Sir. Because if you believe the Lightning Witch, it's not your life on the line—it's the girl's. Any girl you fall in love with."

Liam balled his hands into fists, blood oozing onto the floor from the injured one. "I know, I know."

Jacques patted his shoulder and left.

Feeling much older than a 17 year-old should, Liam leaned his head back against the post and closed his eyes.

Belle had heard enough. She walked back to the table and sank heavily into the chair. Like a key unlocking her own Pandora's Box, this new revelation threw all the "weird" she'd suppressed back in her face, forcing her to confront it all. She had an incomplete box of puzzle pieces and no big picture to guide her.

Lightning Witch? Is that who killed his parents? Only she and her ancestor Abigail are the only ones she knows that have "lightning powers." Were there others in the world like her? And could her own life really be on the line here?

"Violet Wickeby," she whispered aloud, gripping the edge of the desk until her knuckles turned white.

An electronic buzzing sound tore her from her thoughts.

"Thank goodness," she breathed out. She didn't want to spiral down that messy rabbit hole just yet. Retrieving her cell phone from the bag, she saw the following message from Candy: **Lake Party is lit! Get your tush over here! Your Prince keeps asking about you!!!!**

She wrinkled her nose when she thought of laying out on a towel next to Jared and hearing him talk about his cars. And even more so while Marissa looked on in torment. Belle turned to her other side and there was Liam stretched out next to her, a total sun god. He leaned over, his green eyes glittering, and took her hand in his. "I'm drawn to you," he said, so only she could hear and pressed his lips to her hand. "I can't help it." He leaned in and closed his eyes—

"I think my shrink might be able to help you too."

Belle's eyes flew open and she sucked her puckered lips back in.

Liam was standing across from her, with a bandaged hand and a thick black book in the other, his eyes clearly laughing at her. But in the process of being completely embarrassed, she had accidentally knocked her cell phone across the table. Glancing at it, Liam's expression stiffened. He slid it back across the table to her.

Belle caught it and her cheeks burned even more when she saw Candy's message still lit up the screen. "Thanks," she squeaked, and tossed the phone back in her bag. Hoping to change the subject, she asked, "What happened to your hand?" She already knew the answer, but it seemed the natural thing to ask. And she had already forgiven him for the white lie she fully expected to hear.

"I punched a wall."

Her eyebrows shot up in surprise at being given the cold truth. "Why?"

He held her gaze. "Because I felt like it."

And hello Beast, she thought. *Hello* <u>*honest*</u> *Beast.*

He pulled up the chair in front of her and laid the book with a thud on the table.

For the rest of the hour, Liam was all business as they researched for their project. The book he brought was from his dad's private collection. It was all handwritten entries of the Rawlins family history dating back to the 1600s. Searching for the point where the first of his family arrived in Elmridge, he began skimming for the witch trials that Belle had told him she'd read from her book.

"Found it!" He turned the open book over to her. "Knock yourself out." He picked up the last muffin on Belle's tray and popped it into his mouth.

She finished gulping down the remaining orange juice and took the book. Frowning, she slid the notepad and pen over to him. "You take notes then."

He held up his bandaged right hand and shrugged in response. "Sorry, I'm a righty."

She narrowed her eyes at him and huffed, "I am *not* writing up this whole report by myself."

"Chop-chop," he responded with an evil smirk.

Medieval torture weapons started parading in her mind, while the sly smile on his face only grew wider.

He finally rolled his eyes as if relenting. "You write the notes, and I'll have it organized and typed up."

"What do you mean 'have it' typed up?"

He palmed his forehead and looked at her. "Don't worry about it."

When she dropped her mouth open in disbelief, he added, "Look, I'll even read." He moved to take the book from her, but she held on.

"No, it's okay. I like to read." She was so going to use her Victorian English voice.

"So do I."

"You do not," she retorted.

"Netflix reception isn't that great inside a castle. So...." He looked around the roomful of books as if pointing out his last resort.

"Fine," she said, exchanging the book for the notepad. She pointed to the open page in the book and said, "Chop-chop."

He narrowed his eyes at her, but a smile tugged at the corner of his mouth.

"October 24, 1726: I was tasked by Governor Wickeby to scour the Rawlins Forest for this mysterious golden rock that his daughter Violet had spoken of at the Prynn sisters' trial, secure the rock, and have it shipped to his estate in the capitol within a week. He paid me a handsome sum of which I shall have to keep quiet about lest my family stake some sort of claim on it. My uncle's funeral left the family's fortune bone-dry. The gambling debts he had amassed were brought to light and had to be paid. Even in death, the misery Jonas Rawlins spread was boundless. He had my cousin, his own son, William, jailed in secret so that he couldn't interfere while he prosecuted and judged his son's penniless fiancée as a witch. Somehow, as reported by the few witnesses who had seen the trial and punishment through to the end, the Prynn sisters were thankfully able to slip out of their bonds and disappear while Jonas was struck dead by a lightning bolt. There are ridiculously wild rumors about how exactly the girls escaped, but they are simply the symptoms of fevered imaginations. William is out looking for Abigail now...."

Liam trailed off and stared hard at a point above the book.

Belle knew what the mention of lightning had done to his thoughts, but she needed to know what happened next. She gently pried the book from his fingers and skimmed the rest of the passage.

"It says here that this man," she found the author's name at the bottom of the entry, "Edward Rawlins, found the rock in the forest, but"—her finger ran across a paragraph—"he didn't see anything special about this rock and had it shipped off." She turned the page and her eyes ran through the entry. She gasped when her finger landed on "Violet Wickeby."

"What?" Liam asked, coming out of his trance.

"October 31, 1792—"

"That's just a few days later," Liam interjected.

"All Hallows Eve. A great misfortune has befallen Elmridge again. Violet Wickeby's body was found at the base of the cliff just behind Jonas Rawlins's family estate." Belle looked up and met Liam's gaze. "Wouldn't that be here?" A shudder ran though her.

Liam nodded. His mouth drawn in a tight line. "What else does it say?"

Belle swallowed. Her hands were beginning to tremble. She took a moment to close her eyes and think a happy thought. But she only saw Violet Wickeby, looking like her mother with her body broken upon the rocks as the waves rushed in and around her, her lifeless, glassy eyes staring out just like the dead Hammerson brother in the truck.

She felt a strong hand close over her own.

She opened her eyes to see Liam's concerned ones focused intently on her face. "We don't need to read about any more deaths," he said softly.

Belle felt a new kind of warmth radiating from the pressure of his touch that burned in her cheeks. His warmth calmed and blanketed the frenzied heat of electricity that had been building beneath the skin of her hands. Grateful, she squeezed his hand before letting go.

She pushed the book toward him. "Just tell me what happens next."

"Are you sure?" he asked, eyebrow cocked.

"Does it say any more about how she died?"

He skimmed the entry and after a minute, said, "It says this Wickeby chick had come here looking for William.... He was supposed to marry her, but he went AWOL.... Edward told her that William still loved Abigail and not her.... They found her dead, it was ruled a suicide, and now

Edward thinks it's his fault and feels bad about it." He snapped the book shut. "There. Done for today."

Silence hung over them as he watched her finish writing up the notes. If Belle had looked up then, she would have blushed all the way down to her toes.

Her pen stilled at the sound of a buzzing. They locked eyes.

He put his hands up. "Not mine." He pointed toward her bag. "Could be your boyfriend."

"He's not my boyfriend," she muttered, fishing her phone out of the bag.

The screen lit up blue with Candy's message, **Helloooo! Where are you?**

Belle typed back, **Be there soon.** She sighed.

She started gathering her things into her bag. "When can we meet again? You know, to finish up here." She avoided his eyes as she stood up and hitched her bag on her shoulder.

He stood up and pushed the chair in. "You can come whenever, remember?" He gave her a heart-melting smile that made her stomach clench unnaturally. He motioned for her to follow him as he walked her towards the door. "You don't need me here. Just leave your notes on the table. I'll add my own notes." He faced her when they reached the door. "And then I'll 'have it' typed up and ready for Helsing."

"Wait, what? This is a 'together' project, like a you-and-me thing?" She fought the impulse to poke him in the chest, and then turned pink wondering how that would have felt.

He scratched his chin and looked away. "'You-and-me thing,' huh?" For a second, his eyes had a far-away look in them before they cleared and became unreadable again. He grabbed the ornate door handle and said firmly, "You need to be at that Lake Party. Boyfriend's waiting." He pulled the door open for her and called for Jacques.

"Wow! You must be hard of hearing! I've never even had a boy—" Mortified at what she was about to reveal, she turned away from him and changed the subject. "I don't even want to go to this party anymore and parade around in a stupid bikini." She crossed her arms and twisted her lips in disgust at the thought of possibly getting wolfish stares.

When she turned to look at him, she'd caught him mid-scan. His eyes were trailing up along her body, and when they met hers, he quickly averted his gaze. He rubbed the back of his neck, causing his shirt to ride up and reveal a line of hip contour.

When Belle unglued her eyes and met his again, the air between them felt electrified.

"Hmm," he said, as if piecing something together. "How are you getting to the party?" Before the answer left her mouth, he added, frowning, "You're not walking there from here, are you?"

At that moment, Jacques arrived out of breath. "You called, Sir?"

"I sure did." There was a mock business-like tone in Liam's voice. "How far a walk would you say is that lake?"

"A walk, Sir?"

"Yes, a walk to the lake."

Belle followed the exchange between them as she would a ping-pong match.

"Well," Jacques looked up as if figuring a math problem. "A good 45 minutes, Sir."

"We can't allow our guest here to walk such a distance. Wouldn't you agree, Jacques?"

"I like to walk," she inserted.

"She did walk here, Sir."

"Will you drive her to the lake?" Liam asked.

"Absolutely not, Sir."

"Thank you, Jacques. You're dismissed."

He bowed his head and brushed past them into the library and began clearing the table.

"That was not helpful," Belle said slowly, trying to figure out his motive. "I'm walking to the lake. Forty-five minutes is nothing."

Liam closed the door behind them after Jacques stepped out and disappeared into a side hall. He touched Belle's arm, but the wicked glint in his eye did not escape her. "At least let me show you a short-cut. You'll be there in 10 minutes."

"Why do I get the feeling you're up to something?"

His smile matched that glint now. "I don't wear sheep's clothing." He leaned in closer as if daring her. "You can follow the Beast or not."

She blinked at him and frowned. "The scariest thing about that statement is you referring to yourself in the 3rd person."

His intimidating front fell away and he laughed out loud.

Secretly pleased, she rolled her eyes and threw up her hands. "Ok. Lead the way up the garden path."

The "short-cut" turned out to be a motorcycle. Standing in a massive garage with three other fancy cars in it, she said matter-of-factly, "I'm not licensed to drive. Yet."

Liam leaned against the bike, facing her and crossing his arms.

Hello, biceps.

"The idea is for me to take you," he propositioned.

She did a double-take. "I thought you weren't going?"

"Yes or no?"

"Yes!" she breathed out, thrilled.

Her genuine enthusiasm disarmed him. With a boyish grin, he gestured for her bag and when their hands brushed together in the exchange, a static shock erupted again. Shaking his hand, he joked, "I'm gonna have to wear rubber gloves around you." He lifted the seat of the bike and stuffed the bag in it.

She swallowed nervously. She pictured a leisure hand-in-hand stroll with him in the garden, and when he leaned in to kiss her, she fried him to death: the whole cartoonish electrocution scene, skeleton and all.

"You okay?" he asked. He held two helmets in his hands.

She straightened her shoulders. There was no room for romance in her chaotic life right now, so she shouldn't be worrying about accidentally barbequing him. She gave him a hesitant smile. "Peachy."

To put on the helmet, she had to take down her low bun. She cringed as she shook loose the mounds of swirly curls that tumbled down her back. "I know, it's a mess."

She was silenced by the way he stared at her.

"I like it," he said. Those three little words were loaded like a diary.

She bit her lip and looked away. His death was so going to be on her hands.

He approached slowly and stopping in front of her, placed his helmet on the seat. Her breath caught in her throat when he tipped her face up. His searing gaze held her hostage and her eyes naturally traveled to his mouth. He swept her hair back from her forehead, the light brush of his fingertips against her skin, radiating through her, and fastened the helmet on her. He looked down at her mouth.

Belle's breath stalled in her chest. He had only to lean down and, she, to rise on her toes.

But his lips turned up into a wide grin.

Thrown off, she met his gaze and saw the laughter dancing in his eyes.

She took a step back, half-annoyed. "What?"

"You pull off the orange juice mustache well."

Her hand flew to her top lip. There was a sticky mess all around above it. Her eyes widened. "You could've said something before!"

"You had a napkin at the table. It's not my fault you didn't use it."

Dang her Littleton ways. She'd never had to worry about being tidy with food in front of others. Thinking back to how she ate at that table, Liam must have thought she was a Neanderthal compared to the Elmridge girls he'd probably shared meals with.

She wiped her mouth on her sleeve. "Is it gone?" She put her hand up. "Actually, don't answer that. I don't trust you."

With a hard edge to his voice that felt like a jab, he said, "Good."

Ok, so his death might be on her hands, but just not for the reason she originally feared.

He climbed onto the bike and slid on his own helmet with the visor still up. He clicked a remote fob at the garage door, which started peeling open, and held out his hand to her. "Ready?"

She wasn't particularly feeling like going with him anymore, but when the garage door finally reached the top, her narrowed eyes grew wide at the sight of the magnificent stone driveway that looked as long as a state road. But what really made her want to happy-dance on the spot was the sky-high line of statuesque trees of Wychblack Forest that flanked the driveway on both sides.

She ignored the smug grin on his face at her sudden enthusiasm in taking his hand and hopping onto the bike.

"You might want to hold on," he called back, pulling his visor down.

He roared the bike to life and she gasped at the shuddering tremors that rolled through her body.

"Hold on," he repeated in a cautionary tone.

She looked around for some side handlebars. "To what?!"

He reached behind and found her hand. Her whole body clammed up when he brought it to his chest.

He took a deep breath and let it out slowly. "Carpe diem," he said in a low voice to himself. And then he primed the handlebars and took off like a snapping rubber band.

He laughed when she screeched and wrapped her arms around his chest and stomach. While he should have felt the coolness of the wind invade his skin, his body was heated to its core from the feel of Belle glued to him.

The ride was exhilarating. Slowly, as the wind whipped through their clothes, Belle's octopus grip on Liam loosened and after getting over the breath-catching feel of the muscular landscape of his chest and abs under her hands, she could straighten up and enjoy the sights around her. They passed through Wychblack Forest, then rows of mansions of every type, out through the tall ornate gates of the Manor Hill community, and into the town itself. She'd even let out a "whoo-hoo" at one point with her hands in the air.

At one of the stoplights, he raised his visor, leaned back and called out to her, "Still want to walk?"

"No! This is the most fun I've had since..." She wracked her brain, but came up short. "This *is* the most fun I've had."

Liam chuckled and shook his head.

She added, "This must be close to what a roller coaster feels like."

He turned his head so she could see his profile clearly now. "You've never been on a roller coaster?" he asked. When she didn't answer, he added, his voice sounding distant, "Sounds like you're missing out on a lot of 'firsts'."

A car pulled up next to them at the light. The middle-aged driver inside would not stop staring at them.

She leaned forward and said, "I think he likes your motorcycle."

He glanced over at the driver, who faced forward again as if caught red-handed. Liam snorted. "No, he likes *you*."

"What? No way!" She said, flabbergasted. She peered at the driver who looked frozen as he stared ahead. Frowning, she stretched the bottom of her shorts down more to ensure adequate coverage.

The light turned green. Liam snapped his visor shut and reached behind for Belle's hands and wrapped them around himself before taking off.

He smiled as she sighed into his back.

<h1 style="text-align:center">21</h1>

<h1 style="text-align:center">Beach Blanket Bonkers</h1>

Their arrival was announced by the thundering roar of the motorcycle. All eyes were on them as Liam silenced the bike and helped Belle dismount. Once the helmets came off, the rumors kick started through the Elmridge High partygoers like a game of Telephone.

Liam lifted the seat. "Here's your bag."

She pulled a towel and sunblock out of the bag, before offering it back to him. "Can I leave it? It's loaded down with books."

He shrugged and dropped it back in.

Her heart fluttered at the growing list of little details that were connecting them: school project, free pass to his castle, holding onto her bag for her, and as morbid-sounding as it was, even the Lightning Witch.

"Looks like the whole crew's here," he said, slipping on a pair of dark sunglasses.

They started walking down the sandy slope, the pumping sound of techno beats growing louder. She shielded her eyes with one hand and surveyed the scene. "Wow..." she breathed out.

It was like being dropped into a *Beach Blanket Bingo* movie. The music was coming from a DJ in a massive tiki hut, with smoke rising from a large grill and Hawaiian hula-dressed servers going in and out with trays of food and drinks. There were rows of sunbathers, an active sand football game, and plenty of water play going on like jet skiing, body surfing, blob bouncing, and even "chicken" fights.

She paused and held Liam back so she could use his arm as a crutch while she slid off her shoes and socks. "Double wow," she said, closing her eyes and digging her toes into the warm silky sand.

"Heads up!" a distant voice called.

Liam rushed in front of her and caught the football that would have rearranged her nose.

"That better have been your shitty aim, D!" Liam called back, a menacing edge to his voice.

"Dude, it was!" Dmitri yelled, raising his hands in the air proclaiming innocence.

Amir punched him on the shoulder.

The jock, Shawn, who Belle recognized from English class called out, "Bro, show us the cannon!"

Liam smiled as if someone had asked him to show off a prized collection. "Try catching this one, ladies!" he called. He reared his arm back and launched the ball. It sailed over their heads and, like a pack of hounds, they chased off after it with one of them yelling out in glee, "The Beast is back!"

Liam grinned and turning to Belle, asked, "Are you going to be alright?"

She gathered his meaning. He was leaving her. She nodded and smiled, "Of course!" She feigned shooing him away. "Go, run with the pack, Beast."

He peeled off his shirt and Belle nearly choked.

"Here. Hold that for me, please," he said, giving her the shirt. While he patted his pockets and dug out his wallet and keys, Belle, for the life of her, could not look up: she was too busy counting the two columns of muscled squares on his stomach. He deposited the items in her waiting hands and when Belle met his bright green eyes, she blurted out, "Eight."

He raised a quizzical brow.

"Eight...seconds it took you to find your keys." She wished there was quicksand beneath her feet right now.

"Uh-huh," he said, as if he could see right through her. He gave her a swoon-worthy smile. "I'll catch you later," and then turned away to run after the others.

As she watched his retreating back, her mind hit instant-replay on the half-frontal. She found herself inhaling his shirt. Evergreen and spice. She smiled when she looked down at his keys and wallet: the "connection" list had just grown a tad longer. She wrapped their stuff in her towel and tucked it under one arm.

It wasn't even a minute of Belle walking and searching for Candy, before bramble appeared in her path: Kat and two lollipop-sucking minions in neon strips of swimwear looking like poorly wrapped mummies.

"Well if it isn't Jane sans Rochester," Kat scowled, crossing her arms.

Minion #1 whispered to a shrugging #2, "I thought her name was Belle."

"Zip it, simpletons," Kat muttered.

"At least you show signs of intelligence," Belle replied, unable to hide her surprise at Kat's reference to *Jane Eyre*. She moved to walk past the trio, but Kat got in her face.

Belle's hands flared with heat.

"Oh, I'll show you intelligence. Back at that locker, you didn't have a Taser—I don't care what everyone says. You"—Kat poked her in the shoulder—"electrified us somehow. *Freak*."

"Stop," Belle gritted through her teeth.

The sunbathers nearby were watching now.

Kat took a step back and eyed her trembling fists. She snorted. "What? You think you're dangerous?"

Belle gave her a penetrating stare. "I am," she replied in a low, shaky voice. Fueled by fury and fear, she felt like a bomb about to go off.

Kat's snide smile faltered.

"Hi girls!" chimed a voice that sounded like music to Belle's ears.

Millie's megawatt smile and hot pink glasses were a welcome sight. She wrapped an arm around Belle and started drawing her away. "There you are! We've been waiting forever!"

Belle could feel her lungs working now.

"This isn't over, freak!" Kat called after them.

Millie turned around and with an expression of mock curiosity, said, "Oh, how's your dad's embezzlement trial going?"

Kat's jaw dropped.

With fake concern lining her face, Millie added, "I hope he wins. You know bourgees need money to stay at this school, and you're no whiz."

Before Kat had a chance to respond, her two minions descended upon her like harpies.

"Your dad's a criminal?"

"If you're not here anymore, our hierarchy will totally crumble!"

Millie and Belle scooted out of there, but not before Kat yelled after them, "I will ruin you, Millie!"

Millie called back, not even bothering to turn around, "Sorry! But that's my mom's job!"

Then in a low voice, she told Belle as they hurried away, "If you find me dead with my laptop missing, it was Kat. Or most likely her dad's thugs."

"Got it." Belle gave her a quick hug.

They soon reached Candy laid out on a beach chair between two empty ones, fanning herself with an oversized hat. She sat up, her hair intricately braided with little cowrie shells in it. "Hey girl! We saved you this spot." She removed a beach bag from the lounge chair next to her while Millie reclined on the other.

"Sorry I took so long. I was held up by the Gorgon sisters." She smiled at Millie. "Thank God for my knight in shining swimwear."

She dropped her towel and sunblock on the chair and sat. She glanced at the insides of her palms, which were hurting: blood glistened from where her nails had dug in.

Millie gave a dramatic bow. "Millie ex machina at your service."

Belle wiped her hands on her dark denim shorts. She grinned at Millie before sneaking another look at her hands. *Hmmm.* They weren't bleeding anymore.

"Well, what we wanna know is what held you up so long at the Rawlins Castle. Because from what *we* all saw"—Candy waved her finger around—"it was enough to entice Grendel out."

Belle frowned. "Jeesh, you talk about him like he's some kind of monster." Instinctively, she craned her neck to see if she could spot Liam.

"A very hot monster. Like vampire hot," Millie said. "Like a Hemsworth Dracula."

Belle found him just as he sidestepped Dmitri rushing at him before launching the ball.

"We get it, Millie," Candy said, rolling her eyes. "Honestly, girl, just be careful." She touched Belle's arm. "His parents' murder case fits right into the *X-Files*. And you don't want to get caught up in that side show."

Belle gave her a weak smile. "Thanks." If only Candy knew the irony.

Candy leaned back and continued fanning herself. "Is it just me, or is it boiling hot out today."

"It's actually kind of perfect right now, like 77 degrees," Millie said, concern etched on her face. "Are you feeling alright? You've been to the bathroom three times in the last hour—"

"Say no more, Mills," Candy interrupted, holding up her hand. "But, no, I think I might be catching something," she groaned, rubbing her tummy. "Of all days...."

"It must be sweltering underneath that hoodie," Millie said, looking pointedly at Belle. "You're wearing a bathing suit, right?"

Belle nodded nervously.

"Unless you want your tan lines to be worse than Kat's, I'd start stripping." She started lathering on more sunblock. "We're getting into the water in like half an hour."

I'm not, Belle thought defiantly. She didn't know how to swim and she wasn't about to learn or drown in front of an audience. Nevertheless, fighting what felt like stage fright, Belle stood and discarded with the hoodie and peeled off her shorts.

"That is cute!" Millie gushed.

"Briar Rose," Belle and Candy replied at the same time. Belle grinned, feeling more at ease. She grabbed her sunblock out of the towel and started spraying herself.

Millie sighed, looking down. "I wish *I* could pull off the balconette bikini."

Candy clucked her tongue. "Honey, please. Beauty is all shapes and sizes. You have the Kate Moss assets, I rock the apple bottom jeans, and—"

There was a sudden commotion among the football players.

Candy sat up and grinned like the Cheshire cat. "And I believe," she continued, gesturing towards the noise. "Our very own Marilyn Monroe just got Liam sacked. By my man."

Belle shielded her eyes and could just make out what she was seeing and hearing from the fuss. Hans and some other guys were holding Liam back, while Dmitri, with his arms in surrender-fashion, pleaded, "Dude, you were just standing there looking that way"—he pointed in Belle's direction—"and you were wide open so I took the shot!"

Someone teased, "Yeah, man, he was too busy checking out his girlfriend!"

Belle sat down and turned her flaming hot face away. She looked wide-eyed at Candy and Millie.

Millie looked up again and reported, "He's demanding another game." She rejoined their silent "oh-my-God" moment until they collapsed into giggles.

"Oh my," Millie said, sitting up alarmed. When the girls turned to look in her direction, she threw her hands out to stop them. "No! Don't look now." She turned to Candy, and said in a lower voice, "It looks like your pretend-boyfriend is headed this way."

"Dmitri?" Candy screeched.

Millie nodded.

Candy hurriedly smoothed out her braids over her shoulder and propped the beach chair up into a better sitting position. She groaned rubbing her stomach, but as soon as the hulking Dmitri appeared, she was all smiles.

"How's my Hercules?" Candy beamed.

He sat down at the foot of her lounge chair, the fabric sinking to the floor, and huffed, "Liam seriously needs to lighten up." He nodded at Belle and Millie. "Hey."

The girls "Hi'd" back.

Candy scooted closer and twirled her fingers through his ruddy hair. "Well I have something that might cheer you up," she said in a sing-song voice. She pulled a large capped Styrofoam cup out of a small cooler. "I made a shake for each of my closest friends."

Dmitri's eyes lit up like a child's on Christmas. "PBJ protein shake?"

"Where's mine?" Millie asked.

Candy ignored her and nodded at Dmitri. A huge grin on her face.

He uncapped it and took a deep drink. He let out a long sigh of satisfaction and grinned at Candy. "You are an angel. *My* angel." He finished off the drink while Candy melted into a puddle right through the chair.

Belle and Millie exchanged looks.

He stood up and handed Candy the empty cup. "Any of you ladies have sunblock? Time for my second coat."

Belle handed him hers.

He sprayed himself everywhere while the girls' eyes were glued. Belle thought how he must be a good foot shorter than Liam, while Candy looked like she would need an inhaler when he was done.

Millie whispered, "Is anyone else seeing this in slo-mo?" He handed the sunblock back to Belle and thanked her. "No, thank *you*," Millie said.

At that moment, one of Kat's neon clones was passing by. She stopped when she saw Dmitri, her eyes bulging, and screeched at him, "Are you lost?" She turned up her nose at the girls and told him, "If Kat saw you here, she'd have your head."

"Where *is* Kat? I can't find her."

She pointed towards the big tiki hut and walked away, flipping her long pony-tail back over her shoulder.

Dmitri's eyes looked stormy. There was Kat and company bopping around to the music with a few other guys in their midst. A raven-haired guy was dancing a little too close with Kat.

He was about to set off over there, but Belle grabbed him by the forearm and asked, "Why are you with her?"

He looked taken aback. And as if the answer was obvious, he said, "I've *always* been with her." He gently pulled his arm away. "I'll see you guys around."

The three girls watched as he walked away, his figure growing smaller.

"I hope he goes into *Terminator* mode," Millie muttered.

Dmitri hadn't reached the dance group yet when the raven-haired guy caught sight of him and scurried away to Kat's dismay.

"They've been together since they were in diapers." Candy sighed, sounding deflated. She leaned back on the chair and plopped the hat over her face.

Watching Dmitri and Kat argue, Millie said, "They're both from Greek families and they want to combine their fortunes with their marriage, which would be really convenient for Kat since her family's about to go broke."

"How do you know all this?" Belle asked, scary-impressed.

Millie dodged her question. "You know, I've been thinking about giving journalism a shot. Maybe start with the school newspaper, *The*

Peacock Press." She added as if it would be fun, "You should join, too." She jutted her thumb at Candy, "This one here already said no."

"I bake, I don't write," Candy said, grimacing.

"Maybe. I'll think about it." If Belle was doing the sleuthing, then maybe she wouldn't be the subject of one.

Candy groaned loudly and sat up cradling her stomach. "Ok, I'll be back." She headed toward the tiki hut.

"That would be the fourth time," Millie said. "We're probably leaving when she gets back." She peeked in Candy's cooler. It was empty. "Just as I thought. Do you want to go to the hut and bring back some chow with me?"

Belle's stomach rumbled in agreement. "Yes!"

On the way there, Belle thought she spotted Cindy, but it was a false alarm. She chewed her lip as she beat herself up inside. How could she have forgotten? She promised she would help her. She *had* to involve Ernesto and his delta force.

"What are you thinking about?" Millie asked, as she navigated Belle away from smacking into a tiki torch.

"Oh, just something really important I need to do as soon as I get home. Have you seen Cindy around? Do you know if she's here at the party?"

"I highly doubt it. This used to be her scene, until tragedy struck and the Steifschwesters stole the crown. Figuratively speaking."

"Cindy needs help," Belle asserted. "Even if she claims she doesn't want it."

"In an alternate universe, if her dad was still in charge, that's where she'd be," she pointed out a row of what looked like super models sun bathing on lounge chairs, "with the Princess Posse. Oh, look—"

It was Jared Prince coming out of the lake water with Marissa in his arms. They were laughing as she was trying to unwrap her long red hair from him. She was wearing a shimmering pink one-piece that extended all the way down to her feet, but her legs were encased in it.

Belle pointed. "Are those...?"

"'Mermaid fins', yes. They help her swim in the water. She's actually amazing at it. On the school's swim team and everything."

Jared eased her onto a lounge chair with the other Princesses and gave her a kiss on the forehead. He stood up and looked around, combing his wet black hair back with his hands, an action that drew attention to his lean and toned swimmer's body. He looked like he was about to sit next to Marissa, when he spotted Belle.

"Oh no." Belle didn't look away fast enough. They'd made eye contact. "Is he coming over?"

"Yep. Looks like he just told his guards to hang back. And 3...."

"Oh my goodness," Belle's heart started beating rapidly.

"2...."

"He's so flirty. I don't know how to act around him!" she whispered frantically.

"And 1. Hi ya,' Jared!" Millie piped up.

"Hey..." Jared snapped his fingers as if trying to remember.

"Millie. We have First Period together." She turned Belle around by the shoulders. "You know Belle? She's new to the school."

Momentarily distracted by the brilliant sky blue of his eyes in the sunshine, Belle could only manage a sheepish smile.

"Yeah, we've met," he grinned, dimples deepening in his cheeks. His eyebrows arched into his trademark smolder, a look that laid waste to many of the faint-hearted.

Millie sighed.

But Belle's "fan moment" was over when he started eyeing her like a plate of pork chops. He looked her up and down, and pursed his lips as if he approved of what he saw. "I see I owe you a Benjamin."

She crossed her arms and took a step back. "No thanks," she scoffed. "It was a ridiculous bet, anyways."

Millie looked between both of them with a sly grin. "Okay, well, I guess you stay"—she pointed at Belle and then herself—"and I'm going to get food and make sure Candy's still alive."

"No!" Belle said, reaching for her as she walked away.

Millie cast her a perplexed look, as if Belle should be cashing in on a winning lottery ticket, not tossing it aside.

Jared grabbed her by the hand. "C'mon, I'll take you for a ride on my jet ski."

Alarmed, Belle yanked her hand away and stood her ground. "Absolutely not."

He recoiled as if hurt. "What's your deal?"

More eyes were on them now. She swallowed. "It's not personal." He raised an eyebrow as if he didn't believe that. "I can't swim," she blurted out, fulling expecting to get laughed at.

He did laugh.

She glared at him, wanting to kick him in the shin.

"Alright, so it's *not* me." He grabbed her by the shoulders, and said, "Trust me. You have come to the right place." He pointed both thumbs back at himself. "Captain of the swimming team and MVP of the annual rowing competition." He wrapped an arm around her shoulders and started guiding her towards the water. "I'll have you swimming like a champ in no time."

"Hey, Jared, introduce us to your new girlfriend," a coquettish voice called out.

Dread filled her as he hauled her over to the Princess Posse, lined up on their lounge chairs like a page out of an elite swimwear catalogue. She shook off his arm from around her shoulders.

"This is Belle," Jared announced. The girls drew their sunglasses down or lifted their oversized hats to focus on her.

"His *friend*, not girlfriend," Belle corrected, glancing quickly at the red-head, Marissa.

He smirked, giving her arms a squeeze. "Oh, honey, there's no need to be shy." Belle's mouth dropped in outrage, while a few of the girls snickered. She side-stepped away from him. He continued, pointing, "This is Mari, Nieves, Lisa, Fatimah and Rapunzel."

Belle raised her eyebrows at the last girl's name. She even had the long, brown braid coiled down her back to her knees.

Rapunzel rolled her eyes. "I know, I know. My parents are hippies."

Nieves, the girl with the porcelain skin and black crimped curls down to her chin (Belle wanted to ask her how she got her curls to look so angular and *controlled*), giggled through her ruby red lips, and exclaimed with an infectious geniality, "Fabulously rich hippies!" She turned to Belle and grinned, scanning her green bikini. "You're totally rocking the Briar Rose look—I told you'd look super-phenom in it!" She leaned over to Lisa. "We *have* to get a picture of her and Jared. It'll be rad press for the store!"

Lisa frowned. "You do it." She was using a hand to shield her eyes from the sun and craning her neck, as if trying to peer down the beach. Spotting what she was looking for, she lifted off the chair and started heading away from them, her long sheer kimono flowing behind her and her signature scarf woven as a headband barely containing her golden sausage curls. "I've got a beast to bait," she said aloud, catching Belle's eye as she passed, smiling demurely.

Belle's blood boiled. She watched her retreating back, drawing every pair of eyes to her as she passed. It was like the Aphrodite effect. *How could Liam not resist?* she thought with a pang. She looked back to the Princess Posse whispering to each other. They had all been watching Belle's reaction. She unclenched her fists and turned to Jared, "Swim time?"

~~*~~

Jared proved to be an effective teacher and soon had her doggy-paddling with the best of them. "Alright, deal's a deal. I taught you how to swim, or at least not drown, and now you come on the jet ski with me," he said, flashing her a charming grin as he grabbed her by the hand and led her towards a jet ski station. Normally, she'd pull her hand out, but he had just taught her a life or death skill and, admittedly, she was having fun with him. During the swim lesson, he'd been really sweet and funny.

Now, they walked hand-in-hand along the shore line with the water lapping at their ankles. His two beefy security guards followed behind at a distance. Their beach shorts and Hawaiian shirts were not enough to help them blend in with their tell-tale ear pieces, black shades, and constant state of alertness. They looked around as if expecting a hostile invasion at any moment, which from their experience would be a shrieking, estrogen-fueled horde.

While Jared talked on about how his rowing skills would come in handy with jet skiing, Belle resorted to "mm-hmm"-ing and "oh really?"-s. Her eyes wandered to the people on the beach. She frowned. She couldn't spot Liam anywhere. Had he left her? And how was she supposed to get her bag back? Worse yet, was he with Lisa?

"Ow, ow!" Jared stopped walking and pulled his hand away, rubbing it with the other. "What was that for?"

"I'm sorry! I didn't mean to. I was just...thinking of something." She gave him a chagrined smile.

He reached for her hand again, but she casually wrapped her arms around her waist as they continued walking, passing a trio of girls who looked at Belle as if she had kicked their puppy. One of the guards shouted at a girl who had started taking some quick steps in their direction, "Stand clear!" The girls skulked away, one of them answering the guard with her middle finger.

Jared reached for her hand again, but Belle busied herself with squeezing her hair out like a sponge and coiling it into a bun. Those girls' green eyes of jealousy had reminded her that she wasn't going to be known as anyone's Ms. September.

A riot of laughter and cheering erupted from a distance behind them. Both turning to look, they quickly spotted the source: a chicken fight in the water between two couples surrounded by a crowd hooting and howling. "Now that's a match for the ages!" Jared grinned. "Liam can take Dmitri if he beasts out, but Lisa's not much competition against Kat's claws. I say it's a toss-up."

For once, Belle hoped Kat was very skilled with her claws on a certain someone's face. She watched, her vision growing red as Lisa sat on Liam's broad shoulders, her arms entangled with Kat's, while Liam and

Dmitri's arms seemed locked in a stalemate. Their faces showed they were laughing and calling out things to each other. A hot itching in her palms brought her back to her practical self. If she continued with this petty train of thoughts, she'd electrocute everyone in the water.

"What's the fuzz doing here?" Jared asked aloud.

Belle shielded her eyes with her hands. Security forces in black gear swarmed the beach like ants—the same guards that she recognized from the checkpoint outside the town, except POLICE was emblazoned on their chests. Jared's own two guards appeared at his side. "We need to leave, sir." They started to draw him away and leave Belle standing in the water.

"What's going on?" Jared demanded.

"There's been a kidnapping," one of them replied, still pulling him by the elbow.

Alarmed, Jared looked back at Belle. "We'll finish this another time!" He pulled his arms out of the guards' grasp. "I can walk." He shifted direction and commanded they follow him. "We need to get Mari."

Belle scanned the beach for her friends as she made her way back. *A kidnapping? In this fortressed town?* She wondered with growing dread if it was anyone she knew. A thought made her stop in her tracks and clutch her chest: *Is Violet the kidnapper?!* In the last dream she'd had, Violet looked like she was close by outside the town.

"Belle!" Millie almost crashed into her. "Thank God I found you! Come quickly, it's Candy!" She broke into a run with Belle.

"Candy was kidnapped?!" Belle cried out.

"No! She's sick. She won't get up from the chair."

Belle pulled her to a stop and faced her. "Then *who* is missing?"

A police officer next to them overheard and held up a flyer:

MISSING

Have you seen me?

Grace Darling

Under the name was Grace's last school photo. Belle clapped her hand over her mouth.

"Know her?" the officer asked.

She nodded her head slowly in disbelief. "I tutor her. I saw her just yesterday."

The officer scribbled in his notepad. "When, exactly?"

"Last school period of the day."

"Have you seen her since? Seen or heard anything that could help?" He asked looking between both girls.

A shiver crawled over Belle's skin. Could this Peter that Grace spoke of have anything to do with her disappearance? Emilia's Peter? With Grace missing, this wasn't information she could sit on. No matter how ludicrous it sounded. "It could be nothing, but she did mention a boy yesterday. Peter. She said he visits her at night." The officer was scribbling furiously. Belle added, "She also said he could fly, so I'm not sure how real this Peter is."

She watched as the officer wrote, *Drugs?*

"That sounds like her. She's known to be a bit wonky," Millie commented. She faced Belle and pleaded, "We need to go. Candy?" She turned back to the officer. "Good luck!" She dragged Belle away.

The officer frowned darkly as he stared after them.

"Jeez, you don't seem very concerned about a little girl missing," Belle huffed as she tried to keep up with her.

Millie called back, "I'm sure she's fine. This is not the first time she's gone missing and returned saying she got lost in the forest."

Belle slowed down when she spotted Liam surrounded by four police officers, including Ernesto. They were looking at him and questioning him like they already had their suspect backed into a corner. Liam stood with his arms crossed and feet planted wide apart, a stony, patient look on his face as he answered questions. The police intimidation seemed to have no effect on him. He caught Belle's eye, his expression unreadable. Their gaze held as she lagged even more behind Millie. She gave him a questioning look and he responded with a subtle tilt of his chin towards his hecklers as if saying, *Told you so.*

A hard pull from Millie broke the connection. "Can we stay focused here, please?" She didn't let go of Belle's hand this time as she hurried her along.

"Why are they all over him?" Belle asked.

"Well, the forest does belong to him. And he's still the #1 suspect in an unsolved murder," Millie replied in *duh*-fashion, although her voice sagged with worry.

When they reached Candy, all concern for Grace and Liam fled her mind. Candy lay limp on the lounge chair with the hat still covering her face, a pool of vomit on the sand next to her.

"Goodness gracious! Candy, are you alright?" Belle cried as she lifted the hat.

Only a groan signaled she was still alive.

"Oh man, she looks worse," Millie said, crouching by her side and holding her hand.

They looked up as a shadow fell over the three of them.

"Candy?" Dmitri asked, concern creasing his forehead. Behind him, the festive mood had evaporated as the partygoers began packing up and leaving, speaking in shocked, hushed voices.

"She's sick," Millie responded. "I already called the ambulance. They should be here any second."

He leaned forward so quickly that the two girls moved out of his way to prevent being knocked aside. He scooped Candy up in his arms. "I bet my Mustang can get her to the hospital faster." Candy groaned and her head went limp against his chest.

"Then hurry!" Belle cried.

The girls dressed quickly, gathered their things, and the four of them rushed toward the cars.

Out of nowhere, an inhuman screech pierced the air, making every-one freeze in their tracks, "DMITRI MARINO! What the *hell* are you doing?!"

"Back off, babe. I'm helping my friends here." Dmitri turned to face Kat, who was red-faced with fists clenched by her sides. Belle thought how cartoonish Kat's rage looked and imagined angry black puffs of smoke shooting out of her ears.

"You're supposed to be taking care of *me*, remember?! Taking me home?! Not wasting *my* time with these losers and freaks!" At the last word, Kat looked pointedly at Belle.

A wailing siren was heard, growing louder.

"It's alright, Dmitri. The ambulance is here," Belle said, clutching her hot hands behind her back. *Focus on helping Candy,* she thought, trying to calm herself.

"Yeah, we don't have time for your wannabe-Queen-B psychosis," Millie said.

"Shut it, Ms. Nobody," Kat snapped.

Millie's glasses transitioned to black as she glowered at Kat.

A few bystanders were watching them now, some taking out their cell phones and recording.

"You know what?" Dmitri said. "This could be life or death here, and you only still care about yourself."

"You still don't get it, do you? We"—Kat pointed between herself and Dmitri—"are the future." She pointed at Candy's limp form. "She is just a baker. Her 'life or death' is not even important."

Belle's hands sparked to life and her eyes narrowed into slits.

"Whoa, that's low, even for—" Dmitri began, but was interrupted by a swinging punch landing with a crack on Kat's nose.

"Millie?!" Belle cried, surprised.

Millie shook her hand. "Man, that felt good, but, man, my hand hurts."

Several things happened at once: the ambulance pulled up, doors swinging wide open as paramedics popped out; Belle signaled them over, and as they retrieved Candy from Dmitri's arms and prepped her onto a stretcher, some bystanders were hooting about the fight, while some inquired after Candy's health; Kat hollered about her bloody nose as Dmitri led her away, telling her, "Babe, you know I love you, but you asked for that one."

"We can only take one, if one of you wants to come along," one of the paramedics called out, as they loaded Candy onto the ambulance.

Millie spoke up first, "You go. My mother will want to see me right away. I'm sure she's already sensed a disturbance in the Force."

Belle nodded. "Okay, I'll call you."

They hugged, and then Belle joined Candy on the ambulance, holding on for dear life as it sped away.

22

When the Cure's Worse

"Candy, my baby girl!" Candy's grandmother's sob broke through as Belle shut the door behind her. She leaned back against it for a moment, savoring the sweet relief of having survived a whirlwind.

Dehydration and pneumonia were the culprits. Since Candy was contagious, the doctors and nurses had kindly given Belle the boot with the promise that Candy was in good hands and would be fine in a few days. Candy's grandmother wouldn't budge. Belle had left her cell number with her, so she could stay updated on Candy's progress.

As she wandered through the maze-like hospital, Belle's mind was on autopilot playing the director's-commentary version of the events that had transpired so far that day. Soon enough, she discovered she was walking in circles when she passed the same nurses' station three times. She turned into a new wing that had an Exit-arrow sign at the end of the hall. Belle froze. The clear form of a pant-suited, salt-and-pepper hair-styled figure slipped into one of the rooms in the wing.

It was Mrs. Steifshwester.

Belle smelled a rat. *What's she doing here?*

She hurried on tip-toes down the empty hall, her heart beating in her ears. When she reached the door, she peered through its narrow sliver of a window. Mrs. Steifschwester was leaning over a comatose elderly man, talking in his ear, and brushing the white-blonde hair from his forehead.

Belle inhaled sharply. This had to be Mr. Ellerson, Cindy's father. She peered closer. Mrs. Steifschwester was rubbing his arm and still talking. The interaction seemed tender, so was this woman really a threat to him? She recalled the threat the principal had made to Cindy in the bathroom: *I will finish him!* Belle swallowed the acrid taste in the back of her mouth. Cindy's terror had been real.

Footsteps in the hall sent her ducking for cover, but there was nowhere to hide, so she leaned against the wall trying to look casual. It didn't work.

"May I help you, young lady?"

A nurse with a greasy comb-over of the few black hairs he still had looked down on her. His clip-on ID read, *RN: Lucifer*

She shuddered. *Ewww, heebie-jeebies.*

"Um, I'm waiting for my, uh—" She started, pointing back at the door. Stuck mid-lie, she glanced back through the window hoping they hadn't attracted anymore unwanted attention. But her eyes widened when Belle saw Mrs. Steifschwester insert a needle with green substance into Mr. Ellerson's IV line. She gasped, "She's injecting something in him!"

The nurse leaned over and peered through the window, as did Belle. Mrs. Steifschwester was putting the needle away into her purse. "All I see is a loving wife making her usual visit to see her comatose husband," he said, eerily calm.

"But you saw that! The needle?" she pressed.

He glanced past her through the window and replied, as if speaking to a small child, "You are causing a disturbance. You need to leave now."

She looked again and this time, Mrs. Steifschwester was holding his hand and petting it. She locked eyes with Belle, her gaze as sharp as a knife.

"Do I need to call security?" the nurse threatened, still using the kindergartner teacher voice.

Belle was abashed. "For me? I'm not the one poisoning a patient!"

He smiled as wide and creepily as the Grinch. He pulled a small walkie-talkie from his pocket and called for security.

Belle peered through the window again. Mrs. Steifschwester's smile matched the nurse's. Feeling like the helpless victim in a horror movie, she stumbled a few steps away from the maniacs.

"It'll just be a moment," he said, as if apologizing for the inconvenience of the wait.

She turned away and ran. Her inner emergency siren wailing, she followed the exit signs. Her mind made up to seek out Ernesto right away. He had to help her. Help Cindy and her father. She ignored the several people that called out to her, asking if she was okay.

Recognizing a passing blur as a face from school, she backtracked and stopped at a security desk. "Q?" she asked, panting.

He wore a Q-Tech Services shirt and was surrounded by laptops and wires hooked up to the security monitors and a computer. His fingers paused above the keyboard and only his eyes moved as they looked up at her above his glasses. "Hello," he said, in an impatient tone that meant *May I help you?*

"Cindy's dad is in trouble," she spat out.

Without so much as a twitch of a muscle, he replied, "I know. He's in a coma with a 27% chance of—"

"No, that's not what I mean. He's being poisoned!"

His eyes narrowed. "Elaborate, please." She told him what she saw in Mr. Ellerson's room and about Lucifer's interference.

His fingers took off flying over the keyboard as he spoke, "I was called in for a security system reparation, so I will have to do a system check on the cameras in each aisle. I say we start with the cameras in

Mr. Ellerson's wing." He motioned for her to come around the desk and look at the monitor. It was Mrs. Steifshwester and the nurse, Lucifer, outside Mr. Ellerson's room. Q zoomed in on their hands. The principal passed the nurse something that he quickly pocketed. Q rewinded and replayed, zooming in closer. That "something" was a $100 bill.

"I knew it—that snake's been helping her!" Belle clenched and unclenched her hot hands.

"If Mrs. Steifshwester is hurting Mr. Ellerson, then it is logical to conclude that she is hurting Cindy."

Belle chewed her lip. *He had to know,* she thought. "There's more." She filled him in on the verbal and physical abuse Cindy suffered in the school bathroom and the abused-servant-treatment at the mall, all at the hands of what was supposed to be her family. Q's eyebrows had been slowly drawing together like dark clouds amassing before a storm; he bit down on his bottom lip so hard, she spotted blood.

"Q, are you—?" she began, but he held up a hand to silence her as he looked down at his computer screen and stared, the gears in his mind whirring, formulating a plan. When he still hadn't said anything, Belle spoke up as she turned to leave, "I'm going to go tell Ernesto about it."

"No! Please. Leave it to me," he said with an intensity that surprised Belle. "No one hurts Cindy. She is my friend."

When she gave him a questioning look, he added, "I'll get the evidence together from all the camera and cell phone surveillance I will find on Steifshwester and I'll take it to him myself. This"—he cracked his knuckles and actually smiled a little as he poised his hands above the keyboard—"is going to be my greatest masterpiece yet." His fingers began flying and his eyes gleamed. Faintly feeling sorry for Mrs. Steifshwester, Belle gave a weak "thanks" and took her exit.

23

Out on the Town

"**O**h, Lord have mercy," Belle groaned.

She'd emerged from the wrong exit of the hospital and now had to walk the whole way around to get to the front. She was hungry and tired, and since Liam still had her bag, she had no money to buy food and no phone to call for help. She wanted to sit and cry just thinking about walking home—her feet felt like they were about to fall off.

When she finally reached the front of the hospital, she had to snap her mouth shut to keep her heart from leaping out of it. There was Liam. Leaning against his motorcycle like a heartthrob from a chick flick, waving and pointing to her bag sitting on the seat. Belle couldn't help it: as she walked toward him in what felt like slo-mo, the Jefferson Starship song, "Nothing's Gonna Stop Us Now," cued in her mind.

"Hey, thanks!" She grinned as she finally reached him, her face red as the song wailed out its last line in her mind. She noticed he'd changed clothes: from cargo shorts to dark blue jeans, with a black v-neck t-shirt that made his green eyes look gray and clung loosely to his muscular contours. And here she was hoping she didn't smell.

He tucked his hair behind his ears and crossed his arms in front of his chest, distracting Belle again. "No problem. Although I did consider making you a scavenger hunt map to get your stuff back," he said, a hint of rebuke in his tone.

"Wha-why?"

"It took me like an hour to find my keys and wallet. Wrapped in your towel. Under a beach chair. But, hey"—he put his hands up to stop her from apologizing—"it's alright. Things got crazy pretty quick on that beach." He rested his hands on his hips and took a few seconds to analyze her face. "How's your friend? I heard and came straight over here. And Dmitri's asking, too."

As she relayed to him the doctor's report on Candy, she cradled her forehead as a wave of fatigue came over her and clutched her stomach as it let out an embarrassing whine.

He reached out and steadied her by the shoulders. "Whoa, how are *you*?"

She smiled weakly. "I'm fine and dandy. Just a tad hungry and tuckered out," she said, rolling her eyes as if it wasn't a big deal.

"How about we get you some food, and then I'll take you home?"

Grateful, she wanted to collapse into him and just hug him like a body pillow. She inhaled deeply. A spice, evergreen-scented body pillow.

"Uh, Belle?"

Oh. My. Stars, she thought, panicked as her eyes flew open. She had actually done it: hugged and squeezed him and smelled his shirt. Eyes closed and everything. She was still attached to him.

She pushed off him. A surge of adrenaline coursing through her veins from this record-mortifying moment. "Um, you know what? I think I'm good to walk home now." She avoided his eyes as she backed away slowly and turned toward the sidewalk. "You don't really need to concern yourself with me."

He reached for her and grabbed her hand. When she looked up at him, he gave her a teasing smile, but his voice was husky when he said, "Hey, c'mon." He guided her back towards his bike. "All work and no food makes Belle a silly girl." He dropped her bag back into the bike's seat. He mounted and held out his hand for Belle to join him.

She hesitated. Suddenly feeling conscientious, she looked up at him through hooded lashes. "Why are you doing this?"

He cocked his head, waiting for her to continue.

"Why are you bothering with me?" She twisted her hands together. "I mean, this is really kind of you."

His gaze lingered so long on her that she felt a blush staining her cheeks. When he answered, his features softened, "Maybe because of my mom. She was always trying to help people." He shrugged his shoulders. "And she brought home stray cats all the time."

"So, I'm like a stray cat?"

He smiled roguishly. "Yes, now let me do my duty and feed you before I release you back into the wild." He offered his hand again, which she took, hyper-aware of the warm pressure of his grip closing over her fingers, and now the mere inches that separated her body from his back as she sat behind him. Looking past him, she noticed a man in dark shades and a black vest sitting in an unmarked car. Staring at them. She frowned as she watched him. "That guy is staring at us."

"Cop. He's been tailing me since the lake." Liam nodded at him. "Smile and wave or something, so he doesn't think I'm kidnapping you."

She did. The cop looked away and spoke into a walkie-talkie. She settled her hands lightly on his hips, her heart rate picking up speed. "I can't believe it about Grace. I hope they find her soon."

He put on his helmet and handed Belle hers. "Yeah. They're out prowling the forest right now. That's where she said she was last time." He leaned back and angled his head toward her. "Ready?"

Her stomach growled loudly. She hid her face in his back.

He laughed. "I'll take that as a 'yes'." He slid his visor down and roared the motorcycle to life.

~~*~~

When Liam parked and killed the bike at Ridge Rats, a bar and grill that served as the local high school hang-out, Belle's heart plummeted to her toes. The last people in the world she wanted to see right now were hanging out and eating at the tables on the outside deck. Lisa and her fellow princesses, and Kat and her fellow witches. Only Marissa was missing. A few of the guys she recognized like Dmitri, Hans, and Amir made the group less intimidating to her. From what she could see over Liam's shoulder, they'd have to pass right by the pack to get inside.

Or worse yet, would Liam want to hang out with them?

Liam must have read her mind as they dismounted the bike and removed their helmets. "Don't worry. We're sitting inside."

She rolled her eyes with relief. At that moment, Jared walked out of the restaurant with a basket of food and a soda in his hands. He swung his legs over the deck railing and joined the group.

"Unless you want to eat outside..." Liam added, his tone more muted. He watched her face, as if her response was going to decide something very important.

"Inside, please." It was a no-brainer.

His gray eyes brightened as his face broke into a smile that mirrored Belle's.

The plan was to ignore the group as the pair walked past, but Dmitri had extracted himself from a fuming, red-nosed Kat and was waiting for them by the door.

"How's Candy? Is she alright?" He had the expression of a boy who'd just lost his puppy.

Liam held the door open and Belle could hear Lisa commenting in his direction, "Oooh, the famous silent treatment again."

Ignoring Lisa, Liam answered Dmitri instead, "She's at the hospital if you want to visit."

An angry Kat shouted, "Dmitri, come back here!"

"Dang! Chill out, woman!" Amir replied.

"Don't talk to her like that!" Fatimah lashed out at him.

Hans clapped his hand on Amir's shoulder and after throwing a glance Fatimah's way, he said, "Uh, you're helping the neighbor, but neglecting your house."

Amir shrugged him off, and while an argument erupted between Amir, Fatimah, and Kat worthy of an over-the-top reality TV show, Belle reached out and squeezed Dmitri's hand. "The doctor says she'll be better in a few days, but um"—she leaned in and lowered her voice—"a visit from you would speed things up."

Dmitri smiled, understanding.

Just as she was turning to walk through the door that Liam was still holding open, Jared appeared at Dmitri's elbow. "Hey, Beauty." He flashed her a megawatt grin.

"Hi, Jared." She grinned back and then continued toward the door again, but he reached out and grabbed her elbow.

Liam abruptly released the door and joined her side, while Jared just as quickly let her go and stuffed his hands into his pockets. He frowned darkly at Liam before turning to Belle with a charming, please-forgive-me smile. "Sorry for taking off so quickly at the beach. I hope you'll let me make it up to you. I am indebted to you after all." He winked.

Belle bristled at the bikini-bet reminder.

"Dude..." Dmitri warned.

Not even wanting to go there in front of an audience, especially this set, she changed the topic. "How's Marissa? Did you get her home safely?"

"Uh, yeah. Yeah. She's home."

Liam touched her arm, as if signaling they could go inside now.

Jared scowled as he locked eyes with Liam, who simply stood up straighter, towering a full head taller.

Belle swallowed nervously as she felt the tension thicken, and for the first time there wasn't a peep heard in the background.

Dmitri put his hand on Jared's shoulder, who flinched upon contact. "Yo, your fries are getting cold. Amir's eating 'em all."

Jared looked between Liam and Belle before responding, "Yeah, you're right. And I don't like to share." His icy blue eyes held Belle's.

"Me neither." Liam took a step closer, shielding her from Jared's view.

"Ok. Wow," Belle began, backing away. "You two can keep gazing into each other's eyes, but I'm getting a burger." She turned and before she disappeared into the restaurant, she heard Nieves's tinkling laugh. "Oooh, she's hangry."

~~*~~

With a swoosh of the doors shutting behind her, Belle was confronted with rock music, Christmas lights and large TVs everywhere, promising beer, sports and chicken wings. A perky, twenty-something year-old hostess appeared with a clipboard. "Table for one?"

As Belle opened her mouth to respond, she felt a breeze behind her and the crisp scent of evergreen washing over her. "Two," Liam finished for her. He met her gaze, an apology on his lips.

The hostess gasped, a mixture of admiration and fear in her eyes. "Liam Rawlins?"

"Uh, yeah." He shifted uncomfortably in his spot. "It's been a while since I've come in here."

"You used to be here every weekend, until.... Well, I thought you were in prison. They let you out?" She clasped her clipboard to her chest like a shield.

"Look, Jan, we just want a table." He added, in a biting tone, "It's nice to see you, too."

She looked at Belle as if wondering if she was here of her own free will. To answer her suspicion, Belle linked her arm through Liam's and said, "Table for two, please."

Jan frowned at Belle as if suspecting she suffered from Stockholm syndrome. She motioned for them to follow and led the pair through the restaurant to a back booth, away from the glares and not-so-hushed whispers of,

"What's that murderer doing here?"

"How dare he show his face?"

"Does *she* know?"

Belle could feel his arm stiffening under her hand. A glance at his face revealed he looked like he wanted to punch a patron. She looked down at his hands and saw they were clenched, so she slid her hand down his tense arm and wiggled her hand into his.

Their eyes locked. The hard lines in his face relaxed and he gave her a small smile. He took a deep breath and squeezed her hand.

As soon as Liam and Belle slid into the booth across from each other, Jan asked, "Do you two know what you want already?"

Belle exchanged looks with Liam. The menus were still tucked under Jan's arm. Clearly, they were being rushed.

After giving their order, (Belle: a cheeseburger, fries and milkshake, and Liam: grilled chicken breast, vegetables, and water with lemon), a weighted silence fell between the two. He leaned back and laid his arm over the booth, drawing attention to his physique. She swallowed and clasped her hands in her lap. She could feel his eyes on her and she couldn't bring herself to meet them. His presence and attention awoke sensations in her that unnerved her. The last time a significant sensation had awoken, she'd killed three men.

She pushed her curls out of her face and zipped her hoodie all the way up, cringing at the view Liam must have of her. Her hair, washed with lake water and dried with wild motorcycle wind, must be painful to look at, and she was still in her bikini, hoodie and shorts outfit. She scrunched her brain trying to remember if she had even applied deodorant that morning. Would Liam notice if she snuck a sniff?

He leaned forward, resting his elbows on the table, a stoic look on his face. The vintage lamp that hung low over their table cast a soft glow over his features. "Listen, Belle, I understand if you feel uncomfortable around me. I mean, any normal girl would. You're new in this town and you don't need to be...*tainted* by any of the trouble that's dogged me. So, I promise: it's food and then I take you home. Or if you want to catch a ride home with—someone else, I understand."

Belle's heart skipped a beat at his confessionary tone. "Then, I guess I'm not a normal girl."

"That's- that's not what I meant—"

"Because the only thing I was uncomfortable about was being stinky in these clothes."

"Huh," he sat back with a smile, that turned into a teasing one. "But I like your smell."

Her mouth dropped. "I do smell?!" She half-screeched, half-whispered.

His smile grew even more lop-sided. He was obviously enjoying this.

"Well," Belle racked her brain for a response that would salvage her dignity, but could only come up with one that had the opposite effect. "I—you smell, too." She crossed her arms in a huff.

He chuckled in amusement. "I better. It's a $300 cologne." He leaned forward, the light dancing in his gray-green eyes. "Besides, you have a very distinct smell." She was so getting a ride home from someone else tonight. "Strawberries."

She maintained her glare, but couldn't stop her pout from spreading into a smile. "It's my shampoo. My hair requires lots of it."

"Well, you reek of strawberries," he said in mock disgust. She laughed and threw her napkin at him. He caught it and returned it to her. "You hold onto this. You ordered a milk shake, remember?" He gestured towards his mustache area.

Before she could retort, Jan appeared with their food. "Wow, that was fast," Belle said.

Liam nodded and said with an edge of sarcasm in his voice, "The quicker we get our food, the faster we're out of here, right, Jan?"

"Just so you know," Jan's tone carried a warning, "Carlos is the cook tonight." Liam groaned and buried his forehead in his hand. "Hers is safe though." She pointed at Belle's plate and gave Liam an apologetic pat on the shoulder before striding away with her tray.

"What's wrong?" Belle asked. The steam rising from her burger was making her mouth water.

"Carlos hates me." He slowly pushed his plate away. "He's one of the many people that thinks I'm not so innocent. So, there's definitely some of Carlos in that plate." And then he did something Belle didn't expect from the guy who punched a wall to do: laugh.

"I'm sorry. I don't see what's so funny. That's terrible, in fact."

"You know," he said, cocking his head as he looked at her. "If this had happened two days ago, I would have taken this plate into the kitchen and smashed it in his face."

"I don't see how that's funny either." She pushed a straggler fry back onto her plate.

"Something's changed." Something in his tone made her look up. Her cheeks heated as he held her gaze with an intensity that could read into her very soul. And it frightened Belle what he could discover there.

She tore her eyes away. "Well," she covered her food with her napkin. "I don't trust Carlos either."

"Ah, but I promised you a meal...." He eased back against his chair, disappointment setting in.

"Isn't there someplace else we could go where we wouldn't literally get served a revenge dish?" She bit her lip. It hit her that she didn't want to go home yet. Home meant being flooded with the problems and questions she had walled off using today's diversions. And Liam proved to be by far the most successful and pleasant distraction.

His eyes lit up. "Boardwalk's next door. I know of a 'first' you need to have there."

That 'first' Liam spoke of was a pizza pot-pie followed by a chocolate molten lava cake ala mode. Belle thought she'd died and gone to heaven. A heaven that had the feel and sound of a carnival with a long boardwalk lit up like a Christmas tree and flanked by eclectic shops and eateries on one side and the lake a little off to the distance on the other. The sun had begun to set behind the row of shops and a cool air had invaded, announcing the onset of Fall. Belle shivered into her hoodie, but didn't peel her eyes away from the view of the sun's dying rays reflecting across the lake. She sighed with rapture.

Liam leaned an elbow on the table and watched her. They sat across from each other at a picnic table outside *Treats & Eats*. He had just finished clearing the table for them and dumping the remnants of his monthly "cheat meal" into the trash. It was so worth it. And he wasn't even going to tell her about the chocolate 'stache she had failed to completely wipe off. He'd use that later. It was too easy. He enjoyed getting under her skin and rousing that fire behind her innocence. An innocence that was rare in this town. And beautiful. Not to mention the persuasive power her perfect face and hourglass figure emanated. It was out of this world. Something she was oblivious to and he was torturously not. Beyond the purely physical though that constantly evoked him, he had an affinity for who and how she was.

And she wasn't pushing him away either. More than that, she was somehow shining a light into the darkness that he had holed himself up in for more than a year. A darkness that had almost swallowed him several times whenever he stood on the castle's balcony ledge and gazed down into the watery abyss that promised closure, all while his parents' murder at the Lightning Witch's hands replayed in his mind. Her final words to him as he'd stood impossibly petrified in his spot, before she disappeared with his mother's bracelet:

"I let you live Liam Rawlins so that you may know the misery your family inflicted upon me. A misery that ended beneath that cliff. Mark this: whomever you fall in love with, will die by my hand."

Her departing, cruel cackle echoed in his head.

"Liam, are you okay?" Belle had leaned across the table and was shaking his arm.

He had been staring at her, his eyes growing stormier, until it seemed like he wasn't really seeing her anymore. He shook his head and his expression cleared. "Sorry," he replied gruffly. He lifted from his seat and avoided her gaze. "I should...I should probably get you home."

The fun, light-hearted mood they shared over an amazing dinner dissipated. "Okay. I guess." Belle stood and then couldn't help grinning wholeheartedly. "This day, from beginning to end"—she held her hands up and framed the landscape with them—"has been a majestic adventure."

"Nice." Liam knit his eyebrows together as he looked at her. "Makes me wonder though what a typical day for you was like in Littleton."

She swallowed. Littleton meant secrets. And whatever this—thing was that was shaping up with Liam, she didn't want to base it off lies. Her hesitation was noticeable.

"It's okay." Liam shrugged. "You don't need to talk about it. I mean, I know why you had to move here."

They headed back slowly, arms brushing, towards the parking lot. But in the silence that ensued as they walked, it seemed that he was waiting for her to say something. Problem was as she racked her brain for how to even begin, sifting through the details was like slowly unscrewing the cap off a soda bottle that had been shaken: the contents were threatening to explode out. She found herself taking fast, deep breaths.

"Whoa, whoa—hey," Liam grabbed her by the shoulders and faced her toward him. "Easy, now. It's okay."

Tears threatened to spill over, but she was not about to break down. No. That meant explanations. Probably lies. And she wasn't ready. She hadn't figured out enough, yet.

He brought her in and enveloped her in his arms.

She should have responded in kind, but her hands were buzzing and she didn't want to possibly zap or kill him. Her arms remained board-straight at her sides, but she nestled her face into his strong chest and inhaled deeply. That woodsy scent of pines and spice took her mind back to the forest by her house, to this morning's exhilarating motorcycle ride through his forest with the feel of him against her, and then slowly the buzzing in her hands subsided and the soothing thud of his heartbeat relaxed her breathing.

The two were oblivious to the onlookers that meandered by them on the boardwalk and to the gossip that followed and would surely spread around this small busybody town: the new Beauty had fallen prey to the Beast of the castle.

Belle pulled apart from him and looked into his face, his gray-green eyes searching hers. Smiling apologetically, she gave him the most honest answer she could manage, "I haven't unpacked all my baggage yet."

Liam put his arm around her so they could continue walking again. Attempting to lighten the mood, he replied as if impressed, "Hmmm, a girl who doesn't like to talk about her problems." He let his arm fall away and Belle already missed the warm pressure of his touch.

She was in so much trouble.

He gave her a sideways look and joked, "You keep taking a sledge-hammer to the mold of the typical Elmridge girl. Or typical modern girl, period."

"What do you mean?"

"Not once have I seen you check your cell phone tonight. And—*oof!*"

A guy had crashed right into Liam's shoulder.

"Sorry, man." A young twenty-something-year-old guy, slightly shorter than Liam, held his hands up in apology, cell phone in one hand, as if he had been paying attention to it and not where he was going.

Liam, who looked like he had just restrained his fist from flying, quickly relaxed his stance and replied, "It's alright, man." He turned his attention back to Belle. "See what I mean about cell phone zombies?"

But Belle was not hearing him. Her eyes were fixed with horror on the same young guy who walked backwards now, staring at her. His hands stuffed in his crisp khaki pants, wearing a clean-cut yellow polo shirt with the collar popped up, and his all-too familiar face staring back at her, smirking.

His twin joined him. Dressed all in black with heavy eyeliner, his face expressionless as he grabbed his brother's shoulder, prompting him to turn around, but not before the preppy one blew a kiss at her.

"What? What's wrong?" Liam looked in the direction she was staring at, but the twins had already disappeared into the moving crowd.

"Uh," her mouth remained open, speechless. This encounter proved beyond a shadow of a doubt that her dreams were not the stuff of fiction. They were real. The connection to her mother was real. Violet's words from her last dream were coming back to her again, *You will give me what I want, or I will kill someone you love.*

"Belle!" Liam pulled her chin gently, angling her face toward him.

Her eyes refocused on him. "I-I need to get home." Raw emotion broke her voice. She squeezed her hands closed to stop the trembling and quench the burning that'd erupted.

Liam's thumb gently caressed her chin before he let his hand fall away. "Of course."

They resumed their walking. Seeing as Belle moved unsteadily, Liam wrapped his arm around her shoulders. She leaned into him, grateful for his strength and support. He was the only thing keeping her from breaking normal right now. Until she could get home and go to pieces in the privacy of her room and then put together as much of the nightmare puzzle as she could.

24

He Loves Me, He Loves Me Not

Riding Liam's motorcycle with the cool night air rushing over her skin, and snuggling tighter against his back for warmth, eased some of the loose-cannon jitters that plagued her, and she could once again appreciate the moment she was in. With Liam. Who gave her those warm, intoxicating feelings that clouded her brain and kept her in the blissful present.

But the closer she got to home, the louder reality knocked, especially after the encounter with the twins. Her nightmares were real, the threats were real, and that meant that Belle couldn't be selfish and put Liam in the crosshairs over lovey-dovey distractions. For his own safety, she knew what she had to do.

The roar of the motorcycle died as Liam parked it in front of the Historical Elmridge Society. Her heart feeling like lead, she took her time sliding her hands away from his chest, since this would surely be the last time being this close to him. Liam's breathing kicked up a notch. "You really aren't making this easy," he muttered gruffly.

She pretended she didn't hear and dismounted the bike. He slid his helmet off, but hers was terribly snagged onto her hair. "Ouch!" she cried. Wordlessly, he got off the bike and sat against it. He grabbed the hem of her hoodie and drew her closer to help her. "Sorry," she blushed. Their fingers kept brushing, sending jolts throughout her body as she silently prayed she didn't send real ones through his.

"It's alright," he smiled. "I got it." She stopped fumbling with the strap and clenched her hands at her sides. He smirked. "Looks like this thing doesn't want to see you go." She smiled back, full of a different kind of jitters that worried her.

The air between them was heated, electrified even. Liam was at eye-level now and she could feel his soft breath on her face as he focused on gently separating her hair from the strap. She struggled to assert her better judgement over hormones as her eyes roamed his face, admiring the minty color of his eyes down to its yellow flecks, the strong lines of his jaw and dimpled chin which she noticed sported a faint blonde stubble, and the wide M-shape of his tantalizingly full lips.

She would love for those lips to be her first kiss.

"There," he said, the strap coming loose. She held her breath when he swept her hair back, his hand brushing clean across her neck, leaving a trail of goosebumps. He hung the helmet from the handlebar, and as Belle took a step back, he grabbed her hand to keep her from moving too far. Liam cleared his throat and looked down as if he was gathering his thoughts to say something important, his thumb absently making circles on the back of her hand.

Belle's heart beat rapidly, commanding her own thoughts to organize. She couldn't allow this—whatever this was—to continue. For his own safety.

They both opened their mouths to speak at the same time.

"You go first," Liam said, letting go of her hand.

She hugged herself. "No, please, you first. You looked like you wanted to say something first anyways."

"Alright," he passed a hand through his hair. "This is what? Your fourth day here?"

"Third," she corrected.

"Third. And already I—" He put a hand to his chest. "I mean, I really like—" He exhaled gruffly. "What I'm trying to say is...you can't be spending time with me." He looked off to the side. "I know I've already said this, but you're new here and even being seen with me will hurt you." He quickly added, meeting her eyes, "Hurt your reputation."

"You're worried about my reputation?"

"Yes. No. I mean, yes. That's something that's important around here. And you deserve a fair shot at a good one." His shoulders sagged as he concluded, "Without me staining it."

"Staining," Belle repeated absentmindedly, looking down at her hands. She had the blood of three men stained on them and she didn't want to add a fourth.

"Belle?" He grabbed both of her outstretched hands and squeezed them, drawing her closer so she had to look up at him. "Are you okay? You wanted to say something too, remember?"

"It's kind of you to think I deserve a fair shot," she said, barely above a whisper.

Confusion flickered across his face. "You do," he affirmed. Giving her hands one last squeeze, he said softly before releasing them, "And you'll be safer."

It struck her that he was pushing her away for the same reason she wanted: to keep the other safe. He still didn't know she had overheard him speaking of the Lightning Witch's threat to kill anyone he fell in love with. And while she was convinced now that the Lightning Witch and Violet Wickeby and her mother were one and the same, the only thought that trumpeted the loudest in her brain right now was that quite possibly he was falling in love with her! This simple deduction set her heart ablaze, and she couldn't help letting out a laugh of joy.

"Whoa, not the reaction I was expecting," he said, with a baffled grin.

She quickly covered her mouth with her hand, while her eyes watered remembering that she still had to push him away. "This is so messed up," she said to herself. She looked up at Liam's expression, total confusion there. "You must think I'm nuts," she told him.

"It's part of the appeal," he commented lightly, scratching his jaw.

"Ha," she chuckled weakly. "See, what I was going to tell you before"—she paused to see what he might be thinking now, if he'd had enough of her craziness, but he was hanging onto her every word—"was that I simply don't want to burden you with *my* burden. And so it's best you not waste your time on me. I mean, more than necessary."

Whoo, she exhaled. She felt relieved getting that off her chest. It was the right thing to do. Yet, she still harbored that small, but painful, selfish hope that he wouldn't listen.

And maybe he hadn't. Because a change came over him. As if Belle challenging him to stay away ignited the opposite effect. He'd tried to push her away first and expected her to react the same way he'd seen other girls do: sulk and get huffy about it. Instead, she laughed in his face and had planned to be rid of him just the same. As if she was pretending she didn't want him around just as much as he wanted her. Frankly, it was insulting. And in some twisted way, this challenge turned him on even more.

"Hmm..." he began, the light minty hue in his eyes darkened to a smoldering emerald, turning up her temperature and cracking her resolve. "Define what you mean by 'more than necessary.'"

"Um, well," a nervous laugh escaped her. "We do have that school project, so...."

"Yup. Nothing more important than school." His lips gathered into a knowing smirk. "And?" he prompted, raising an eyebrow. He knew what was coming.

"And...." Belle repeated, taking a step closer. "You did—quite graciously, may I add—extend an open invitation to your garden and library." She held up her hands for emphasis, adding, "Unfettered access."

She knew she was obviously sucking up now, but losing that venue would be like cutting off her air supply.

Liam nodded in mock seriousness. "'Unfettered,' huh?"

She gave him her most charming smile and hoped she didn't come across as too scandalously opportunistic. What ever happened to scaring him off? This fake act of hers might do the trick. And then mission accomplished: Liam would be out of harm's way. But she got the feeling that not even *this* was working. Because as if by magnetism, she kept inching her way closer to him as she spoke, and the look in his eye got even sultrier. "And the last place we'll be forced to meet is in English class. I mean, you do sit right in front of me. Otherwise, I think we can manage to stay out of each other's hair and...avoid...problems."

Their faces were mere inches apart. Her skin tingled all over and her heart beat wildly. Belle watched as Liam's lips parted into a roguish smile. He straightened, creating slightly more distance between them, and said with an air of innocence, "If it helps, I could always sit in front of Lisa, instead."

To his utter delight, Belle's response was instantaneous. Her eyes narrowed and she recoiled a step back. "You'd like that, wouldn't you?"

His eyes shining with pleasure, he added more fuel to her fire and pointed towards her mouth. "And you've still got some of that chocolate dessert around there." He shook his head in mock disapproval.

"Yeah, right," she hissed. She wiped her mouth with the back of her hand and was supremely irked to find chocolate smudged on it. "What in tarnation?" Her mouth dropped. "Again?! This whole time? And you didn't say anything?!" She wanted to clock him. He was so under her skin right now.

He grinned broadly at her idiosyncrasy—something else he relished about her—but his playful taunting soon eased into something else, as he grabbed her hand and pulled her gently towards him. Her feet mechanically obeyed, but she still scowled at him. He held her gaze like an adult waiting for a child to finish throwing a temper tantrum. As she looked back at him this up-close, the anger melted away until the only heat left was more of a need that yearned to be met. She watched his eyes drop to her mouth. "Is it gone?" she whispered. "Did I get it all off?" He shook his head a fraction, unable to tear his eyes away from her parted lips. Desire flashing through her, she looked straight into his eyes and breathed, "Well, aren't you going to be a gentleman and help a lady out?"

It was a challenge he couldn't resist, a challenge he welcomed with all his being. He squeezed her hand, lacing their fingers together, while his free hand brought her face to his and he closed in on her mouth. Tasting her lips lit a spark inside him, a simmering warmth that slowly spread and melted the numbness in his soul from the past year, and when she leaned into him, curling her free hand through his hair and let him deepen the kiss, the spark turned into an inferno that seared every part of his being.

A real burning sensation in his hand like it was on fire started to distract him.

Belle abruptly pulled away and cold air rushed in between them.

"Hey," he protested gruffly. Still in a haze, he reached for her hand again, but she quickly pocketed her hands in her hoodie. The smell of burnt paper and a scalding pain in his hand cleared his head, and turning his palm up, he saw that a burn had ripped through the bandage and a patch of the exposed skin was a bright red, as if he'd just pressed it against a hot stove. He blinked twice, trying to make sense of it.

"Are you hurt?" Belle moved closer again, cringing with guilt.

"Nah, are you?" He looked at her pocketed hand as if he wanted to examine it, but she didn't move it.

"I'm fine," she said a bit too quickly.

He didn't want to lose the moment they'd just had. He cocked his head as he looked at her, with those incredibly long legs that curved out into round hips and then back into a tiny waistline and back out again. He saw that the zipper on her hoodie was halfway down, the result of his absentminded handiwork while their lips were busy. The green bikini top was too flattering on her. And very distracting for him. With his good hand, he beckoned for her to come near. A faint smile appeared on her lips while her eyes narrowed with suspicion. Her feet didn't budge. "I just want to help you with something," he said in peacemaker fashion.

"Yes, because you were so helpful before." Sarcasm lined her voice, but she was smiling now and her eyes shone. Everything inside her was still reeling from that spine-tingling kiss.

"I was. Chocolate's all gone now," he replied innocently, gesturing towards her mouth.

A slight breeze blew into them. Belle shivered and hastily zipped up her jacket, her cheeks reddening at the realization of how the zipper had been moved.

Sighing, Liam stood and lifted her bag out of the motorcycle. "I believe this belongs to you?"

She took it from him, and she noticed he'd checked out her hand and frowned. It was obvious her hand had not been burned like his. "Thanks," she said, quickly concealing her hand beneath the strap of the bag. She grunted under its weight.

A silence descended. Liam grabbed his helmet and held it in both hands, hesitating. He looked off into the distance in the direction of his castle, a hardness coming into his eyes.

Belle watched him. Thinking she knew what he was thinking: that this couldn't happen. It wasn't safe. And as difficult as it was, she had to let him think that. Because it was true. And this was the page they both needed to be on. Despite what their hearts and bodies may be screaming, their lives were more important. She broke the silence. "So, thank you...kindly...for everything today. Truly." She gave him a small smile and began to turn away. But as Liam shifted his gaze to her, she paused as if waiting for his reply. He looked at her, thoughts churning behind those muted green eyes. He still hadn't said anything, and she felt like she needed some parting words or something from him before she could go inside. She added, "And...you've been a, um...a really good friend. So, thanks."

That elicited a raised eyebrow from him, as if he found that statement amusing. His contemplative mood evaporated. "You're welcome." He eyed her bag, which had gradually sunk down to the ground beside her feet. "Come on," he reached forward and swooped her bag up. "I'll walk you to your door. That's what good friends do, right?"

She couldn't help grinning to herself as she followed him up her driveway. "You are just so helpful," she muttered.

When they reached her door, he set her bag on the porch and faced her. "So...'no more than necessary'." He gazed down at her and gently pinched her chin. *Uh-oh*, Belle thought. He had that look in his eye that landed her that first kiss. She could feel her breath catch and before the last of her brain turned to mush, she thought with a pang that their "keep-away" plan was never going to work. As if reading her mind, Liam let go and stepped back. "Listen, um," worry creased his forehead, "I'm gonna be checking in on you. Don't ask me why. It's- it's just necessary."

Belle knew why. But before she could say okay, an electronic buzzing interrupted them. She reached down into her bag and dug out her phone. The screen was lit with several missed calls and texts. "Hey! It's Candy! She says—" But when she looked up, Liam was already halfway down her driveway. "She's feeling better...." She watched as he put on his helmet and mounted his bike. She didn't know what she was hoping for. A wave goodbye? But she didn't get one. Not even a look in her direction as he tore off into the night.

Maybe their keep-away plan would work after all.

25

Down the Rabbit Hole

"He *what?!*" Candy screeched.

"Kissed me," Belle repeated, breaking into a grin. "Well…I actually kind of dared him into it." She cringed with embarrassment now that she thought about it.

She was curled up in her bedroom window nook in her PJs, gazing out at the turrets of the Rawlins castle, while on a three-way phone conversation with Candy and Millie. They first tried to direct Belle into getting a face-to-face chat session going on the laptop, but to no avail, so the girls opted for the "old-fashioned" method.

"Seriously?" Millie sounded incredulous.

"Yes," Belle responded.

"Wow, you are *bad*. And here we thought you were little Ms. Innocent." Millie couldn't keep the admiration out of her voice.

"It was my first kiss," Belle admitted.

"Aaaagh!" the two squealed.

"I do feel better that *you* kissed him, instead of the other way around," Candy said. "Means you're in charge. Go girl!"

Millie sighed. "I need details now to satisfy my vicarious existence."

"Yes, spill them!" Candy said.

Belle's cheeks flamed replaying the kiss in her mind, how tentative it was at first, questioning, and then a new kind of fire had started under her skin, turning her thoughts hazy, her problems blissfully forgotten and the only thing that existed was the feel of his hand tightly interlaced with hers, his other hand squeezing her waist closer to him, and the soft, commanding pressure of his lips. And then she lost control, and if it hadn't been for the bandage, she would've charred his hand to a crisp. It had been too close a call.

"Belle? Hello?"

"Yes?" Belle replied, sounding blank.

"How was it?" Candy pressed.

"Um, it- it was nice," she said.

"You're killing me, Belle," Millie said.

"Okay, okay," she relented. "I don't know, he- he kissed me like he hadn't had a drink of water in a week."

The two girls sighed, satisfied.

Belle grinned, feeling dopey herself. "Now, can we change the subject?" she asked. "Candy, how are you feeling? Are you still in the hospital?"

"They're discharging me tomorrow." Candy added in a sing-song voice, "Guess who came by to visit earlier?"

"Me," Millie said drily.

"Yes, you did and thank you, but you know who I mean." Candy said. "A word that starts with 'M' comes to mind when you look at him...."

"Meathead?" Millie said.

"Girl, you lay off my man, now," Candy chided. "You know I mean 'Muscles.'"

Belle chimed in, "Dmitri!"

"Yes!" Candy gushed. "He brought me a little brown, chocolate-scented teddy bear and said it reminded him of me because—"

"Oh my God, he didn't—" Millie gasped.

"—it smells like my bakery," Candy finished.

"Whoo, okay then," Millie exhaled.

The sound of a door clicking open out in the hallway grabbed Belle's attention. "Emilia?" she called out.

No answer. Only the pitter-patter of feet.

When she first got in the house, she assumed Emilia was asleep in her room, since the door was shut and no light shone from underneath. "Um, guys?" Belle half-whispered. "Do you know anything about this place being possibly haunted?"

There was silence on the other ends.

Candy finally spoke up, "We didn't want you to be scared since you just moved in—"

Millie interrupted, "It's not 'possibly,' but 'definitely.'"

"Millie!" Candy chastised.

"What? The girl deserves to know!" Millie said. "Visitors have reported seeing a fleeting shadow."

Candy sighed as if giving in and added, "Things being knocked over, people tripping from having both their shoelaces tied together—"

Millie cut in, "One guy reported actually getting his underpants pulled up into a wedgie, you know, old-school bully vs. nerd-style."

"Come to think of it," Candy said. "It seems like it only picks on guys."

"Casper, the mischievous, misandrist ghost. Why do you think no one visits that museum?" Millie asked pointedly.

Belle tried swallowing against the lump of fear growing in her throat. "I-I have noticed what I think is a shadow moving out of the corner of my eye sometimes, but I thought it was just my over-active imagination." Her ears suddenly pricked up. "Shhh!" she commanded the girls.

They held their breaths. The sound of humming, loud and clear, could be heard.

"I hear it," Candy whispered.

"Me too," Millie said.

Belle breathed a gigantic sigh of relief. It was the same tune she'd heard yesterday morning. "It's Emilia. I better go say 'hi.'"

"Millie, you stay on the phone with me," Candy ordered. "I can't sleep after this. Tell me about that cartoon you like to watch so I can fall asleep."

"It's anime," Millie said defensively. "And it's rated higher than your *Teen Hearts in Paradise* show."

"I'll talk to you girls tomorrow." Belle disconnected as an argument broke out between Millie and Candy. She shivered against the frosty A/C and tightened the fleece throw around her shoulders as she ventured out into the hall. Emilia's door was wide open and the lights were on. Grateful for some family time, Belle hurried forward to greet her. "Hey, Emilia? I wanted to tell you about my day at—" She froze just outside her room. She didn't see Emilia. She stuck her head in, not wanting to break the stern "no trespassing" rule, but a quick check around the room and...still no Emilia.

Those familiar icy fingers of foreboding started trailing down the back of her neck making the hairs stand on end. She looked around the whole house and even checked downstairs. Emilia was nowhere to be found. The only logical explanation was that Emilia left the house for a walk or something. But wasn't she supposed to be staying out of the public eye?

Belle was used to being alone for long periods of time. Papa would sometimes go away for days at a time, and she was okay with it. She knew what it was like to be alone. But standing here now in front of Emilia's open bedroom door, she *knew* she wasn't alone. She couldn't put her finger on it, but she felt like she had been drawn out of her room to this very spot. Just as she had been led to that open book in the hallway to that very story about her ancestors. And now, here was this open door.

It was an invitation.

"Emilia?" she called out as she stepped into the bedroom, certain she was going to be yelled at any second now for trespassing. Surveying the velvety, plush Victorian furniture in the room, four-post bed, and the massive fireplace that could fit a sofa, made her feel like she'd time-warped into a bygone era. She noticed that the mantle of the fireplace was lined with silver frames all laying face-down, and the walls of the room had a few squares of a darker shade of paint where hanging frames would have been—as if they had all been recently removed.

After taking one last glance around the room for Emilia, she moved to the fireplace and lifted the first frame back onto its leg. It was a color photo of a much younger-looking, very handsome Ernesto, smiling with his arm around who she assumed was Aunt Emily, since she was an exact replica of Emilia, but with a '50s hairdo and poufy poodle-skirt outfit. Her bright red lips were spread into a huge happy smile and her arms rested around a young boy leaning against her front, facing the camera, with a mischievous grin on his face, and his ruddy brown hair sticking out everywhere. They stood in front of a classic yellow car, a few luggages beside them, as if they were about to embark on a family trip.

"That's Peter."

Belle jumped as she swiveled around, gripping the picture frame in her hand. Emilia stood by the window gazing in her direction. The same white nightgown, black shawl, and vacant expression she wore when Belle first met her. *How did she make it all the way to the window without my noticing? And where was she this whole time?* Belle wondered, her heart beating wildly at the sudden fright.

Emilia never took her eyes off the frame as she approached and took it gently from Belle's hand. Her eyes watered and she smiled sadly as she peered at it. Belle stepped closer and pointed at the woman in the photo. "Is that Aunt Emily? Your mom?" She looked at Belle and only smiled before returning her focus to the photo, caressing the image of the boy. "Is that Peter?" Belle asked softly. When she gave a small nod, Belle swallowed the lump in her throat. This must have been Emilia's older brother. "What happened to him?" Belle whispered.

Emilia placed the frame back on the mantle, up-right. "They took him." A solitary tear trailed off her face as she continued to gaze at it.

Belle placed a hand on her thin arm. "I'm so sorry...."

"First, they came for James, Abby's son. And then they came for Peter. Your first-born in exchange for powers and eternal youth."

Belle knew she shouldn't ask, that Emilia must be entering some sort of neurotic episode that she shouldn't encourage, but she pressed on. "*Who* took them?"

Emilia looked at her. Her round, vacant eyes luminous. "The Neverfairies."

Belle's breath stalled. The story she'd read in the Elmridge history book also mentioned fairies. *Fairies. This, this was just too ludicrous,* she thought. *It belonged in fairy tales.* But shooting electricity from her hands was also a break from reality, so given what her new state of normal was.... Could what Emilia be saying be possible? She needed to know more.

"Do you know anything else about my mother? Did I really have a brother James?" *Was he dead?* Belle wanted to add.

Emilia sighed raggedly as she continued to look at the picture. "I can't, I can't explain anymore. I get lost."

Belle stepped in front of Emilia to force her to focus on her and not the picture.

As if something clicked into place in her mind, Emilia gripped Belle's shoulders and looked wildly into her eyes. "I've left you clues. The book in the hallway—you must read it. Only then, will you be ready for the final piece and be able to put the puzzle back together. I wasn't going to tell you, but she's coming. I can feel it. You have to be ready. You are the only one who can stop her. Others have tried—and died. It's difficult enough keeping Ernie safe...."

Belle's growing shock exploded exponentially. Emilia, the protector? She pried Emilia's hands away, her fingers had been digging painfully into her arms.

Emilia took a deep breath before continuing, bringing the hysteria down a notch. "And then your father and I tried to keep you safe. But I feel as if...she's finally found us." Emilia blinked and the urgency in her eyes dissolved into an emptiness, and Belle could see that she was going vacuous again. She couldn't lose her now.

Belle grabbed her shoulders and shook her. "Who's found us? Who needs to be stopped? My mother?"

Blinking rapidly, Emilia focused on Belle again. "Abby? No. It's Violet. Violet Wickeby."

Belle gasped. Her dreams. So again, it was all true. All real.

Emilia considered her reaction. "You've seen her in your dreams, haven't you?" She nodded to herself and moved to a small nightstand by the bed. "Then, you will need this now." She unlocked a drawer in it and pulled out a worn-out leather book. "This is the final piece. Not even Ernie has seen this." She placed it in Belle's hands who opened it to random pages. All handwritten diary entries.

Emilia answered what Belle was wondering, "Your mother's." Turning away, she added, "I picked up where she left off."

"You?" Belle asked, stupefied. "Why, you?"

Emilia ignored the question. "You were going to inherit this eventually. But I'm- I'm losing myself faster than I can hold on. This will explain everything. I-I wish I could tell you myself, but I can't do it. It would kill me." She moved to the fireplace and gently touched the picture of Peter. "I've lived so long." Her voice broke. "All these centuries...." Emilia began flipping up each picture frame, and with each one, the floor felt like it was shattering and threatening to give way beneath Belle's feet.

Belle stumbled and gripped the back of an armchair. Each picture showed Emilia with the woman from her dreams in different time periods. The oldest one was in brown hues and they were dressed like Quakers, both girls sitting and looking stoically into the camera. The latest one was of the two girls in modern streetwear and make-up; long, flowing hair, smiling like models and taking a selfie in front of the Statue of Liberty.

Ageless. Her mother and....

"Aunt Emily?" Belle croaked, tears stinging her eyes.

But Emily was lost on memory lane. She slowly walked back to the beginning of the line of pictures, her finger trailing along the mantel until she stopped again in front of the picture of her with Ernesto and Peter. "I thought sisterly love could conquer all, even more than romantic love, but a mother's love...." She gripped the mantel with both hands and let out a wail of such agony that Belle's own heart broke and she rushed forward to support Emily, who had sunk to her knees, her shoulders shaking in between sobs.

"I just, I just want my boy back," Emily wept, as Belle helped her onto her feet. "More than anything in my entire existence. I would give up an immortality of lifetimes just to share *one* with my Peter." She hid her face behind her hands. "Those twelve years with him were a mere 12 minutes to me...." Emily's sleeves fell back to her elbows, revealing the red scars that branched down her forearms. Like the scars of a lightning strike victim. Violet had said in her last dream that her mother had tried to kill her as a baby and that her aunt had gotten in the way. *Struck with lightning*, Violet had said.

Belle knew this wasn't the moment to ask, but the twins' arrival in town meant Violet was here too, and Emily's warning confirmed that this was life or death, so two big questions remained. "Emily," she ventured delicately. "How can Violet Wickeby and my mother Abigail be one and the same?"

Emily looked up with such intensity that Belle took a step back. "October 31st, 2004."

"Wh-what do you mean?" Belle asked, confused.

Emily repeated it. "October 31st, 2004. All Hallows Eve." Her eyes were losing their lucidity again.

"And the gemstones," Belle said quickly. "Violet said she's using certain gemstones to make her unstoppable and, um, she needs pixie dust?"

"I-I can't, dear," Emily said backing up. "But she must not be allowed to complete her plan, especially with another Halloween coming up soon...."

Belle reached forward and gripped her shoulders. "How am I supposed to stop her? How?!"

Emily looked at her, all clarity in her eyes just about gone, and touched an index finger to Belle's forehead. "Happy thoughts."

Belle's heart plummeted. She opened her mouth to respond, "What? How can—?"

"Your Aunt Emily is tired, dear," she cut her off in a sleepy little girl's voice.

Belle could only watch feeling helpless as Emily sidled into bed. She yawned and stretched her arms outward before patting the spot next to her and looking towards the open bedroom door, "Come along, Peter, time for bed." Belle gasped and covered her mouth in terror when a shadow flitted into the room and disappeared under the blanket. "It's quite alright," Emily said soothingly to Belle. "It's only his shadow." She pointed towards the door. "Be a lamb. Do turn off the lights and shut the door on your way out."

Belle clutched the diary to her chest and backtracked out the door, her feet weighing like cement. Just as she switched off the light and grabbed the doorknob, she heard Emily whisper into the darkness, "Father will be home soon, isn't that right, Peter?"

26

The Possession of Abigail Prynn

Belle did not sleep that night. She sat on her bed with all the lights on in her room, even the TV, its white noise drowning out any distracting things that might go bump in the night like Peter's shadow. Her door securely locked and herself wrapped in a thick blanket, she felt shielded enough from the new frightening realities to continue digging for more through her mother's diary—anything to help her piece together what she already knew with all the revelations Emily had unleashed upon her an hour ago, trying to form one clear picture, even if it did end up looking like a Dali.

The first entry she'd flipped through the diary for was October 31, 2004, but she found that her mother's short, quick handwriting ended the day before that, and Emily's long, script writing picked up on the next page, 5 years later. Her heart weighed like lead to think of the personal cataclysm that could have caused the extended absence and abrupt change in authors.

October 30, 2004

Today was tiresome, to say the least. My body feels as ragged and abused as on the morning after we survived the Titanic. And today was only because Lisselle is teething and <u>nothing</u> will sooth her. Enzo and I have tried everything, but the poor dear can only cry herself to sleep. Nothing pains me so much as to have my daughter in pain and my not being able to help her. How torturous upon one's soul! Her pain is my pain magnified by a million!

The only pain that overshadows all for me, though, has been the loss of James. Thirty-three years with my son. The most precious years of my life...before he was ripped from me. But I've numbed that part of my soul so that I can continue on functioning (I won't say 'living.').

I dare not think on it further.

Motherhood has proven to be the most challenging role I have ever played and, yet, the most gratifying (as I've had to remind myself often today, when Lissi's constant wailing threatened to shatter my sanity).

In fact, tomorrow night, Em and I are taking a break from our domestic duties. Enzo and Ernie think we're going to the cinema, but it's really a different sort of theater we're visiting, one our men would never approve of: a mass séance hosted by the Divine Zoraya! Em is quite hesitant, but of course she will please me and go. It's amusing to watch how easily the audience is fooled by these charlatans. Em and I have always been on the lookout for anyone claiming to be magical of some sort. And every single one, after some discreet testing on our part, have proven to be false. Seems Em and I really are alone in our specific set of peculiarities. At least on <u>this</u> planet.

Lissi's crying again. She's awake from her nap.

Until next time, my dear William.

Belle's head was spinning. She really had a brother. And her mother *did* love her. So why would her own mother try to kill her? And was this the same William that her mother and Violet Wickeby fought over?

She continued reading.

March 13, 2009

It has been 5 years since Abby last wrote. In fact, 5 years since Abby hasn't been Abby. I did not want to keep a diary. I warned Abby against leaving any evidence of us, but she said it would be "criminal" not to document our extraordinary lives. Besides, she wanted the truth recorded lest anyone should say differently.

In my sister's honor, I, Emily Prynn, take up this pen. I will begin by saying that the child is safe with her father. And a secret she shall remain for her own safety.

I have left France and taken up residence again in my childhood home of Elmridge. My darling Ernie refuses to leave my side. While Abby had been so candid with Enzo about the details of our history, I refuse to endanger Ernie with that much knowledge. He understands only that my sister and I do not age.

I've decided to make myself useful in this town, where no one will grow suspicious of me until in about 15 years and then I will have to recluse myself. It's either that or move and start fresh again. Although "fresh" has become stale with habit by now. The Darling family lives in my home now, the home where I had Peter.... So, I've taken up residence in the abandoned Historical Society and intend to bring new life into it as a museum, although some townsfolk have warned me its haunted. They may be right. But that's another mystery for another entry.

I've put off writing about it long enough. I've never shared this before. Ernie believes I was struck by lightning, but it isn't the whole truth. Enzo knows. He was there when it happened.

I will tell <u>you</u>, Lisselle. My sister chose to continue "speaking" to her dead "first love" in this diary, but you, my niece, my blood, Lisselle, will be my audience. You will know everything. As rightly you should. Enzo has already informed me that you do not dream. Consider it a blessing. God help you should your mind connect with Abby's now, for it is not Abby's, but a demon's you'll find.

You are special. As you will come to find out soon enough.

But I digress. Let me tell you about the night that your mother became the Lightning Witch.

The details of what followed in the entry played out in Belle's head like a movie:

"You are ever the flirt," Emily chided her sister.

"What?" Abigail said innocently, her big brown eyes going wide. "I only smiled at him." She flipped her long, black hair over her shoulder and gave their tickets to the guy behind the counter.

"His wife doesn't think so," Emily pointed out.

A fuming lady nearby elbowed her husband in the ribs, causing him to cry out, "Ow! What's with you?"

"His wife isn't wearing this dress," Abigail replied, winking.

Emily rolled her eyes. "You're incorrigible."

Abigail linked her arm through Emily's as they turned away from the counter and passed through the double doors.

"Oh, come now, Em. Let me have my fun," Abigail began. "It's harmless. I'll be back to married, maternal Abby when we return home tonight. This sister-date is our mini-vacation, you know." She pecked Emily on the cheek, who smiled back as if won over.

As a sign she was ready to enjoy herself, Emily replied in a Yoda-voice, "Right, you are."

Abigail groaned. "I still don't get what you see in that sci-fi non-sense."

They sidled down the aisle into their seats and Emily grabbed her sister's hand with an earnestness that surprised Abigail. "Because," Emily began, "it's a future I can look forward to. If Peter and James *have* been taken to another world as we have come to understand, then you and I know that we can eventually commandeer a spaceship and find them."

Abigail waited for the "just kidding" part, but when it didn't come, she frowned with worry. "Em, dear, that was a touched thing to say." She looked forward as Emily's eyes narrowed. "Besides," Abigail added, "our children are not immortal. They'll be long dead by the time your *Star Trek* becomes a reality."

"But, I have theories, Abby, and I think that in this other place, they live just like us and—"

"Hush!" Abigail hissed. "How *dare* you? I don't want to hear another word about it. Ever. Do you understand?"

Emily's eyes brimmed with angry tears as she yielded to her older sister's demand, something that never changed. She faced forward in a huff. After a minute of stony silence, she muttered, "And it's *Star Wars*, not *Star Trek*."

An expectant hush came over the audience as the dark curtains pulled back, revealing a tiny, round elderly woman standing beside a solitary two-seater table with only a small crystal ball sitting on it. Momentarily forgetting her pledge not to speak to her sister for the rest of the night, Emily whispered, "No mirrors and smoke so far."

"Paid actors in the audience. Guaranteed."

A deep voice reverberated throughout the room, introducing the Divine Zoraya. The woman on stage curtsied as everyone applauded. She looked more like a friendly school librarian with the high bun, long khaki skirt, button-down blouse, and cardigan than a mystical seer.

"Welcome," she announced, in a kind, grandmotherly voice. "I know that many of you are here...simply because you are bored." A small titter of laughter broke out. "And you expect to be entertained. And, well, that is fine. Most, if not all, of you doubt my gift. And that is okay too. It is to be expected."

Abigail grumbled, "She talks too much."

"But are you really here because you're bored? Or is it really because you are in pain? And even though you doubt from what you've heard about me, is a small part of you, in actuality, hoping that I can help you? Well then, let me tell you. The answer is yes, I can help you. That is what I use my gift for: to help ease your pain by reconnecting you with your lost loved ones. Even if it is only for a moment. That can bring you relief for...."

At this point, Abby whispered angrily to Emily, "I'm going to expose her. She's another charlatan profiting off people's grief."

"Hear, hear," Emily responded.

"Let's begin, shall we." Zoraya sat at the table and placed her hands on the crystal ball.

Abigail snorted derisively.

"I shall hone my gift to seek out the individual suffering the most and then call you to the stage." Zoraya began humming an eerie tune and then chanted some words in another language, one the sisters didn't recognize, which was odd since they each knew over 20 languages. "I sense someone with more pain than anyone has ever suffered...in one lifetime. And even...more?" Zoraya muttered, as if responding to herself, "That's impossible." She raised her voice to speak to the audience again, "There are two of you here. Sisters." Abigail and Emily looked at each other. "And the pain will go on... forever," Zoraya said, surprise lining her own voice.

The audience murmured.

Emily whispered, "I never spoke with her. Did you?"

"Of course, not," Abigail whispered back.

Emily gasped with alarm. "Do you think she somehow got ahold of your diary?"

"Don't be ridiculous." Although Abigail did not sound so sure of herself.

Zoraya sat up straight and squeezed her eyes shut as if that would help her concentrate better. "Sisters, do these names seem familiar: William, James, Peter?"

The sisters blanched and gripped hands.

"How does she know?" Emily squeaked.

"How do I know?" Zoraya repeated. What she said next made a chill run down their spines, "Because I was there."

While Emily shrieked, Abigail felt emboldened and concluded that she must be what they've been searching for all this time: a magical sort like themselves. She leaned in close to Emily and said, "I'm going to test her now." Standing up, she called out to Zoraya, "You've perfectly described me. Shall I join you on stage now?"

With eyes wide with panic, Emily grabbed her hand and held her back. "What are you doing?!"

"Maybe she knows something we don't." And then Abigail pulled her hand away and strode on to the stage. The audience applauded as Abigail took her seat across from Zoraya and the microphone hanging above the crystal ball was lowered further. Abigail began right away. "How were you there?"

Zoraya rubbed her hands together as if reveling in a secret delight. "So much power," she rasped in a low voice that was barely picked up on the mike.

Emily was getting a terrible feeling about this.

Abigail repeated her question.

"I have another name for you," Zoraya replied, her mouth spreading into a haunting smile. "Violet. Violet Wickeby. Know her?"

The blood drained from Abigail's face, and after clearing her throat a few times, said, "Yes. I know *of* her. She lived a long time ago."

"And died a long time ago," Zoraya added meaningfully. "You asked me how I was there." Abigail nodded. "That's because Violet was there."

"I don't, I don't understand," Abigail stammered.

"She stood on the edge of the cliff that night. Thinking how you had driven her to that point by stealing William from her. You, a convicted witch, a penniless nobody. She and William had been set from birth to be married, but you twisted his mind somehow and he ended up running off with you." Her voice was taking on a manic quality and her eyes gleamed with a hatred that frightened Abigail. "I don't know how you and your sister escaped that night, but Violet escaped too. Those rocks below freed her, and she made a promise that she would find you and make you and William and their whole family line pay for the misery you caused her." She punctuated the end of her sentence by landing her fists on the table causing Abigail to jump and Emily to cry out, "Abby, get away from her!"

The audience applauded as if on cue, clearly thinking it was staged. This seemed to bring Zoraya back into the present. "Am I right?" she asked politely.

Abigail was reeling. "H-how—?"

Zoraya looked at her, and in the syrupy, sweet voice that belonged distinctly to Violet Wickeby, said, "Why, hello Abigail Prynn."

Abigail jumped up and knocked her chair backwards while Emily rushed out into the aisle towards the stage, but was caught and held back by an usher.

Zoraya stood and gestured for Abigail to take her seat as a stagehand rushed out and righted the chair for her. In her regular grandmotherly voice, she said, "I do apologize. This is a common reaction at each show. I promise you, we're almost done." She turned to the audience and asked, "Did I not say I can reconnect you with loved ones who have passed on?" They applauded a roaring approval, while the usher directed Emily back to her seat and Abigail reclaimed hers.

Abigail took a deep breath. "What about James?"

"You live an extraordinary life," Zoraya remarked offhandedly. And then she whispered so only Abigail could hear, "Long and powerful." Her smile was snakelike. Abigail swallowed nervously, wishing she was back home where her secret was safe and not under a spotlight, but the old woman hooked her in again with her next move. Zoraya raised her voice so all could hear, "Abigail, would you like to reconnect with James?"

"Yes," was her immediate response.

"Well, then." Zoraya whispered so only Abigail could hear, "If you want your secret to be safe, I will need to transfer my thoughts directly to you."

"You can do that?"

"Yes." Zoraya leaned in closer, a gleam in her eye and whispered, "Do I have your permission to transfer directly into you?"

Someone in the audience complained aloud, "Hey! We can't hear!"

Abigail, with some hesitation, responded, "Yes."

"You need to say all the words," a note of impatience lined Zoraya's voice. "Repeat after me: I give you permission to transfer into me."

"Abby, what's going on?" she heard Emily call out from the audience. "You've been up there long enough! Let's go home!"

Zoraya sunk in her final hook. "James is alive. I can tell you where he is."

The effect was immediate. Abigail replied, loud and clear, "I give you permission to transfer into me."

The audience's complaints turned into screams as Zoraya opened her mouth unnaturally wide and a column of black smoke streamed out and shot straight into Abigail. Zoraya slumped forward, her forehead banging loudly against the table, and did not move. Abigail stood and stretched her arms wide, an ecstatic grin on her face. "This body will do nicely." She looked at her hands. "This is perfect.... With this power, I can have my revenge!"

The audience began quieting and most were resuming their seats, thinking this was all part of a very convincing act. But Emily knew better. She fought hard against the usher, but his linebacker hug would let her nowhere near the stage. "Abby! Abby!" she called out frantically.

"And what *is* this power?" Abigail wondered aloud. She pointed a hand at the massive chandelier hanging above the audience.

"Abby, noooo!" Emily cried out. She had vowed she would never use her own power in public, but she had no choice. She disappeared from her spot, leaving the usher hugging air, and reappeared next to Abigail on stage, knocking her hand upward.

But it was too late. A bolt of lightning had already shot out of Abigail's hand and severed the chandelier's chain, sending it crashing down onto the audience's heads.

Screams filled the air. A look of shock and then utter delight seized Abigail. She laughed in hysterical triumph as she gazed at the electrical sparks dancing along her hands. And then she turned to the horror-stricken Emily next to her. "And you?" she asked, incredulous. "Teleportation?" And then she added in an ominous tone, "I think I shall come for *you* one day."

Emily backpedaled a few steps.

A stagehand tried to wake Zoraya, but she slid to the floor with a *thud*. "She's dead!" he squeaked.

The scene before them was a madhouse of panic and terror. An usher rushed at Abigail, but she shot a bolt at him that left a hole in the center of his chest.

"No!" Emily cried out, as she caught the young man sliding to the floor.

Abigail giggled with glee. "This is just fantastic!" And then she looked dead straight into Emily's horrified eyes. "And now my revenge can begin." But before the bolt left her hand, Emily had already disappeared.

I reappeared back at the house. Ernie was not there, so my concern was for you and Enzo. Quickly, we packed our most valuable things. I thought we had enough time for at least that, thinking that Violet did not know where we lived. But I soon found out that she now knew everything Abby knew.

As soon as we were out the door, you, all bundled up in your father's arms as he headed down the path towards the car, and me, behind, locking up, Violet had already made it to the house in a stolen car. She held out her hand as if to strike the both of you with lightning, but for some reason she couldn't, and her hand trembled violently. I do believe that Abby was still fighting inside. But I couldn't take that chance. I reappeared in front of her, blocking you from her path and I knocked her down.

She let out an inhuman roar and let her hand fly toward me. I blacked out in a blinding flash of white.

Later, after a few months of coma, Ernie was by my side and told me I had been struck by lightning and was lucky to be alive. In a letter from Enzo, I learned the truth: Violet had blacked out as well, as if Abby had shut her down from the inside. When she came to, it was Abby. She told Enzo to take their daughter and flee, hide, live somewhere else, far away and keep themselves safe. That she couldn't keep Violet from taking over. She didn't have the strength to, especially believing she had killed her own sister. After Enzo saw me to safety, Abby had already disappeared when he returned to the house. All that was left was you. You, to live for.

Now you know the truth. Violet tried to kill you, and your mother saved you.

27

Detective Belle

Belle waited for the first sign of sunlight in the sky. She stood before her window, staring in the direction of Rawlins Castle, her next stop for answers. She read the entire diary last night and even though her eyes ached something fearsome, the movie marathon in her head of the Prynn sisters' farfetched lives had made sleep impossible.

Most of the puzzle pieces had finally fallen into place, except for one: how to stop Violet Wickeby and save her mother. Emily's wild plea played in her mind, *You must stop her from finishing her plan!* Okay, but how? And it had to be done within a month since Halloween was right around the corner. Belle knew from her last dream that Violet's scheme involved four rare gems, a blade, and fairy dust. Violet only had two gems as far as she could tell, so maybe if she could figure out which other two gems she needed and then get to them before she did?

Belle had no idea how to make that happen.

And then there was the issue with her mother being held hostage. How does she separate Violet from Abigail? This was dipping into the realm of the supernatural now, not just the fantastical. She was thinking she'd need a priest's help. But before she'd go that route, she wanted to exhaust her natural resources. And right now, those were books. She'd scanned through all the historical books and documents downstairs, searching for anything that would help her stop Violet, but other than finally feeling qualified enough to curate the museum, she'd come up with zilch. She had to get to Liam's private collection. Maybe his ancestor-cousin, who'd served as a confidante to Violet at one point, had written down something useful.

Which was why she now stood like a sentinel watching the sky for her signal. She dressed comfortably: high-top sneakers; something called "yoga pants" that the tag promised would *feel so comfortable, you'll forget you're wearing pants*; a baseball tee with purple quarter-sleeves and the school's peacock mascot on the front, it's feathers outlined in rhinestones; and her trusty school hoodie. She'd braided her mane back away from her face.

As she was envisioning how she'd ask Liam for his books without seeming like an eager beaver who didn't know how to stay away, the sound of the upstairs landing door opening and closing grabbed her attention. Leaving her bedroom and poking her head through the hallway's arched entrance, she locked eyes with Ernesto as he dropped some files and a briefcase onto the kitchen table.

"Hey, what are you doing up so early?" He glanced over at the clock on the oven. "It's 5:45 in the morning."

Dagnabbit, she thought. She couldn't slip out now without an explanation. When he invited her to take a chair at the table, she plodded toward him and chewed her lip as she paused at the chair. He looked at her questioningly upon noticing she was already fully dressed for the day, with a messenger bag slung across her shoulder as if she was going somewhere. Just as an excuse was about to leave her mouth, she noticed the two files on the table: one was labeled *Grace Darling* and the other *Lena Steifshwester*. "You're investigating the school principal?"

Ernesto tugged the file out into view. "Yes. Can you believe it?" He pulled up a chair and sat. "All this video surveillance was emailed to me of her allegedly poisoning her—but, ah," he cleared his throat, "I'm not at liberty to discuss these details, of course."

"Of course," Belle repeated, but she stood rooted to her spot waiting for more information.

He entered a combination, clicked his briefcase open and pulled out a large laptop. He leaned back in his chair and sighed raggedly, as if about to face another round in the ring. "There's so much surveillance to go through. Normally, one of the techies working in *Evidence* would do this, but since she's such a high-profile member of this community...." He pointed at himself to indicate he got stuck with the load.

When he opened Steifshwester's file, Belle caught a glimpse of a large red stamped word, "Closed," outside Grace's file. "You found Grace?" she almost shouted.

"Oh, yes. Same story as last. Took a trek through the forest chasing butterflies. Got lost." He threw the file back in his briefcase a little too forcefully. "Her parents ought to put a tracker on that girl," he muttered. "Save us the manhunts."

Belle exhaled a giant sigh of relief. "That's great!"

"Only odd thing was she purportedly escaped through the window with a boy. Actually, 'flew out together,' according to the sole witness."

Her eyes widened. "Who was the witness?"

"Her 3-year-old brother."

"Oh."

"So, case closed. That's that." He tapped his briefcase for emphasis. "It's her parents' problem now."

She felt uneasy. There had to be a connection between Grace's Peter and Emily's Peter. A plan formed in her mind and she decided to just go with it. "Um, could you give me her address? I'm actually her tutor, so I could swing by and help her catch up with what she missed in school."

"That's not a bad idea." He peeked at her file again and copied the address onto his legal pad. He ripped the page off and handed it to her. "Maybe you could talk some sense into her while you're at it."

"Also," she continued, swallowing nervously, "I'm working on a family history project with a partner for Dr. Helsing's class."

"Hmm." His brows knitted together. "Not too keen on digging up our private family matters and publishing them."

"It's just for a school project—" she began before Ernesto cut her off.

"Who's the partner?"

Yeah, this wasn't going to go over well. "Liam Rawlins," she replied, bracing herself.

The effect was instantaneous. He threw his pen down and stood to his feet. "Absolutely not. I forbid it. I'm talking to that teacher right now—"

Something snapped in Belle. "Oh, excuse me, *Dad*."

Ernesto flinched.

She continued, her hands trembling with heat, "*What* is so terrible about Liam?! He's innocent and, yet, he's treated like a pariah in this town!"

Ernesto's eyes bulged. "Innocent?" he repeated in a low, edgy tone. "Is that what he's been telling you?"

Belle crossed her arms across her chest in defiance.

He inhaled a deep, ragged breath through his nostrils. He sat down again and gestured for Belle to do the same. "I think you better sit down for this one." He propped his elbows on the table, tenting his hands beneath his chin.

"I'll stand," she replied curtly. And then she added more softly, "I have to go soon anyways." She was not liking being at odds with her uncle. It reminded her too much of her argument with Papa. Right before he died.

"What I am going to tell you, no other civilian, besides your aunt, knows. But I am going to tell you because we, your aunt and I, care about you, and also," he frowned darkly, "because I see that you've taken a certain interest in Mr. Rawlins," his frown turned into a scowl, "and it is clear to me that he has also noticed you."

She was frozen in time, waiting for the bomb to drop.

"There were two crime scenes that night: one in the West Wing and one in the Rawlins' bedroom bathroom. Liam says a female intruder encountered him and his parents in the West Wing and demanded a certain bracelet of his mother's or she would kill Liam. The mother obliged, and here, Liam claims," his tone grew increasingly mocking as he continued, "the perpetrator called down lightning from the sky and struck his parents dead and he thought it had also killed him, but instead the force of the blast had knocked him out."

This only strengthened her belief in Liam's version. This crime had Violet's signature all over it. But, still, Belle had to know. "What was the other crime scene?"

He responded automatically, "Mr. and Mrs. Black dead in their bathtub. A smartphone with charger attached to the wall had been thrown in. The bodies bear the electrocution marks." He leaned back and crossed his arms as if that was open-and-shut enough.

But it wasn't to Belle. "How does Liam figure into that?"

"Glad you asked. He was found unconscious on the floor next to the bathtub, OD'd on pills. The only fingerprints on the murder weapon, the cellphone, were his."

Belle was aghast. Her eyes brimmed with angry tears and her breath caught in her throat. She hadn't been appalled by what Ernesto thought was Liam's murder-suicide in the bathroom, it was the evil monstrosity of what Violet was capable of, the nefarious lengths she took to stage that scene. It made her objective to stop her more urgent than ever. She had to get to Liam's family diary and hopefully find some answers.

Ernesto continued, more gently, "Now, do you understand why Liam is not welcomed in this house? The only reason he is walking around a free man and not sitting on Death Row is because of your aunt." He banged his fist on the table as his agitation rose, "She swore on our son's life that Liam was telling the truth and that if the truth was exposed—" His eyes grew round and his mouth fell open by his own admission.

"'Our son's life'?" Belle repeated.

He sighed deeply and passed his hand over his face, as if incredibly burdened by another dilemma. She spoke up before he could try to explain. "I know," she said simply. "It's okay. Aunt Emily a.k.a. Emilia told me last night." She exhaled with astonishment, as if believing it for the first time and said, "She's hundreds of years old."

He shook his head, amazed. Leaning back in his chair, he hung his arms at his sides, as if a thousand pounds had been taken off his chest. "You know," he repeated.

"Yes," she exhaled, gripping the back of the chair. The weight of the revelation bowling her over again.

Ernesto leaned forward suddenly as if the world's fate depended on it. "I hope you understand why we had to lie to you. If anyone was to find out about Emily's secret, she would be taken away from us and turned into a science experiment. I know you don't want that, do you?" He looked at her pleadingly.

"You can trust me." She placed her hand over her heart. "Fort Knox."

He sat back again. After a pause, he added, "And I hope I can also trust you to stay away from Liam for obvious reasons."

She pinned him with her eyes. "If I can believe that Emily's immortal, I can believe in Liam's Lightning Witch."

He barely contained an indignant humph.

Belle turned to go, but then remembered Grace again. "Um, so for my history project, I need pictures. I already had a talk with Emily in her room"—she swallowed nervously for what she was about to do—"and Emily said it was okay if I borrow the picture from her mantel of you, her, and Peter." She looked down at her shoes, watching them squirm against each other. She felt terrible about lying, but there was something extremely important she needed the photo for.

It was a long moment before Ernesto responded. "It's been awhile since I hear anyone talk of Peter as my son...." He was absentmindedly rubbing the table with his hand. Perhaps remembering a time when he ruffled his son's hair. "It feels good." He cleared his throat. "But we don't need to disturb Emily." He pulled his wallet out and withdrew a small, cracked photo and handed it to Belle.

It was a wallet-sized photo of the same one on the mantel.

"Thank you," she said softly. "I'll make sure you get it back."

"Keep it." He sighed deeply and before she could object, he said, "Be nice for you to have a photo of your cousin."

She pocketed the photo, nodding and smiling gratefully.

"You're going to visit the Darling house now, right?" he asked suddenly.

"Yes."

He drummed the table with his fingers. "You know, we used to live there. Emily and I. It's where Peter was born. Where he grew up, until...."

She held her breath, waiting.

"Until one day he went outside to play. Took his favorite action figure, Captain Bang-A-Rang. I could hear him playing outside. And then I remember realizing that, after a while, it had been too quiet. We looked for him everywhere...." He exhaled roughly, and then his voice wavered as he spoke, "Disappeared without a trace."

Belle laid a hand on his shoulder. She had been drawing close to him as he spoke.

"We built the walls around the town that year. Recruited our own private army. But...it didn't bring Peter back. Instead, the rich and famous flocked here." He shook his head. "Makes me nervous when that Darling girl goes missing. She being from the very same house and all."

"Thank you kindly...for telling me. I'll go and try to talk some sense into her now."

He nodded and squeezed her hand on his shoulder.

She left him, sunken in his chair, staring shiny-eyed at a spot on the table. His mind replaying his last moments with his son.

28

And the Truth Shall Make You Faint

Rawlins Castle felt deserted. She'd been buzzed in through the back gate, but she saw no one in the garden, not even the gardener, and even the birds seemed quiet, as if hiding from the storm they sensed followed her. She dragged her feet through the rose garden and collapsed onto the bench at the foot of the wisteria tree. "Thanks, Grandmere. I needed this." She leaned back against the tree and took slow, deep breaths. With the walk to Grace's house and then the castle, her lungs burned and she could no longer feel her legs.

The reception at Grace's house hadn't been too welcoming. She'd been met by a haggard-faced Mrs. Darling, dark circles under her eyes, but dressed as if the First Lady-look was her lounge wear. String of pearls and all.

May I help you?" Mrs. Darling asked, frowning and holding the door open enough to only step halfway outside.

"Hi, I'm Belle, Grace's tutor at school. I, um, brought her homework. May I see her?"

"You may not. She's grounded and not allowed any visitors. But I thank you to leave the work with me."

Mrs. Darling's response threw a monkey wrench into Belle's plan and left her scrambling to think on her feet. "Oh, oh, well, um—" She began digging through her bag to buy time. An empty composition notebook gave her an idea. Using the notebook as a cover, she discreetly wrote a message on the back of Ernesto's photo: 'Is this Peter?' And then added her address as the Historical Society, plus her phone number. She slid the photo into the pocket of the notebook and, on the first blank page, wrote a made-up math assignment. She closed the notebook and handed it to Mrs. Darling with as charming a smile as she could muster. "The work's in here."

Mrs. Darling only nodded curtly and retreated back inside, the door shutting loudly with an abrupt finality.

Belle hoped with all her might that Grace got the message, and then maybe, just maybe, she'll be a step closer to solving the flying, girl-kidnapping, house-shadow Peter-mystery. If they were even the same person. Or even existent, at all.

Now, though, she was focused on stopping a Lightning Witch and freeing her mother somehow. And for that, she needed information.

No one met her as she left Grandmere's lap and let herself in to the castle, navigating herself toward the library. Passing through its corridors, she forced herself to focus on her mission—the eerie quiet of the dark castle had been tempting her to stray into one of her Gothic reveries.

She paused before entering the library, and facing away from the grand doors, she called out one last time, "Jacques? Liam? Anybody?"

No response.

She was convinced no one was home. Unless they slept like rocks. Just as she was about to pull the door open, the memory struck her of Liam retrieving a book from his father's private collection. And it hadn't been from the library.

She wrung her hands. She'd have to snoop around.

Silently thanking God that no one was around, she headed upstairs, thinking the best place to find this collection would be in his father's office or study. The utter terror of being caught kept her from dawdling inside the rooms, as distracting as much of the grandeur was. She already had an excuse ready in case she did run into someone, *"I got lost trying to find the bathroom!"* Even though she'd already peeked inside at least three of them.

The sight of yellow crime scene tape forming an 'X' over two giant, ornate doors almost stopped her heart. *Was this where...?*

The West Wing.

She swallowed and felt her hands getting clammy. She had to check. The books could very well be in there. As she pulled the doors open, she winced as the yellow tape snapped apart. She hoped Liam would forgive her. There was no way he wouldn't figure out now that she had intruded and snooped around like a thief. Especially into the West Wing, which he had expressly forbidden her from. She could kiss her free pass to the castle goodbye.

The room looked like the ghost of a grandiose family gathering place, with a black, gaping fireplace at its center, and couches and furniture covered in sheets gray with dust. The more Belle's eyes adjusted to the dim glow of the room, the more it became clear that disaster had struck: the dark wood-paneled walls were lined with empty display cases, but most of the glass had large, spidery cracks or had been completely smashed in. As her eyes trailed upward, an enormous crystal chandelier reflected a faint kaleidoscope pattern on the walls from the only source of light streaming into the room: two large holes in the roof, each sealed from the outside by a clear tarp—where two killer lightning bolts might have torn through.

She clutched her chest at the terrible realization. One for each of Liam's parents.

"What are you doing here?"

Belle shrieked, stumbling backwards as she turned to face the voice.

Liam stood in front of the door, a football in one hand and a gym bag in the other, his face half-hidden in shadow. His voice was low, measured, as if he was using immense willpower to keep rage from seeping into his words. "I thought. I told you. To stay out. Of the West Wing."

"I got lost looking for the books, I mean, bathroom." Her cheeks flamed. She now thought it possible to die of shame.

As he prowled towards her, she instinctively backed away with each step he took. He continued in that disturbingly controlled tone, like the growl of a dog before it bites, "Was the crime scene tape on the doors not clear enough for you?"

"I'm sorry, I—"

"Or did you decide to do some private investigating? Maybe Panzinski sent you. Find some new clues so he can finally lock me away for murder."

She stumbled on something and her arms flailed, but Liam stepped forward and caught her arms, steadying her. His face was clear now: his jaw was set like steel and his bear-like grip on her arms hurt, but there was an anguish in his eyes that cut through her fear. She shook off his hands and looked directly into his eyes. "You are *not* a murderer."

Surprise registered on his face for a fraction of a second before the iron mask formed again. He leaned in and with cold decisiveness, said slowly, "I *am* a murderer." He backed away from her and held up his arms as if inviting her to survey the room. "I mean, how else can this be explained?"

"Exactly how you first reported it," she responded firmly.

"Oh yeah, and what's that?" he challenged, drawing near to her again.

She swallowed. "You know how."

"And you believe it?"

"Yes," she shot back.

He considered that for a moment. "Then, how come no one else believes it? I mean, I don't even think I believe it myself anymore." He scoffed. "A witch who shot lightning bolts out of her hand and then called two more down from the sky." He walked over to one of the broken display cases and peered at his reflection in the cracked glass. The image of his face appeared fractured. "This room is the only thing that keeps me from going insane. It's why I haven't changed anything about it since that night. But"—he smashed his fist into the glass, causing Belle to jump—"it's getting harder and harder to believe that I didn't kill them in that bathroom and then took those pills...."

By this time, Belle had walked up behind him and when she touched the hem of his sleeve, he flinched and almost shoved her away as he turned, facing her. He held his hands up, as if warning her. "Stay away. I can't, I don't want to hurt you, too."

The despair in his voice was heartbreaking. Liam was a walking, talking, open wound, painfully infected after left festering for so long, robbing him of peace and normalcy, and now, it threatened to steal his sanity. She couldn't allow it. She owed it to him to help him. The only way to do that was to rip the lid off her secret and expose it to him. Tell him the truth. The unbelievable, terrifying truth. "Liam, please," she caught one of his hands.

The desperation in his eyes subsided as he focused on her and the small, but strong, grip of her hand in his. Her gentle earnestness dispelled the mania that he'd been losing himself to. "I'm dangerous," he said weakly, trying one last time to warn her. But at the same time, seeing as she wasn't afraid to be this close to him, to still touch him, he was getting the faintest glimmer of hope that salvation was standing right in front of him.

"No," she responded, her tone suddenly changing as she dragged her hand out of his and stepped away. "*I'm* dangerous."

His features twisted into befuddlement. "What?"

Belle's hands began shaking. This was more nerve-wracking than she thought. "I need, I need to tell you, but—" She looked around at the gloom and doom surrounding them and hugged herself. "But can we get out of here?"

He nodded slowly. "Alright." He held out his hand. "Follow me."

She took it. And like a warm blanket stifling the shivers, her nerves subsided.

He led her to the one place he knew she could relax in: the library. But this time, he'd shown her to a large bay seat tucked away into a corner that she'd completely missed before. They sat on its plush cushions, and when Liam pulled back the curtains, she gasped. It was a perfect view of the garden and even had a glimpse of the ocean in the distance.

"Wow," she breathed.

"If my mom wasn't sitting underneath that tree, we could find her here."

"This must be the best view in the house, er, I mean, castle."

"House will do."

Belle quoted absently, "Home is where the heart is." She watched mesmerized as the white birds dipped and soared in the sky in perfect concert.

"Yeah, my heart might definitely be here."

Something about his tone made her look at him, and then she quickly wished she hadn't because his smoldering gaze entrapped her and the tiny cove they were in suddenly felt smaller and warmer. His massive figure was leaning back against the wall, eyes trained on her, while one foot rested on the floor and the other leg was pressed tightly against hers on the bench, heat radiating from the touch.

He was the first to look away. "Look, Belle, uh, I need to apologize for the way I behaved up there. You just, you surprised me." He added with a note of rebuke, "But I did warn you not to go there."

She flinched. "I know. I'm sorry."

He leaned in closer so that he was at eye level with her and continued in a serious, but softer tone, "What I want to know is"—his breath tickled her cheek and elicited goosebumps along her neck—"why you didn't seem surprised when I talked about OD'ing on pills." She looked sheepish, but before she could respond, he guessed, "Pan?"

She nodded. "He told me everything." He leaned back against the wall and exhaled. "Sorry," she murmured.

"No, don't be." He looked at her and gave her a half-smile. "You know everything and yet, here you are. Sitting a foot away from an alleged suicidal psychopath." He paused as he looked at her in a new light. "It's very telling." His corner lip rose into that snarky twist that had angered Belle numerous times before. "You're either hopelessly in love with me, or—" All humor fled his face as he added slowly, "You *are* more dangerous than me?"

She held his gaze and swallowed. If she had acted insulted, he would've known it was the "hopelessly-in-love" part, but since she didn't....

His eyebrows furrowed with dark understanding. "So, if I'm supposed to be a Menendez brother, you're...worse than that?"

She nodded. She felt her skin growing cold and clammy, and her insides felt like they wanted to hurl out of her. She stood up and took a few steps away from him, rubbing her arms to invite back some warmth. *Better to have some distance between us for when the truth bomb drops,* she thought.

Liam watched as she paced back and forth, her abject nervousness contagious. He realized with a pang that what he knew about her was mostly of his own construction. And it was all threatening to come crumbling down. "So, 'worse' like Hannibal Lecter worse?" he asked, half-chuckling, half-worried.

She took a deep breath and exhaled, stopping behind one of the long tables, wringing her hands and not quite meeting his eyes. "It's the worst thing you can imagine."

His face blanched. "You're, you're a dude?"

"What? No!"

His relief was almost comical.

She bit her lip. "Think..." she closed her eyes and concentrated on letting the dreaded words slip out of her mouth, "Lightning Witch."

His response was immediate. Liam's eyes narrowed and he whispered, "What did you say?"

She opened her eyes and was grateful for the wide, solid table between them. "I'm going to explain." She gripped the edge of the table to steady herself. "This is, this is just so crazy. I've never had to explain to anyone, but myself, and even I didn't believe it, I mean, I thought I was going crazy myself."

"I'm listening," he said in a tone that sounded like a warning for Belle to get to the point and fast.

"The Lightning Witch. It's not me, but my mother. But it's kind of not even my mother, I mean, well, it's her, but not *her* at the same time." She laughed out loud, in disbelief at how delirious she sounded.

"You're rambling," he said coolly.

She straightened her arms at her side and clenched her fists. "My mother is possessed by a spirit or demon, Violet Wickeby. And, and she needs these gems to, I don't know, increase her power or some sort." She paused to analyze his reaction: he was listening and his expression was not so cold and iron-like. "She's been collecting these gems and the last one was from, from—"

"My mom," he finished.

"Yes! A black serendibite bracelet."

His eyebrows shot up and his eyes clouded in suspicion. "How do you know this?"

Belle felt herself backpedal. She sounded like an accomplice. A lunatic one. "Um, ah, well, we're connected through dreams." Despite his expression growing darker as if his intelligence was being insulted, she plodded on. "When I dream, I can see through her. I hardly ever dream though. And that's how I know her plan. Only I don't know how to stop her, which is why I need to see your father's private collection of history books for any mention of Violet Wickeby's weakness. You know, since she was mentioned in your ancestor Edward's diary. That's, that's why I was in the West Wing—I was trying to find those books."

He shook his head slowly, his indignation melting into pained bewilderment. "How can you go on like this? I knew you weren't whole, like me, but this is just..." he finished weakly, "sick."

Oh no, she winced. This is what she feared from confessing to him. "I'm not trying to hurt you...I'm trying to help you." She had to get him to understand.

He exploded, "By twisting my parents' murders into one of those fantasies you get lost in?!!" Belle jumped, her hands flying protectively in front of her. Slowly, like an old man weighed down with a heavy load, he sagged and looked away, the fury on his face giving way to grievous disappointment. "I'm sorry. I didn't mean to frighten you." He added bitterly, "Again."

Her own throat choked with emotion, she began, "It's okay, I know—"

But he cut her off, "You need to leave." He folded his arms across his chest and looked down at the floor. He would not look at her.

Belle blinked back tears, but it was no use. They forced themselves through. Just as she turned to go, her misty eyes landed on the gold lettering along the thick spine of a giant book on a nearby shelf, *The Holy Bible*, and she recalled one of its prominent adages, '*You shall know the truth, and the truth shall set you free.*' Even if it hurt like hell.

She faced him again and quickly drew her sleeve over her eyes. "I'm not done." He looked up at her with indignant surprise, but she continued before her resolve evaporated. "When the Lightning Witch was here that night, up in the West Wing, did she give your mother no other choice but to say with her *own* words that she could have the bracelet? Insisted, *or else*, that your mother say the words?"

His eyes widened, as if remembering. "The witch said she'd kill me if my mom didn't say the words." He squeezed his eyes shut. "She'd already killed my dad with lightning. She threatened to kill me, if my mom didn't repeat after her." He opened his eyes, his expression distant. "So, my mom did it. Then, second bolt. And then all went black for me. Until I woke up in that bathroom." He stared absently into the distance, in the direction of the West Wing.

Belle walked around the table and crossed over to him. When she gently squeezed his fingers, his attention wandered over to her until his eyes regained their clarity. She looked sadly at him, her hazel eyes shining with sympathy. And again, he was struck by her beauty and instantly regretted being so beastly with her. But one question remained....

"What do you know about the lightning?" he asked. Wanting to calm the tension in the room, he returned to the bay seat and patted the spot beside him, which she took.

They sat close. Their faces a foot away from each other, their confessions of the heart and soul inviting a friendly intimacy that was beginning to feel natural. The blonde shadow along his jawline was thicker, and the curves of his lips and yellow flecks in his mint green eyes were fast becoming a familiar trail that Belle's eyes roamed over.

He continued, "Let's say I drink this Kool-Aid you're offering." He ran a harried hand through his hair. "Let's say we're both telling the truth, as crazy as it sounds. I get the 'witch' part, but what about the lightning? I mean, even though I saw it, how can that even be possible? And you say she's your *mom*?"

Secret-government-experiment-gone-wrong was a tempting explanation to give him, but she decided to stick with the only explanation that made sense. And that definitely didn't include the bits about the fairies and immortality. "The way I think of it, the ability to conduct electricity with our hands is in our DNA. Like a genetic mutation." Professor X had made it sound so easy.

He looked pointedly at her. "You mean *her* DNA."

She shook her head and bit her lip. "Our DNA," she repeated.

His eyebrows shot up as he looked at her in a new light. But then the skepticism crept back in as his lips turned up at the corners and his eyes narrowed slightly. "Prove it," he said.

Belle looked at her hands. "I can't call it at will," she said, exasperated.

"Make a lightning bolt strike in that garden," he suggested, pure doubt in his voice.

A shiver ran through her as she remembered the only time she'd inadvertently called for lightning. She cleared her throat, still in great disbelief that she was sharing this out loud. And with Liam, no less. "I mostly just produce these electric sparks from my hands," she said, holding them out before her.

Liam carefully took her hands in his and examined them as if trying to search out its secrets. He turned them over and back and traced the lines in her palms and then flattened his own hands against them, which dwarfed hers in length, before he closed his hands over hers, lacing their fingers together.

This made Belle breathless and her cheeks flushed. And for a moment, she forgot that she'd just revealed her deepest, darkest secret and could only focus instead on his touch. She soon felt her hands heating up unnaturally and quickly ripped them away from Liam's.

"I felt that," he said pointedly. He reached for her hands. "Can you do it again?"

She kept her hands away at her sides and shook her head. "It only happens if I'm really scared or angry, or, I guess—" She looked toward his hand, the one that she'd accidentally seared last night as they kissed.

He noticed. He held up the hand, a bright pink patch of skin at the center of the palm. "Or..." he repeated as understanding dawned on him, and before she knew it, he was leaning in, gently pinching her chin with his thumb, pausing right before her lips, as if allowing her the chance to withdraw or proceed. She didn't flinch or pull away, but glanced from his eyes down to his lips.

Green light.

It was the lightest kiss, soft and sweet, almost polite. And then, what felt like too soon, he stopped and looked directly at her hands.

Nothing.

Disappointment registered on his face, while she, on the other hand, was uneasy. She felt like a guinea pig being kissed for an experiment, even though she knew he was just trying to help her prove the truth. "I'm sorry," she said. "I'm just really tired. I literally didn't sleep last night. Like at all. I came straight here at sun-up."

He smiled at her, but seemed to be thinking about something. "Hey, um, I've never mentioned this to anyone, except Jacques, and only the hospital people knew, but, uh—" He suddenly peeled his shirt off and her jaw dropped before she automatically snapped it shut.

"What are you—" she began, but he said, "I wanna show you something." He gestured towards his chest. "You can't really see them well, but if you look hard enough...."

She stared, but only saw an impeccably defined upper body that made the muscles clench low in her stomach and her cheeks feel like fire. "I think you should put your shirt back on."

He pulled the curtain even farther back, letting in a brighter blast of sunlight.

Belle gasped. There was a very faint network of spidery white lines radiating from a baseball-sized mark in front of his shoulder. "That's where a ricochet blast from the bolt that killed my mom hit me," he said. "Knocked me out." Without thinking, she reached out and let her fingers trail along each white streak. "Over the past year, I've had the red scars removed...." Her fingers followed the trails over his powerfully built arm. "I know I should've left them as evidence," he continued, his voice dropping an octave. "But it was too painful a reminder to have my whole life."

"I can't believe I didn't notice before at the beach," she murmured. She thought of each line as a painful accumulating debt she owed him for the cruelty her family secret had caused him.

"I got a tan that day, so the white lines are clearer now." The rise and fall of his chest became perceptible as his breaths deepened.

"This is the longest one," her finger chased the long, white sinewy line down over the contours of his chest, over the first pair of abs, eliciting a shudder from him.

He caught her hand.

Her eyes flew wide in embarrassment. "I'm sorry—I wasn't thinking."

His gaze was smoky and penetrating, and stilled her clamoring. He pulled her hand towards him and placed it on the white patch on his shoulder. "It's fine." He cupped her cheek with the other hand and his voice became husky, "It's more than fine."

Her lips parted with a small gasp as he drew in and met them with a hunger that spread like wildfire under his skin. But he didn't let his need dictate his speed. He kept it slow, savoring the deep intensity of the kiss, the way their mouths melted into each other, and when she curled her fingers through his hair as if she wanted to be closer, he readily obliged and wrapped a hand around her bottom and the other on her hip and lifted her into his lap. Her eyes flew open in surprise, but they quickly fluttered shut as he moved his mouth down her neck and focused on the spot beneath her ear. When a small moan escaped her, his lips closed over her mouth again.

Belle's mind had clicked off, her body humming with the delicious burn of passion. But when the sweet fire in her blood raged hotter, and the darkness behind her closed eyelids started to go white, she stiffened and promptly extricated herself from Liam's lap.

A crackling sound was heard and once the haze in his eyes cleared, Liam found himself staring at Belle's outstretched hands: a flurry of electrical sparks dancing around in her palms. He blinked harder. The sparks were growing as if inflating into an electrical orb. Alarmed, he met her anxious eyes.

She gave him a sheepish look. "Told you."

"No kidding," he croaked.

"Um," her skin was pale and a sweat broke out on her brow, "I'm not feeling so good." That was the last thing she said before the sparks fizzled out and her world was plunged into darkness.

He caught her just as she slumped towards the floor, unconscious.

29

A Killer Dream

"She's at the castle," the goth twin reported, turning toward her. He had just gotten off the phone with his brother. "Sounds like she'll be out of your way for a while."

They were sitting in a car with darkened windows. Belle felt herself reach out and stroke his cheek with one sweep, but the hand did not look like hers. Strangely enough, while Belle was conscious that she was mind-melded with Violet again, she felt nothing herself. She was a numb observer.

"Well done, my pet," she purred.

A hairline trail of blood appeared on his cheek. "Ow!" he flinched and touched the area. He looked with disgust at her black lacquered nails, which had been filed into sharp claws. "Watch it," he growled.

She violently shoved his head and sneered, "I'll sort you out later." She exited the car and barked out before slamming the door shut, "Wait for me here."

Gravel crunched beneath her Louboutin heels as she strode up the driveway. Lifting a hand towards the ornate sign post, she muttered a curse and smirked with satisfaction at the loud *crack* that followed. Another ancient utterance and the front door to the Historical Society of Elmridge unlocked and opened soundlessly.

She paused in the presence of the museum relics.

Memories flooded her. Abigail's memories. A rocking chair her father hand-made for her mother with the single doll she owned as a child sitting in it. A large frame on the wall displayed a dress she knew belonged to her sister, Emily; it had the dark patch on the sleeve where she had spilled the molasses the morning they'd attempted to make breakfast for their parents. In a glass case, sat the gavel that belonged to the Rev. Judge Jonas Rawlins. The same one he used to condemn her and her sister to the stake, with the help of Violet Wickeby's testimony. And *still*, Wickeby's lies continued to destroy her family. Abigail felt her blood boil. She opened her mouth to scream, but Violet forced it shut and only a muffled cry came out.

Violet focused on the stairs she knew led to the second floor and took a step forward, only to be locked in place.

Abigail clenched her fists and spoke through gritted teeth, "I know what you're trying to do and I won't stand for it."

"I need him out of the way," Violet gritted back. "He is still Jäger, and will kill us if he can."

"No! I won't allow it."

"Oh, what? And the other killings you allowed?" Violet hissed. "Selfish girl. You always have been. William would have lived a long, successful and important life, with *me*, but instead you charmed him with your penniless, pretty looks, and then what?"

Abigail felt her strength wane.

"That's right," Violet continued viciously. "He died a drunk. In despair. His son taken and his wife absent." She spat on the ground. "You should have been the one tossing yourself off that cliff. Not me."

Ernesto's voice boomed from upstairs, "Em? Is that you?"

Abigail seized up again, not allowing Violet to move forward, and cried in a hoarse whisper, "I won't let you!"

Ernesto called out again, "I'll be in the shower, Em." There was the sound of shuffling upstairs and the bathroom door opening and closing.

In a burst of strength, Violet managed to reach the top step.

Abigail suddenly grabbed her own throat and pierced her claw-like nails into her flesh. Blood oozed from the wounds. "I will rip my own throat out if you continue."

Violet choked out a laugh. "I thought you knew by now. Weren't you listening when I gave my boys the order? They're enchanted to carry out my bidding: if this body dies, your daughter dies."

Abigail still didn't let go.

Violet narrowed her eyes. "Or, you know what? Maybe, I'll just take over your daughter and make her do all sorts of fun, bloody things that will blacken her soul. I think that sort of torture would be worse than death for her, don't you think?"

Abigail gasped in horror and let go.

"But, you know what? I'm tiring of your defiance. Maybe it's about time I let you go and take Emily instead. She's right upstairs, sleeping. And with a weak mind like hers? She's easy pickings, and I can have my way...new wicked ways with her invisibility powers." Violet became mesmerized by the possibilities that danced in her mind.

"No!" Abigail croaked. "Keep me. Please! I won't fight you anymore. Just leave Lisselle and Emily alone."

Violet felt Abigail fade away, as if slipping under dark waters to un-reachable depths. "Finally," she muttered impatiently. She winced when she felt the puncture wounds at her neck. Blood dripped onto her fin-gers, and she pursed her lips in extreme irritation when she looked down and saw the streaks of blood staining her silk blouse. She knew she shouldn't have dressed up for this kind of messy task. But then again, funerals required formal attire.

At the top of the stairs, she opened the door just wide enough to poke her head through ever so slowly, soundlessly, until she could see that the coast was clear. Only the bathroom across the way showed any signs of activity; its door was cracked slightly open and the sound of a running shower could be heard. She sneered in delight. Soon this town's security force will be running around like a headless chicken, and she'll settle in unnoticed. She crossed through the space, stifling a gag at the disastrous décor, and paused outside the bathroom door. The shower turned off.

She had to act now.

She swung the door open as Ernesto pulled the shower curtain back. "Hey!" He shouted, wrapping the curtain around himself. "Who are you? What are you doing here?!" Instinctively, he eyed his gun on the counter.

She wagged her finger disapprovingly. "Is that anyway to treat family?"

His forehead wrinkled in concentration and as recognition dawned, his face slacked in horror. "Abigail?" At once, Ernesto's military training kicked in and he knocked a shampoo bottle in her direction while he lunged for his gun with the other hand.

She dodged the bottle, but he was not as quick as he used to be: her bolt struck him clear in the chest while his bullet grazed her arm. He fell onto the floor, contorting as the blue electricity snaked all over his wet body still wrapped in the curtain, until he shook no more and his eyes stared blankly at the ceiling.

"What a mess," she griped, setting her hands on her hips and thinking how she was going to clean up this trail. Her ears pricked up at the sudden movement in the room next door. Emily was going to show up any second now. She caught her reflection in the mirror and, despite the ruined expensive shirt, took a morbid pride in her *Carrie* appearance. But as she continued to gaze at her reflection, that familiar feeling of being haunted gripped her. Her mouth twisted into a cruel smirk. "Were you watching, little girl?"

When she felt no response from Belle, she taunted, "I know you're there." She faked a gasp, and waved a hand toward Ernesto's lifeless body. "Has my latest masterpiece made you speechless?" She narrowed her eyes in the mirror when she sensed no reaction from Belle. "You see too much. And it's already crowded in here as it is. I don't know why I can feel you, but can't hear you." She touched her chin with a bloody finger and smiled as if struck with an idea that pleased her. "Ah, yes, well, maybe this will make you sit up and take notice: how about we leave this scene as a murder and leave a nice convenient blood trail back to the room of the crazy invalid that Ernesto secretly keeps locked up? Who wouldn't believe that?"

She laughed aloud with glee, but suddenly gulped in a large breath of air as if breaking the surface of deep waters and thrust herself against the mirror, catching herself with two bloody palms pressed against the glass.

"Lisselle!" Abigail gasped desperately. "You have to stop her! Wake up!" She pounded the glass with a fist.

"Ernie?" Emily called from outside in the hallway.

"Wake up, now!" Abigail screamed.

30

Game Over

N"ooooo!" Belle bolted upright. Her heart thundering in her ears, she instinctively flailed against the hulking figure trying to hold her. "Get away!"

Her fist connected with something hard.

"Ow!" He cursed and let go.

For a second, she stilled and took in her surroundings. "Liam?" They were still in the library's bay window, but a pillow and blanket were added, and a pile of open books on the table before her where someone had evidently sat and pored through the books.

Liam stood before her, cradling his jaw. "Are you okay? You were completely out for two hours and then you wake up throwing punches like Mike Tyson."

"I passed out?" She rubbed her eyes. Without having a night's sleep, her powers must have drained her. She'd slept so deeply that she hadn't even reacted to Violet in her dream.

"Yes. I had Jacques check on you. He's certified and all that. I figured you wouldn't want a hospital, since"— he gestured at her hands—"well, you know."

"Since I'm a mutant," she finished for him. She suddenly stood up and grabbed him by the arms. "But never mind that."

"'Never mind that?' That's a pretty big deal—"

"My family's in trouble! I need you to take me home! I need to stop her from hurting Emily!" She clutched her head with agony at the memory, *She already killed Ernesto.* Her eyes burned with tears.

Liam lifted her chin. "Stop who?"

"Violet Wickeby." She gritted her teeth with anger now. "The thing that's inside my mother."

He glanced at the books behind him. "I think I know her weakness. After you fainted and I knew you were okay, I started reading through my father's books, and...." He pursed his lips.

"What?"

He looked amazed. "You were right. Edward did know something."

"What is her weakness?" she pressed.

"C'mon," he grabbed her hand and a small leather-worn book off the table. "I'll tell you on the way."

~~*~~

The town was a blur as they sped through in the fastest car Liam owned. He wasted no time. He tossed the small leather book into Belle's lap. "Edward Rawlins's journal. I wasn't done reading it, but there's mention of a secret society of hunters."

"Hunters?" She swallowed nervously.

"They called themselves Jäger."

And there it was. Papa's final warning to her, *"Beware of the J—."* Her breath hitched in her throat as she remembered something that Wickeby had said in the last dream, *"He is still Jäger and will kill us if he can."*

Ernesto? He was Jäger? Her chest tightened. *But he's dead now....*

Liam hadn't noticed her reaction, and continued excitedly, "They approached him two times: once, after the Prynn sisters escaped the stake, and second, after his cousin, William, died. I left off reading when he was mulling over the pros and cons of joining them." He looked like he was doing the same in his mind.

Belle grabbed the side door as he shifted a gear into place that propelled the car even faster through a yellow light. "What did they hunt?" She feared she already knew the answer, but she needed the crazy thoughts validated by someone.

He glanced at her and hesitated. "Monsters." He added quickly, "Like that Wickeby witch."

"What were Edward's exact words?"

He exhaled slowly and gave her a sympathetic look. "'Unnatural creatures of the otherworldly kind.' Edward said the hunters only eliminate the ones that have killed people." He half-smiled at her. "That rules *you* out."

Belle felt herself shrivel up inside. Lifeless fish-eyes in a rusted green truck flashed in her mind.

"So, I was thinking," he continued, becoming more animated as he spoke. "This Lightning Witch is real, so these hunters must still exist somewhere. I say, we contact them somehow and let them know about Wickeby. They should be able to take care of her."

"I don't want hunters 'taking care' of my mom. It's that thing inside her that needs to be taken care of." She bit her lip. "I'm thinking we need a priest. Is there a church in this town?"

Liam scoffed. "The mall is the church here."

The mood darkened when the Historical Society came into view down the road. A lead weight dropped into the pit of her stomach. He reached for her hand and squeezed it. "She's in your house right now because you dreamed it?" he asked softly, but doubt colored his tone.

"I saw her companions in my dream before. A set of twin guys. And then I saw them yesterday on the boardwalk. One of them winked at me like he knew who I was." He raised a disapproving eyebrow at this. "I knew then the dreams—the nightmares—were real," she finished.

"Let's see if she's really here then." He set his mouth in a determined line as he stared at the house looming closer, but she could tell he wasn't fully convinced yet about her dream visions. And she couldn't blame him. She was grateful for how far along he was willing to come with her. But it wasn't going to be far enough to put him in danger. She wasn't going to allow that.

With the entire property in full view now, there was something that didn't match up with her dream. "The car I saw in the nightmare...it isn't there." A hysterical note crept into her voice. "Maybe she left, and Emily is—"

"Emily's fine," he assured her. He pulled up to the house and threw the car into park.

Belle grabbed him before he could open his door. "What are you doing? Leave me here and go. This doesn't concern you."

He looked insulted. "This, in every way, concerns me. It concerns my dead parents and it concerns you. And if you're right, I'm not letting you walk in there by yourself." He pulled his arm away and got out of the car.

She hurried out and met him by the trunk, where he pulled out a bat, his expression dead-set, and she knew he wasn't staying out of it. "At least, stay behind me," she pleaded. He looked slightly offended again, but finally nodded. Something over his shoulder caught Belle's attention. "Wait a minute," she said. She walked over to the signpost of the Historical Society. "It's not cracked."

Liam stood behind her. "Is it supposed to be?"

"In my dream, she said a spell at it as she walked by and it completely cracked at the center." A suggestion started forming in her mind, one that gave her tremendous hope. "What if...?" She took off running up the path.

"Hey! Wait up!" He caught up as Belle opened the front door and ran up the stairs to the second floor.

"Whoa! What is going on here?" Ernesto jumped and cursed in Spanish, closing his bathrobe tighter as Belle burst into view. A vein bulged in his forehead when Liam almost crashed into Belle from behind. "What's he doing here?" Ernesto said icily.

Liam looked to Belle for help, but all she could say was, "Ernesto, you're alive!"

He looked utterly confused. "Well, of course, I am." And then he narrowed his eyes as if suspecting he was being pranked. "What is this?"

"Ernesto, wait." She held her hands up in peace offering. "Just answer me this: are you going to take a shower now?" He looked like he wanted to walk out of the room. "Please, just answer: yes or no."

"Yes," he said exasperated. "I was going to set my microwave lunch and then take a shower."

"Oh, thank Heavens!" she breathed out, and then laughed with relief.

"What is it, Belle?" Liam said, touching her arm.

"Hands off," Ernesto growled.

He complied.

"I see it, before it happens," she said. "I dream it, and *then* it comes true."

"What are you talking about?" Ernesto asked her. He looked menacingly at Liam. "Did you give her drugs?"

"No!" "Of course, not!" Liam and Belle responded at once.

Another voice piped up, startling them, "She's a Dream Seer."

Emily had appeared in their midst.

"What the—" "Em, how did you—" Liam and Ernesto began, but she held up a hand to silence them as she moved towards Belle and reached for her hands. Emily smiled proudly at her. "It's her special gift, apart from what she inherited from her mother. Abigail must have started the link." Concern clouded her wide eyes. "She must be getting very desperate, or else she wouldn't have brought you into this."

"Belle, who is this?" Liam asked, sounding lost. "Is she who we came for?" There was a steely edge to his voice.

"No," Belle responded firmly. She held his gaze and hoped more truth wouldn't hurt. "This is Aunt Emily."

He looked dumbfounded.

Ernesto slapped an authoritative hand on his chest. "There is nothing here you need to know about. Leave, now!"

Liam pushed his hand away. "I'm not here to deal with you, Pan."

Meanwhile, Emily drew Belle into an embrace and whispered in her ear, "She's here. She's outside. The boy doesn't stand a chance. She'll kill him on sight." Belle gasped and tried to pull apart, but Emily held her tighter. "I will take him to a safe place. Keep Ernie safe. She won't dare harm you." She let go, and Belle stumbled back.

"But how do I keep him safe?" Belle whisper-shouted. "I can't hurt her—she's my mother!"

"The pixie dust. You'll have to give it to her."

"But—"

Emily cut her off. "It's the only way. For now."

The ground-floor front door opened and clicked shut.

Ernesto opened his mouth to speak, but Emily silenced him with a finger to her lips.

A female voice was heard in the stairwell.

Liam wrinkled his brow. The intruder sounded as if she was arguing with herself in a hushed voice.

Belle felt the hair rise on the back of her neck. The dream was playing itself out. She knew what would happen next. She looked to Emily for help.

Emily gave her a small nod. She crossed to Liam and grabbed ahold of his wrist, who gave her a befuddled look. Looking at Ernesto, she said, "I will come back for you." And then she and Liam disappeared into thin air.

Belle and Ernesto both jumped at the sudden vacancy before them, but they didn't have enough time to dwell on the shock. The second-floor door clicked open and the top of a raven-haired head poked through, slowly. Belle moved to shield Ernesto from the door, and he gave her a quizzical look and then gestured towards his gun in its holster on the kitchen counter. She shook her head and mouthed, *No. Trust me.*

Violet emerged into full view looking like a business fashion model who'd been fed on by vampires. The blood that stained her blouse at the collar matched her crimson lips and her long, charcoal black hair hung stick-straight past her shoulders. A pair of black, rhinestoned sunglasses kept her hair out of her face, as if she was stepping out of the car for a quick errand: get in, kill, get out.

Belle was stunned. As bloody terrifying as her presence was, this person was still her mother, in the flesh. Despite her horror, she felt a lump swell in her throat.

Surprised flickered on Violet's face when she saw Belle. "Well," she drawled out, "this certainly changes the game."

"Abigail?" Ernesto whispered, shocked. He grabbed Belle's arm and his voice shook as he warned, "She's dangerous, Belle. Stay close."

Violet held up her index finger to indicate a pause as she looked around at the space, wrinkling her nose in disgust. Then, she placed her hands squarely on her hips and locked eyes with Belle. "I just had another odd dose of déjà vu in that staircase and, lately, they always have to do with you. And now here you are...meddling."

"I won't let you hurt Ernesto," Belle blurted out.

"I'll be fine," he grunted. "You distract her while I get to the kitchen."

"Stay," she muttered back.

"And you even know *why* I'm here," Violet mused, a bloody index finger on her chin. "Well, partly." She started to stalk closer.

Belle moved back still shielding Ernesto. She had an odd feeling Violet was trying to figure out the extent of her dream power, as if she wasn't aware that she was the starring villainess of Belle's nightmares. How could she not know? Was her own mother still somehow protecting her from Violet? Again?

"I want to speak with my mother," Belle demanded.

"Hush, girl. If Abigail interferes, I kill you. She knows it." She tapped her chin as if thinking. "I see now," she mused aloud, and then her eyes lit up and she spoke as if divulging a secret between friends, "Did you know your mother is a Dream Catcher?"

"What do you mean?"

"It means that Abigail has been sneaky. Clever, but sneaky: catching visions of me and sending them to you...a Dream Seer. And it won't work, now that I know how you've been spying on me. I'll make sure to divert your attention into someone else's mind. Oh, don't worry, I'll pick an interesting one. Are you a fan of the horror genre?"

"That's enough," Ernesto said, stepping out from behind Belle. "You need to leave."

An electric bolt whizzed by his ear and shattered the door behind him in a deafening blast. He and Belle were thrown to the ground in a shower of wooden shards and splinters.

"That's a warning," Violet said icily. "No sudden moves."

They picked themselves off the ground, the wooden splinters cutting painfully into their hands.

Belle felt her hands heating up as her anger swelled. She pressed harder into the wooden shards, hoping the pain would distract her from the emotion. If she was forced to defend herself or Ernesto, she would have to be in control enough to gauge her electrical release—she didn't want to kill her own mother, Hammerson-style.

"She murdered the Rawlins family," Ernesto whispered raggedly. "The kid was right." Regret weighed heavily in his voice.

Violet heard him. "That pathetic family got what they deserved." She laughed. "And I got what I needed." She held up her hand and stroked the serendibite bracelet.

Belle felt herself trembling with rage. She clenched her red-hot hands into fists.

But Violet was still admiring the bracelet. "The Rawlins father was the most pathetic, just like every Rawlins man before him." She mimicked Mr. Rawlins, "'Take me and spare my wife and son.'" She snarled. "William couldn't bear to be without his son either. Weakling."

"Please...stop." Belle tried to think happy thoughts, but the images filled her mind of Mr. Rawlins begging for his family's life while Liam helplessly watched, terrified.

"Why, little Prynn," Violet sounded amused. "You seem all worked up."

Belle was shaking all over, straining to contain the white-hot needles piercing out of every pore in her body. *No!* she thought, anguished. She squeezed her eyes shut and gritted her teeth as she concentrated on pushing out the Rawlins's gruesome murders with anything that had made her happy, but instead the Hammerson brothers' lifeless eyes stared back at her.

"Belle?" Ernesto sounded concerned.

"Don't. Touch. Me," she whispered in warning. She felt faint, as if she could no longer feel her body.

"How interesting...how very, very interesting," Violet cooed. "Am I upsetting you? Oh, I would love to see what kind of show *you* can put on."

Tears squeezed out of Belle's eyes, but they evaporated as they trailed down her steaming cheeks.

Emily re-appeared next to her. "Belle! Think happy thoughts! This is what your father tried to save you from. Focus, Belle. Focus on what is good and joyful." She lowered her voice. "We only need to give Violet the dust. Her plan still won't be complete, so there's still time to stop her." She drew closer and whispered, so that only Belle could hear. "Do *not* let her see the full extent of your powers, or she will *take* you."

Violet spoke up, "Emily, dear, kindly step away. I will have my way no matter what. The pixie dust can wait. I most assuredly need to see the new rising Prynn star's grand finale."

"Abby!" Emily called toward Violet. "Abby!"

"Shut. Your. Mouth," Violet gritted back through her teeth. Her amusement had contorted into a deadly stare.

"Abby, please! We need you now! Your daughter needs you!"

Electrical orbs erupted around Violet's hands, but she grunted as if her arms were forcibly pinned at her sides. Suddenly, a maniacal laugh escaped her. "You fool, I don't need my hands!"

Belle sucked in a breath of air that allowed her body to calm down enough for her vision to clear again: Emily stood close by but was restraining Ernesto by the arm, who was still trying to reach for his gun, while Violet stood immobile wearing a twisted, exultant expression.

"Where is the Rawlins boy, huh?" Violet taunted Belle. "It wasn't too kind of me to let him live and suffer the aftermath of his parents' murders, wasn't it?"

And just like that, Belle was seeing white again and Emily's soothing, desperate voice seemed farther away. "I. Can't. Control it," Belle whimpered.

"This little family reunion has made me want to turn over a new leaf," Violet continued snidely. "I think I *will* do him the kindness he deserves after all."

"Abby, please! Before it's too late!"

Violet snarled, "I'll put Liam Rawlins out of his misery and let him join his dead parents!"

Abigail finally broke through and shouted, "Lisselle, no! You must stay calm!"

But it was too late, for Belle had not heard. She cried out, her control shattered, and with it an explosive blast left her that felt like the rush of a nuclear wind obliterating everything in its path. Over in an instant, the roar in her ears died away and an eerie quiet soon descended. Only the sound of Belle's short spasming breaths could be heard. She felt in control again, but she was terrified of what she might find if she opened her eyes.

A voice rasped in her mind, *"Open them, Little Prynn, and lay eyes upon your exquisite handiwork."*

Dread filled her soul. Only one person called her "Little Prynn."

Finally, she looked.

Her breath stilled in her chest and she froze, a cold sweat blanketing her skin. The entire upper half of the second-story, including its roof, had been torn clean away. Only the second-story floor, some heavy furniture, and its jagged perimeter remained.

Panicked, she turned and turned searching the exposed outdoors for her family. She gasped when she spied three thin columns of smoke rising in the distance. "No!" she cried, collapsing to her knees. From their clothing, she could tell...even her mother was gone.

"Yes! Bravo, well done!" the voice applauded in her mind.

Belle sobbed into her hands. "Oh no...what have I done?"

"Don't be rude when I'm speaking to you. Look at me."

"Huh?" She looked.

Hovering a few feet before her was a dark shadowy outline of a woman she didn't recognize. But it could only be..."Violet Wickeby?"

"The one and only," she continued speaking in Belle's mind as the phantom held her gaze with a cold stare. *"I say, what a marvelous performance you've wrought. Couldn't have topped it myself."* The phantom slowly smiled, never blinking once. *"And what supremely magnificent powers you have...."*

"No, no!" She started scooting away from her. "You can't have me. I'll never give you my permission!"

"Look around at the deaths you've caused. You've surpassed my own number now." Violet laughed. *"We are so similar now, 'kindred spirits' you might say (See? I'm already getting to know your mind.) that I don't even need your permission. Nor the blade and the gems. With all your powers, no one can defeat me."*

"Stop! I'll kill you, too!" Belle aimed a hand at her.

Violet snorted. *"You can't kill a ghost, dear."* The phantom pointed a finger at her. *"Now that I have your mind, all I need is the rest of you. Oh, yes, Little Prynn, you'll do nicely. Much better than your mother."*

As Belle screamed, the phantom shot into her mouth in a column of black smoke. And then there was only darkness.

31

Reset

"Send her back, now!" A deep voice commanded.

Belle faded in and out of consciousness. The edges of her vision shimmered with gold.

"We must hurry, Master William. If she fully awakens here, the cataclysm will be irreversible."

The same deep voice, William, snapped back, "I know. Here, inject her."

Belle's eyes fluttered open. A syringe filled with a shimmering gold liquid was passed from one gloved hand to another. Her eyes closed again. A sharp needle stabbing through her chest jolted her. She gasped awake and beheld the same man from one of Violet's memories—the same beautiful, despondent man who stared over the edge of the cliff with a bottle in hand, before he plunged off it. William. Abigail's William. She wanted to ask if she was dead, but the thought could not even reach her tongue.

William held her down gently by the arms and spoke soothingly while people moved about with urgency behind him, like an E.R., but the people here seemed enveloped in shimmering gold that trailed them as they moved—no, flitted. Her eyes failed to make sense of the background, so she tried her hardest instead to focus on the painfully handsome man before her with dark shaggy hair and the same angular jaw and clear green eyes as Liam.

Her eyes were fluttering shut again as her body felt heavier and heavier, as if she would just sink right into this table.

William spoke with great urgency and concern, "The Never-fairies consented to one do-over. Only one." He cupped her face, forcing her to focus again. "When you go back, no one will remember what just happened except you, vaguely. This will feel like a dream to you." His tone became insistent, "Everything will turn out fine if you follow two rules: do *not* lose control, especially in front of Violet, and trust no Jäger, except Edward. Edward will help you defeat Violet and bring Abby back to me."

Belle's eyelids were far too heavy to keep open now. The last she heard him say before she sank into blissful oblivion was "Do not kiss him, or he'll be rendered powerless, and any hope of...."

~~*~~

"She murdered the Rawlins family," Ernesto whispered raggedly. "The kid was right."

Belle blinked and looked sideways at Ernesto. She stared at him. She had the oddest sensation of just having woken up, the remnants of a dream fast dissipating.

"That pathetic family got what they deserved." Violet laughed. "And I got what I needed." She stroked the serendibite bracelet encircling her wrist.

Heat flashed in Belle's hands, but the overwhelming sense of déjà vu distracted her from feeling any further outrage. A masculine voice from her dream floated back to her, *Do not lose control, especially in front of Violet....* She hid her hands behind her back and took in a deep breath, letting it out slowly as she felt the warmth leaving her hands.

Violet narrowed her eyes. "Don't be rude. Keep your hands visible."

She showed Violet her palms. Only blood trickled at the wounds.

"Hmm," Violet said. Satisfied, she sidled over to a couch and sat on its arm, crossing her legs and folding her hands in her lap. "Now, let's talk business."

The surreal feeling left Belle, and the fear and very real danger of the present slammed into her. Her heart rate spiked. Another glance at Ernesto's face told her he was calculating the moment he could spring for the kitchen and get his hands on his gun. He was waiting for Violet to be distracted. But Belle knew from the dream she had in Liam's library that he wouldn't be fast enough.

She grabbed his wrist and squeezed. The message was clear: *Don't move.*

Violet sat like she was conducting a meeting, and watched them like a cat ready to pounce. "Little Prynn, *I* have something you want, and *you* have something I want. So, let's make a trade."

"The only thing I want from you is my mother, free of you."

Violet widened her eyes in feigned surprise. "So you don't want Ernesto to live?"

"What?"

Violet replied slowly, as if Belle was a toddler, "Ernesto's life for the pixie dust."

"You promised my mother would be free."

Violet casually picked off a lint from her pants and flicked it away. "And she will be...as soon as my plan is complete."

"I don't know what dust you're talking about." Emily's former manic warning replayed in her mind, *"She must not be allowed to complete her plan."*

Violet smiled patiently. "'Lisselle, keep the dust, keep it safe.' Daddy's words, remember?"

The dream. Belle *had* seen her at the cemetery. Of course, Violet figured out the message Belle's father had left her on his gravestone—seems Abigail had not been able to shield *that* from Violet.

Violet clucked her tongue at Belle's hesitation. "You know? It's better for me in the grand scheme of things to have an ex-Jäger police chief out of the way than alive and sniffing around, so if I were you, I'd get a move on and fetch the dust." She held her palm up and an orb of crackling electricity burst forth. She narrowed her eyes and snarled, "Now."

Ernesto spoke up, "The dust—it's in the kitchen. I'll get it."

"No!" Belle held on to his wrist. She shook her head. He was going to get himself killed. "*I* will get it." She said firmly, "Stay put." She looked at Violet. "Do *not* hurt him. I will be right back."

"Good girl." She snapped her crackling hand shut and stared cat-like at Ernesto as Belle disappeared into her bedroom.

Belle didn't know how much longer she could stall. Besides not wanting to give her the dust, she feared how Violet would react when she discovered the dust wasn't golden anymore. That it was used up. Dead. More than that, though, *what* could she do to stop Violet without hurting her mother? She felt so woefully unprepared. Her only course of action was to follow Emily's last direction to her. Hand over the dust.

As she returned with the jar, Violet had just asked Ernesto, "So, where's Emily?"

"Who's asking?" Belle responded before Ernesto could. He looked like he wanted to jump out of his skin toward the kitchen.

"A-ha, clever," Violet grinned, and then became dead serious when she spotted the jar in Belle's hands. "Now, slowly, place the jar on this couch," she gestured toward the spot.

Belle gave Ernesto another *'stay here'* look and approached Violet slowly. She and her mother had the same nose, lips and eyebrows, but as she drew closer, any connection she was hoping to make with her mother was squelched by the cold, piercing stare Violet held her with. It was disturbingly inhuman. She set the jar on the couch and stepped away.

"Stay," Violet ordered. "I want you to see this." She reached for the jar and held it up: the dust began to swirl and shimmer with gold.

"How...?" Belle trailed off as confusion and even envy set in.

"The pixies...always wanting to go up...toward home." She held the jar to her face and peered closer. "They come alive when—"

Ernesto made a sudden move, and at once, Belle felt disappointment over the interruption in the story and horror at the certain fatal consequence he would face. Violet let loose a bolt and Belle screamed out as it hit him dead-center. But to everyone's utter shock, Emily appeared out of thin air in front of him. The bolt broken up into a million electrified sparks that snaked around her body, she collapsed onto her side, seizing.

The realization struck them all: Emily had been acting as an invisible shield for Ernesto this whole time. Belle rushed to her side as Ernesto collapsed to his knees beside her. Emily's eyes fluttered shut as the electricity subsided. "You monster!" Belle screamed at Violet.

But Violet paid no attention, for Abigail seemed determined to claw her way out. "Em!" she wailed. "Em!!!" She suddenly stiffened as stone-cold fury paralyzed her, her hands clenching into fists at her sides. Guttural rage filled her voice, "I'll. Kill. You. Violet!!!" Her hands flew to her own neck with a ferocious clench.

"No!" Violet croaked out. "Don't!" Blood oozed from where the nails pierced through. One hand shot to the side of her face, nails digging through, scraping down trails of open flesh. Blood streamed freely from her head and neck as Violet cried out in pain, begging for Abigail to stop.

Ernesto gasped out with relief, "Emily's alive!"

Belle tore her eyes away from the horrifying scene and looked down to see Ernesto with his fingers pressed against Emily's neck. "She has a pulse," he said, his eyes shining. "And look—" Emily's chest rose and fell slightly.

"She's alive!!" Violet pleaded, as if that would get Abigail to cease her attack. She screeched in agony as she yanked out fistfuls of her own hair. Bolts began flying out of Violet's hand. Blasts of household items exploding into pieces rocked the air.

Belle dodged one that singed right through her hair.

"I'll kill the girl, if you don't stop!" Violet shrieked.

As if Abigail finally relented control, Violet's hands suddenly fell to her sides and she collapsed onto her knees with a cry of relief. She looked at her bloody hands and screeched with disgust as she tried unsuccessfully to shake out the tufts of flesh and black hair that stuck to her fingers. She slapped her hands on the floor in indignant frustration and screamed, "Abigail Prynn! You bitch!!"

Still crouching over Emily's supine form on the floor, Belle and Ernesto were too stunned for words to do anything but watch wide-eyed as Violet gathered herself up, a bloody gruesome mess, and swipe the jar off the couch. She hobbled towards the door, paused and cursed as she ripped off her high heels, and towed them in hand, limping down the stairs and leaving a blood-spattered trail in her wake. Only until they heard the sound of a car door slamming shut outside and tires peeling away did they dare speak.

"Think she'll be back?" Ernesto asked.

"I think my mom made it clear to her not to mess with us," Belle replied with a spark of pride. "No, she's not coming back...at least, not for a while. I hope."

32

Huddle

Belle swept up the first mound of shattered pieces of furniture and wall paneling and whatever remained of her bedroom door which had been blasted into bits. She could still hear the two men speaking in low voices where Emily lay in her bedroom. Belle stood closer to the door, which was slightly ajar. She was waiting for a break in their rapid Spanish-speaking before she knocked. She wanted an update. The last one had been an hour ago: Emily was in a coma but would live. The only question was what state her mind would be in when she woke up.

Ernesto emerged from Emily's room, worry lining his face, and headed to the kitchen.

Belle pounced. "How is she?"

He withdrew a glass from the cupboard and began filling it with orange juice. "Same as last time. Sleeping and recovering. She's had some water, so we want her to take a sip of this next time she wakes up."

Satisfied with Emily's progress for the moment, she asked another question that had been plaguing her, only she wasn't sure how he'd react. "You know, Violet called you 'ex-Jäger police chief.'" He stiffened.

"What's a Jäger?" she asked point-blank. A name from a dream floated back to her, '*Edward*,' but she brushed it off.

He tightened the cap back on the OJ and put it away, but his movements were mechanical. Turning back to face her, he paused with the glass in hand. "Another reason to protect Emily and keep what she is a secret. The Jäger are hunters. We, I mean, *they* are each assigned an 'unnatural' human target to eliminate." When Belle made a move to reply, Ernesto cut her off, "It is a long story for another day. I was very young, Emily was my first...assignment. I didn't understand the ins and outs of this secret military force. Not even governments know about it. It's like Illuminati, but more secretive because it operates as if it doesn't exist. It goes back hundreds of years. They recruit you and once you're given a target, you're bound to it somehow, like an on-switch you can't turn off. The pursuit is relentless. You sleep, eat, breath thinking of the target and the only way to be rid of it is to kill it. Needless to say, my deadly obsession with Emily...well, she showed me another way to channel it: love. I was lucky enough to have her love me back."

He put a hand on her shoulder. "Another day, we'll sit—you, Emily, and I—and we'll have a nice, long family talk over dinner."

Belle could only nod her head slowly, still processing what he said as he disappeared into Emily's bedroom.

Tap.

Belle's ears pricked up.

Tap.

She wasn't sure what direction the sound was coming from.

Tap.

What new devilry is this? Icy dread snaked its way around her heart. *Perhaps Violet's already recovered and wants revenge?*

Her heart hammering in her chest, she followed the taps and ended up in her bedroom.

TAP.

Her window! She opened the curtains an inch.

TAP.

She flinched as the sound struck the glass loudly, but when she looked down, she saw Liam with a handful of the tiny rocks that coated the driveway. She threw open the window.

"Finally!" he exclaimed, flinging the rocks down and throwing his hands in the air. "You're alive!"

"I'm going to open the front door for you," she called back.

"But, what about—" he began.

But she was already gone.

Her heart felt like it was about to burst. She was so happy to see him...and it scared her. She forced herself to take a deep breath and smoothed out her hair as best she could before opening the door.

As soon as she opened it, though, her "Why didn't you just knock?" was smothered by Liam enveloping her into a tight hug, her feet lifting clear off the floor. Her senses fired into overload as her face flushed against his strong chest and his woodsy man-scent filled her lungs.

"I thought you were dead—all of you," he said into her hair.

"We're all okay. Except for Emily—ow, you're crushing me now." Liam released her, an apology etched in his fine features, but his eyes couldn't stop drinking her in. Belle continued, sucking in a ragged breath of air, "The doctor says Emily will recover."

"Recover from what?" She quickly filled him in on the Violet vs. Abigail stand-off and how Emily got caught in the cross-hairs. "So, she gave you the ultimatum, huh?" Liam said darkly, more a statement than a question. "You know, she would've killed him anyways. After she got what she wanted." He swallowed, his face grim. "I wish I had done for my mom what Emily did for Ernesto."

She touched his arm. "You wouldn't have survived it."

He looked like he wanted to ask her something, but his eyes grew round when he spied the blood on the staircase wall behind her. He brushed past her. "Whose blood is this?" He reached a hand toward the bloody trail, but stopped short of touching it.

"Violet's, my mother's," she replied, coming up behind him.

He followed the trail up the staircase through the open second-story door and halted abruptly as if he'd run into a wall. He muttered a curse under his breath as he surveyed the damage before him, "Like déjà vu." As she stepped to his side, he turned to her, grabbing both of her hands and squeezing, his face lined with urgency as he looked pleadingly into her eyes. "Listen, I know why she's doing this. I-It's because of me."

"That's not true," she said quickly. There was so much more he needed to know.

"It is," he said firmly, squeezing her hands to his chest, bringing her within inches of his face. "The night she killed my parents, she told me if I ever fell in—"

They were interrupted by the sound of loud movement in Emily's room and the two men's voices raising and then quieting.

"Let's talk in my room," she suggested, her face feeling unusually warm. As they stepped over the large splintered doorframe pieces that still scattered throughout the living room floor, he placed a protective hand on her lower back, as if ready to catch her if she tripped. As they walked into her bedroom, she became hyperaware of what Liam might be thinking as he surveyed the room and she suddenly was very glad that it wasn't her Littleton bedroom that he was checking out.

As if by instinctive pull, Liam immediately headed for the telescope poised by the window, still aimed toward the last view she had been scoping out. And it hadn't been the stars.

"Uh," she reached out as if to stop him, but it was too late. He was already peering through it, and when he looked back at her, he sported a smile of satisfaction. "Nice view of my balcony," he said, with a bit of the snarky attitude that angered her so much. Gone for the moment was the urgently concerned Liam.

But she quickly averted her eyes, her cheeks flaming and busied herself with straightening out the pillows and comforter on her bed. She tried to sound nonchalant as she replied over her shoulder, "I was admiring the architecture. What style is it in?"

"Body building," he answered, a hint of smugness in his tone.

"Huh?" she replied, straightening and facing him. Her mouth gaped open as his meaning sunk in. "That's *not* what I meant."

He sat at the desk, the chair creaking beneath the weight of his large stature and casually leaned back. "Ah, but you *did* understand what I meant and that could only mean—" The open laptop's screen on the desk lit up on its own, as if activated by his motion. Belle stifled a gasp that turned into an embarrassing gurgle. The last screen she had visited stared back at them: Liam's Peacock Profile. "That you're obsessed with me," he finished, swiveling around to look at her. He shook his head at her as if she'd been caught doing something naughty, but his sly smile and smoldering eyes told her something else that made her heartbeat race and her stomach turn somersaults.

Belle knew she should feel indignant, so she acted accordingly. "Do you know what I could do to you?" She waved her hands and wiggled dangerous spirit fingers at him, while she tried her best menacing face. She realized with a pang that the banter his digs instigated from her were fast becoming something she secretly enjoyed, but she could never let him know that.

Liam slowly stood up to his full height and approached her so that only inches separated them. "Are you threatening me?" He lowered his face closer to hers, his lips spreading into a devilish smile. "Like you want to punish me?"

She could feel the heat rolling off him and her lungs suddenly felt like they weren't working properly. "Why do I get the feeling it wouldn't be a painful punishment for you?"

He inched even closer, her heart threatening to choke her, until his breath was on her lips when he spoke again in a whisper, "*This* is painful."

The only thing she could think to say as he gripped her waist and squeezed was "I'm sorry?"

Her eyes fluttered closed as he brushed his lips along her cheek and whispered, "I'm not."

She fought her body's impulse to lean into him and wrap her arms around his neck in surrender. "I can't," she breathed out barely above a whisper, her last shred of control about to disappear.

Slowly, he stepped away as if it cost him immense willpower to do so. He brought Belle's hand to his lips, and as he pressed a soft kiss to the back of her hand, he held her gaze with all the fiery intensity that the next few moments had promised.

She reminded herself to breathe.

He let go of her hand and turned his back to her, keeping his head down. After a moment, he shook his head and his broad shoulders sagged.

"Liam?"

"You're right," he said, as if defeated. Facing her again now was the same Liam who'd arrived at her doorstep moments ago. His sense of urgency returned. "Listen, that witch—she told me something the night my parents died. Threatened me with it actually." He paused and sucked in a breath before exhaling slowly. "She said she'd kill any girl I fell in—" He shook his head and quickly corrected himself, a slight blush staining his cheeks. "Um, any girl that I found special."

"That's awful."

He took a step toward her and added softly, "So, you see, she tried to kill *you*."

A moment passed as she fully registered his meaning. "Oh." She had known about this since she overheard him speaking to Jacques in the castle, but hearing him say it to her...well, that unleashed a legion of butterflies inside her. "So, I'm *special* to you?" she asked in a tiny voice.

"Yes," he huffed out. "Obviously, there's no denying it. But—" he pointed through Belle's busted bedroom door at the destruction in the living room. "That witch was trying to make good on her promise." He approached her, grabbing her gently by the arms, his eyes full of pain as they gazed into hers. "This was all my fault. I can't allow you to be hurt because of my selfishness." He straightened and turned away. "Um, so what I'm really trying to say is...you can't associate with me anymore. It's too dangerous."

Oh man. Belle could feel something vital slipping through her fingers and, without thinking, her instinct was to try and snatch it back. She didn't want to lose Liam. So, she told him the truth that would ensnare him even deeper into her perilous world. He was wrong about one thing. *He* was the one in danger. But something inside her had panicked and she wasn't thinking too altruistically now.

"Um, actually..." Belle began.

This wasn't the reaction Liam had braced himself for. But then again, Belle was not like any girl. Period. Sparked by curiosity bordering on amusement, he turned and stared at her expectantly.

"The witch, Violet—she's not allowed to hurt me. It's kind of like a deal she has with my mom, the body that she's possessing. From what I understand, if Violet hurts me or my aunt...my mother, Abigail, will kill herself. Essentially killing Violet. Um, I don't know how that all makes sense, but in there"—she pointed at the living room—"my mother almost physically tore herself apart to hurt Violet when she struck Emily and threatened me."

Some myriad questions rushed into Liam's mind, but the one that mattered to him most was, "So, you're pretty much the only girl that the witch can't touch?"

Belle shrugged her shoulders. "Yep."

"You're the loophole?"

"I am the loophole."

Allowing the revelation to sink in, a noticeable change came over Liam as he stared at Belle. Doors of opportunity that had been sealed shut before, on pain of death, were being thrown open. Even his spirit was feeling considerably lighter. Like a fervent prayer his mind had always refused to acknowledge, but his heart had earnestly prayed, had finally been answered.

"Maybe there is a God after all," he remarked.

A beat passed between them as they gazed at each other, and then the sound of a throat clearing loudly broke the spell.

Ernesto stood in the doorway of her room. She blushed when she realized how close she had been to Liam and what Ernesto must be assuming about them. He probably thought they had just been about to kiss. Given their track record when less than a foot away from each other, Ernesto might've been right.

"I'll be gone soon, sir," Liam said, straightening.

"That won't be necessary." Ernesto stepped slowly into the room. "I'd actually like a word with you."

Liam threw Belle a questioning look, but she nodded encouragingly. Watching the two men face each other now reminded Belle of an old Western showdown.

Ernesto dug his hands into his pockets (he'd changed out of the bathrobe, thankfully) and looked Liam in the eye, as if what he was about to say took a lot of effort. "You were right about that night."

Liam looked down at the floor before meeting Ernesto's eyes. "I'm guessing the person on the phone responsible for convincing you to let me go that night was Emily."

Ernesto nodded.

"Makes sense now why she believed me." Liam cast a glance at Belle as if saying they had a lot to talk about and then looked at Ernesto. "So, what happens now?"

"We don't tell a soul, *anybody*, about what happened or what it all means. This remains between us." Ernesto cast a glance out the door and said, "The doctor owes me a favor. No questions asked." He turned his attention to Belle, cocking his head sideways as if remembering something important he wanted to ask her, but then instead motioned for them to follow him out. "Come, let's talk at the table." Once settled in at the kitchen table, Liam and Belle side-by-side, and Ernesto across from them, he leaned forward and asked Belle the question that was on his mind. "What 'dust' did you give her, Belle?"

"I don't even know. All I know is it was important enough for Papa to inscribe a warning about it on his gravestone telling me to keep it safe. Emily warned me too. Said to make sure Abigail—well, Violet Wickeby—didn't get her hands on it." She bit her lip. "Obviously, I failed. She has the dust."

"Violet Wickeby?" Ernesto asked.

"Violet Wickeby's spirit is possessing my mother. At least, that's what I've concluded."

Liam spoke up. "Is this what you were trying to explain to me back in my library? When I thought you were drinking the crazy sauce?" Belle nodded sheepishly. "So... it's all true then." Liam's voice cracked in disbelief. "And this Violet, she's the girl from Edward's diary. Threw herself off a cliff because some guy didn't love her back. Right?"

Belle nodded again. *'Edward.'* There was that name again. It sounded familiar for another reason she couldn't quite put her finger on.

"Uh-huh," Ernesto said, doubt lining his tone. "And you're supposed to be a Dream Seer and Abigail a Dream Catcher?"

Belle bristled at how weird she was appearing to be, especially in front of Liam. She glanced over at him and found him staring at her, unblinking, waiting for her answer. "Like I told you in the library," she told Liam, before turning her attention to Ernesto, "I dream of what Violet is doing sometimes. Now I know that my mother was purposefully showing me what Violet was up to."

"And what have you learned?" Ernesto asked, sheriff-like.

"Violet has a plan." She told them about the red Queen of Hearts diamond ring and the black serendibite bracelet. "She wears them on her hand like trophies."

Liam leaned back in his chair with a stormy expression.

"And tell me again exactly why she needs these jewels?" Ernesto pressed.

"She said she'd combine them with the dust to become unstoppable."

Ernesto stared at her, astounded by this new level of surrealism.

"It's true," Liam said, breaking his stony silence. "That night at my place, she gave a villain-speech thinking none of us would live to tell." He looked at Belle. "She said the same thing and some more. I thought it was a lunatic's rant." He shook his head.

"What more did she say?" she asked, reaching over and squeezing his hand under the table.

Liam looked like he was having a rough time with the information overload. One of his legs wouldn't stop its frantic ticking. "She said her spell was from a mermaid's siren song. She even sang it." He shuddered at the memory. "I only remember something about 'a blade of jade.' And there was something about gems and some mythical island."

Belle just barely caught herself from reacting out loud. That line was strikingly familiar. She was sure she read it in one of the books from the museum downstairs.

"If I hadn't seen her shoot a lightning bolt from her hand, I wouldn't believe it." Ernesto dragged his hand over his tired face. "I knew the Prynn sisters were special, a phenomenon of nature, but this? This is brujería, sorcery. I am not equipped for this."

"There's more," Belle said in a small voice. Both men looked at her expectantly. She told them about her visions of the twins and how they came to be her henchmen. "It's like they're under some spell. So, Violet really has three people held hostage." She didn't remember their names but described what they looked like.

"Did these guys help her kill my parents?" Liam asked, his eyes hard. Belle could tell what he was thinking: if he couldn't make her mother pay, then the twins were ripe for picking. He was out for blood.

"No," she said quickly. "They were entranced just a few months ago." She turned to Ernesto. "There has to be a missing report on them or something."

Ernesto was processing everything quietly and when all the gears finally clicked into place, he spoke as if he was in a briefing room with his police officers, "I'll put out an APB on her and the twins, cross-reference the missing kids' reports in this country and Interpol's and begin tracking down any missing rare jewelry." He stood up from the table, resolved. "If we can trace back her trail, we can figure out more to her plan. And *when* we catch her, I'll make her talk."

"You can't hurt Abigail," Belle said firmly. "She's still my mother. And Violet said that if the body dies, I die."

"That's kind of important to know," Liam interjected, wondering why she hadn't brought it up sooner.

Ernesto smiled patiently at her. "I promise I won't hurt your mother. And if I can contain her, she won't be able to hurt anyone else. And if I find the twins, I'll make them sing." He retrieved his gun belt from the top of the refrigerator and buckled it on. "Anything else I need to know?" he said, resting his hands on his hips.

Belle and Liam exchanged a look. Liam still hadn't said anything about his earlier suggestion for dealing with Violet. Belle wasn't going to bring it up because, unlike Liam, she already knew what Ernesto would say.

"Um, yeah," he said, tearing his eyes away from Belle's silent pleading stare for him to keep quiet. "We learned from an old diary that there are hunters who hunt these violent, 'unnatural' kind." He used the finger quotes.

Ernesto stared icily at him.

"Again," Belle said, "we don't want to hurt my mother."

"Belle's right," Ernesto said a bit harshly, causing Liam to narrow his eyes in confusion. Ernesto continued, eyeing him. "We don't want anyone else involved. This"—he jabbed his index finger against the center of the table—"is the trio of trust. No one else is to know what we know."

Liam's fist landed on the table with a heavy thud causing Belle to jump while Ernesto didn't flinch. "That witch murdered my parents! I need to do something about it! These hunters may be our best chance—"

"At what?" Ernesto challenged. "Killing Abigail? Emily? And then Belle? All the 'unnatural kind'?"

"'Violent ones,' the diary said."

Ernesto smiled cynically. "And these hunters get to decide what counts as violent or not."

Disappointment etched across Liam's face, and after a moment, he sighed in defeat. "You're right." Liam noticed Belle release the breath she'd been holding in, so he reached over and squeezed her knee. "Hey, I'm sorry. I'm just trying to offer a solution. But if it's anything that ends up with you hurt, then it's off the table." Belle smiled her thanks. He continued, "It's just hard, you know. I know she's your mom, but all I can think of is—I want justice."

"And there will be," Ernesto affirmed. "Let's do this my way. My people and I will find her, confiscate the jewelry, and then she won't be able to work her spell. Then, we'll figure it out from there." His cell phone beeped. He looked at the message, and his eyebrows flew up. "Looks like your school will be getting a new principal soon. Lena Steifschestwer's just been arrested."

"What?" Liam said in surprise, at the same time Belle enthusiastically said, "Really?!"

"I'm sure you'll hear all about it on the news soon. In the meantime," the chair scraped the floor as he abruptly got up, "we'll need to set up shifts until Emily's better." He grabbed his keys off the counter.

"I'll be here," Belle said. "So, I guess I have the first shift."

Ernesto frowned as if unsure about leaving Belle alone.

Liam spoke up, "I'm going to run home and then I'll be back soon to keep them company." He turned to Belle. "If that's alright with you."

Belle nodded. The temperature in the room felt much warmer now.

In a rare sign of approval, Ernesto clapped him on the back. He turned to go, saying, "I'll be back later tonight," but stopped and turned around at the top-landing door as if he forgot something, and looked straight at Liam. "Oh, one more thing: you have a 'strike one.'"

Liam's eyebrows furrowed in confusion. "I thought you believe me now about—"

Ernesto shook his head. "No, just a minute ago," he said pointedly. He raised an index finger at Liam, as if in warning, "Don't *ever* lose your temper around my family."

He held his gaze until Liam spoke up, "Of course...I'm sorry."

Ernesto suddenly piped up, "There's left-overs in the fridge." And he shut the door behind him.

Liam turned slowly back to Belle. "What happens at strike three?"

Belle grimaced. "I wouldn't want to know."

33

XOXO

Soon after Ernesto's departure, Belle walked Liam out to the front door. "You know, you don't really need to worry about me. I'll be fine here with Emily. I'm almost sure Violet isn't going to bother us for a while." She dipped her chin as if embarrassed. "She already has what she wants. She's got the pixie dust."

Liam pulled down on one of Belle's curls and watched it bounce back into place. He'd been looking at her intently. "From what I remember from her villainess song, she's still missing a few things. One's a jade-blade."

"I think what she sung may be a poem I read in one of the museum books. We can check it out when you get back."

"So, you *do* want me to come back?" he said, inching closer. His minty green eyes searched hers out and held them, while his lips smirked in the way that infuriated or titillated Belle. At this point, she wasn't sure which.

"Well, it would be, uh, productive," she stammered, the heat crawling down her throat. Those yellow flecks were so distracting. "We could

find that poem and then there's that project we're supposed to finish...."
She'd trailed off, her eyes fluttering closed because Liam had wrapped
a hand through her hair and around her neck, and with his other hand
intertwined with hers, his lips slowly brushed a trail from her ear to the
corner of her mouth. The feeling was intoxicating and almost succeeded
in smothering the cautionary words from Ernesto that surfaced in her
mind: *"...once you're given a target, you're bound to it somehow- like an
on-switch you can't turn off.... You sleep, eat, breath thinking of the target...the only way to be rid of it is to kill it."*

"Why are you doing this?" she whispered, just as his lips hovered over
hers.

Slowly, he pulled away, pinning her with a questioning look.

"It's, It's only been three or four days since I've known you," she
took a deep breath, her voice growing stronger. "Heck, only four days
since I've moved here. And I am honestly not experienced with romance, unless you count the ones in my head with my book-boyfriends,
so I'm not altogether too sure if I'm reading all of your signals cor-
rectly."

"Book-boyfriends?" Liam repeated, a smile tugging at the corners of
his lips, but anxiety over her objections tinged his gaze.

"Mr. Darcy and Gilbert Blythe," she rattled off automatically.

Liam asked lightly with a wicked glint in his eye, "So I can't bash
their faces in?"

Her jaw dropped. "See? *That* is not normal." Then, she gestured between the two of them. "*This* is not normal. This attraction between
us—" She stopped at her confession, shutting her mouth and feeling her
cheeks fire up.

The worry lines left Liam's face. "You're right. I do have..." he paused
as if searching for the right word, "an *affinity* for you."

"Oh. That, that sounds nicer than 'attraction'."

"It's the truth." He leaned back against the side of the doorframe,
and for a moment was deep in thought before he said, "Wanna sit with
me for a minute?"

"Sure, but just for a few minutes. I need to get back to Emily." She wondered what more he could say to her. Already, though, that insidious suspicion about Liam, himself, possibly being Jäger was fading. He led her to the swinging porch seat outside. The air was cool against her skin, and the night sky was painted with a few stars and the glittering lights of the boardwalk shops. "I can't believe you live there," Belle remarked, with a pinch of envy in her voice. She was gazing at the Rawlins Castle. Its imposing peaks and turrets jutting into the sky, cast a vast, oppressive shadow that obscured the bright, fancy lights of the Manor Hill mansions sitting at its feet.

"I literally live like in one room in that place."

She looked at him as if he was making a mistake. "I would turn that big, beautiful castle into a school for orphans."

Liam bit back what he wanted to say because it would have sent her running for the hills. She was already suspicious of his quick attachment to her. *Then the castle's yours,* is what he'd wanted to tell her. Instead, he focused on helping her understand what was going on between them. Maybe, it'd help him understand too.

Belle misinterpreted the thoughtful silence between them as awkward. "Are you really okay with all of this?" She waved her hands around and jutted her thumb behind her, as if indicating all the weirdness that had just taken place in the house behind them.

Liam leaned his large frame forward, resting his elbows on his knees. "I have been completely lost in the dark since my parents died. Alone. With no one to completely trust, not even myself." He cradled his forehead with one hand, as if what he had to say next was difficult. "I, um...." Belle inched closer to him and laid a hand on his shoulder. He drew in a deep breath and exhaled roughly. "I almost jumped off that balcony ledge a few times." She squeezed his shoulder as a lump formed in her throat. "Whenever I had convinced myself that I had killed my parents, especially my mom," his voice cracked on the last word, "I didn't think I was worthy of life." He stayed silent for a minute, shouldering the burden of the once familiar gloom that had descended for what he hoped was the last time. "And then you showed up," he said suddenly.

She felt compelled to meet his eyes. They glittered with an intensity that made her catch her breath. He was so close now. The blonde stubble along his strong jaw was thicker, his lips tantalizingly close and his eyes liquid sea green. She was suddenly hyper-aware of the feel of his solid shoulder beneath her hand and she slid it off slowly, only to accidently have brushed the back of her hand down the length of his bicep. It sent the blood rushing to her cheeks and a fiery sensation in her hands. She quickly clasped her hands together.

Without breaking the connection their eyes held, he reached for one of her hands.

"Don't," she pleaded.

"It's okay," he said gently and he interlocked his fingers through hers. By the way his eyebrows lifted and he glanced at their hands, she knew he felt the jolt that this physical contact had wrought. She bit her lip. *Think happy thoughts, think happy thoughts.* But as he continued talking, she was drawn out of her head and into his words, and her hand eventually relaxed in his. "I mean, I admit, at first you caught my attention for very natural reasons," he smiled slyly as she frowned at him. "And then...." Belle felt his hand becoming sweaty. "And then, um...sorry, uh, I've never sat around and talked about *feelings* with anyone. Except with my shrink, but even that didn't last very long." He let go of her hand and dried his hands on his lap. "Wow, I've never gotten nervous around a girl."

Belle couldn't help it—she was Eizabeth and here was Darcy before her struggling to pour his heart out to her. She sighed and smiled dreamily.

Liam narrowed his eyes playfully at her. "You're role-playing in your head or something right now, aren't you?"

Belle's eyebrows flew up in surprise. "How'd you know?"

He shook his head and laughed. "Your eyes kind of glaze over and you have this little faraway smile."

She blushed at how observant he apparently was of her. "Sorry. It's a bad habit from my loner days."

He nodded. "Well, we're a lot alike there."

She leaned in, pressing for him to continue. "What were you going to say after 'And then'?"

He pushed back a thick strand of her curly hair that had fallen over her eye. "And then," he met her eyes, "you kept drawing me in, just with the way you are." He held her wide-eyed gaze. "And then you became a light in my darkness. You gave me the answers I needed. And slowly, I feel like you're helping me piece myself back together...."

Belle was stunned. She had no words. All she could do was imagine showing him how those words had made her feel. She would cup his chiseled cheeks in her hands and press her lips against his pillow-soft ones. He would readily kiss her back, fulfilling the one thing he'd wanted to do since returning to her house and finding her alive.

"You like kissing, huh?" he said, his voice low and husky. His lips, wearing a hint of a playful smile, were only an inch away from hers.

Belle's eyes grew wide. She hadn't just imagined kissing him, she'd actually done it. Normally, she would have felt ashamed for what she thought would have been a lack of propriety, but somehow, with Liam, it felt right. He wasn't a Jäger. He was just a guy who *really* liked her and appreciated her, even with all the mutant defects that would send normal guys running away faster than they could scream "Freak!" But Liam wasn't a normal guy...he was actually an incredible guy.

Holding his minty gaze, she boldly replied, "I think...I just like kissing *you*." And she kissed him again.

If she had to pick one kiss with Liam to remember forever, it was this one. This one held the sweet thrill of promise behind it. There were no doubts or disconnects in the back of their minds miring this kiss. Their hearts were on the same page, in a strange, fantastical tale that Fate had seemingly ordained for them to play out together. But as the kiss deepened and Belle gravitated even closer to him, the sudden reminder that she could burn him with her touch caused her to abruptly pull her hands away from his cheeks.

"Don't," Liam said, catching her hands. He held up their hands and interlocked them. "Don't think about that," he said gently. "Just think about," he pressed his lips against hers, "how my lips feel against your lips," he pressed a kiss beneath her ear, "how they feel against your neck..." A sigh escaped Belle. "And there..." he murmured, placing a soft kiss on her collarbone.

A hot, buzzing sound drew their attention to their joined hands. Little white bolts of electricity vibrated between their hands as harmlessly as placing a hand on a plasma globe.

"I don't think your method works," Belle pouted. "I'm still zapping you."

"But it doesn't burn." He suddenly withdrew his hands away. "Until now." He blew air onto his hands.

"It's hopeless." She got up and remained standing, crossing her arms in front of her, and staring dejectedly into the distance.

In one swift move, Liam stood and encircled her in his arms, tipping her chin toward him. "Hey, if there's one thing I've learned since I met you," he pressed a light, warm kiss against her lips, "is that there *is* hope."

That comment just about reached deep inside her and hugged her heart. She rewarded him with an endearing smile and they stood gazing at each other for a minute, until Liam abruptly pecked her on the lips, smacked her behind, and hopped off the porch. "Now go take care of Emily," he wagged a finger at her as he walked away backwards, "and when I get back, no more kissing, young lady. And hands off all this—" he referenced his body, while cracking a wicked grin. "I don't want to feel like my virtue isn't safe around you."

Belle laughed out loud. "Oh, so what you're really saying is that *my* virtue isn't safe around you."

He paused, and from the short distance that had already been created between them, Belle could feel the heat in his words, "You're in charge, angel."

"Angel?" Belle repeated, looking dubiously at him.

He looked at her incredulously. "You still don't get it, do you?" He shook his head. "Well, then, I need to make you understand again, huh?" In just a few wide strides, he was on the porch again.

"What are you—" Belle began, but he'd caught her mouth in a searing kiss. He grabbed her hands and looped them behind his neck, his hands trailing down her arms to her waist, squeezing her to him, until her feet lifted off the floor.

When he placed her back on her feet and let go, she was breathless. And she could swear she saw stars in her hazy field of vision.

"Do you get it, now?" he panted, holding her steady by the elbows.

She looked up at him after a minute and scrunched her face. "Kind of," she said, doing the "so-so" gesture with her hand.

He laughed. "A-ha, you bad girl."

"Hey," Belle suddenly remembered something she'd been meaning to ask him. "Where did Emily take you after she—"

"Pulled that Harry Potter stunt?"

Belle nodded, curiosity written all over her face.

"She left me in a dungeon I didn't even know the castle had."

Her eyes popped with excitement.

"You like that, don't you?" Liam smiled and shook his head. "You weirdo."

"Hey!" Belle threw a light punch against his arm, which actually hurt her more than him.

Liam chuckled and withdrew the semi-injured hand she'd started cradling and dropped a seductive kiss against it. He held her hand as he continued, "When I finally managed to get a bar on my cell, I called Jacques. A few wrong secret passageways until the right one finally led him to me. And then I ran straight here. I didn't want to risk making a sound by bringing a car." He exhaled with relief as he looked at Belle, standing here alive. He looked like he wanted to hug her again.

"So, you were in the castle's dungeon with secret passageways that whole time?"

"You may have enjoyed it if you'd been in my shoes, but it was tearing me up the whole time thinking the witch had killed everyone in this house." A dark look passed over his eyes and he pressed his mouth into a firm line as he remembered.

Belle touched his face.

He focused back on her and his features relaxed into a smile. "I guess our next date's in that dungeon." His eyes roamed her face as if committing to memory every detail.

"I'll bring the picnic basket," she said just as seriously as he had been looking at her, but this only made him laugh again.

"Of course, you will," he replied, grinning. And then after a moment, he sobered and wet his lips before leaning in and giving her a slow, gentle goodbye kiss that she felt all the way to her toes.

"I'll be back," he said huskily.

"Like in an hour?"

"More like 30 minutes," he corrected.

She looked at him skeptically.

"What? I'm motivated," he replied with feigned innocence.

Slowly, he let go of her hand as he stepped off the porch. And then a mischievous smile spread across his face. "I'm going to blow your mind right now, Belle. You ready?"

She looked at him like he had sprouted alien tentacles. "Okay, who's the weirdo now?"

He stood there a good ten feet away with his hands in his pockets, but the look he pinned her with captivated her. For a moment, it felt like they were the only two people in the world. He gave her his most smoldering bedroom eyes and said softly, "Parting is such sweet sorrow that I shall say goodnight till it be morrow."

"Oh. My. Lanta," Belle whispered, her heart stuttering.

He grinned with pleasure at her reaction and chuckled. "See you soon."

She watched until his finely formed figure retreated into the shadows of the night. She listened as he got into his car, started the engine and then peeled away like a man on a mission.

She shook her head to herself and touched her raw lips as she turned to head inside. *If Liam keeps sweet-talking me in Shakespeare, I am in serious trouble.*

34

Truly Beastly

Liam had arrived home in record time. He felt like wings, not his car, had carried him home. Even with the maelstrom that he and Belle were deep in with the Lightning Witch, and even though he still didn't understand everything about the insane, sci-fi nature of the Prynn family, he was never happier than he was now. And it was all thanks to Belle. No woman has ever had this effect on him. Hell, he could see a future with her. Every other girl had been just a temporary fix. Did this make him a terrible guy? He knew it. But now he felt like just knowing Belle was making him a better man.

If his football friends could see what he was thinking right now, he knew what they'd say about him.... He was whipped.

But with the hesitations that Belle had expressed on that porch over how fast they were moving, he knew he'd have to slow it down Matrix-style or risk scaring her off. So, tonight, he was serious about the hands-off rule he'd jokingly mentioned to her. Just homework, stop-the-witch research, and a Batman-movie marathon to catch her up to speed on some essential knowledge.

Unless Belle made a move on him. Then, it was game over with the good-behavior plan.

He sped through the shower and threw on some cargo shorts. Running a comb through his damp hair, he figured it was time for a haircut. This past year, he'd only cared enough about his appearance to keep his facial hair in check, and channeling his anger and depression into weight-lifting and boxing had done the rest for his body. And for the first time in a year, he could look in the mirror now and nod at himself and say, "Who's that sexy beast?"

He glanced at his cell phone clock. Eight minutes left.

While towel-drying his hair, he stepped out into the secondary part of the vast bedroom that was attached to the large balcony and spied the dark long-sleeved Henley shirt he was looking for in the "clean pile" on the floor. Just as he reached the pile, he froze. An odd, cold breeze had swept over him, eliciting a barrage of goosebumps along his exposed torso. Turning his head, he saw that the glass balcony doors, which he kept locked, stood wide open, its curtains billowing with the intruding ocean wind.

Ignoring the deep chill that coursed through him, he listened and scanned his surroundings for anything out of place. Jacques was out doing whatever he does at this hour. And those heavy deadbolt locks on the balcony doors could only be opened manually, which could only mean one thing...he wasn't alone.

A whisper. Out on the balcony. Or was it the wind?

His aluminum bat was too far away, propped against his night table by the bed. He crept toward the open windows, his senses painfully heightened, until he stood at the entrance of the balcony.

Nothing. The empty expanse of the balcony gaped back at him and the only sound was the incessant low roar of the waves battering the rocks below.

He turned to check the rest of his bedroom and was startled at the sight of three dark figures standing just within the room.

"Hello, handsome. We meet again."

Liam ground his teeth. "Witch," he spat.

Violet stood wearing a skin-tight suit as black as her short, newly cropped hair, and beneath a white Phantom of the Opera-like mask covering the half of her face that was shredded by Abigail, she sneered at Liam. The two tall, dark figures who flanked her were dressed like the typical nighttime robbers, all in black, except for the masks they wore: one wore an exaggerated "happy-face" drama mask and the other wore the "sad-face" version. They stood with their hands fisted and their feet apart, as if waiting for the signal to pounce.

Shifting her weight onto one foot and placing a hand casually on her hip, Violet drawled out to them, "I promised you some fun tonight, boys, didn't I?"

They nodded vigorously and began shifting impatiently on their feet like two dogs catching the scent of prey and anxious to give it chase.

Liam shifted slightly into a defensive stance and clenched his fists.

Violet's eyes roamed over Liam. "Hmmm. I see you've inherited the famous Rawlins male physique. Something William loved to show off any chance he got. I bet he didn't care that I used to watch him bathe in the river." She suddenly screamed out in pain, her head moving as if someone had grabbed her chin and wrenched it aside. Frozen in that position, she whispered, her voice trembling with rage, "Let go, Abigail.... You won't give me the girl, so I *will* take the boy. Let go...or I take them both!" She slouched forward as if released and let out a low roar of frustration.

Happy-face reached for her in concern and she snapped, "Don't touch me!"

Liam took a step toward the door, but Violet pinned him with a murderous look and gritted out, "What are you waiting for, boys? Get him!"

At once, the two darted at Liam. He side-stepped to his right and connected his fist to Sad-face's jaw with a terrible crack, sending him straight to the floor with a thud.

Happy-face paused, momentarily stunned as he looked from his brother knocked-out cold at his feet to Violet, as if unsure what to do, which was unfortunate for Happy-face because Liam did not hesitate: down went Happy-face with an iron left hook.

Liam continued moving toward the door—he knew his fists were no match for the witch's deadly lightning bolts—but as Violet looked in shock from her senseless henchmen sprawled on the floor back to Liam, she quickly recovered and shot out one hand toward him.

Liam had braced himself for the death bolt that would surely kill him, but as he peeled his eyes open, he found that he was suspended in air, frozen, only his toes brushing against the floor. He tried moving his mouth to say something, but—nothing, not even a twitch of muscle. No part of his body responded to him, except his eyes. He could only look on in horror as the witch walked past him out onto the balcony with her hand still pointed at him.

"Come, join me." Automatically, his body floated toward her. "It's such a nice night out." She walked to the edge and peered over it. "Much nicer than the night I last stood at this very spot. No stars were out. None to inspire an inkling of hope. Only a wind that kept pushing this way, nudging me...as if the universe was whispering to me, 'Do it.'" She turned back and faced him. He hovered, paralyzed, in the middle of the balcony. "Now, I understand why. The universe needed me."

She pressed a finger against her temple as if remembering something. "How did that line go? Oh, yes. 'For ye shall rule in eternal youth and be granted one wish in all sooth.' I have followed its commands so far...." With her right hand still stretched out toward Liam as if holding him in place, she opened her left palm and watched as electricity danced in her palm, illuminating her half-masked face and the maniacal gleam in her eye. "And, like a dutiful daughter, I've been rewarded with this power." She snapped her left hand shut. "Now, you will help me complete the plan and then I will be immortal and rule over all."

She raised her free hand in the air and muttered, "The reddest rose, come to me."

She stepped closer to him and looked up at his face. "I'm going to release you now. Are you going to behave? Blink twice if that's a yes, or not at all if I'll have to kill you."

Liam defiantly refused to blink.

"Pity. I thought you cared for the girl." She shrugged her shoulder. "I'll just have to use her then."

He quickly blinked twice.

"Wise choice," she sneered. She dropped the right hand and Liam fell to the floor with a grunt.

"What do you want?" He groaned, rolling onto his side and propping himself up onto his knees. His whole body ached all over from the crushing grip that had held him suspended.

A long-stemmed red rose flew out above the balcony and straight into Violet's outstretched hand. "Your servitude," she replied. "You obey me, and no one gets hurt."

"Why? Why me?"

"I am owed a Prynn or a Rawlins slave." She shrugged her shoulders. "Let's just say, it'll add joy to my day."

Liam watched, entranced, as the rose hovered before her, and as she chanted a spell, the long stem unseamed itself like ribbons and wove into a webbed circle with the red rose petals affixed at the center. It looked like a dream catcher.

She grabbed one side of it and held it before him. "Grab the other side." She splayed her free palm toward him, as if ready to strike him should he dare try anything.

He could see now this up close how much she looked like Belle. With a pang, he thought how the past hour had been the most amazing time he'd had in a long time and now it was threatening to become his last. He had so been looking forward to spending more time with Belle. He had already been planning to take her to his secret getaway spot in the forest, right where it met the base of the mountain...but he couldn't let anything happen to her. Belle had already saved him, so now it was time for him to return the favor. If he was killed for it, at least he'd die a happy man.

He met Violet's steely gaze. "You said 'no one gets hurt' if I help you. I know you, yourself, cannot hurt Belle, or Abigail will kill you, but how do I know you won't bewitch me into hurting Belle?"

Violet shrugged nonchalantly and smirked. "You'll just have to trust me then."

With his palms up in surrender, Liam shook his head and slowly began walking backwards away from her, towards the edge of the balcony.

She narrowed her eyes in suspicion and released a slow bolt of electrified light that lazily stretched out from her hand, following Liam and threatening to latch onto him. "What. Are. You. Doing?"

"You see, that's the problem. I don't trust you. I'd rather jump off this balcony than help you hurt Belle." The back of his legs hit the ledge. He put one hand on it as if ready to prop himself up.

"Stop," she gritted out.

He continued climbing the ledge.

A lightning bolt crashed against the ledge, shattering it to pieces. The explosive force tossed Liam back onto the balcony, away from the edge. "You can't stop me," he grunted, gathering himself off the floor. The concrete shards had pummeled him. He winced as he stood. He probably had a broken rib. "You're just gonna have to kill me."

"No, I won't. You won't even want to kill yourself after what I tell you."

"There is nothing you can say, Witch, that I'll believe."

She lowered the dream catcher and the blood from where the thorns had punctured her palm dripped onto the floor. With her other hand, she tapped a finger against her cheek. "Oh, no? If you are willing to die for her, then you are *not* her hunter. And if you are not her hunter, you are *not* her true love."

"What?" He scowled in confusion.

"Only her hunter is her true love. And he'll hunt her to her death."

He shook his head. "How does that make any sense? You're lying."

Her eyes flashed, and she smiled nastily. "*I'm* lying? I think your sweet Belle has been the liar all along. I may be wicked, but a liar, I am not."

"And she won't have any hunters after her," Liam continued, his heart hammering against his chest, "because she isn't violent. Jäger only hunt the violent kind. My ancestor, Edward, said so in his diary."

"Hah! You Rawlins men. Even now, you can't resist a Prynn skirt. You think I'm a witch? Well, the Prynns are sirens leading men to their deaths."

He backed away, shaking. "Y-You're insane."

"Oh, but I'm not finished. You haven't even heard the best part." She laughed gleefully. "Belle is just like Mommy Dearest, except Abigail has only killed one person, Jonas Rawlins." She stepped closer to him. "Ready for the kicker?"

Liam knew he shouldn't listen to her. That this witch was just messing with his mind, trying to get him to yield. But he had a heartbreaking feeling that the witch wasn't totally lying. Because, because how much did he really know about Belle anyways?

Violet batted her eyelashes in mockery. "Poor, innocent Belle..." she grew serious and snarled, "murdered three men."

Liam stumbled backwards. "No. Th-That can't be," he replied weakly.

"Well, four men if you include her father."

He felt as if the air had been sucked out of his lungs.

"Now," Violet held up the dream catcher again. "Grab. The. Other. Side."

When he hesitated, she said, "How about this? Just to prove I am telling the truth, when you are under my service, you will not be able to harm your true love, whomever it may be."

Groaning sounds from behind them caught their attention. The twins were waking up.

"Vi?"

"What the hell happened?"

"Over here, boys," she called over her shoulder to them. She pinned Liam with a fierce look. "My patience has run out." She held the dream catcher up to him. "Take it. Now."

Liam took one tentative step closer.

The twins straightened out their masks and joined Violet on either side. They breathed hard like they wanted another go at Liam, but they knew not to interfere.

"And for the record," she said just above a whisper. "I don't need Abigail. Abigail needs me. And I am really, *really* tired of Abigail. The young, inexperienced Belle seems so much more...inviting. Catch my meaning?" She squeezed her hand tighter on the dream catcher and held it up closer to him. Blood seeped out between her fingers. "But if you promise your servitude to me, then no one gets hurt. Especially your true love."

Something in Liam snapped. With her evil, twisted words, this witch just robbed him of the newfound bliss he thought he'd found with Belle, and now his father's charred body and his mother's screams re-played in his mind, and he felt that deep dark pit looming up again to swallow him. And he was having none of it.

"I'll pass," he said, with a hard stare. He stepped away and threw a look at the twins. "I won't be another one of your lap dogs."

They lunged at him, but Violet commanded, "Stay."

Liam smirked. "Maybe you can get them to 'roll over' now."

The twins roared in protest.

"Patience, my loves," Violet said with an eerie calm. Her hand suddenly shot out and Liam was once again frozen and suspended in midair. "You see, I don't *really* need your permission." She flicked her wrist and he began turning 360º before her. "It's just a bit of a power boost for me when what I want is willingly given. I can get what I need from you with just a fraction of your allegiance."

Liam came to a stop, facing her again.

She narrowed her eyes at him. "Oh, but you *will* be punished now for your insolence."

Liam's eyes burned with rage.

She spoke over her shoulder to the twins, "How would you both like a pet? I think you boys have earned it." She looked at Liam with a smug smile. "Lapdog, no?"

"You're gonna turn him into a dog?" Happy-face asked.

"Not just any dog," she replied, running a finger down the length of Liam's chest. She drew closer and whispered, "I hear you like to be called 'Beast.'"

An angry tear escaped and rolled off Liam's face.

"Well, then," Violet continued, stepping back and raising the dream catcher, "a beast you shall be."

With a flick of her free hand, Liam's hand moved and latched onto the other side of the dream catcher. He squeezed his eyes shut as he felt the thorns pierce into the flesh of his palm. His hand felt slick and wet and like it was on fire. When he opened his eyes again, the twins had stepped away, giving Violet a wide berth as she chanted in a language that did not sound earthly.

The dream catcher tore out of Liam's hand and he crumpled to the floor.

As she continued the melodic, unnatural chant, she tossed the dream catcher and it hung in midair, spinning above where Liam lay.

He tried to get up, but he could only groan and writhe with the excruciating pain that felt like lava scorching its way through his body. At Violet's word, "bestia," he let out a gut-wrenching cry at what felt like every bone in his body breaking and shifting at once. His limbs stretched torturously, sharp claws tore through his fingers and toes, and he flipped on all fours with unnatural speed as his spine elongated out of his body into a tail and long, dark blonde hair grew out of every pore of his skin. His screams were silenced as his face contorted and stretched before him.

"Now, Beast, just one more step," Violet cooed as if trying to soothe him. "I have a nosy little Prynn to transfer into your mind. Let's see how she likes *this* horror show." She chanted again as she circled him, the dream catcher descending until it touched Liam's forehead, and when it did, a blinding flash of pain erupted in his head, and he blacked out.

35

When the Wild Things Come

Belle jumped in her chair. She clutched the book to her chest and gazed out Emily's bedroom window, searching for the source of the long, mournful howl that had startled her. It had sounded like a wolf. But there were no wolves in Elmridge, unless they were beyond the town's wall in the forest or mountains. And how can a wolf be loud enough to hear from so far away? Perhaps, if it was a monstrous-sized wolf....

But she shrugged off the fright. It'd been an hour now and Liam still hadn't showed. With each passing minute, the potential for a disappointing no-show warred with the excitement of his arrival at any moment. Her cheeks burned when she remembered how it felt to be in his arms. She so enjoyed his kisses and didn't haven't an ounce of regret. The feeling was more than she'd imagined from her romance novels.

But, and it was a big 'but,' she learned enough to believe that marriage was sacred, and she'd decided that she'd never "go all the way" unless it was with her husband—the man who'd truly love her enough to take that sacred oath with her. Call her old-fashioned, but that is what felt the most right to her. Her husband would be her true love. Hopefully, her traitorous body would obey her mental resolve. Which was why, when Liam arrived, no more smooch-fests— just Lightning Witch research and family history project.

She'd already started on the research. She found a poem about the blade of jade in an Elmridge fairy tales book, which was currently cradled against her chest. She settled back onto the plush chair and before cracking the book open again, looked over at Emily's sleeping form in the bed before her. Ernesto's doctor-friend had hooked her up to machines that monitored her vitals. The moonlight shining through a large bay window by her bed, cast a soft glow on Emily's face, making her look like an angel.

Satisfied that all seemed fine with Emily so far, Belle returned her attention to the page she'd been reading. There was a picture of an ornately illustrated mermaid with long flowing, green hair, sitting on a giant rock on the shore of a sea. She was looking back over her shoulder at the reader, and her mesmerizing, exotic face had a pair of eyes that were inhumanly large for her face and otherworldly: instead of a typical eye color, they were like two starry night skies. On the opposite page, she re-read the scroll-like writing of the poem:

Come close, wayfarer, and lend me your ear;
Though you be from afar, from the second morning star,
You'll find eternity here, if our rules, you adhere.
For we know all mysteries, timeless secrets and histories,
From the roots of this Island to your own world's end.
Peer now into our endless eyes and learn of the Island's highest prize.
A warrior, who can fly, fight, and crow, and rid us of a most pestilent foe:
A bearded enemy sailing these seas, pillaging, plundering, ignoring all pleas.
Come, Savior, save us from slaughter!
Our pixies go far, recruiting son or daughter!
The first contacts, they'll choose, and the Chosen pay dues:

Immortality, powers for their first-born child;
On the Island, they'll test in the Wild.
Hearken, Leader, pass this grand test,
And prove to this Island that ye are the best:
Red diamond from romantic spice,
Serendibite from a life's sacrifice,
Fire opal from vengeful rage,
Taffeite from one pure and sage.
Gather all as gifts and mount them on this:
A blade of jade and sealed with a kiss.
For ye shall rule in eternal youth, and be granted one wish in all sooth.
A word of caution to this truthful tale: face down a Hunter and ye shall fail.

The message seemed loud and clear to Belle. Violet needed two more precious stones: fire opal and taffeite. Attach the stones to that blade of jade, and she'd somehow become some eternal ruler. And it looked like a hunter, perhaps the Jäger, was her weakness.

Incredulous, Belle shook her head. A few months ago, this all would have been just the sort of ludicrous fantasy she would have lost herself in for hours, but now astonishingly this was real life for her.

She sighed loudly, frustrated. *Where's Liam?!*

She had so much to tell him already. Remembering her cell phone, she nearly bounced out of the chair to retrieve it from her bag. Maybe he'd been trying to call her? Sitting back down with it, she turned it on, and, instantly, her phone's screen lit up with unanswered messages.

Her heart sank.

None from Liam. His name didn't even appear in her Missed Calls list.

It was way past an hour already. Feeling deflated, she decided to check a text from Candy: **Thank you, girl!!!! You got the Stiff fiiiiiii-iiiiired!!! Woot-woot! Check out the video of her arrest, lmao! It's gone viral!** She included emojis of laughing/crying faces, a police man, handcuffs, and a witch-face.

Belle played the clip Candy had included and watched with growing satisfaction as the police escorted an enraged Mrs. Steifschwester from her home, through a throng of reporters, and then into the cruiser. Belle giggled when she saw that the police had not even given her a chance to change out of the two-piece pajama set she wore that was covered in "I♥Prince" script and neon-colored hearts.

A reporter had shouted out a question, "Is it true you tried to poison the comatose Mr. Ellerson, and that you've been endangering his daughter this whole time?"

Stony-faced and with her chin stubbornly held up high, she turned an icy glare upon the reporter and said, "That is an outrageous accusation. And the girl is a delinquent liar." The police began shoving her along, but she continued and yelled out, "I know people in high places! My people will have me out in no time!" The video cut off with the police slamming the car door in her face.

Belle grinned when she thought about Cindy not having to deal with the Stiff anymore. She hoped Mr. Ellerson would be able to improve now that he wasn't being poisoned anymore, and maybe life could really start looking up for Cindy.

The next message she saw was an unknown number, but when Belle read the message, she quickly saved the number as a new friend in her contacts.

Hi, it's Cindy. I just wanted to say thank you. So much.

Belle texted back, **I'm just glad to be your friend. You deserve to be happy.**

She saw some older messages that she had never opened from Jared. They were all quick one-liners.

Hey.

What's up?

What you up to?

You and Liam a thing?

See you at school.

She decided she'd talk to him tomorrow at school. She didn't want to risk responding to his texts now and opening a dialogue this late. Especially when Liam was on her mind. Although if Liam did show up late, she wrestled with the idea of telling him to just go home for keeping her waiting past what he'd promised. Or maybe she just needed to ease up a bit on her expectations. After all, whatever this was between them was just a few days old. It was probably better if he didn't come.

She felt her soul pout in response, and she knew then she couldn't lie to herself about this. She *wanted* Liam here.

An incoming text filled her cell phone screen.

It's Grace from school. I got your photo. That IS Peter.

Belle's breath hitched.

Another text chimed in.

He showed up just now. I showed him the pic and all he said was "Mother." He took the pic from me and flew out the window.

A shadow fell across the room and the window rattled by Emily's bed.

I think he's headed to your place.

Belle drew her legs up to her chest, and peering over the edge of the book pressed against her chest, she hoped the darkness of the corner she was in obscured her presence. Her ears perked at the sound of the bolt on the window sliding open from the inside.

She swallowed. Only magic could have done that.

She knew the bay windows opened when the curtains billowed and a soft breeze fanned Emily's hair from her face. She stifled a gasp when a boy flew in, followed by a trail of shimmering gold dust that evaporated when he landed silently on his bare feet. He looked wild, with reddish hair that stuck out in every direction, clothed in animal skin and thick green leaves.

The window door flapped against the wall and the boy reacted instantaneously—he spun back, swiftly pulling out a dagger as he faced the window. With the moonlight illuminating his face, Belle could see the striking similarity he bore to Emily, only he appeared more elfish with his pointy ears and prominent almond-shaped eyes. He was a handsome boy, who looked strong and salient for his age. But when Belle saw the dagger he brandished in his hand, her eyes went round: it was green just like jade. She watched as he sheathed the blade back in its holster, and as he took one sweeping look around, Belle closed her eyes. If he did see her, then hopefully he'd ignore her if he thought she was asleep.

She counted to 5 in her head and then slowly reopened her eyes.

He was beside Emily, peering down at her. He withdrew Belle's photo from a pocket and looked from the image to Emily.

"Mother?" he whispered.

He touched Emily's arm, but she did not stir. He furrowed his eyebrows and pressed his lips into a firm line, and Belle knew that he had noticed the branching red scars on her arms. He reached into a small pouch that hung from a makeshift leather belt around his waist, and pulled out a pinch of gold dust that he released over Emily in a shower of tiny golden sparkles.

Belle's protective instinct kicked in, but she remained still: she knew this boy wasn't here to cause any harm.

Emily stirred, and the boy took a step back.

Her eyes fluttered open. It appeared she was trying to focus and orient herself to her surroundings and time of day. But when her eyes landed on the boy standing beside her, they popped open.

"Peter?" she croaked out.

He did not move.

"Peter?" she moved more urgently now, struggling to sit up. "Peter? Is it...is it really you?" She suddenly covered her eyes with her hand. "No, no this can't be real. I must be dreaming. Or, I've finally gone insane." Her voice cracked on the last word. But when she looked again, Peter had drawn closer. He peered at her, as if suspicious, while she stared back at him, ghostly pale and her eyes bright and luminous.

Peter showed her the photo. "Mother?" he asked softly.

Emily's eyes spilled over with tears as she gasped out with a sob, "Yes! Yes, my darling boy! Come, let me feel you and make sure you're not just a dream!" She held out a hand to him.

Slowly, as if all time stood still, Peter slipped his hand in hers and squeezed.

Emily cried, tears of joy streaming down her cheeks.

Peter's face softened. He offered her his other hand, which she gladly took, and he gently pulled her up into a sitting position with her feet touching the floor. She pushed the heavy blankets away and pulled off the monitor-wires that were attached to her skin.

Peter watched, concerned. "Are you hurt, Mother?"

She smiled rapturously at him. "Not anymore, Peter." She took his hands again. "Where have you been?" she asked, failing to mask the pain in her voice.

He smiled, an impish dimple appearing in his cheek. "I'd like to show you, Mother. May I?"

She nodded, her happy tears unceasing.

"We'll need some more fairy dust," he withdrew another pinch of gold dust from his pouch, "and you just need to think happy thoughts."

"*You* are my happy thought, Peter."

He held her gaze as he opened his palm before her and gently blew the shimmering dust onto her. She squeezed her eyes closed as she relished the shower of gold.

When she opened her eyes, Peter stood by the window, one foot on the ledge, and one hand extended toward her. She didn't feel the bed beneath her anymore. She was floating! She cried out in glee and stretched out her arms and legs, enjoying this new sensation of freedom from gravity's clutch.

"Come, Mother."

She floated toward Peter, but just before taking his hand, she looked in Belle's direction and smiled, as if she knew Belle was there the whole time. "Thank you," Emily mouthed.

Belle blinked, and the tears that had pooled, finally spilled over.

Emily took Peter's hand, and, together, they flew out and onward toward the second brightest star in the night sky, followed by a shadow that chased after them.

~~*~~

Around midnight, long after Peter and Emily's departure, and while Belle slept in her bed and dreamed of herself running desperately through the forest like a wild animal, a tall hooded figure emerged from the pouring rain, stopping beneath the canopy of the security booth outside the town wall.

The police man, alarmed by the stranger's appearance, placed one ready hand on his holstered gun and called out over the roar of the pounding rain, "Freeze! Put your hands up and do not move!"

The stranger slowly showed his palms. He wore a long, hooded trench coat that obscured the top half of his face so that only a strong, square-cut jaw was visible. A large duffel bag, half his size, slung over his shoulder.

"Now, slowly, remove your hood."

"Of course, Officer," the stranger replied, his voice low and measured. With one hand still raised in the air, he used the other to push back the hood, which fell heavily against his back. A rugged, handsome face with messy pieces of black hair and amber colored eyes stared back at him. "I have my documents, if you'd like to see."

The officer shone a flashlight on him and nodded.

The stranger squinted and grimaced at the light in his face but withdrew his documents from his coat pocket and handed them over.

"Keep them up," the officer warned as he shone the light on the paper.

"My uncle's expecting me. He said everything's in place for my arrival."

"Edward Helsing. 18 years old. Says here your registration at the high school is already completed." As if satisfied, the officer handed him back the documents. "Looks like you're all set. At ease, son." He flashed the light on the bag. "I just need to check that bag now."

Edward hitched the bag tighter against his shoulder and looked the officer straight in the eyes. "You don't need to check my bag."

"I don't need to check your bag."

"In fact," Edward continued, "you're going to wave me in now."

The officer turned and signaled a code to the police watching from the wall. The gate began opening.

"Thank you, Officer. Have yourself a fine night." He slid his hood back up.

"Welcome to Elmridge, Mr. Helsing."

Edward strolled past. He retrieved a damp paper from his other coat pocket. It was a printout of a Peacock Profile. He looked at it again for the hundredth time, although he had already memorized every curve and line of that face and knew every word of the profile by heart.

"See you soon, Belle."

THE END

Liam Rawlins had been dreaming of Belle Montague again. Finishing that night they'd started three weeks ago, cuddled up in each other's arms on the living room couch watching a Batman movie. But they hadn't really been paying much attention to the television in the dream, what with all the lip-locking and carnal exploration they were absorbed in. Something his gentleman side had promised not to dive into with her so soon.

But dream-Belle had made the first move, so who was he to deny his girl?

He knew the real Belle, or even he himself, would never have let things progress so soon to where they had. Clothing landing on the floor, a shoe tugged off and hitting the TV, and two heated bodies collapsing on the couch together. Impossible, he knew from Belle's character, but thankfully it had still been his dream.

Only, it'd turned into a nightmare. The same nightmare every dream of Belle always turned into.

He cupped her face as he kissed her neck, his other hand roaming down the soft skin of her back.

"Ow," she winced. "That hurts."

He loosened his grip on her and concentrated on keeping his cursed fingernails from sharpening into claws.

But, damn it, he was losing control. Again.

He could feel the hot passion coursing through his blood, morphing into a boiling rage that felt like it was taking hold of his very bones, twisting and pulling at them until the only relief was to allow himself to succumb to the animal within.

"Ow, Liam!" She scuttled away to the far end of the couch and felt her neck. "You bit me." Her horror-stricken eyes met his, at the warm blood seeping through her fingers.

He opened his mouth to beg for her forgiveness and to try and explain, but the searing rip inside his belly wrenched the words from his mouth. He collapsed to the floor, writhing and clutching his stomach.

"Liam!" She tried holding him as convulsions wracked his body. "What's wrong? Please, talk to me!"

One strangled word was all he could manage before he lost human speech. "Run."

"What? No, let me help you!"

He meant to say the word again, but what erupted from his throat was an unnatural snarl that made her recoil.

The transformation happened quickly now, a familiar physiological process his body had memorized. The blonde fur sprouted out of every pore of his skin as his joints snapped, bones lengthened, and jaw stretched.

It was excruciating. Every. Single. Time. Like his body was undergoing every medieval torture at once.

Even in these nightmares, his subconscious writhed with the agony.

His human form never remembered what he did as Violet Wickeby's cursed canine beast. But in these dreams, his mind felt conscious during the whole ordeal, so he knew what would come next.

He was the beast now, and it pinned Belle with a feral stare, growling its warnings.

She clambered to her feet, her face frozen in terror. Palms up like a guard, she backtracked slowly.

The sight of such easy prey made the hairs arch on his back and his claws elongate with anticipation, and with a snapping bark, he rushed at her. He sank his sharp canines into her throat, until her screams grew silent.

Liam pinched the bridge of his nose and squeezed his eyes shut. He waited for the painful white spots to flash, the only thing that worked in clearing the remnants of the nightmare from his thoughts.

He'd dwelled achingly on the first part of the dream, raking in his lower lip at the memory. But the ending—Belle's bloody and lifeless body—always served to remind him why he'd made the decision to cut her out of his life.

For her own safety. He wasn't going to give his nightmares a chance to become reality.

He looked down at the feminine hand bedecked in expensive rings and bracelets trailing up his inner thigh. With a grunt of disgust, he snatched the hand and cast it back towards its owner. "Do not ever touch me, witch."

Violet Wickeby laughed as she let herself fall back against the limo seat perpendicular to his. "I can't help myself when it comes to a Rawlins man." Her eyes trailed over him. "And that suit you're wearing makes you extra delectable."

He grimaced. Violet and her twin minions had ambushed him on the balcony outside his bedroom three weeks ago. The twins hadn't been a problem, but she'd bent him to his knees with her threats to possess Belle. She'd cast a spell on him then: a beast at her beck and call. But he'd never given her his permission, so he'd kept his free will.

Only problem was she used threats to manipulate him into obedience.

...Finish the story in *Nightmare Hunt*, Book 2 of *A Nightmare in Elmridge* series!

Continue the Elmridge saga with Belle, Liam, and newcomer Eddie.

A ginormous 'I love you' to my husband. You complete me (said in Dr. Evil voice).

Thank you, from the bottom of my heart, to:

My parents for their never-ending love and support.

My brothers for being amazing bros.

My cousin, Crystal, for being the first to enthusiastically hear out this story. Your excitement kicked off my own for this series and gave it momentum.

My students for being bright sparks of potential who daily motivated me to pursue my own path of potential in writing. Yes, cheesy, but true.

My teen beta-readers (Nina, Kai, Eva, Amelie) for devouring the original manuscript in a day and responding so quickly with helpful feedback.

The readers—You!—who made it all the way to the end of the book to this very point and will hopefully love Belle and Liam enough to continue reading what happens to them in the next book! I have so much more in store for these characters, and even more world-building, character-populating to come! And if you can, it would mean the world to me for you to hop on over to Amazon and Goodreads and leave a review; I appreciate every single one.

ABOUT THE AUTHOR

Ileen Martin lives in the vibrant city of Miami, FL with her husband, son, and two dogs, embraced by her large and lively Cuban family. A language arts teacher by day, she spends her free time writing in her zen spots around the city, salsa dancing, enjoying funny viral videos, and indulging in paranormal and mystery romances. Nightmare Beauty is her debut novel, launching the A Nightmare in Elmridge series, which promises to thrill and enchant readers.